TOMORR

IS ANOTH⌐R

DAY

A novel by

John Talman

TOMORROW IS ANOTHER DAY
First published April 2006
ISBN 1-85215-061-0

Printed by
Published by Heritage House (Publishers) Ltd
Steam Mill Road, Bradfield, Manningtree, CO11 2QT
www.heritage-house.co.uk
e-mail: sales@heritage-house.co.uk

Cover: Keith Mirams

Acknowledgements

Many people and countless organisations have helped with this book in a whole variety of ways including:

The Ipswich Museum
The Imperial War Museum
The Ipswich Record Office and Library
The Dedham Pharmacy
Dorothy Gunnel at Clifford Road School
Jenny Spanton and Jean Garrington for their literary comments
All the members of The Untapped Writers Group
Roger Freeman
Keith White
David Jones' excellent book – Ipswich in the Second World War
Julia Stainer for her wealth of information on Red Oak, Iowa

1939

'You must not be taken by surprise' – *Ministry of Information leaflet.*

'Now trying telling me there won't be a war.'

They were seated around the kitchen table sipping a cup of tea after cycling back from the Empire Day celebrations at RAF Martlesham Heath.

'I mean the Hurricanes and Spitfires put on a wonderful display but we're not building that lot for nothing, are we? Or a whole load of new airfields. I don't like it any more than you do but I'm telling you there's going to be a war all right.' Jack fumbled for his pipe and scooped some tobacco into the bowl from a worn leather pouch.

Vera watched him quietly, 'I just don't want to think about it, that's all. We've got Kitty and Jimmy settled into jobs, the house more or less how we want it, what ever do we want a war for?'

'I not saying I want a war. I was the one who always believed that the last one was the war to end all wars, and I wouldn't wish that lot on anyone.'

He glanced around the table and then hurriedly struck a match.

'We can't have a war dad, Ipswich Town have only just got into the league.' Jimmy attempted to lighten things.

Jack couldn't help laughing but looking at his son he remembered that in 1914 he too had been young and innocent.

'Ouch! If you stand on my feet again you're going to have to carry me home.'

'Sorry,' Alan muttered, trying to count to the music. *Slow, slow, quick, quick, slow.*

He could never fathom out how people like Fred Astaire made it look so easy.

With a final crescendo the five piece band finished the fox trot, the dancers parted, stood around the floor of the British Legion hall and applauded. Kitty reached down and rubbed her ankle, 'I've heard of people with two left feet but I think you've got three,' she muttered, glaring at him.

To Alan's relief the leader of *The Mellow Tones* announced the last waltz. Alan was better at the waltz, he could simply shuffle around whilst Kitty swayed close to him to the tune of *Moonlight Serenade*. When the music stopped she gave him a quick kiss and then disappeared with a throng of girls to the cloakroom.

It was a clear night and they decided to walk up Bishop's Hill along by the park. Kitty affected a limp but when he looked concerned she grinned and squeezed his arm.

'Next time you come round to my place we'll go in the front room, put some records on, and I'll teach you to fox-trot,' she promised.

'I know all the steps; it's just that my feet won't go where I tell them. I don't think I have natural rhythm.'

'You can say that again but practice makes perfect, as they say, and we do both like going to dances don't we?'

Alan wasn't so sure but decided not to say anything. He knew how much Kitty loved the new swing music. She seemed to come to life as soon as the band struck up. His mother said she would settle down once they got married.

Kitty changed the subject. 'Mum and dad and Jimmy all went to that air display at Martlesham Heath this afternoon. It really set dad off about this war thing again. I'm getting so fed up with it all. He talks about nothing else these days.' She was puffing a bit as the hill became steeper and tightened her grip on his arm.

'Too many people keep assuming its inevitable,' Alan said, ' but I think they should keep talking to the Germans. It should be possible to sort things out between civilised people without having a war. Mr Fisher, the chief clerk at the bank, was saying so only yesterday and I agree with him.'

Kitty paused and looked up. 'You are so serious sometimes Alan,' she said.

'This is serious, Kitty, very serious. I don't want to go and fight in some war they could have settled by talking. In fact I don't want to fight at all. I'm not the fighting sort.'

'Oh. Stop being such a misery. If you don't want to go then don't go.'

'It won't be as simple as that,' he quickened the pace, nearly dragging her off her feet.

'Steady on. First you bruise my ankle and now you're pulling my arms out of their sockets. And stop going on about this war thing. I told you I'm fed up with hearing about it.'

'I believe it is peace for our time.' - Neville Chamberlain

'That was a lovely film', Doris was sniffing into her handkerchief, 'I think James Stewart is wonderful, so handsome and so tall.'

Jimmy stood on the tips of his toes and attempted a drawl, 'I guess I am pretty tall, at that.'

'Don't be so silly, you don't sound anything like him.' she said.

Jimmy thought that girls were an odd lot. No sense of humour. But Doris had cuddled up to him in the dark and held his hand even when the lights came up for the interval and her hand had stayed in his as they came out into the wet night.

They crossed Lloyds Avenue and joined the queue for the number 6A trolley. It was lucky that Doris lived in Avondale Road so he wouldn't have far to walk once he had taken her home. His mate Steve had advised him never to take a girl out who lived the other side of town. Jimmy had little experience of such things.

It had been raining and the upper deck of the bus smelt of cigarettes as people lit up and talked in muffled voices. There were a lot of couples like Jimmy and Doris and quite a number of girls in groups leaning back over their seats to talk to those behind them. It seemed that all of them had been to the pictures.

After the usual rattle and a few sparks the bus started on its way pulling out from the long line at the Electric House depot. The conductor clattered up the stairs and Jimmy fished in his thick grey trousers for the return tickets.

'Did you think Jean Arthur was lovely?' Doris asked.

'Yea, she was .....very pretty.' he stammered.

Doris laughed, 'Very pretty! You're not very romantic Jimmy Wright,' then she leant over and whispered into his ear, 'Do you think I'm very pretty?'

He felt himself colour up as he tried desperately to conjour a reply. What would James Stewart have said? 'Of course I do. I mean why else would I have asked you out?' was the best he could manage.

'Because Steve Simpson dared you to, 'she laughed.

'No, because I wanted to. But I didn't think you'd come, if I'm honest.'

'So why do you think I did then?'

Girls do ask a lot of questions he thought. His sister wasn't like this, she either ignored him or argued with him. ' Because I have the same name as Jimmy Stewart,' he suggested.

Doris laughed again, 'I'll say this for you. You've got all the answers.'

By now the trolley bus was swinging down Tacket Street, rocking them close together. She grabbed his arm and stayed that way as they straightened up when the bus stopped swaying.

'I'm glad we didn't use our bikes,' she said.

Eventually, they reached her stop and Jimmy pulled the bell cord above them. The trolley shook to a halt and they clambered down the stairs. He took her gloved hand and they jumped off together. It had stopped raining but there were puddles everywhere and the wires sparked into the black night. Jimmy looked up still holding her hand.

'Do you think they'll be a war?' he said. 'My dad says there is no doubt about it, Churchill is right.'

'Oh. Jimmy, don't be so morbid and anyhow Neville Chamberlain says there won't and he's the Prime Minister.'

For a while they walked in silence; across the wet road, then onto the grass where an island of trees separated Avondale Road from Clapgate Lane. Doris pulled at his arm and guided him out of the glare of the nearby houses and close to the trees. He found himself leaning on the wet bark and she was leaning against him. She took off her gloves and stuffed them into the pockets of her blue serge coat, then placing her hands either side of his face pulled him towards her and kissed him. Automatically he put his arms around her and kissed her back and then, in spite of the cold, they unbuttoned their coats to get closer to one another. Mmm, I am Jimmy Stewart after all, he thought to himself , and then went on with the kissing.

After what seemed for ever, she pulled away, 'I really have to go,' she said, ' My mother will be looking out.'

'Yes, all right,' he said, and they walked hand in hand from the trees and across into Avondale Road. The lights were on in the front room of number sixty four where they paused and she kissed him gently on the cheek.

'Thanks Jimmy,' she said, 'You're nice.'

'So are you,' he said, ' very nice.'

She laughed and skipped up the path where the door opened before her and she was whisked into the warmth.

Jimmy felt good. He walked very slowly along the road, kicking his boots in the puddles like a toddler. She was a really good kisser that Doris Harper; really good.

He couldn't quite work out why she had said yes to his tentative suggestion of the pictures. There were plenty better looking blokes than him at the youth club and they all seemed to be more grown up, somehow. Then there was the question of his spots; just when he thought they were disappearing another ripe one would crop up in some obvious place. He fingered his neck where a particular nasty volcano was establishing itself just beneath his collar.

Digging his hands deeply into his pockets he went down Wye Road and into Severn Avenue; the beginning of the Rivers Estate where he lived. The street lights played interesting reflections in the pools on the pavement and he executed a silly dance. Who cared about those other blokes, he was the one who had taken Doris Harper to see *You can't take it with you*. No doubt when his mates found out they would pull his leg and refer to her as Ginger Harper but so what, he loved her red hair and the scatter of freckles on her nose. Maybe when his spots went he'd be left with freckles too.

He'd see her at Youth Club next Friday and then he would ask her out again. What if she wouldn't come? What if she said it was only a one night stand? No, of course, she'd come. She would never have kissed him like that if she didn't want to come out with him again.

When he reached Trent Road it began to rain more heavily. He turned up his collar and ran to his house. Once at the porch he looked back at the black, wet night and hoped that just for once his father and Winston Churchill were wrong and that Neville Chamberlain was right.

Jimmy tapped on the door gently and saw the outline of his mother through the coloured glass panel.

'You're late dear, we were beginning to get a bit worried but Kitty said it was a long film'.

'You didn't tell Kitty!'

'Well only when I was a bit worried. She came home from Alan's at about ten o'clock. They go to bed early there, Mr. and Mrs. Birdwell.'

He took off his wet raincoat and hung it on the hook inside the door.

'Look at you, you're all wet. Is it raining that much? You'd better go and hang up those trousers or they'll go all baggy at the knees. And dry your hair before you come down, your father will wonder what you've been up to.'

'Tell you what I'll go straight to bed if you like. Big match tomorrow,' Jimmy said , needing to be on his own.

'Well call in on your dad and say goodnight first. He's listening to the wireless in the front room'.

Jimmy ran his fingers through his hair and opened the door gently. His father put a finger up to his mouth leaning his head closer to the wireless. The room had hardly changed since Jimmy was a young boy. Two patterned armchairs stood either side of the fireplace where the remnants of the evening glow were reduced to hot ash; a heavy mirror hung above a solid looking mantelpiece on which the gently ticking clock stood flanked by two pictures made out of butterfly wings. His father always declared that they were worth a bob or two. To the right of the door, where Jimmy's head remained bent inwards, was a two seater leather sofa which had seen better days since some horsehair protruded from the arms. The only pictures on the walls were a print of a curly headed boy blowing bubbles and an embroidery of St. Pauls Cathedral which his mother had made prior to her marriage. The wireless, to which Jack Wright was listening intently, was perched on a table in the corner behind his chair.

After a while Jack's father turned the volume knob down and stared at his son, then he stood up tapped his pipe on the hearth and spat into the remaining fire causing it to hiss.

'Churchill has made another speech to the House of Commons and, at last, they are starting to listen.

They'll all be made to look fools once he's proved right, you mark my words.' he paused, and placed his pipe back into the pocket of his hand knitted cardigan, 'Your mother tells me you've been out with a girl. Nothing but trouble, girls, I didn't go out with one until I was well past twenty one. Stick to football, that's my advice. You can't get into a muddle with football'.

'Right dad, I'll remember,' Jimmy said. 'I'll be off then. See you in the morning.'

'Right. And don't go using that toilet in the middle of the night and waking everyone up.'

Jimmy withdrew and clumped up the stairs.

'I'll bring you up a mug of cocoa', his mother called from the kitchen.

'Making Whoopie.' – *popular song*

The lemon sun disappeared behind black trees and for the first time that afternoon Francis felt the cold. He shivered.

'No wonder you're cold; you never wear enough clothes. Look at you, coat flapping in the breeze, no scarf, no gloves.'

'Blame it on a private education,' he said, ' cross country runs on freezing afternoons, playing rugger on frosty pitches.'

Sylvia looked at him closely, ' You never strike me as a rugby player'.

'I wasn't. Only made the second fifteen, thank God.'

'But you were quite good at sport. There are trophies and things on the sideboard with your name on.'

He took her gloved hand in his, 'Tennis. I am a fair tennis player. You just wait until the Summer, I'll have you scampering about the court'.

'Don't you be so sure,' she said. They had swung through the kissing-gate that led from Christchurch Park into the Arboretum and were strolling along Mayors Walk.

'A couple of Grimstones planted trees along here,' she boasted, ' How about the Camerons?'

'Just Uncle Bertram, I'm afraid, 1929.' He was peering at the metal plaques, stooping as he walked.

Old Ipswich names lined up beneath the trees like soldiers on parade, Alderman Hunt, Councillor Wilson, Councillor Callaghan, Alderman Harrington.

Old Ipswich names. That's how he and Sylvia had met. Introduced at a party of Old Ipswich names. His forefathers, had come down from Scotland in the middle of the last century and become part of Andersons, joining in the success of early agricultural engineering. Her family went back even further and although known for the three fine department stores that bore their name they also had invested in the Port of Ipswich and in particular the flour-mills. With his father now a director of Anderson and her father and uncles directors of Grimstones Francis and Sylvia were a highly suitable match and local society would smile favourably if an engagement were to be announced.

'So here are the tennis courts waiting for our first encounter', Sylvia chirped as they came past the little thatched hut where a park keeper would be on duty during the summer months.

Francis looked up at the bare trees and noticed a squirrel jump across the branches.

'I always thought squirrels hibernated but I never was much good at natural history. Look there's one up there.'

'Oh. I do love them. Look at his cheeky little face.'

'But do they hibernate?' He was persistent; didn't like loose ends.

'Really Francis, I don't know. They do collect a lot of nuts though.. You would think that would be for the winter. We'll have to ask Vicky, she'll know, won't she.'

He didn't answer, still brooding, wanting to work it out for himself. He'd always had this fierce independence, wanting to mull things over before deciding whether or not to share his thoughts with others. Sylvia, he realised, was different; she came right out with things, not afraid to ask questions, not afraid to look silly in a quest to understand. There were times when this irritated him.

There are four courts in the lower Arboretum with a track between the third and last that leads to a tunnel. Sylvia tried to slow down their pace, wondering whether he would seize the opportunity to kiss her, but Francis seemed keen to get going.

Crossing the road he opened the gate leading to the upper Arboretum and they climbed the moss covered steps together. Here the park opened up to a large lawn with a bandstand on the northern edge but he chose the southern route that took them past the fountain, where icicles glinted like Christmas decorations in a Grimstone Store window. They paused before large wrought iron gates.

'There it is,' Sylvia announced, ' the old school where the famous Francis Cameron was educated.'

He laughed,' I'm not so sure about the famous.'

'One day,' she said and squeezed his arm.

He looked at the great red brick building with its impressive towers and turrets. A group of young students, first years by the look of them, emerged from the entrance in the company of a master Francis didn't recognise and proceeded in single file up the Henley Road.

'Do you miss it?' she asked.

'Not at all, I'm much happier working for a living.'

It was true. His time learning to be an auctioneer was proving to be really enjoyable or perhaps he was just growing up. Far happier now than at school where he never really felt he fitted in. Being more creative than sporty he wasn't held in much esteem by the other boys and even when he was a prefect he went about his duties in a thorough but unremarkable way.

'I miss St.Felix,' she confided, ' We boarders did have such fun. I'm still in touch with a lot of my friends, of course.'

Maybe that was it, Francis thought, most of his contemporaries had gone onto University but he had chosen a different route. He saw some old class mates when they came home for the vac but they were full of University talk and in his opinion, rather frivolous. But there again Francis found most people of his own age, frivolous. There was also the question of Miller; now up at Oxford, Miller with his flop of fair hair, pale blue eyes and the fingers of a pianist. He had been both surprised and worried when Miller first confided that he was attracted to him but had not discouraged him. Their brief foray into the forbidden had both intrigued and excited him but he was relieved at its brevity.

'Come on dreamer, let's go down to Limmers for tea and tea-cakes'. Sylvia was piping in his ear.

'Yes let's', he said. 'That would be splendid.'

They walked down the hill into town and onto the Buttermarket where a news vendor was shouting 'Churchill warns again about Hitler'.

That Saturday was the night of the annual Rugby Club Ball, a rather grand title for a dance held in The Crown and Anchor Hotel in the middle of Ipswich. It was a black tie affair and Sylvia told Francis that he looked like Lionel Barrymore; rather belatedly he responded that she, in her taffeta gown with her hair piled high, could have been mistaken for Merle Oberon.

Leaving their coats with reception they decided to have an early drink in the downstairs bar where they were joined by a crowd of

Sylvia's old school friends and their partners. To Sylvia's disquiet, the main conversation was of impending war. Once drinks were dispensed Francis was soon agreeing that the Government had all but abandoned the hopes of Munich and that the country was in a state of preparation for some form of invasion. The obligatory carrying of gas-masks by children and the distribution of Anderson shelters were practical indications of the thinking in high places.

'Even my mother has joined the Red Cross', Francis admitted, 'though what use she'll be in an emergency, heaven knows.'

'My old man's busy as a bee organising something to do with Civil Defence,' chipped in the boyfriend of Beatrice Witherspoon, former St.Felix hockey captain.

'Will you be joining up ahead of conscription then, old boy?' someone asked Francis, 'An awful lot of my old school pals are dead set on getting in at the beginning'.

On over-hearing this shocking piece of news, Sylvia tugged at his sleeve, 'Come on, let's all go up to the dance,' she urged.

A seven-piece band was doing its best to be Tommy Dorsey and couples swayed easily to the music as a large crystal ball twinkled above.

It happened in Monterey warbled the Suffolk crooner trying to sound like Frank Sinatra as Francis and Sylvia took to the floor.

'You're not going to do anything stupid like volunteer for the army, are you?' she whispered loudly in his ear.

'Not tonight', he said.

'Don't be silly.'

'Let's not spoil a perfectly good evening by speculation', he said, knowing that it was a feeble response. The truth was that although he had had much discussion with his father about the prospect of war he had decided to wait before applying for a commission. His father seemed keen for him to join his old regiment but most of the chaps Francis knew were talking of the Suffolks. The dance ended and they rejoined their group. Some of the girls were sitting on the gilt painted chairs that circled the room leaning forward chatting, laughing, and exchanging news and gossip. The men stood above them smoking, drinking and talking loudly.

Raymond Charlesworth asked Sylvia for a fox-trot and, after seeking a nod from Francis, she joined him on the floor. When they returned she came and took his arm,

'Raymond is joining the R.A.F. Says he's going to learn to fly.' she said, 'Francis, I had no idea it was all getting so close.'

'It's only precautionary, may never come to anything, just precautionary,' he said, searching in the pocket of his DJ for his cigarette case, ' here have a cigarette.'

She took one and allowed him to light it for her, then after gently inhaling extended her arm in an exaggerated manner, 'I had such plans', she muttered.

'What do you mean plans?' he said,

'Well if you can't guess I'm hardly going to tell you,' she said and inhaled again.

Sylvia was the only girl Francis had ever been out with and he was beginning to realise that women, at times, were difficult to fathom so, following the interval waltz, he was pleased to return to the bar to get some more drinks. Charlesworth had come with him but had then headed for the toilets and Francis found himself in a throng of smart young chaps attempting to attract the attention of the bar staff.

'I say, I thought it was you. How are you, dear fellow.'

Francis glanced over his shoulder, 'My God, Miller, what are you doing here, thought you were...'

'Up at Oxford. Well I am and was until yesterday but a chap is allowed the odd week-end to come home and see the family and old friends, you know. So how goes it, still up to your ankles in Wedgewood and Spode?'

'Yes, something like that. Here I've just got to get an order in. Four Gin and Tonics and four pints of Tollys Best'. The bar man took his money and Francis placed the drinks on a tin tray just as Charlesworth arrived back.

'Look, I'll take these up if you want to have a chat to your chum', he volunteered.

'No it's .....thanks old man', he managed and Miller deftly drew him away from the crowd.

'Now, you would simply love Oxford, Francis, my dear.' he confided, 'I mean as long as one is discreet anything goes and one doesn't feel at all in the minority, if you know what I mean.'

'No I don't and I don't think I want to. Listen Miller I'm upstairs with my girlfriend and can't hang around here chatting. So good luck and all that, right?'

'Sorry, no need to be so touchy. I just thought if ever you fancied a little dalliance then you might like to get in touch. St. John's college will find me, Toodle pip, old thing,' and he glided off into the sea of black jackets.

Francis took a large gulp of beer and went up the stairs.

As the evening progressed he found himself taking quite a number of large gulps of beer and was admonished at one stage for trampling on Sylvia's feet whilst attempting a deft spin turn.

'Someone has had rather a lot to drink,' she laughed as he held her a shade too tightly during the last waltz.

'I'm fine, just fine,' he said but was aware of a certain unsteadiness, ' You are a very lovely girl, Sylvia', he told her and she laughed again.

'My friends all think you're a bit of a catch', she confided.

'A bit of a catch', he repeated, ' sounds a bit fishy to me,' amused at his own bright wit.

After the last waltz Sylvia suggested that they should get their coats and take a breath of fresh air before summoning a taxi. He nodded in agreement, his head spinning like the twinkling ball in the middle of the ballroom.

Outside it was misty but not cold and she took his arm and guided him up Westgate Street and into a shop doorway. Then she placed her arms around him and kissed him with far more passion than he remembered from previous experiences.

'You did mean it when you said I was lovely, didn't you?' she whispered,

'Absolutely. Loveliest girl at the dance,'

'And what are you going to do about it ?'

'Kiss you again, if you like.'

'You could kiss me like that for ever if you wanted.'

'Damn fine idea,' he said and proceeded to put this idea into practice.

After a while she pulled away, 'That's not quite what I meant' she said.

He had a momentary vision of Miller looking at him and smirking. Then he gently extricated himself from the embrace and stood staring down the street.

It had been raining and the reflections of the lights danced in the puddles making him feel even more unsteady. If there's a war, they say all the lights will go out but then nobody really knew what would happen, nobody really knew anything any more. He shuddered and turned round,

'Sylvia,' he said, 'You wouldn't think of marrying me, would you?'

'If we are engaged in war our contribution will not be half-hearted' -

Leslie Hore-Belisha, Secretary of State for War

'Of course I know her, she was that little ginger girl two years down from me at primary school. So that makes her nineteen, same as Jimmy.'

'Jimmy says her hair is auburn, like Rita Hayworth. Now give me a hand with the fish paste sandwiches, there's a good girl or I'll never be ready in time.' Vera was fussing.

Kitty stopped leaning on the small kitchen table, turned and started to cut the large loaf into neat slices; in spite of herself she was a practical girl.

'What other sort of sandwiches are we having?' she enquired.

'I thought we could use some of the strawberry jam that Mrs. Green gave me and there's the trifle with the last of the tinned peaches and the Dundee I made is in the oven.'

'We are putting the boat out for Rita Hayworth, aren't we. She only lives in Avondale Road you know.'

Her mother ignored her and continued counting the cutlery, placing it on the draining board, 'So that's six of us,' she said,' You and Alan, Jimmy and his young lady and your dad and me, that's nice isn't it, Kitty?'

'Very nice. Now, where's that strawberry jam or are you sure you don't want to save it for when war breaks out. Mrs. Green won't be giving away her jam then, from what I hear.'

Vera looked out of the window at the jasmine straggling the fence. What did Kitty know of war? What did she know of war? Jack seldom mentioned the last one though she knew that it had left its mark in a hundred little ways. She was worried.. Worried about what would happen to Jimmy if he were called up.. Worried about Kitty's boy, Alan. And now here was young Jimmy bringing home his girl for tea. In normal circumstances that would have made her feel good but the threat of war made it impossible to think optimistically about anything.

'Right where's that jam then, Alan will be here in a minute and I haven't got any make up on.'

They worked together finishing the sandwiches and carrying the food, cutlery and plates into the dining room where Sunday tea would take place. Kitty skipped upstairs to prepare for the arrival of Alan evicting Jimmy from the bathroom where he was examining his face for spots. Vera popped her head around the front room door where Jack was listening to the radio – a pastime that he indulged in a lot these days.

'Hitler and Mussolini have signed that pact but there again we knew it would only be time,' he announced as if he had become the Prime Minister.

'Kitty's been helping me prepare the tea' she said.

'Well we better enjoy it since they've announced that the farmers are to plough up grazing land and go in for more arable production. They're worried that imports of food will dry up once the war starts.'

'If it starts'.

'When it starts, woman, don't be so naïve.' He stood and knocked his pipe out on the hearth and then produced a penknife and commenced scraping the bowl, ' and I thought we'd finished with war, after the last lot.'

There was a knock on the door and Vera peered through the net curtains, 'It's Alan', she announced.

'Well I didn't think it was Hitler,' Jack murmured, filling his pipe from a worn leather pouch. Vera scuttled out shouting up the stairs to Kitty before opening the door to Alan who stood hair plastered flat on his round head and wearing his suit.

'Hello Mrs.Wright, hope I'm not early.'

'Not at all, Alan,' she said and ushered him into the front room. 'Here, go and talk to Jack he needs cheering up especially since the Town lost yesterday.'

Shouting upstairs again to Kitty, she padded into the back room and looked at the table. I do hope they talk about films and things and not war she thought, not realising that Jimmy had joined her.

'It all looks very nice, mum.'

'Thank you Jimmy,' she said, hoping he hadn't detected the tears in her eyes.

Another knock on the door had him hurrying to open it and then ushering in a nervous looking Doris. When he took her coat he noticed that she was wearing a simple cream blouse and a straight green skirt.

'So this will be Doris. Yes, I do remember you now dear,' Vera said.

Kitty came tripping downstairs smelling of inexpensive perfume.

'Hello Kitty', smiled Doris still standing just inside the front door.

'Come and meet my Alan and my Dad', Kitty said taking her elbow and Vera sighed and smiled. Jimmy, by then, appeared redundant and followed them into the front room.

To Vera's surprise Jack immediately switched off the wireless and stood up smiling.

'Very nice to meet you....Doris,' he beamed. My God, thought Vera, the old devil can still be charming when he wants to.

Kitty and Doris were soon chatting easily about films and film stars and swing music. Jack was debating with Alan recent performances of Ipswich Town Football Club now that they were in the Third Division South and Jimmy tried, somewhat unsuccessfully, to join in both conversations. From time to time Doris, who was sitting next to him and opposite Alan and Kitty, would glance at him and smile. Vera noticed this and thought to herself that young Jimmy was truly smitten with this redhead from Avondale Road.

'You work for French's the Chemists don't you Doris?' she asked.

'Yes, on Majors Corner, opposite the Regent.'

'That must be interesting.'

'Yes, I enjoy it really. Mr. French is very good to me and is teaching me how to mix the medicines and things. Then there is Joyce, that's the other girl who works there, she's a real comedienne at times.'

'Has to be more fun that being on the line in Phillips and Pipers, I can tell you,' said Kitty and for some reason everyone laughed.

The sandwiches quickly disappeared with Vera worrying if she had prepared enough but by then everyone was tucking into the trifle with gusto. Doris pointed out to Jimmy that he had missed his mouth and had custard on his chin. He laughed and wiped it off with the back of his hand.

Vera brewed more tea and all but Kitty had some Dundee cake.

Jack, who clearly approved of Doris, only touched on the subject of war once.

'When will you be twenty, Alan?' he asked.

'July, Mr. Wright, July. He fiddled with his Dundee cake, 'To be honest I'm worried about it, Mr. Wright, I have no idea what it might be like.'

Jack stroked his chin, 'Don't think anyone does,' he said, 'Somehow I don't think it'll be like the last one. Hope not, anyway.'

'Our Jimmy is twenty in August,' Vera said, looking at Doris. ' Seems only yesterday he started shaving.'

'Mother!' Jimmy was clearly embarrassed when everyone laughed. Doris secretly dug him in the ribs.

After tea Kitty and Doris helped clear away and Vera put the kettle on for the washing up. Then they all sat round the table and played pontoon for matches. Doris had never played before but Vera observed she got the hang of it very quickly.

Just before the nine o'clock news the party broke up. Doris thanked everyone while Jimmy got their coats; Jack and Vera went back in the front room to listen to the wireless and Kitty persuaded Alan to take her for a drink at *The Margaret Catchpole*.

'Your parents are very nice.' Doris said as they walked hand in hand up the road.

'Yea, they're all right, I suppose,'

'Alan's really worried about getting his call-up papers, isn't he? And I'm worried about you getting yours,' she squeezed his hand.

'I'll be OK.'

When they arrived at the top of the road where the woods bordered one side of Elmhurst Drive he stopped and pulled her to him.

'I'll be OK', he repeated and they held each other very tight.

The Margaret Catchpole sat solidly next to the Cliff Lane entrance to Holywells Park and enjoyed a steady trade from the residents of the Rivers estate. Alan and Kitty popped in from time to time as did the other members of the Wright family. They selected a table in the far corner of the panelled lounge bar under a fading Constable print.

'You haven't even noticed my hair.' Kitty patted the new bob with her hand.

'I did, I told you earlier you looked very nice.'

'Very nice. I bet Errol Flynn doesn't say *you look very nice* to Greer Garson.'

Alan toyed with his drink,' No one seems to agree with me but I still think we should negotiate a peaceful solution with this Hitler.' He gazed at her over the top of his pint awaiting an answer.

'If I lived in Hollywood I'd have my hair done every week,' she said.

'I hate the whole idea of war. I've tried to talk to my father about it. I told him, if there is a war I am not joining up.'

'I might even have it dyed blonde. I mean it is too straw coloured, don't you think?'

He looked at her seeking her attention, 'You're not listening to me are you?'

'Yes I am. You said something about your father joining up.'

Alan swigged the remainder of his pint and stood up, 'I wish you wouldn't make jokes about important things. Do you want another drink?'

She drained her glass and thrust it in his direction, 'One for the road, you old misery.'

When he came back she thought he still looked grumpy. 'The point is I am not cut out for killing people. I don't think many people are if they're honest. So I really don't want any part of it.'

She took his hand,' I do understand Alan, it's just that I'm getting fed up with all this gloomy war talk. My dad going on and on about it, even the girls at the factory are worried. The way I see it is if there is a war and you don't want to go then don't bloody well go.'

He sighed, 'It won't be like that Kitty, There won't be any choice. Like my dad says they shoot cowards in the back and put conchies in jails.'

She touched her hair again, 'So should I become a peroxide blonde then?'

Alan banged the table so hard that his fresh mug of beer toppled over. 'For Christ's sake stop going on about your bloody hair. I'm trying to tell you that I don't want to fight in this bloody unnecessary war and you keep talking about your hair.'

The pub went quiet. The landlord looked over at Kitty and Alan not wanting any trouble. Kitty stood up, took hold of his sleeve and led him to the door. He was normally such a mild boy. She had never known him lose his temper before.

'Happiness in marriage is entirely a matter of chance.' - *Jane Austin*

On the twenty first of May, nineteen hundred and thirty nine the sun was shining at three o'clock causing Officer Cadet Cameron to blink as he emerged from the church of St. Mary Le Tower with his bride on his arm. The bride, Sylvia nee Grimstone, did not blink. She was far too happy. She smiled at the small group of well-wishers gathered outside in the company of a photographer now hidden beneath a hood.

The wedding itself wasn't quite what she had in mind when she first decided that Francis was for her but at least she was married in white and at the premier church in Ipswich. The country was involved in planning for what seemed to be the inevitability of war and she was not alone in having grandiose wedding plans reduced to intimate family affairs.

Francis had chosen a fellow Officer Trainee, Freddy Pearce to be his best man. He had formed a close friendship with Freddy at Mons Training School over the past few weeks during the rigours of officer training. His parents considered the choice most suitable and his mother was heard to say that she thought the two young men in officers uniform would look very impressive on the photographs.

Lining up to come out of the church, Freddy was happily chatting to the chief bridesmaid, Victoria Cameron, and thinking how much he was going to enjoy this forty eight hour break from training, when Sylvia looked over her shoulder and hissed.

'Photographs Freddy. Could you be a lamb and get that chap organised.'

'Oh right. Absolutely.' The potential commander of men stammered and the small family gathering formed up in a series of traditional groupings whilst the man under the hood slid in his plates and flashed his magnesium.

The party had decided to walk from the church to The Great White Horse for the reception much to the pleasure of the denizens of Ipswich hurrying about their meagre shopping.

'A spring wedding in pure English sunshine who could believe that war is just round the corner?' Robert Cameron confided to Elizabeth Grimstone, as she took his arm.

'At times it does rather feel like some hideous dream, Robert,' she replied, ' but the signs are all there aren't they. That awful man Hitler is not going to stop?'

'No my dear, he isn't. We must enjoy days like this since, in my view, nothing will ever be the same again.'

'Oh dear Robert, I can see we'd better get you a glass of champagne pretty quickly.'

'Sorry, Elizabeth. Didn't mean to spoil the party. Difficult to get this threat of war out of my head at times. I've been to meetings you see, there's going to be an awful lot for people like us to do.'

'Well I'm not thinking about it today. Let's just rejoice that these two splendid young people have got together and that our two families are now even closer as a result, shall we?'

The Great White Horse put on a good spread. Best Man, Officer Cadet Freddy Pearce, made jokes about officer training and Hitler and was particularly gallant in his remarks about the bridesmaids. Francis, replied in more serious vein and Sylvia looked pleased with herself. At five o'clock the newly wedded couple left from the back of the hotel in the groom's green MG on their way to Bournemouth for a brief honeymoon. Francis had been given the customary seventy two hour pass by the army.

They had booked a small, but comfortable, hotel on the Boscombe side of the town and sat down for dinner soon after arrival. Sylvia knew it was perfectly obvious that they were honeymooners and smiled confidently at the sprinkling of guests in the dining room. Francis, she thought, looked a trifle embarrassed. They dined on oxtail soup, roast pork and charlotte rousse washed down with a bottle of Chablis recommended by the headwaiter.

Sylvia thought she would be a bit nervous as she cleaned her teeth in the bathroom, but looking at herself in the mirror realised that she had got what she wanted even if he did have to go tearing off back to Aldershot after a couple of days. She was now a married woman and what's more married to a handsome officer who was a member of one of Suffolk's best known families. She was confident that this silly war thing would all be over in no time at all. Finishing her teeth she looked at herself in the mirror again. She was, of course, a virgin but had read loads of books and had sensible conversations with her mother.

She came from the bathroom and Francis, clad in a rather dull looking dressing gown, almost knocked her over as he rose from the bed where he had been sitting smoking. Sylvia giggled at the awkwardness of it all.

She slid out of her silk dressing gown and arranged herself primly in the bed and waited. She could hear him splashing about behind the door and wondered just what was taking him so long. Eventually he emerged smelling of toothpaste, his sandy hair newly brushed. He removed the woollen dressing gown revealing a pair of blue and grey striped pyjamas. Then he got into bed beside her and they sat upright, looking at each other for what seemed to her an awfully long time.

'My, you are beautiful,' he said eventually, snuggling his head into her neck, ' and you smell divine.' Thanks to mother's gift of French perfume, she thought. He kissed her at first gently and then with more vigour. Sylvia found herself unbuttoning his pyjama top and slipping it off his shoulders and they slid down beneath the cool sheets. She felt his hands moving under her night-dress exploring her body, soft hands caressing her breasts and she started kissing his neck, whispering to him.

'You do love me don't you?'

'Of course I love you.' he said.

With a little help, he removed her night-dress and she wondered whether she was expected to pull the cord on his pyjama bottoms but decided to let him deal with that.

It seemed to her that the love making itself was all over rather quickly but, in spite of her reading, realised that she'd had no idea of what to expect. Francis had groaned a little and she had felt a slight jab of pain as he entered her. After a while he had fallen away and lying on his back had asked if she was all right. She'd said something like 'Wonderful' and then she had gone to the bathroom. When she returned Francis was propped up in bed smoking.

'Would you like a cigarette?'

'No thanks, I'll just have a puff of yours.'

And so they sat, Officer Cadet and Mrs. Frances Cameron, sharing a
Craven A and grinning at each other.

'We'll be all right, won't we darling?' she asked.

'Of course we'll be all right', he said.

'This country is now at war with Germany. We are ready.' -
Neville Chamberlain

'We've been ever so busy. People coming in all the time with cuts and bruises all on account of bumping into things in the blackout. Joyce made me laugh she says she goes out at night all the time now hoping to bump into a nice young bloke. Says he won't see her big nose in the dark.' Doris was chattering away happily, hanging onto his arm.

'The paper says the hospitals are full up of people injured on the roads. Stupid really, I mean we've been at war now for over a month and haven't seen as much as one German plane yet we go round killing each other in the blackout,' Jimmy replied.

It was a Sunday, a mild autumn Sunday and they walked idly kicking at the parchment leaves that fluttered gently from oak and beech; a squirrel leaped across the path causing them to laugh. There were other young couples in the park as well as families wheeling babies in prams. Children played on the grass and a crowd of teenage boys were kicking a football over by the swings watched by a group of giggling girls. Only the echo of hammering disturbed the softness of the day and rounding the bend towards Holywells Mansion they saw a group of workmen building a municipal air raid shelter.

'The war doesn't care about it being Sunday,' Jimmy said.

Doris was quiet and then looked up at him, 'What you said just now is right, it is funny isn't it? I know we are at war and I know that those Germans are doing all sorts of awful things in Poland and the like and I know people say they're out to rule all of Europe but it's ever so difficult to believe it,' Doris said, echoing the thoughts of a nation.

'I've got a feeling I will know soon enough. Any day now I'll get my call-up papers. Every time I get back from work the first thing I do is ask Mum if they've come. The waiting is worse than the signing up. I mean Alan has gone now, done his training and is somewhere in France. He must be hating it. I mean, you cannot imagine Alan being a soldier, can you?'

Doris gripped his hand and they walked off the path across the sloping grass towards the pond. Youngsters were throwing bread to the noisy mallards.

'Some official will stop us wasting bread like that soon, you mark my words,' Jimmy said, 'My foreman at work said the only thing we're being bombarded by at the moment is regulations.'

'I know and the signs are up everywhere and they're piling up those sandbags around the town hall and other big buildings. Mr. French says we're not having sandbags in front of his shop.'

'They were testing searchlights up at Nacton airport last night. Eerie they were.'

'My dad says he's going to volunteer to be a fireman. What's your dad going to do?' Doris asked, changing the subject, not wanting to think about Jimmy going away.

'He's already applied to be one of those Air Raid Wardens. Starts next week going around shouting 'Put that light out' – I can just hear him, can't you?' As long as he remembers where he is and doesn't yell 'And don't make a noise going to the toilet.' Doris knew he was trying to make her laugh.

The light was starting to fade and she pulled her scarf tighter around her neck. She felt warm inside her heavy blue coat with its silly label stating her name in bold letters. The government had promised identity cards by the end of the month and then people wouldn't have to all go around labelled like those poor evacuees. Looking up now that they were away from the trees she saw three barrage balloons over towards Felixstowe. Three great elephants in the sky.

'One broke free last week and made a right mess of the trolley bus wires in Fore Street,' she said, ' Loads of people were late for work.'

'I saw the photos in 'The Star.' Hilarious I thought.'

'Not if you'd been on the bus, it wasn't.'

A bell rang signalling that the park would be shutting in fifteen minutes.

'Come on,' he said, ' race you up the hill. Mum will have tea ready.'

The next Saturday Jimmy's papers came calling for him to report on the first of October to a camp at Whitchurch in Hampshire. He read them again and again in his bedroom and then announced to his parents that he was going for a cycle ride. His father started to say something but Vera put a finger to her mouth and he kept quiet. They knew what the brown envelope was about. Jimmy didn't get many letters.

Instinctively he made for Nacton and propping his bike up in a hedge walked down the muddy track to the shore. The tide was out and the watery sun shimmered on the shore causing it to change colour, blue, brown, purple, and silver. He knew if he walked too far out he would curse the mud as it sucked over his boots but standing there, just gazing at it, he marvelled at the colours. His eyes swept down the Orwell towards Wolverstone and Pin Mill where in the distance he could make out one or two sailboats bobbing in the breeze.

Jimmy chose to walk on the drier ground, where tufts of grass and shingle provided a firm footing. He made his way towards the skeletons of dead trees that strung out along the shoreline like dinosaurs. When he was a young boy he used to fight them with his wooden sword. Very soon his fighting would be far more real and yet he had no idea what war would be like. Like Alan, he didn't think he had it in him to kill another man, even a German. He doubted whether he had the stomach for war, the appetite to go out there and kill for his country. But there again, if he didn't go and others didn't go, they said this Hitler and his Germans would make them all slaves and that seemed even worse.

He shrugged, kicked a stone, and wandered up as far as the first dinosaur. Leaning on it he felt the wind on his face and his eyes watered. His father had never talked of his experiences in the First World War, the war to end all wars they'd called it. The odd comment from time to time but he'd never talked to Jimmy about it and Jimmy had never asked. He didn't think he would have an opportunity to now that his papers had arrived. It would have to be the Army who taught him what to do and like all the others he'd just have to go and do it.

Large, well-fed gulls suddenly swooped from the river towards the land, squawking loudly above him like a squadron of German fighter planes. Funny how everything reminded him of war.

He began to think about Doris. His Doris she had become over the last few months. He couldn't believe how well they got on. Apart from his sister, Jimmy's world had been a man's world, football, the factory, sometimes the pub; even at the youth club he'd tended to stick with the lads. But then Doris had appeared and they had become inseparable -apart from football, of course. Whilst they chatted together about all sorts of things he had deliberately not confided in her his confusion about becoming a soldier. He was aware that she had tried to bring conversations around to the subject but he had always managed to make a joke of it and move on. He decided he'd cycle down the town later and meet her from work.

A couple with a dog approached. The dog came up to him, sniffing at his trousers and they called him off. They'd never had a dog. His dad didn't like them.

Doris saw him looking through the window. His face peering above large receptacles of red and green fluid, his body dissected by pills, potions and pastes. He always did that, searched for her through the window, sometimes sticking his nose against the pane to make her laugh. Why didn't he just come into the shop like a customer? Mr. French wouldn't mind. Without thinking she smoothed her hair and then beckoned to him to enter the shop.

'The war has closed down Ipswich Town Football Club, so I thought I'd call in and cycle home with you,' he said, grinning.

'That'll be nice,' she said, then making sure Mr. French and Joyce were out the back, 'We'll be shutting in ten minutes. Here, sit over there by the scales and I'll ask if I can leave a bit early.'

Jimmy liked her in her white overall. She looked like a nurse. He heard the hum of voices from the dispensary at the back of the shop and then laughter. Then Mr. French's bald head peeped round the corner, glasses on the end of his nose. Jimmy always thought he looked like pictures of Mr. Pickwick that he had in a book at home.

'Hello Jimmy, she won't be long. Been such a nuisance today, the pair of them, so I've packed them off to get their coats.'

'Right then, Mr. French.'

After a while she came back into the shop and he noticed that she'd applied some lipstick and powder; he thought she looked like a film star. Joyce, who had an unfortunate nose and protruding teeth, greeted him, grinning.

'Glad to see you're looking after my friend,' she lisped.

'Right, Joyce, but only because the Town are no more. Just think four league matches, all those new signings and it's closed down. They say the manager, Scott Duncan, has got a job at Churchmans. At least he can see the ground from there.'

Joyce looked a bit blank. If I want a boyfriend I'm going to have to learn about football she thought.

They went through the door together and Joyce set off towards Majors Corner to get her bus. Doris took Jimmy's hand and led him down a narrow passage way to the back of the shop where her bike was stored in a wooden lean-to. She stopped and looked at him.

'It's come hasn't it. Your call up, it's come?'

'Yeah. First of October.'

She threw her arms around his neck and kissed him. 'They won't let anything happen to you, Jimmy Wright, because I love you.'

'I love you, too.'

It was the first time they'd said it.

Hall Farm had been in the family for two generations and although it came with just over a hundred acres the Grimstones had never farmed it preferring to let it out to Peter Phillips whose family owned nearly a thousand acres in and around Playford.

There was a shingle drive up to the house dissecting fine lawns and mature trees, herbaceous borders cosied up to grey Georgian walls. Twice a week Old Moore tended the garden and his wife helped up at the house; both under the supervision of the benign but firm Elizabeth Grimstone.

About a mile down road, on Grimstone land, was a farm cottage and this had been recently renovated to provide a marital home for Francis and Sylvia until such time as they purchased a place of their own. With Francis now away at war Elizabeth had declared the arrangement an admirable one allowing Sylvia to alternate between the two properties.

Francis had now completed his training, passing out as Second Lieutenant Cameron and after the briefest period of leave had embarked with the B.E.F. to France to join the other one hundred and fifty thousand British troops waiting for something to happen. Sylvia received matter-of-fact letters from him in neat handwriting to which she replied in warmer terms. Francis, she knew, was a serious man but she loved him for it and was convinced that once this wretched war were over they would find themselves a splendid house and settle down with a family of their own. Sometimes, she wished he would laugh just a little bit more, sometimes she wished he would be just a little more demonstrative, but he was a steady man and a thoughtful one and she had plans for him.

Much as she missed her new husband years at boarding school ensured that she was a resilient young woman and she began to give some thought about what her particular war effort might be. Since leaving school, some two years ago, she had become a trainee manager at the major Grimstone Department Store in Tavern Street but had always viewed this as a diversion. Her main plan had always been to become a wife, a mother and a central figure in appropriate circles of Suffolk society. However this war was changing things and, in spite of herself, she realised that she needed to consider what her particular contribution should be. After all, she calculated, it didn't have to be all gloom and doom, it could even be fun.

She sat, with her mother, in the drawing room of the main house sipping tea, thumbing through *Picture Post*.

'Your father is almost enjoying this war, you know, he's already getting involved setting up the new Local Defence Volunteers.'

' That's good I suppose but my problem is I'm not sure what it is we are getting prepared for. One moment it's barrage balloons and barbed wire to keep Hitler away from our shores. The next moment it's building shelters and stumbling about in the dark because of Air Raids.'

'Well, it's probably both Sylvia, they go together really. Your father says Hitler's plan is likely to entail softening us up with lots of bombing from the air before launching an attack across the channel.'

Sylvia munched a Rich Tea biscuit then wiped her mouth with a small handkerchief.

'It really is going to happen, isn't it?'

'We are not supposed to even think that way but it does look pretty grim. Your father also says it depends how effective the BEF is, so it's down to your Francis and his chaps to send Hitler back where he came from.'

'Poor old Francis, I do hope he is all right. His letters never really tell me what he is doing let alone what he is thinking. I lie awake trying to imagine it but I have no idea of what it can be like.'

'Men never tell us about war. Never have,' Elizabeth said quietly.

Sylvia sighed, ' So mother, what can I do whilst he's away?'

' Womens Voluntary Service, that's what you can do. Or you could become a land girl. I've agreed to put together an Ipswich branch of the WVS. You can help me get it all set up if you like. For example, there's a number of jolly useful vans garaged at Grimstones and we know they won't be used much if the war really gets going. I suggested to your father that he could donate those for a start for conversion to field canteens.'

'Who are we going to feed, for heaven's sake, mother?'

'The poor people who are bombed, of course.'

'Oh. My God, you do really think it will come to that, don't you?'

Elizabeth sipped her Earl Grey and looked out onto the lawns where Old Moore was concentrating on his edging.

'Your father has been going up to London quite a bit. He's on some committees set up by the Government.'

'I see,' Sylvia paused, 'Then count me in. I agree to be a WVS person.'

'I already have, darling, you're on my committee.'

Both women laughed realising how alike they were.

'In the meantime there are a host of fund raising activities to organise and you, Sylvia, though inexperienced, are a natural organiser.'

On the Sunday before he went off to Whitchurch Training Camp Jimmy helped his father put up an air raid shelter in the garden. There was a bit of drizzle about but they worked in shirt sleeves clearing the rockery and digging down about three feet along dimensions worked out by Jack and indicated by taut string boundaries. After a while his father stood back and leaned on his spade.

'That's the bulk of area dug out,' he puffed, 'Perhaps we'll get a cup of tea out of your mother before we bolt the thing together'.

The shelters had been delivered earlier by lorry during the week and it seemed that every household was employed in assembly on that particular weekend. Looking across the garden fence Jimmy observed that their immediate neighbour's garden had already been disfigured by the corrugated steel contraption and further up the road he could see and hear similar work going on. Men were calling to each other across the gardens and what surprised him was the amount of good humour with which this gruesome task was being undertaken. Apron clad wives stood at doors and watched or brought tea out to their men folk. Flower beds, lovingly tended over the years, lawns weeded and cut to perfection were disappearing as the landscape took on the appearance of a battlefield.

On cue, Vera appeared from the back door with two cups of tea.

'Fred's going to give us a hand with the construction,' Jack confided.

'Well, I should think so too, you helped him yesterday.'

Jack took a sip of tea, 'That's better,' he licked his lips and looked across at his son.

'This time tomorrow you'll be on the parade ground,' he laughed.

Jimmy looked down at his spade, 'Can't really believe it,' he said. 'Don't know what to expect. What's it really like, dad?'

Vera stared hard at her husband. He looked a bit taken-a-back by the directness of the question and fished in his pocket for his pipe and tobacco. 'It'll be different this time,' he muttered, eventually. Then he looked up at the sky and blinked, ' You'll be fine boy. Just don't go taking any silly risks, if you get my drift.' With that he lit his pipe and clamped it securely into his mouth,' 'Right all this gossiping won't get the job done. Come on let's go and get the roof.'

The next morning Doris got permission to be late for work and came to Ipswich Station to see Jimmy off. Small groups of soldiers, returning from weekend leave, grouped together eyeing up the latest recruits with leather strapped suitcases and girls hooked to their arms. The train steamed in on time and she clung to him, clumsily kissing his mouth, as he broke free and climbed into the train with a couple of other boys. He tried to prise his head from the window but the others got in first and all she could see was the top of his head as the train moved out of the station.

She stood on platform two crying into her handkerchief and thinking how silly she was. It was only a training camp. He would be back in a month.

1940

'I have nothing to offer but blood, toil, tears and sweat.'
Winston Churchill

'She's not too well, Mrs. French, is she?'

'It's her stomach, poor woman. Cancer I think, though he never says. I don't know how he keeps so cheerful.'

'He could do without all that worry, especially in wartime. At times like this it's a shame he doesn't have any children to talk to.'

Doris took another bite out of her sandwich,

'Joyce? I mean, I know he's a really nice old bloke, Mr. French, and I do feel sorry for him with his wife and that but does he ever, *you know*, with you?'

Joyce nearly choked on her hard boiled egg, rocking up and down on her stool, 'What do you mean, does he ever *you know?*'

'You know very well what I mean. Like he gets very close, comes up behind me when I'm mixing some elixir or pounding away at an ointment and sort of fondles me.'

Joyce stopped giggling, 'Well, all old men do that a bit don't they?'

'I don't know, do they?'

'Yeah, well I'm sure he's harmless enough.'

'Oh. I know, I wasn't meaning...it's just that...yeah, you're right.... We'll just have humour him, after all he is a good boss and I like him. Just wish he wouldn't...No, sorry I'm being silly I'll just have to lay back and think of England,' Doris concluded, remembering something her sister had said once.

'Well I wouldn't go as far as that,' said Joyce and they both got the giggles.

They were sitting in the dispensary enjoying their packed lunch, Mr. French had gone home to tend to his wife promising to be back as soon as possible. The shop bell clanged heralding a new customer and Joyce tipped off her stool and tripped out of the dispensary. Doris abandoned her lunch and looked at the prescription book, kaolin and morphine mixture, she could almost do that in her sleep; two grams of kaolin, half a gram of sodium bicarbonate, a drop of chloroform and morphine tincture, fill it up with water, shake it about and Mrs.

Stephenson's tummy would be as good as new. More and more, these days, Mr. French allowed her to put into practice what he was teaching her about pharmacy. She had a thirst for knowledge and thought that she should stop moaning about the occasional amorous advance from a man who, in all other ways, she respected. Joyce returned grinning,

'I love it when them young lads come in for a packet,' she whispered, ' I hope you and that Jimmy were careful before he went to France, Doris.'

Doris looked up, her face red, 'Joyce Underwood, if you weren't my best friend I'd be very angry with you.'

'Whoops, sorry.'

Doris looked up from measuring out a dose of cough medicine, 'If you must know, and I wouldn't confide in anyone else, we didn't do it.'

'Look I'm sorry. Nothing to do with me. Let's talk about something else, Doris.'

Doris ignored her, 'Actually, I decided in the week before he went, that I wanted to very much. I even sneaked a packet from the shelf and put the money in the till in case he hadn't done anything about it. You know what boys are like.'

'Unfortunately I only know what the boys are like who come in here, but go on..'

'In a way it was all laid on a plate for us. Mum and Dad and my sister Alice had all gone to Gran's for Sunday tea. I think Alice fixed it without them realising and after our walk I took Jimmy back to my room.'

'And?'

'And, we didn't do it. That's all. We decided we wouldn't do it until, well I don't know, until things were more settled, I suppose.'

Doris was saved from further embarrassment by the bell and Joyce went back into the shop, walking slowly.

Doris stared at the wall. Her mother was always saying that her bedroom was a tip and Doris had surprised her by tidying it up that Sunday morning. Later, after the briefest of walks, she had urged Jimmy to come back to the house with her. He had been so nervous that her parents might return in spite of her re-assurances that tea at Gran's was a long drawn out affair. They had kissed in the hall for simply ages and then he had taken off his coat, jacket and shoes and she had led him by the hand up the stairs. They had tumbled onto the bed and in a frenzy started to undress each other. Eventually she was in her undies and he his pants and they started to kiss again, touching each other with a sort of pleasure she had never experienced. It was as though they were in some private world. He had managed to undo her bra and she felt her breasts squash under his chest. She found herself licking his neck and he made little noises which excited her even more. Then his hands pulled at her knickers and his fingers explored between her legs. He started to move on top of her and then, for reasons she would never completely understand, they stopped for a split second and she opened her eyes and stared at him.

'Are you sure we should be doing this?' he whispered.

'I want you so much, Jimmy,'

'And I want you ....but I'm not sure we should.'

She sat up, leaving him lying with his legs spread over hers.

'Oh! God, Jimmy Wright, why are you so decent. I love you very much.'

He managed to sit up next to her, 'I know and that's why I'm not sure. Not yet. What if you had a baby or something and I didn't come back from the war and...'

She threw her arms around his neck, 'Don't talk like that.'

They stayed that way for some time eventually being disturbed by a garden door swinging shut causing Jimmy to jump out of the bed in one leap. Doris burst into helpless laughter, 'It's next door's gate, I told you mum and dad won't be back for ages.'

He managed to laugh as well, 'Sorry, you must think me very stupid.'

'No. I just think you are so right for me. You don't think I'm, well.... loose, do you. Trying to lure you into my bed.'

'Don't be so daft.'

'Oh.. Jimmy, I know you're right and the sensible side of me didn't really want to do it just yet either, it was just the thought of your going away and my needing to show you how much I loved you.'

They kissed again, dressed hurriedly and went downstairs where she made him a cup of tea. She never told him about the packet hidden in her bedside drawer.

When Joyce came back from the shop Doris was crying. Joyce put her arms around her friend.

'I'm sorry, Doris, I never meant to pry. I can understand that someone like you would want to wait until you were married. I'm sure Jimmy understood as well.'

Vera was getting the washing in and her hands were red and wrinkled. She dumped the damp shirts, trousers, undergarments into a wicker basket, arms, legs, no heads. She shuddered.

Glancing at her watch she muttered to herself that it was nearly five. The hooter would go off at any minute and Jack and Kitty's dinner needed to go in the oven.

No sooner had these thoughts crossed her mind when she heard the familiar sound echoing through the unseasonal mist. It was Friday, Jack would be pleased to be coming home and she would be pleased to get her housekeeping. It had been a long week. Then, she smiled to herself in the knowledge that things might change a bit if she went for that telephonist job; a bit of extra cash for the family, a bit of a change to her routine, a bit of independence. She knew Jack was not happy about it but with so many young men away at war Mr. Churchill said women had to do their bit.

Down the town at Back Hamlet the great factory gates swung open and men swarmed out like an army charging over a drawbridge. Cloth capped, grey, stooped men pushing bicycles or walking across the road to join the trolley-bus queues. Jack mounted his bike and peddled alongside George Simpson, one of the other foremen.

'Things look pretty bleak over in France,' George said.

'That Gort got it all wrong, I reckon. Now Holland has gone the Germans are going through Belgium and France like a dose of salts.'

'Heard from your boy lately?'

'No, not for a bit but like I keep telling Vera I reckon he's got his hands full at present, not much time for letter writing.'

'Poor little sod. Still he's a sensible boy, your Jimmy.'

'Doesn't matter how sensible you are if you're hemmed in on all sides with all manner of shit being chucked at you by the enemy.'

They were quiet for a while, turning right into Fore Hamlet, then joining the mass of cyclists competing with the trolley buses manoeuvring towards Bishops Hill. Most of the men dismounted and pushed their bikes up the steep incline, coughing as the factory smoke settled on their tobacco ridden chests. The air smelled of Andersons Engineering and it would be good to get away from it for the weekend.

'And what about your boy, how's he getting on?' Jack asked, once he had his breath back.

'Oh he's OK, working all the hours God made on those aircraft at Biggin Hill. But he enjoys it, he's a good mechanic, John.'

Jack couldn't help wishing that Jimmy had gone into the RAF. He wasn't a bad mechanic either but he changed the subject.

'And here's another thing. Vera is talking of taking a job as a telephonist. I can't say I like it. When we got married I said to her *Vera, that's the last time you have to go to work. I'm the provider now.*'

'I know just what you mean, mate, my Iris says she's going back to nursing. I said I understood the war effort and all that but I still expect my meal on the table when I come home.'

At the top of the hill one of the arms had come off a trolley bus and the driver and his conductor were manipulating a long pole to nudge it back onto the wires. The air was fractured with sparks and crackling.

'As if we haven't got enough problems,' said Jack, spitting into the gutter before remounting his bike.

As long as anyone could remember Holywells Mansion had been semi derelict. Owned by the council it had, at one time, been used as offices and later the Y.M.C.A. had commandeered it as a Headquarters. In 1940 it served as an ideal place for converting into a hostel and refuge centre for local people made homeless as a result of enemy bombing.

Sylvia still found it difficult to imagine such a thing as enemy bombing but she entered into the challenge of heading up a group of WVS members to put the place in order with her usual exuberance.

A Grimstone's removal van stood parked on the drive outside the vast front doors and green clad young and middle aged women pulled, pushed and lifted the contents into the Victorian building.

'Come on, four of us strapping girls should be able to lift this old sofa,' Sylvia shouted, ' one, two, three, there we go.'

After about an hour of what Winston Churchill would have called blood, sweat and tears the front two downstairs rooms were full of second-hand furniture scrounged by Sylvia and her team from the better-off citizens of Ipswich. She went to the driver and banged on his cabin. 'Thanks, Dobson, you can go now.'

'Right, Miss Sylvia, and good luck.'

She then went to the smaller van and opened the rear doors, 'Blackout materials, ladies,' she announced.

'Good old Grimstones,' whooped Audrey Blackthorpe, 'I'll never shop anywhere else.'

Inside the hall those with a head for heights set about climbing stepladders and measuring windows, whilst others began preparing the black curtains. A small team, encouraged by Sylvia, were painting the surrounds of the windows with special black paint provided by the council.

Sylvia consulted a small note book and called Audrey and Grace over from their tasks.

'We've a whole load of camp beds coming up tomorrow but we need to concentrate on the kitchen. I've made a list of what I think we need as advised by WVS headquarters and ticked the items we have been promised. So search your brain boxes for any other sources, would you? In the meantime I'll get some tea organised, I think we all deserve a cuppa, don't you?'

Having got everyone involved she wandered outside and lit a Craven A . It was now early evening and the park looked peaceful. She wondered about Francis and where he was. She hadn't had a letter for more than two weeks when he had been at Lille. Correspondence was subject to censoring and so all she really gathered was that he was OK and that the other chaps were a good bunch and that he had made a special pal out of someone called Bruce. Oh and to her slight annoyance he was apparently now called Frank. Well, she would have none of it. He would always be Francis to her. She smiled to herself thinking about how much she missed him. Of course she missed him, her new husband, her future, the intended father of her children. But she had become very busy and in her secret moments wondered if she missed him enough. She was, after all, having quite a good time with her war effort.

Kitty arrived home before her father and went straight to the kitchen where Vera was putting the finishing touches to the cottage pie and peas.

'Hello Mum.'

'My, you sound weary.'

'No, not really. We had quite a laugh today with all the new uniforms we're trying to make. The girls kept holding them up and prancing down the aisles until Old Mrs. Turpin told them off. But it was funny to see them strutting about like soldiers.'

'You've got to laugh, haven't you,' said Vera.

'Look on the bright side,' added Kitty, ' there must be one, somewhere. Talking of which I don't suppose there's a letter for me from Alan?'

Vera opened the oven door with a tea cloth and peered in, the steam made her face wet. 'No news is good news.'

'Yes, you're right. Talking of which I'm going out with Doris on Saturday. Tea at Grimstones and then the Pictures. She gets in the doldrums worrying about Jimmy. Droopy Doris I call her, that makes her laugh, at least.'

'That's nice, Kitty. You weren't sure about her at first were you?'

'I didn't know her, Mum, not properly, she was two years younger than me at school. But she's all right when she's not all broody about Jimmy. So I'm going to cheer her up.'

'There's a whole lot more Alans and Jimmys out in France with their girls worrying about them back here. But we just have to believe it'll all work out. That's what Mr. Churchill says, doesn't he. Oh Good, there's your father.' Vera tapped on the kitchen window as the silhouette of Jack appeared through the steam, on his way to the bicycle shed. Then he retraced his route and let himself in the front door. 'Anyone home?' he called.

'Why does he always say that?' whispered Vera. 'He'd have the shock of the devil if no one answered, we're in the kitchen, Kitty beat you home.'

'You might not be at his beck and call once you start your telephonist job', Kitty whispered back to her mother.

'That subject is barred at present so don't you go mentioning it, my girl, anyhow I haven't got it yet. Got to go for an interview first. Now go and lay the table in the back room and tell your father the meal will be ready in five minutes. He's got ARP tonight.'

After their meal Vera made a cup of tea and the three of them went into the front room to listen to the six o'clock news. Jack, as usual made comments throughout the bulletin in his best politician's voice; at the end he summed up the situation in case the women hadn't understood.

'It's the Belgians fault we're in this mess. If they hadn't given in so easily General Gort would not have been forced to retreat to this Dunkirk place. The only thing is that Hitler seems to have slowed things down a bit because he thinks his tanks will get stuck in the mud. Best place for them, I say. So, some of our boys are getting out by boat.'

'Let's hope Jimmy's one of them.'

'And Alan,' whispered Kitty.

'Of course and Alan, sorry dear,' Vera added.

'Deutschland siegt auf allen Fronten.' From a banner displayed in Paris.

'Good Evening, this is the six o'clock news read by Frank Phillips. Operation Dynamo continues, as thousands of boats crowd the channel evacuating British troops from the French coastal areas.....'

'Did you hear that,' Jack proclaimed, ' all those boats, bringing our forces home. No other country in the world could have done that, you know.'

They were sitting in the front room, Vera, Kitty and Doris who had called round to see if there was any news of Jimmy, huddled around the wireless awaiting Jack's summing up of the situation.

Vera stood up, adjusting her apron in preparation for making yet another cup of tea.

'I keep wondering what it's like out there. All those Germans firing at our boys and them trying to get on the boats. I mean how many of them are there for God's sake?'

'They said on here the other night that there are about 750,000 Germans and about 350,000 of our lot.'

'I don't know how to work that out,' Kitty said. ' How many people live in Ipswich, dad?'

'About 50,000 I reckon. So just imagine it was Felixstowe beach and about seven times the number of people who live in Ipswich were crowded on there waiting to get on boats with a whole load of Germans shooting and bombing at them.'

Doris stood up. 'I think I'll be going home now, if you don't mind.'

'Oh. Stay and have a cup of tea first dear, I was just about to put the kettle on.'

Reluctantly, but because she was polite and because she liked them, she sat down. ' Just a quick one then, Mrs. Wright, then I'll be off.'

Kitty moved closer to Doris on the sofa and put her arm around her, 'They'll be fine, just you see.'

Doris smiled at her, she wished she could be as bubbly and optimistic. She hoped she didn't take after her dad, who was now one of the Local Defence Volunteers and inclined to be a pessimist, convinced that Hitler would invade Britain any day. He and other

Local Defence Volunteer's had been out changing all the signposts to confuse the enemy when they landed. She and Jimmy would have laughed at that but she dare not let her father see how absurd she thought the whole thing was. Sadly, she had never found her mother easy to talk to and there had never been much physical contact between them. More and more, over recent weeks, she found herself calling on Jimmy's mother. She knew that her own mother resented this by the odd comments made but Doris realised that she could talk to Vera and, as a consequence, had become very fond of her.

They sipped their tea in silence and when Doris announced it really was time for her to go home Kitty stood up and said she could do with some air and would go with her.

It was a warm afternoon and the trees in Trent Avenue were still full of pink blossom.

'I think about old Alan more than I admit, you know,' Kitty said.

'I know you do.'

'He's such a decent, steady sort of bloke. Far too good for me in that respect.'

'Well, it's good that you're both different. I mean when your'e married and that.'

'Married. I never said anything about marriage. Don't think I could marry Alan. I said he was decent but he is a bit boring, if you know what I mean.'

Doris laughed. Kitty had a look of Jimmy when he had teased her about something. She knew she would never find Jimmy boring.

'It's obvious, even to me, that Jimmy and you are a couple,' Kitty continued, ' though what you see in the cheeky little sod, I've no idea.'

' I like him being cheeky. Like your Alan, I can be a bit serious and he takes me out of it.'

'Yeah. I suppose so.'

They turned into Derwent Road and were aware of the steady clink of spades, the squeak of wheelbarrows, the murmur of voices from the gardens of the semi-detached look-a-like houses.

'Dig for Victory,' laughed Kitty, making a gesture with her arms.

'By the end of this lot we will have forgotten what flowers look like,' said Doris but she, too, was laughing and they skipped together down the road miming the men in their gardens.

'Two no trumps.'

'Pass.'

'Three spades.'

'No bid.'

'Four spades.'

'Pass.'

'Four spades it is then, I hope you know what you are doing.'

The Camerons and the Grimstones sat hunched over the card table in the lounge of Hall Farm; a shaft of late afternoon sun lit up the patterned carpet, dust mites flitted in the bright light like aeroplanes in a dogfight.

'We need to win this one to keep in the rubber,' said the competitive Robert Cameron, picking up the first trick.

Elizabeth Grimstone studied her cards, her face impassive. She seldom spoke, apart from bidding, when a game was in progress.

The door opened and Mrs. Moore appeared with the tea tray which she set down on the nest of tables by the French windows.

'Thank you Mrs. Moore, I should trot off home now if I were you,' Edward said, glancing at his wife for approval.

'Well played, Robert and you too Valerie, of course.'

'Yes well done, two games each, all on the third. I'll tell you what let's break for tea.'

The four rose from the bridge table and settled in comfortable chairs.

'How are your Local Defence Volunteers doing, Edward?' asked Robert Cameron.

'Well, we're certainly not short of volunteers, it's the equipment that's in short supply. If Hitler does arrive on our shores he'll be met with a lot of old buffers repelling him with pitchforks and garden hoes.'

'But there are plans to improve things, aren't there?'

'You would know the answer to that more than me, old boy, I'm just an old Major who's trying to revive a bit of military discipline into a willing bunch.

Now you, Elizabeth, are doing wonders with your WVS, I gather.'

'We're getting ready. Though I'm not sure for what. There, I sound just like Sylvia, who is working like Billy O by the way, and enjoying every minute of it. Just wish she'd stop asking her father and me questions that we can't answer. More tea Robert?'

'No thanks, my dear. I have to say I think Francis has found himself a brick in your Sylvia, such an enthusiast.'

Elizabeth sipped her tea; 'I don't suppose you've heard anything?'

'Not a word. Not a word.'

Doris was perched on a high stool muttering to herself, '300 milligrams of light Magnesium Carbonate, 500 milligrams of Sodium Bicarbonate,' when Joyce burst into the dispensary.

'Ladylike, Joyce, try being ladylike,' Mr French looked up from his mixture.

'Doris, quick, come into the shop.'

'I'm in the middle of......'

'Now,' shouted Joyce and Mr. French shrugged, he'd never make a lady of her, might as well give up.

Under protest Doris followed her friend into an empty shop.

'Well?'

'Look.'

Doris followed Joyce's outstretched hand and there was a face squashed against the window. A grotesque face. Jimmy's face. She screamed his name and ran to the door just as he was about to enter. She threw her arms about him and hugged him like she would never let him from her sight again. They almost fell into the shop together.

'Got anything for blisters, Mr. French?' Jimmy said to the proprietor who had left the dispensary to see what all the fuss was about.

'Welcome home, young man, welcome home,' he said.

'Oh. Yes, Jimmy, thank God you are safe,' said Joyce. 'This one has been driving us nuts.'

'Oh Jimmy, you are all right aren't you?' Doris asked, looking the young soldier up and down.

'Apart from the blisters I'm fine', he said.

Mr. French looked at his watch. 'It's four o'clock. You might as well be off then Doris. I'll finish Mrs. Western's medicine. You Joyce, I'm afraid, will have to stay 'til the bitter end.'

'My pleasure,' Joyce said doing a mock curtsey.

Doris and Jimmy left the shop, their arms tightly around each other. They walked together up Westgate Street towards the Electric House Trolley Bus depot, unable to say very much. The details could wait until later, Doris thought, wiping her eyes with a free hand.

There was a slight sea breeze at The Ferry but not enough to spoil the golf. Fairways and greens were in excellent condition in spite of limited attention from a depleted ground staff. The Martello tower stood sentinel and firm and a high barbed wire fence straddled the seashore as far as the eye could see. Gulls swooped and cried, welcoming local fishing boats back from Dunkirk.

'After all of that you can still hit a decent ball Francis,' Robert said as they stood on the fifteenth tee.

'You taught me all I know about golf, father. I don't think I'll ever be in your league.'

'Nonsense, I'm only one up with three to go having given you a meagre four shots.' Robert had just turned fifty but had always kept himself in good shape. He looked every inch a gentleman in his plus twos and tweed hat rammed solidly on his greying hair. He tee'd up, took a relaxed practice swing and then propelled the ball down the fairway adjacent to the sea wall.

'Good shot, father.' Francis took a couple of swings before striking the ball in a rigid fashion causing it to hook towards the gorse.

'Came up on it again,' he muttered.

They walked together, father and son; both delighted to be in each other's company again, neither admitting it in so many words.

'No ill effects then?' Robert eventually asked.

'No, I'm fine, father. One of the lucky ones. A lot of my men didn't make it'

'Who's looking after the wounded?' Robert, the experienced World War One veteran asked.

'I couldn't believe it,' Robert told him, ' the doctors were drawing lots as to who would stay and who would get on the boats. God knows what will happen to those who stayed behind..'

They reached the gorse bushes together and spied a ball nestled in the thick branches.

'Better take a drop,' said Robert.

By the time they reached the eighteenth, Robert was two up and the match was his.

'I'll let you off the drink since we better not be late for this dinner party your mother-in-law is so keen on.'

'We'll keep it light won't we, father, I still haven't really spoken to Sylvia about how it was. Don't think I will actually. No sense in making her worry about next time.'

'Where next time? Defending the home soil or off to try to stop the enemy in some other part of the world?'

'No idea, and that's not being secretive, I have to report back to barracks on Monday.'

'So tonight it's the Grimstones, Sylvia's pal and her husband and your mother and me and, of course, you two. Do you know these friends of Sylvia's?'

'Met them once, Sylvia has become great buddies with this Audrey, WVS and all that. I think I met him, Roger, before the balloon went up. He's a second lieutenant in the Royal Engineers, got back a couple of days before me. You know the engineers.'

'War-time grub, I'm afraid,' said Elizabeth, ' but I did manage to get a decent bit of beef for the steak and kidney pudding.'

'Steak and kidney pud, wonderful,' said Roger, licking his lips at the prospect.

'And we won't go short on vegetables, Old Moore is growing enough to feed an army.'

'He might have to do just that,' muttered Francis and they all laughed unsure whether he was making a joke.

'So who is this Old Moore?'

'Mr. and Mrs. Moore have been with us for years, too old to do much else in terms of the war so they are staying on helping out.

Obviously we will spread any surplus vegetables around the village if things get tough.'

'Sound absolute treasures.'

'They certainly are. Now then Audrey you haven't got much.'

Sylvia glanced around the familiar room, with its thick embossed wallpaper, pictures of men with guns resting on their knees, pheasants and hare dead at their feet. Men and guns, she thought, why did they go together? Way before the war little boys ran around with wooden guns playing Cowboys and Indians now they had changed to being soldiers fighting the Germans. She looked at Francis talking quietly to Audrey at the end of the table; competent Francis, deep-thinking Francis, but somehow she still couldn't imagine him with a gun blazing in his hand.

'Audrey has been giving me the low-down on what you girls have been up to whilst Roger and I have been holed up in France. Sounds very useful stuff. ' Francis was attempting to open up his conversation with Audrey to the rest of the gathering.

'Your Sylvia is amazing, she is the driving force of the WVS,' Audrey bubbled.

'You girls might be busier than you think before long. We're pretty sure that Jerry's next move will be to send the Luftwaffe to drop a few bombs on strategic targets. Airfields, docks and engineering works are bound to be on their lists. A few stray bombs could cause havoc to nearby houses. That's why all this preparation is so important. Just about everyone is getting involved.' Robert had a captive audience but felt he had gone on long enough at a dinner party meant to be a welcome home for his Army Officer son, 'Enough of that. Had a damned good game of golf today, didn't we Francis?'

'It was good to be out there. The Ferry seemed just the same, apart from the odd bit of barbed wire.'

'They hadn't taken the sand out of the bunkers for sand bags then?' Sylvia chimed in.

'Not yet. But I bet they will as soon as somebody thinks of it.'

Sylvia took a swig of cider,' Who won then?'

'Oh. Dad. He always wins,' said Francis.

Plates were cleared and they had the last of the tinned peaches as a treat before going out onto the terrace for a glass of port. The women lit up cigarettes and Edward handed round cigars for the men. Francis and Roger had separated from the rest of the group.

'Did you have a tough time, old man?' Roger asked, glancing over his shoulder.

'It was a bit tricky towards the end. We were about ten miles from Dunkirk trying to march in some sort of orderly fashion alongside throngs of refugees when the Luftwaffe swooped. I shouted to the platoon to disperse and ran into a farm building. A few minutes later it was hit and I was partially buried in the rubble. Good news was nothing broken, eventually I got up and went outside but couldn't see my men anywhere. I assumed that Sergeant Little had got them back to the road.'

'Christ. So what did you do?'

'I went back to what shelter was left but the Germans were all around by then. Then I had a bit of luck. Saw this Hun on a motor bike so I took a shot at him and got him in one. Bit of a shock, actually. Didn't have much time to think. Got on his motorbike and rattled off down the road towards the beaches.'

'Good God, old man, I heard about some chap who came into Dunkirk on an enemy motorbike, that was you?'

Sylvia and Audrey spotted their men chatting together and came over.

'So what is all this army talk then?' Sylvia said.

'Francis is quite the hero, you know. He was telling me that...'

'Nonsense. I just managed to commandeer a motorbike that's all.'

'Didn't know you could ride a motorbike, Francis?'

'I can now,' he laughed, 'Come on let's go in, it's getting a bit chilly.'

The party broke up at ten thirty and Sylvia and Francis went back to Limes Cottage. They were both tired and went to bed immediately. Sylvia wanted to ask him more about his experiences in France but as soon as he got into bed he wished her a hurried goodnight and fell asleep. A few hours later he woke up; he was sweating profusely, he couldn't stop shaking. Not wanting to disturb Sylvia he got out of bed and walked, unsteadily, downstairs to the kitchen. With some difficulty he made himself a cup of tea.

He sat for a while on one of the two wooden chairs in the small kitchen gripping the sides of his cup. His head was spinning. Then it seemed to clear and he was back in France.

He was at the head of the platoon as they picked their way along the rubble strewn road when suddenly there was a roar. A German fighter swooped. He heard the noise of machine gun fire, saw bullets hit the road in front of him, shouted out to the men as he threw himself down. From where he lay he could see farm buildings close by and managed to crawl towards them seeking shelter. Another fighter appeared from nowhere and began to spray the barn with bullets; he thought it was a *Messerschmitt*. Then, with an eerie groan the wooden structure collapsed on top of him. There was dust in his nose and mouth and he couldn't move his leg. After a while he managed to shift a smouldering beam that was trapping him and wriggle free. His leg was sore but appeared intact. Crawling back towards the road the area seemed like a ghost town. His men were nowhere to be seen. Then he saw a solitary figure. A German motorcyclist leaning on his bike, adjusting his helmet. Instinctively, he picked up his rifle, checked that it was loaded, aimed and shot. The German fell, the motorbike slithering on top of him. Francis looked around and then ran towards the German. He knew he was dead. He knew he had killed him. Momentarily he had looked at the face. Blood was oozing from nose and ears but above all what he saw was the face of a young boy. He, Francis Cameron, had shot a young boy and nothing in his training had equipped him for this. Vomit appeared in his mouth, his head was spinning but instinct and survival took over. He jumped on the bike, kicked the starter and flew off, weaving down the road and somehow arrived at the beach to join his cheering men.

When, eventually, they got back to England they had been taken to their barracks and instructed to clean up and report for dinner in the mess. He hadn't seen Bruce for some days and was relieved to find that he was OK. Later Bruce had come to his room for a night-cap. They'd talked together about the chaos and panic of it all and, before long, Francis started to open up about his feelings after shooting the German; he remembered he had begun to shake uncontrollably. Bruce had come to him and taken him by the shoulders, 'It's all right, Frank, it's all right,' he had said. They were very close and for a

second he thought Bruce was going to kiss him and for a second he
had wanted him to.

Earlier on that same June day Jimmy and Doris had been enjoying
home made lemonade, manufactured from powder that Doris had
discovered and brought with her to Trent Avenue.

Jack had gone inside in readiness for the next news bulletin and
Vera, as always, was in the kitchen. They sat on a couple of old chairs
outside the back door. The garden had changed shape over the last
few months. The shelter stood ready for occupation to their left, the
lawn had been dug up and linked to the rest of garden forming an
impressive vegetable patch.

'Someone's digging for Victory,' Doris nudged Jimmy.

'If he gets any keener he'll be digging for Australia.' He took a swig
of his drink.

'Not too bad this lemonade.'

'Thank you kind sir, it's your treat for being a hero,' Doris paused.
'You were a hero weren't you, Jimmy. You haven't spoken much
about it since you've been back.'

He rocked back on his chair causing it to creak, 'We were all heroes,
thousands and thousands of heroes but the best were the chaps with
the boats. I've never seen so many boats.'

'A lot went from round here, you know,'

' I think I now understand why my dad never talks much about his
war. It is like nothing you have ever experienced and I was one of the
lucky ones. We weren't too far from the coast when the order came
down the line to retreat. The CSM was near to us and started barking
out instructions to B Company and our Sergeant yelled at us to get
fell in and marches us briskly back to the shore. We were one of the
first lots to arrive though there were burnt out vehicles and medics
taking away the wounded on the beaches when we got there. The
noise was ear shattering, there was this awful smell of burning and the
whole beach seemed to be exploding. Then, in a very British sort of
way we went and queued up, standing in the water like we were
waiting to get into a football match. Luckily, we didn't have to wait
long before they packed us onto this destroyer and we set sail. We

didn't celebrate or anything. Just looked back at the beaches where more and more were coming with the Germans still screaming over head firing at them. So you see I was lucky. I'm always lucky.'

Doris got up from her chair, sat on his lap and kissed him.

'Steady on. My Mum thinks you are such a nice girl.' he said.

'I'm nice to you, Jimmy Wright, and don't you forget it.'

'Oh, Doris, and one more thing. Don't go telling any of this to my parents, will you?'

When they went back into the house Jack informed them that there wasn't much on the news for a change. No one seemed to know what Hilter's plans were. The Germans were still lording it around their new territories, especially Paris. Paris seemed important to them. Suddenly they heard a fierce knocking on the door. Vera scurried off and they could hear Kitty's voice in the hall. She came into the front room and stood framed in the door. For a long time she didn't move. Just stood there, staring.

Vera came up behind her placing her hands on her daughter's shoulders.

'It's so unfair,' Kitty blurted out. 'He hated the idea of war. Never wanted to go. He was such a decent bloke. Much nicer than me, he was. I was horrible to him but he just smiled at me and came back for more.' She rounded on her mother, ' But in my funny way I did love him, you know, I did,' and she burst into uncontrollable tears, violently shaking her mother's comforting hands away.

Jack sucked on his pipe, his eyes lowered, there was nothing he could say.

Doris stepped forward, 'Oh. Kitty I'm so sorry,'

'You're so sorry,' Kitty shouted, 'You're bloody sorry. You're all right you are. Got your Jimmy back in one piece. And you, Miss bloody Goody Two Shoes, are so sorry'.

She almost knocked her mother over, rushing from the door and up the stairs.

Vera turned to Doris, 'She didn't mean it dear. It's just such dreadful news.'

Doris was sobbing in Jimmy arms, ' I'll give her a while then take her up a cup of tea,' Vera said and went to the kitchen. Jack fiddled with his pipe, ' We don't swear in this house.' he said.

IOWA

'Little towns are mighty big places to be from.' – Wright Morris

Karl and Lois drove the Buick into Red Oak and parked in front of Brown's Shoe Fit. It had been another hot, humid day and at six o'clock in the evening the temperature was still in the low eighties.

A whole range of vehicles lined up outside the red brick Victorian stores, Buicks, Pontiacs, Cheverelets and since it was Saturday all of them had been polished by their owners. A crowd of women had gathered under the awning of Hayes Clothing following a rumour that new supplies had arrived whilst, further up the sidewalk, a similar number of men sat waiting their turn for a haircut. It was a matter of pride, in Red Oak, to be smartly turned out for church on Sunday.

Karl climbed carefully from his car and walked around to the passenger side to open the door for his wife, stretching his six-foot frame.

'I know why you parked by Browns,' Lois said, ' You're after a new pair of boots.'

Karl laughed, 'There's nothing wrong with my present boots, they're good and comfortable. I might just have a look though, see what's on offer.'

'Well, I'm off to Earl Mays so I'll see you back here in a while. I put some lemonade and cookies in the trunk box.'

He watched her walk away. You're a lucky man Karl Nelson, he thought, that wife of yours looks as slim as the day you got wed. She's had two children and struggled with you through the depression. Then he chuckled to himself; they had been through some hard times but were out of it now, the farm was looking good, this year's corn healthy and his daughter Ellen was about to make him a grand-father. Still smiling he went to check out the boots.

Fountain Square was always busy on a Saturday evening and they had difficulty locating a spare bench on the north side in the shade. Children ran around on the grass, teenagers teased and taunted one another by the fountain and on the south side the Salvation Army band played well known hymns. As always, during the long Iowan summer, it had been a busy week and Karl and Lois were content to sit and listen to their town relaxing.

'That crop of yours is looking good.' They hadn't noticed the Linquists approaching. Karl stood up, 'Why it's good to see you both, here Patty have a seat next to Lois.'

'Yeah, so far so good Lester, a lot can happen before harvest, but so far so good. And your crop looks fine to me. Let's hope they're right and this is the year the farms start making money again.'

'God willing,' Lester replied. Both men were tall; Karl carried a bit more weight than the wiry Lester. They were fair, tanned and had the blue eyes of their Swedish pioneer ancestors.' 'That boy of yours is making a good job of repairing the large barn. Every time I've been past your place I see him working away.'

'Tom, yeah he's never happier than when he has a hammer or a paintbrush in his hand. I just wish he'd be as keen on his books.'

'I shouldn't worry too much about that, if I were you,' Lester murmured, 'Letha may be keen on her books but she's not a lot of help on the farm.' He thought a bit, 'Maybe that's a bit unfair, she does help her mom in the house with bottling and pickling and all that stuff. Where is Tom tonight, by the way?'

'He's up at Chautauqua picnicking with some friends. He said he'd be down at the Square early evening.'

'He'll probably see Letha up there. Seems to be the natural meeting place for the young folk. They're lucky to have Chautauqua.'

'Lucky to have a lot of things. This is still a good a place as any to live. We've just got to hope the Government is right and we are, at last, getting out of this Depression. They talk on the radio about there being more jobs. America getting back to work again so, I guess, we have to believe them.'

'President Roosevelt seemed pretty positive on his 'Fireside Chats' last week, and I have a lot of faith in him.'

'Sure, I'm not sure I follow his comments about this war in Europe though. Why are we worrying about all that?'

'Well I can tell you I'm not worrying about it. Don't know much about it and don't want to. Got far too much to concern us back home, if you want my views.'

Patty Linquist stood up, 'That's enough politics for one night boys. Lester we promised to find the Petersons, if you remember. Now then we must have a meal together soon with you folks.'

Karl lowered himself onto the bench, his movements always slow, deliberate.

'I like Patty Linquist, she seldom talks about herself, always thinking about other folk,' Lois said. Karl smiled, held her hand and closed his eyes and felt the warm evening sun on his face.

The Chautauqua Pavilion was one of Red Oak's major buildings having been erected in 1907 when its tented predecessor had blown down in a storm. When not used for concerts and official gatherings it was a natural meeting place and in the heat of day provided an excellent shaded picnic area. Tom Nelson and Letha Linquist were two of a crowd of local youngsters who had met there on that particular Sunday.

'How's it going Tom?' Letha had walked away from her group, deciding it was time to go down to the Square, when she noticed Tom.

'Fine, just fine. And you Letha you O.K?'

'Sure am, off to university in the fall. To Lincoln, you know Lincoln, Nebraska.'

'Yeah, I heard, that's real nice for you.'

'How about you?'

Tom could never quite make Letha out. She was without doubt a looker. He loved the way she fixed her fair hair back from her gently tanned face and those eyes of hers gazed right at you. She seemed pleased to see him, 'Don't have to make my mind up yet', he muttered,' but my dad keeps on at me about the value of education. He would really like me to go to college but I really love it on the farm. I don't know why he isn't content with that. He knows I will probably take over from him one day.'

She looked at him with those eyes, ' It's the Depression. Our folks are scared for us in case it don't go away or even if it comes back again one day.'

'Maybe that's it then,' he shrugged and for some reason she smiled at him.

'I'll see you around then, Tom', she said, and with a swirl of her skirt was gone.

Tom walked out of the Pavilion and watched her go down the hill. He stayed for a while looking across the town to fields that went on forever; a light breeze ruffled the great sea of corn. Maybe one day he would suggest to Letha Linquist that she came with him, into the heart of it, and together they would listen to it grow.

'Music while you work.' – Radio programme

Vera

'So you want to be a telephonist, do you?' He leant across a bulky oak desk and looked at her over a pair of rimless spectacles. 'Yes, I do. I want to be a telephonist,' Vera replied as confidently as she could muster.

The room was small, airless and stuffy; a poster stating that the speed limit in the blackout was 20 mph. created the only diversion. Mr. Hargreaves sat on a large winged chair behind an impressive desk.

'What did you do before?' He fingered through the papers in front of him, then looking up, 'you were married?'

'I worked at Andersons, in the office.'

'A clerk?'

'Yes, a clerk.'

'Good, and since being married you have not worked.'

She thought about saying that apart from washing, scrubbing, cooking, ironing, dusting, bringing up two children and budgeting on a pittance, he was correct but decided not to pursue such a line, 'No. My husband believed that the man should provide.'

'And what does he think about you applying for this post, then?'

'Oh. He is a patriot and understands that women have to do their part what with all our young men being in the services.' It was a white lie but Jack would come round.

Mr. Hargreaves made a show of shuffling his papers into a neat bundle, 'Well Mrs. Wright, I would like you to put these headphones on and then speak the words on this card to me in your clearest voice.' He handed over the headphones, which Vera found rather off putting. Then she read from the card *Category One Emergency at Cornhill 0800 hours.*

'Now I would like you to put on this gas mask. You will note that it has been specially designed to enable you to speak.' She pulled on the gas mask just as Jack had always instructed and read the second card in a muffled voice, *'Red Warning, enemy aircraft imminent, Alert Fire Stations one, four and six.'*

59

'Good, you can take the mask off now. Right, here is a browser of files in alphabetical order. I want you to search for the following as quickly as you can. First Waterbeach, good, now Shetlands, thank you and now Leeming. Well done, that's fine.

Thank you Mrs. Wright, I am happy to say that your credentials are fine and you do have a good clear voice, very important in a telephonist, and your speed of obtaining information is perfectly adequate. In the event of any invasion it will be a critical role but one which I feel sure you will adequately fill. We would like you to report for training at our Burrell Road Centre next Monday. The details are all here, including information on pay, shift work and overtime.' He handed her a large brown envelope.

When Vera left the building she was aware that she was smiling. She looked at her watch and decided that just for once in her life she would give herself a treat.

The young waitress in Lyons was mouse-like but very polite and Vera took time over her tea. The restaurant was half-full, a few well-to-do ladies with neat little hats, a table of soldiers on leave after Dunkirk, even some airforce boys, presumably from Martlesham. Vera was not a great smoker and so did not contribute to the already heavy atmosphere but enjoyed herself simply doing nothing for a change. Eventually she rose and decided she would complete her special morning with a brief walk in Christchurch Park.

She chose to go up Fonnereau Road and into the Lower Arboretum commencing her stroll along Mayors Walk taking in the names of the various Aldermen and Councillors who had been Ipswich mayors since the late 1800's. She remembered how on Sundays when she was a young girl her father would take her to the park after church. How smart he had been in his three-piece suit with pocket watch chain glowing across the waistcoat and bowler hat plumped solidly on his bald head. She couldn't remember him ever having hair. He'd loved Christchurch Park, particularly the Arboretum and repeatedly told of its grand opening in 1895. She was pleased that not much had changed. On this calm, warm Summer's day it was impossible to imagine that the country was at war.

Her route opened up so that she could see the two croquet lawns where elderly ladies were seriously engaged in combat. Croquet, her father had said, was a vicious game but she liked the noise of wood on wood, the whiteness of the women's attire and the jauntiness of their straw hats. Moving away from the main route she went down a slope to where a wooden bridge provided a vantage point for the main pond which linked the wooded area with Christchurch park proper. She stood leaning, wishing she had just a morsel of bread since, on spying her presence, the mallards dive-bombed the water skidding to a halt in front of her. Ashamed, she moved away and sat on a small bench by the tiny waterfall. A breeze caused the bamboo and reeds to rustle but it remained very warm and she closed her eyes hearing only the chatter of birds and the echo of distant mallet on ball.

She wondered what Jack would say when she announced that she had taken the bull by the horns and got herself a job. She knew his foolish pride would get in the way but that he would be pleased for her provided his meals were still on the table and his shirts ironed on time. He would also be pleased (though he would never admit it) with the prospect of a bit more money coming into the household. He understood, of course, that in this war-changed world women everywhere were training for all sorts of jobs, many of which had been the preserve of men. Why Jack himself had told her that Andersons intended to eventually train four hundred women to be engineers, adding that he didn't know what the world was coming to!

This war, she thought, was an awful thing and still difficult to fathom since apart from all this preparation Hitler's armies had not invaded our shores nor had a single bomb been dropped on Britain. But she knew, from recent experience, that the war was indeed very real. She thought back to the evening when Kitty had returned from visiting Alan's parents with the news that he had been killed on the beaches of Dunkirk. She remembered, only too well, how she had lain awake listening to her daughter sob the night away; how Jack had said he had not known what to say to his daughter leaving Vera to find what ever words of comfort she could manage in the morning.

When Jack had gone to work and Jimmy was out of the house she had taken the customary cup of tea to her daughter. She sat on the bed, after a while Kitty had wanted to talk and Vera had let her. Offering no advice she had eventually suggested a bath and Kitty had nodded. The geyser wouldn't light first time and when ultimately it exploded into life with a loud boom she found she was shaking.

About an hour later Kitty had come into the kitchen, she was wearing her newest flower print dress and had put her make up on. She had hugged her mother saying, 'Don't worry mum, I'll be all right.' Then she'd gone into the front room and switched on the wireless.

Vera shook herself and got up from her seat wandering back past the tennis courts and through the tunnel to the Upper Arboretum. She could see silhouettes of people sitting in the bandstand reading newspapers, she wondered where they came from. She paused before leaving by the gate opposite the fine school, taking a final deep breath, enjoying the scents of the park. It was a perfect afternoon so why did she have this empty feeling in the pit of her stomach.

'If only they'd tell us what to do?' – cartoon in newspaper.

Sylvia

Sylvia had cycled to the meeting. The lanes around Playford and Rushmere were always lovely in Summer, warm and fragrant and travelling on a bicycle was an excellent way to enjoy them. She went down Grove Lane into the town itself freewheeling down the hill to The County Hall which she noticed was encased in a wall of sandbags. She parked her bike in the shed at the back and gathering up a leather document case from the useful basket attached to her handlebars made her way to the basement. She was looking forward to the meeting in a selfish way, quite pleased that her mother had a headache and was unable to fulfil the role of WVS co-ordinator. She knew most of the committee and with her father-in-law in the chair she would not feel overawed.

She took a vacant seat at the oblong table in between a senior policeman and Anna Catchpole from the Red Cross. Father-in-law, who was shuffling his papers, had not seen her come into the room; eventually he looked up, 'Why hello Sylvia, this is a pleasant surprise.' Others around the table looked at her with interest.

Robert then assumed his official face and explained that the purpose of the meeting was to ensure that all arms of Civil Defence were properly co-ordinated and ready to deal with air attacks from the Luftwaffe. He pointed out that obvious targets included the docks, the engineering works, HMS Bunting and local airfields. Then he added that Suffolk was situated over the flight-path for London and the Midlands and that the Germans would jettison any unused bombs in our vicinity on their way back to their European bases. Robert then went to a chart and explained how Ipswich was divided into a number of specific areas with services allocated accordingly. One or two homes, including his own, were now equipped with telephones in order to co-ordinate activities and each individual service would need to create their own alert system responding to the sirens and using, for example, messengers on bicycles.

He then asked various representatives around the table to elaborate on their duties and Sylvia scribbled diligently into her notebook. She learnt that ARP wardens would deal with incendiary bombs alerting their HQ, in the case of more serious missiles. They would in turn call in the army bomb disposal people in the case of any unexploded H.E bombs or mines. The police, together with the ARP wardens would keep the public away from buildings and houses that had been hit. The fire service would be at the forefront putting out fires and rescuing victims; he added that an encouraging number of local people had volunteered as auxiliaries.

Sylvia was just thinking that she had never noticed before what a commanding voice Robert had when he consulted his agenda and asked her to say a few words on behalf of the WVS. She briefly explained their role in providing tea, food and comfort for both victims and helpers. She explained that WVS vans would be present immediately a raid had taken place but would continue to serve in bomb damaged areas as long as there was a need. She went on to explain the siting of Rest Centres throughout the town which would be run by WVS and other volunteers. When she had finished she noticed that her hands were clammy.

Robert thanked everyone for attending and told them, sounding almost Churchillian, that he had every confidence that the people of Ipswich could deal with anything Hitler threw at them.

Having walked her bicycle up the steep hill of Grove Lane she was pleased to get out of the town proper and back along the hedgerows of Humber Doucy Lane and on through Rushmere to Playford and the cottage. She let herself in and put the kettle on, deciding to report back to her mother later in the afternoon. Tea wasn't yet on ration but rumours suggested that it would soon join sugar, bacon and butter. She felt stuffy in the little kitchen and opened the window above the sink, after what she had learnt today she would have to set about taping her windows at the weekend.

With tea balanced in one hand she opened the back door and dragged out an old wooden chair to the garden. She sat thinking about the meeting and couldn't resist chuckling to herself, then wondered whether she was being unpatriotic. There was no doubt that father-in-law had conducted the affairs in a serious and appropriate manner and the enthusiasm from all, including herself, was never in question. But, mingled with an underlying fear of the unknown was a feeling that they could just as well have been

64

organising a village fete. At the same time, she rationalised, that this ability to pull together, as already demonstrated at Dunkirk, could be the hidden strength of the British.

Dunkirk made her think of Francis who was currently up in the north of England at somewhere called Catterick undergoing even more training for whatever the War Cabinet had in mind. She smiled to herself at the irony of it all. Francis far away from any obvious enemy targets whilst she was attending meetings about what to do when the bombs fell around Ipswich. As always, she questioned herself about how much she missed him? Like so many war time marriages it was very different from what she had anticipated. He had been sent to France almost immediately after their Bournemouth honeymoon and since Dunkirk he had spent most of his time in remotest Yorkshire. She'd tried to talk to him about France, out of curiosity as much as concern, but he'd made light of the subject. She sensed, however, that something significant had happened and had even asked Audrey what Roger and Francis had been talking about on the evening of the supper party. Audrey had shrugged and muttered something about 'army chat'. Francis would be coming home on a 72 hour pass in a couple of weeks and she hoped that somehow she could get closer to this deep man who she was sure she had married for love.

Looking down she found she had let her tea get cold and admonished herself for daydreaming. She picked up the cup and saucer and walked back into the cottage. She would cycle down the lane to Home Farm and, in the hope that her mother had recovered from the headache, deliver a blow by blow account of the meeting. Being tidy minded she washed up the crockery and put it away in the small wooden cupboard with the other Royal Worcester pieces, a wedding present from an Aunt Mary.

She was smugly aware that she had enjoyed herself representing the WVS at the meeting though she realised that she had no real idea of what to expect from this war. She was certain, however, that the peace of summer afternoons such as this were about to be shattered by more than a headache.

'True friendship must undergo and withstand the shocks of adversity.' – George Washington.

Doris

'Someone to see you,' Joyce stuck her head around the back door of the Chemists shop, calling to Doris who was sitting in the yard enjoying her lunch. The walled area, which housed the bicycle shed and another lean-to that was used for storage, was a real sun-trap. Doris was pale skinned and burned easily so she had placed an old straw hat on top of her thick red hair. 'Who have you got out there, Joyce, Rita Hayworth or Katherine Hepburn?' said the visitor and Doris looked up and saw that it was Kitty.

She jumped up, 'Kitty, here bring out one of those stools. You've got time for some tea, haven't you?'

'About half an hour left before I'm back to the grindstone.'

After a bit of manipulation the two girls sat together in the paved yard, Doris insisting on perching on the stool looking down on Kitty. Joyce had put the kettle on before disappearing back into the shop.

'This is nice,' Kitty said, 'I've only ever been in the shop before and here you are with your private sun terrace. See, just like on the pictures. Especially you in that hat.'

'It's an old one of Mr. French's. Been hanging on a hook in the dispensary for as long as I've worked here,' she cocked her head at a jaunty angle, 'Do you think it suits me?' Kitty looked up and laughed.

'Talking of pictures I really came to see if you fancied coming to the Odeon with me on Friday after work?'

'I'd love to. It's the new Lionel Barrymore one, isn't it?'

'Yeah. He's a bit of all right isn't he?'

'It's his eyes isn't it and he's got wonderful teeth. Hang on the kettle will be boiling. I'll be back in a jiffy.' Doris climbed down from the wobbly stool and went inside whilst Kitty looked around the walled yard; a large laburnum bush hung over the brickwork in the far corner trailing over the sheds. Cabbage-White butterflies flitted busily like a ward full of nurses in starched uniforms.

When Doris returned, Kitty took the tea and looked at it for a while, 'Doris, I never really apologised for my outburst, you know, when I heard that...'

'For goodness sake, Kitty, you've no need. God, I'd hate to think how I would behave if anything happened to Jimmy. Sorry, that's not really the way to put it but you know what I mean?'

'I know what you mean. Anyhow I'd be a bit upset about Jimmy too, he is my brother after all, even if I don't quite see him in the same wonderful light as you do'.

Doris sipped her tea rocking on the stool, 'Funny, Jimmy and me, neither of us ever had another steady but we just click somehow. We probably seem a bit soppy to other people.'

Kitty didn't reply, 'He's due for leave soon, isn't he?' she asked.

'Three weeks he said in his last letter. He's training as a gunner. Not sure whether I like that much but he seems to be enjoying it. Afterwards he'll be posted somewhere near the coast he reckons.'

As they spoke two spitfires roared overhead drowning out their conversation.

'I shall never start a war without the certainty that a demoralised enemy will succumb to the first stroke of a single gigantic attack.' - Adolf Hitler.

Sylvia got out of the WVS van and stood leaning on the mudguard surveying the scene in Myrtle Road in total disbelief. The whole docks appeared to be on fire; a pink cloud with an angry red centre lit up the sky, grotesque yet in an awful way beautiful.

Every now and then there was a loud explosion from the burning warehouses, fireballs like footballs bounced from the buildings and the noxious smell of burning rubber pervaded everything. Scores of fire service personnel had scaled ladders from official fire service vehicles and from makeshift versions adapted from private cars and vans; they were hosing gallons of water into the heart of the fires and as they did so rafters and timbers came crashing down. Even more intense activity was taking place along Myrtle Road itself where houses immediately in front of the dock area were affected. More firemen aided by rescue squads were hosing into the crumbling homes. ARP wardens in their white and black tin hats were shouting at onlookers to keep back, to go home unless they were involved. Ambulances had driven through flooded roads littered with debris and teams of first aiders were searching out the victims and bringing them to safety.

'My God, Audrey just look at that,' Sylvia shouted to her colleague, then trying to be resolute she added, ' I suppose we better ask someone where to set up our centre, get some tea on, sort out these poor people and get them up to the Holywells Rest Centre.' She ran over to the nearest ARP warden, 'WVS,' she announced, 'Where should we set up?'

A sooty face looked up at her and grinned, ' Don't really know miss, but I would suggest further down the road towards Cliff Lane safe from debris. Then you could come back and take the survivors with you. We'll label them up. The sooner they get away from all this the better.'

'Right. We'll be at full strength pretty soon.' She turned and went back relieved that two other WVS vans had arrived containing a number of the green clad volunteers.

'OK they want us to go back away from here about one hundred yards towards Cliff Lane. We'll need two persons for each van to provide tea etcetera and the rest are to come with me.'

As she spoke there was a tremendous crash and a section of an elevator fell into the heart of the flames, then everyone seemed to be shouting at once.

Sylvia gathered a group of about twelve women around her and proceeded back along the road towards the damaged houses, water gushed over their feet and mud splattered their skirts.

'Please move away,' a warden was shouting at a crowd of people who had left their homes wanting to help, hating being helpless. 'It would be far better if you all went home and left us to deal with things,' then seeing the WVS,' Right ladies go up as far as the group of my men in white helmets with the first aiders, see them down there. They've got some people needing you.'

Coming nearer to the destroyed homes Sylvia thought they looked like gigantic dolls' houses with their fronts ripped out, personal possessions exposed for all to see; pictures hanging crooked on walls, smashed vases lying in the corners of sloping floors, a bath that had crashed through a ceiling wavering precariously against a burning sofa and a toy wooden car slowly smouldering in what had once been the front garden.

About three houses appeared to have been completely devastated and another six or seven badly damaged. A First Aid helper saw them approaching, 'I've got twenty two people here,' she said indicating the group huddled together under blankets, we've labelled them up. About another twenty have been taken to hospital. Most were in shelters and survived, quite a few were injured, we've treated some for minor abrasions and such and,' she bent towards Sylvia,' I'm afraid at least three have been killed.'

Sylvia attempted to clear her throat, 'We're going to get you a cup of tea and then take you somewhere safe and warm,' she said to the group in the most purposeful voice she could muster and then instinctively put her arm around the nearest woman, 'What's your name dear?'

'Mrs. Fisher, we're all here except my Simon and they've taken him to hospital they said. They wouldn't let anyone go with him. He's only six, he'll be frightened to death.'

'I'm sure they know best Mrs. Fisher, we'll find out how he is as soon as possible.' Sylvia looked back,' Let's all get away from here shall we?'

'Bloody Germans' said an older woman clutching a blanket, 'that's our home they've destroyed, we never did anything to deserve that.'

Gradually Sylvia led the party of Myrtle Road residents and WVS volunteers back to the vans where tea was waiting.

'Daft isn't it. A cup of tea works wonders even in all this,' said an elderly man with a bandaged hand.

'Yeah, thank you dear' a younger woman said to Audrey, ' it don't bear thinking about do it?'

'They've taken Grand-dad to hospital,' a small girl no more than four or five told Sylvia,' Will he be all right?'

'I'm sure he will. Now what's your name?'

'Ruth and this is Shirley,' she said holding up a charred doll.

When she was certain they were ready Sylvia asked four of her ladies to escort the group up Cliff Lane to Holywells mansion. As she was saying the words she had a flash of memory of the fun they had had getting the Rest Centre ready. It wasn't much fun now.

The party set off on the short walk to the park, to the Centre, to a hot bath and a warm bed. The realisation and the shock would set in later.

Sylvia grabbed a cup of tea herself and refused a rock bun managing a smile to Hazel behind the counter, ' Don't think I could do it justice' she said. Then she went back along the road where the ARP had been reasonably successful in dispersing the crowd and order was starting to emerge from chaos. There were four more victims wanting help at the Assembly Centre, two very old women and two younger ones.

'We can't find Yvonne. She went out of the shelter to get a drop of grog and she never came back. No one can find her,' tears streamed down the women's blackened face making absurd lines.

'They'll let us know if you come with me to Holywells,' Sylvia said,' they've got all your names and they know you're going to the Rest Centre.'

As they picked their way back to the vans the other younger woman said to her,

'I've never heard a noise like it miss. After the wail of the siren we were all huddled in the shelter and there was this sort of drone getting nearer and nearer. We heard the crack of the ack ack guns and then a sort of muffled boom followed by bloody great crashing and banging and people screaming. It was bloody terrible. We daren't come out not even when the all clear eventually sounded.'

'I never imagined it would happen you know,' Sylvia confided holding on to the woman's hand.

'Nor me miss. But when we came out of the shelter and looked up our house had gone, smashed to smithereens. What on earth are we going to do?'

'For a start we're getting you somewhere safe and warm and then we'll have to find you somewhere to live. There's a lot of women up at the Centre to look after you and in a day or so they'll sort something out, I'm sure.'

The woman looked at her and Sylvia thought she had a pretty face, she was probably in her mid thirties, 'Will you come up to the Centre sometime, miss?'

'Yes, I'll be coming up there quite a bit, I expect,' and she peered to see the name of the label but couldn't make it out.

'Mrs. Howell' she said, 'My name is Mrs. Howell.'

An hour or so later Sylvia went up to the Holywells centre where her colleagues had worked tirelessly in organising baths, food and beds. They told her most were sleeping, if fitfully, and it was decided that three WVS members would stay on duty to be relieved early the next day. Sylvia got a lift back to the cottage.

She let herself in and went straight to the bathroom. She pulled off her hat and looked at the dishevelled, dirty face in the mirror. She started to shake and tears tumbled down her cheeks; still looking in the mirror she spoke to the person looking back at her, 'Now you know what it's all about.' she said.

'Never in the field of human conflict was so much owed by so many to so few' -

Winston Churchill

'Here they come, waves and waves of them. Spitfires, Hurricans, what a wonderful sight.'

Jack's head appeared in the shelter giving his audience an up to the minute commentary, like a war correspondent.

'Jack come in here with the rest of us. You're not on duty now' Vera shouted above the noise.

'Don't you want to know what's happening then?'

'Yes but' she turned to Kitty and Doris, 'I'm wasting my time with him and he's not even wearing his tin hat.'

'Leave him mum, he thinks he's Richard Dimbleby.'

The shelter had a strange smell since Jack had insisted in applying the last of his supply of distemper to the walls at the weekend. Mingled with the creosote that he had liberally applied to the wooden door and supports it made Vera hope that the all-clear would wail out before she was sick. She said as much to Doris and Kitty.

'It won't be too long, Mrs.Wright, all the fighting is taking place over the south coast according to the wireless.' Doris had been visiting when the siren went off and Vera had bundled her through the newly stained shelter door with Kitty in her wake.

Jack appeared in the doorway again.

' I'm going to call you Jack in the Box if you keep popping in and out like this.'

'No laughing matter girl,' he snapped,' unless, of course, you're laughing at old Goering losing all his airforce.'

'Goering has only got one plane and Gobbels has no balls at all' Kitty parodied a well-known ditty of the time.

'Kitty, hush your mouth. I don't know where you get it from, and with Doris here too,' Vera chimed in but Doris was giggling in the corner.

'The RAF boys from Wattisham, they sing it all the time.

Hitler has only got one ball, Himler has two but very small...' Kitty stopped singing as Jack's head appeared again.

'That will do my girl. Thank you very much. This all comes from women doing the work of men,' and he glared at Vera before disappearing once more.

'Since when did men operate sewing machines at Pipers?' Kitty laughed.

Doris was enjoying the family banter but added, ' My mother has enrolled on that course at Andersons so she can help there. She's learning to be a welder.'

'You better not let Jack hear that. He's been going on and on about the subject all week.' Vera said, ' Here pass me one of those cushions girls, I'm getting a sore bottom what with sitting in front of my switchboard all morning and now this.'

The wireless had been giving a blow by blow account of what was referred to as The Battle of Britain over the last two weeks with enthusiastic commentators sounding like they were attending football matches. Although many British fighters had been lost nearly 700 hundred German aircraft had been shot down and they were certainly finding their quest to destroy the British airforce much more difficult than envisaged. Whilst this was good news for the long-suffering British the Wright family was not alone in continually worrying about the possibility of invasion.

After another half an hour the all clear went and they trundled into the kitchen. As usual Vera put the kettle on, insisting they had enough rations for a quick brew before Doris. left for home.

'My dad still thinks Hitler is going to invade,' Doris ventured, 'what do you think Mr. Wright?'

Jack had already lit his pipe. He took a noisy suck, puffed out rings of smoke and holding the bowl pointed the stem at Doris, 'The first thing I'd say to your father is that if Jerry does come, we are ready. Only yesterday Mr. Churchill said *Britain now bristles with two million soldiers ready to resist invasion.* Bristles that's what he said, bristles. The second thing is that Hitler lost his chance in July, they say he was all set to come at full moon but altered his mind, decided that he needed to destroy our airforce first. But we are putting up such a magnificent fight that my guess is he's got a job on his hand if he still wants to come over here.'

'This is Jack Wright reading the six o'clock news,' mimicked Kitty.

'Watch your tongue, young lady. Doris asked me a question and I answered it, that's all. Now if you don't mind I'm going to get my head down, I'm on the early morning shift this week.' Ramming his pipe back into his mouth, he stomped out of the room.

'You shouldn't tease him so,' Vera said to Kitty, 'He's working so hard both at the factory and with his ARP. Poor old chap is looking washed out.' Secretly she was pleased to see Kitty back to her chirpy self though she realised that to some extent it was her way of dealing with Alan being killed.

'He doesn't mind. He knows I don't really mean it,' Kitty replied.

'He'll be pleased to see Jimmy when he comes home next week,' Doris reminded them.

'Oh my, we've hardly mentioned poor old Jimmy. It will be wonderful to see him. Seems ages since his last long week-end.'

'I can't wait' Doris whispered.

'Hark at you two. All this fuss about little Jimmy,' Kitty chipped in. Doris tried not to talk too much about what Jimmy was up to when Kitty was around saving her joys and worries for when she was alone.

'Is he still on guns?' Kitty persisted.

'Yes. He's been transferred to the Royal Artillery based at Folkestone.'

Kitty got up from the kitchen table and put her hands on Doris' shoulders.

'Hope the poor little sod is all right,' she said, 'Tell you what I'll walk home with you. I could do with some fresh air to clear away the effects of dad trying to turn our shelter into Buckingham Palace.'

They walked along the quiet roads in the late afternoon sun. A few people were talking over their fences, comparing notes on the progress of the war in the air.

'I didn't say anything to your mum but I've joined one of those Mobile First Aid teams. You see, working in the chemist shop I know a bit about first aid and the course was pretty straightforward. Mr.French encouraged me and my dad thinks it's all right but he's so doom and gloom you don't get much out of him, these days. Mum is so excited about her welding I don't think she'd care if I joined the

WACS. So I went ahead and did it. Already been on a couple of call outs but they were just incendiaries, minor casualties.'

'Good for you, I just do my fire watcher shifts at the factory,' said Kitty.

'Have you thought of doing anything else?'

'Me? That's all I can fit it in really what with all the extra shifts and seven day working at the factory. We're making parachutes now, as well as all those uniforms. I'll say this though, when I'm not working I give my time to cheering up the RAF boys, that's my war effort. They're a laugh they are and it's no good being gloomy all the time is it?'

'No you're right. I think I've become a bit of a misery these days.' Doris looked at Kitty for confirmation.

'You should come out with me and meet the RAF then. Why not tonight? They'll be at The Bluecoat Arms near the Cattlemarket. If nothing else you'll have a good laugh.'

'Not tonight thanks, it's nice of you Kitty but I think I'll stay in and write to Jimmy.'

'Well tell him even his sister is looking forward to seeing him soon.' Kitty laughed.

They came to Doris' front gate and she gave Kitty a hug.

'Thanks Kitty.'

'I don't know what for,' Kitty said.

A few days later Doris called on Vera again.

'Something smells good.'

'Come in dear, excuse the mess.'

She had gone round the back of the house, admiring the neat rows of vegetables leading up to and indeed over the Anderson shelter. She had carefully latched the side gate behind her before poking her head round the open door. Vera, she noticed, was bending over a small recipe book and frowning.

'Something else you've copied from *Kitchen Front?*'

Vera smiled, 'I don't get all my ideas from the wireless, young lady. This one comes from *Potato Pete.*'

'Oh. Mum's got that one. She swears by it but there again she's not the cook you are, Mrs. Wright. We've all flatly refused to eat her 'Wooton Pie', war or no war.'

'This one could be almost as bad, it's called Vegetable Pudding but there's hardly a vegetable in it,' she consulted the book again, ' now let's see, I've got to line this dish with bread crumbs before I put in the macaroni, peas, cheese and this sauce I've made. I'll just get this bit done and then we'll have a cuppa.'

Vera grated some cheese and sprinkled it on the top of her concoction and then placed it carefully in the oven, 'Matches, matches, where the devil are they. He will keep pinching them for that damn pipe of his.'

'There's a box over here.'

'Thanks. Now look that is typical of him, at least half of them are dead. Why does he always put the dead ones back.' Vera extracted a live match, turned on the gas tap and the oven lit up with a minor explosion.

'So, what did I smell in the saucepan when I came in?'

'Oh, just some soup made up with all the left overs.'

'I think you should be on Kitchen Front, Mrs. Wright. You could do Vera's Vegetables. Sorry I shouldn't be so cheeky, should I?'

'Nonsense I get enough cheek from Kitty and I used to get even more from that Jimmy, so you make up for him being away,' she paused and wiped her hands on her apron, 'another week then he'll have some leave, that's right isn't it, Doris?'

' Yes, and I can't wait.'

Vera filled the kettle and put it on the hob, ' Right my girl just put that swill in the pig bin will you and I'll fix us a cup of tea. Mind you I'm even having to watch my tea supply these days, I don't know what things are coming to, I'm sure. I said to the girls at the exchange I said that Hitler knows how to get at us English, making us ration our tea. That made them laugh.'

'I reckon Jimmy will spend all his leave sleeping judging from his letters; he's on duty most nights and still finds it difficult getting his head down in the billet with the others coming and going. It's probably me but he sounded really down in his last letter.'

Vera poured the tea and they sat round the small kitchen table, 'Oh he'll bounce back. Never down for long that Jimmy.'

'Now then, I've got something to tell you. I saw one of the German parachutists that bailed out when their Dornier crashed in Holywells Park on Monday. Funny old thing that turned out to be.'

'You saw a German? How exciting. How close were you? What did he look like? Did he try to kill you?' Doris was enthralled.

'Hang on, hang on and I'll tell you. You see I was on mornings and I had come home and was chatting with Mrs. Otter down the road on my way home and she said there was a Jerry plane up there but the siren hadn't gone. She said she thought it was a Dornier (Jack would have known what sort it was) but it was pretty high up by now. Then, one of our Spits came out of the clouds and we heard the crack of the machine guns. Next thing this Jerry plane is falling out of the sky, making a Dickens of a noise and black smoke billowing from it. Silly really, Mrs. Otter and I just stood there, spell bound I suppose, and we watched it until there was this tearing sound and then an explosion. *It's fallen in the park* I said. Then, I don't know why, we looked up and, calm as you like, there were four parachutes drifting down like feathers. So peaceful after all that racket. *Bloody hell,* she said, sorry dear but those Otters they do swear a bit, *Bloody hell* we'd better be ready for them. By then loads of other women were out in the street looking up. They had all armed themselves with carving knives, rolling pins, garden forks and such. *We'll have to get them before they get us* they explained.

Three of the parachutists drifted quite a way east but the nearest one seemed to be heading for the park itself. Mr. Brownlow and Mr. Pizzy had finished shifts so they came out in their Home Guard uniforms carrying their rifles and I must say I felt a bit better. So with the Home Guard leading the way this army of women with knives and such all hurried to the park. Going down Cliff Lane hill we spotted him stuck on the top of *The Margaret Catchpole* pub. Large as you like, an evil German soldier on the roof of our local. By the time we got there the Home Guard had their rifles trained on him and one or two wardens were keeping back this hoard of women brandishing knives. *Has he got a machine gun?* Someone shouted out. *Shoot him before he kills us all* a female voice yelled. Then the fire engine came and before you could say Jack Robinson they had a ladders up to the pub roof and with the rifles trained on the Jerry invader they climbed up and got him down. Then the Home Guard surrounded him and marched him to their vehicle. Well the amazing thing, Doris, was this. By chance they came very close to me and I got a good look at this so-called evil enemy. And do you know what? He was just a boy. Just a boy like our Jimmy, only he was German and he looked scared out of his wits.'

The next day Doris told the story of Vera and the Germans to Joyce and Mr. French.

She had been given increased responsibility at the shop since Mr. French was having to spend more time with his sick wife and whilst she enjoyed the challenge she knew she had to concentrate hard on what she was doing. She also knew that since she was not qualified Mr. French was taking a risk in relying on her to deal with the medicines.

She wasn't sure whether this was because he took pleasure from her enthusiasm or because it allowed him time with Mrs. French. It was probably a bit of both, she thought, after all, he had also lent her books to read and suggested that when the war was over she should consider becoming a qualified chemist herself. She reasoned that she was, in some ways, the daughter he never had but wished he would resist the temptation to touch her when they were together in the dispensary. One day he might go too far and she was unsure about how she would deal with such a situation.

However, it was Mr. French who had encouraged her to join one of the Mobile First Aid teams and she had added to her medical knowledge through the training. She also enjoyed the camaraderie of a lively group of women and now that she had attended a number of incidents she felt she was doing something useful to help with the war.

The last time she had been called out had brought home to her how fragile life could be. The H.E. attack had been in Landseer Road where the bomb, probably intended for the factories in that area, had strayed and destroyed two houses, damaging four more. Thankfully no one was killed but at least twenty people were injured and Doris had put her training into practice, giving treatment on the spot and ensuring that those who needed further help were swiftly taken to hospital. She felt part of a team, as ARP wardens, policemen, firemen, rescue squads and WVS women worked around her.

Doris missed her sister Alice. They were never that close but they were sisters. Alice had announced to the family that she was going to become a land-girl and before they knew it she had left home and seemed to be enjoying life up in North Norfolk. The house seemed empty without her. Doris found her father's continual pessimism draining and couldn't help comparing him with Jimmy's dad who could be really pig-headed but at least he was always optimistic. Both men, she reasoned, in their different ways were responding to the difficulties of wartime Britain including accepting the idea of having working wives. Her mother didn't help since she was positively revelling in her skills as a welder and wasted little time in boasting of her new found expertise. She'd taken to wearing slacks which she said were purposeful causing Doris's father to comment that it wouldn't be long before she was playing football for Ipswich Town.

In contrast, though she knew Jimmy's father remained unsure about his wife working but she felt that deep down he was proud of her and the banter between them was of a much friendlier nature. Increasingly Doris found herself drawn to Jimmy's family and in Kitty she had found a genuine friend. She knew that in spite of their teasing they were all as excited as she was about seeing Jimmy at the weekend.

He came round to see her after breakfast on the Saturday of his forty eight-hour pass. Her father had gone off to Home Guard practice and her mother was busy in the kitchen. She threw her arms around him and held him tight. They didn't say anything, just looked at each other long and hard.

Her mother came out of the kitchen and, after asking how he was and failing to wait for the answer, suggested they went into the front room and she would bring them a cup of tea.

Jimmy was always surprised at how neat and sparse the Harper's front room was and sat, somewhat nervously, on the edge of the settee. Doris sat next to him holding onto his arm like a mother holds a child to stop it falling. She looked closely at his face and thought that though she might look tired he looked totally exhausted. His lips were dry and cracked, there were telltale rings under his eyes and his fair hair, cut short by army barbers, was sticking up in tufts.

'Oh Jimmy, it is so good to see you,' she said, giving his arm another squeeze.

'And you, Doris.'

'And you said in your last letter you'd been promoted. Clever old you.'

'Nothing really but Lance Corporal sounds a bit better than private, I suppose.'

'Very impressive I reckon.'

She leant over and kissed him even though she knew he was nervous in case her mother came in.

'So what plans have you for the week-end, then?' he asked.

'I just want to send everyone else away and have you to myself but I suppose that won't happen, will it?'

'Fraid not since dad is insisting I go to the football with him this afternoon.'

'And you don't want to go I suppose?'

He laughed, it was the first time he had laughed she thought, 'Of course I don't. I mean it's not the same watching the Navy play the Army is it?'

'Of course you must go,' she said. 'Your dad is really looking forward to it. I see quite a lot of your mum and dad these days. And Kitty, of course.'

The door opened and Mrs. Harper appeared balancing two cups of tea, 'No sugar, I'm afraid,' she announced, 'so you've been all right then, Jimmy. Judging by the number of letters you write you can't be too busy.' Doris opened her mouth to say something but changed her mind.

'That's right Mrs. Harper, shoot down a few Jerries then write a few letters, that's me.' Doris was pleased with Jimmy's reply, which was lost on her mother.

'I've become a welder, you know,' she said placing a hand on her hip,' Not that folks round here are that impressed.' Having made this important statement she left, closing the door.

'Now you can see why I go round to your house so much,' Doris said.

Jimmy shrugged, 'War does funny things to people' he said, ' So what are we going to do?'

She took a sip of tea, 'Well for a start, I thought it might be nice to go into town and have a cup of coffee at the Picture House. Then after you've been to the football your mum has invited me to yours for tea. Tonight your parents want us to go down to the 'Catchpole' with them for a drink. Then tomorrow we could get out our bikes and go somewhere nice, like Flatford.'

'I knew you'd have it all worked out,' he said and took a large gulp from his cup. Doris wasn't sure whether he was praising her organising abilities or being sarcastic.

They took the trolley bus into town and recalled their first date and how they felt when they came home from the pictures that night. She whispered to him that she loved him and thought he said the same but the bus gave a sudden jolt and she couldn't be sure.

The Picture House Restaurant looked as comfortable as ever but more dowdy than they remembered. Doris recalled that before the war, they always seemed to be giving it a new coat of paint and the waitresses would wear white starched aprons. Now they moved slowly in well-worn black dresses, the paint on the arms of the Lloyd Loom chairs had flaked and the glass-topped tables were in need of a good clean. All sorts of uniforms were present, servicemen and women on leave, sailors from HMS Bunting, airforce chaps and girls from any number of nearby stations. Chatter seemed cheerful. People were making the best of things.

'I should have worn my First Aiders uniform,' joked Doris.

'Oh. Yes, like you said in your letters, you've joined up as well. What's it like?'

'I like it. If 'like' is the right word, sometimes it's really grim when the air raids are really bad. But I enjoy doing my bit, as they say.'

He took hold of her hand, ' I think your terrific,' he whispered, 'Sorry if I'm a bit quiet. To be quite honest, Doris, I don't think I've ever felt so tired. Trouble is I work nights mainly and I'm not good at getting my head down in the billet what with the lads coming and going and that. Sorry, I'll be fit as a fiddle after I had a sleep in my own bed again.'

She put both her hands on his, 'Don't worry Jimmy,' she said, 'It's just wonderful to see you. Nothing else matters,' then she added, 'Would you rather we didn't go to the pub tonight. I could come round and you could get an early night.'

'No, no, I'll be fine. It will be fun. And nice for mum and dad. Mum said something about Kitty and some RAF bloke coming as well. You don't mind do you? You and Kitty are O.K. and that?'

'Kitty and I are good friends. We talked about poor old Alan and that made us closer somehow. I think she's decided just to have as good a time as possible nowadays. She's probably going a bit wild but that's her way of dealing with it. She's determined she won't settle down with one particular bloke. Safety in numbers is her motto.'

'Yeah, that's what mum said, 'You don't want that, do you Doris? What with me being away all the time I wouldn't blame you if you wanted to go out a bit and...'

'Don't be so ridiculous. I want you and nobody else. Don't you ever listen to me Lance Corporal Wright?'

He laughed, 'Sorry Sir,' he said and clicked his heels under the table.

Back on the trolley bus again she put her head on his shoulder and they began to relax.

In the evening Doris went to see Jimmy at five o'clock as arranged, only to be met by Vera with her finger to her mouth.

'He went up to his room about an hour ago for something or other and when I peeped in he was fast asleep on the bed. So I left him. Poor lad he looked all in.'

'He hasn't been getting much sleep,' 'Doris said, Oh. I've brought you a spot of tea and some jam. Mum said to bring it.'

'That's kind of her,' said Vera, though knowing Mrs. Harper she reckoned Doris had had to scrounge it.

They went into the kitchen. 'He's grown about five years in five months,' Vera said, ' the only time he laughed was when I told him the army was good for his spots. They've nearly all gone, you know.'

Doris laughed, 'Good job you didn't embarrass him in front of me like when I first came to tea.'

'Oh. I did didn't I. What a scream' said Vera, grinning to herself as she started to cut the bread into thin slices.

'Is Kitty coming to the pub with us?' Doris said, taking the butter dish from the cupboard by the sink.

'She says she'll see us in there later. Bringing her latest, whoever he is. I can't keep up with them. Still I suppose she knows what she's doing. She says she's keeping her head screwed on tight. I told her I was more worried about her legs being tightly together than I was about her head. Sorry Doris, but you know what I mean.'

After a while the simple tea had been prepared and Vera told Doris to go and sit in the front room and wait for Jack to return from the allotment and Jimmy to emerge from upstairs. Doris did what she was told and slumped into the worn leather chair.

She'd been looking forward to Jimmy coming home so much that it hadn't really occurred to her that he might, in any way, be affected by his duties on the south coast. Somehow she had viewed his short leave as providing a cure for her feeling low, for everyone around her feeling tired, for the way in which this war was changing people. She had given him a God-like status and it had taken her a while to realise that he had suffered more than anyone. She must get him to talk about what he'd been through.

She must stop being so selfish. Tonight, the pub with its patriotic jollyness, would be a help but tomorrow she would get him to talk and she would listen.

'Run rabbit, run rabbit, run, run, run'

They entered the Margaret Catchpole to the well know tune being thumped out on the piano by Sam Evans, the local butcher, accompanied by quite a number of the locals seated at wooden tables in the lounge bar. Jack and Vera waved to friends and the four of them found seats in the far corner near a wilting pot plant. Pictures depicting the sad life of the lady after whom the pub was named hung at various angles on the panelled walls.

'So what's everyone having then?' asked Jack, standing, whilst fiddling with his pipe preparing to add even more fug to the smoke filled bar. Vera ordered a stout, Jimmy a Tolly's light ale and Doris a shandy. Doris grabbed for Jimmy's hand under the table and grinned at him, 'You look better after your doze.' she said.

'Yeah, sorry about that. But once my head hit the pillow I was away.'

'Now you're ready for anything?'

'I certainly am,' Jimmy grinned back and started joining in the song.

'He never made the school choir,' Vera said nudging Doris but Jimmy didn't hear and continued unabashed.

Jack returned with the drinks and the pianist stopped, turned round on his stool and asked for requests. 'Give us something under the counter, Sam' someone shouted out and the whole pub roared approval. Vera produced a packet of Navy Cut and offered them around saying she had bought them with her wages. Jack sucked on his pipe.

The butcher-cum-pianist struck up *If you were the only girl in the world* and, this time, they all joined in the singing.

They were having a good time. Jack was talking to some of his mates who were in the Home Guard, which, they told him proudly, was now part of the Suffolk Regiment. He was intrigued to learn that the local C.O. was still forecasting an imminent invasion but he told them, in his view, the RAF had done enough to make Hitler think again. Vera had another bottle of stout and sang along happily, and in tune.

'Oh. So there you are, hiding away in the corner.' Kitty appeared, hand in hand, with an RAF sergeant. Doris thought she had already had quite a bit to drink, 'This is Peter and these, Peter, are my parents, my brother and his girlfriend Doris.'

Peter shook everyone's hand and then offered to buy a round of drinks, Kitty pulled a couple of chairs to the table and sat down, ' Gin and tonic for me' she said, 'and I'm dying for a fag. Anyone got any, I'm right out?'

Vera opened her handbag and produced the Players Navy Cut, 'Here,' she said, adding, 'seems all right, your Peter.'

'Not my Peter, just a friend. Mind you he's always got a load of money. That's why I go for sergeants, always flush they are.'

Doris squeezed Jimmy's hand again and he gave her a knowing look.

'If you don't mind Doris and I will be getting along in a minute or two,' he said, 'No offence, Kitty.'

Kitty looked at Doris and grinned, 'Don't be daft. You two have hardly seen each other since the little buggers been back.'

'Kitty! Good job your dad's not listening.'

Peter arrived with the drinks, an unlit cigarette hanging from his mouth. Doris decided she didn't care for him much and then rationalised that maybe she was being a bit unfair. She was not a drinker but knocked back her shandy fairly quickly. Jimmy took the hint and they said their farewells to the tune of A nightingale sang in Berkley Square.

They didn't discuss the evening on their way back home. They were far too close to each other to have opinions about anyone else.

Sunday was a perfect late Summer day and Doris and Jimmy started off early on their bike ride to Flatford. As they went through Wherstead, Tattingstone and then Bramford they noticed tell tale signs that their country was at war. Following the harvest the fields had been ploughed up in readiness for replanting, every house they passed was cultivated for vegetables and the now familiar shelters dominated the gardens. Nearing the river Stour they noticed a string of pill boxes and in the distance barrage balloons bounced over Harwich and Felixstowe but what really mattered was that the early sun was already warming them as they pedalled towards Constable's birthplace.

On reaching Flatford they stacked their bikes with a few others on a grassy stretch before the bridge and then, as was the custom, they went and looked at the ducks squabbling in the river. Hand in hand they walked along the tow-path to the mill, sombre cattle stood in the water meadows their reflections divided by tufts of bright green grass and birds chattered from pollarded willow.

'This is more like it,' Doris remarked.

'Yeah, I feel so much better today. All I needed was a good nights sleep.'

They linked arms and continued in silence passing the mill and sluice gates and moving on through high reeds and wispy grass. When they were well past the more popular area she took his hand and led him down a steep bank and they lay down in the soft undergrowth. She moved towards him and as they kissed she closed her eyes and was at peace again. After a while she propped herself up on one elbow, her red hair falling over one side of her face. 'Do you want to talk about it?' she asked.

He knew what she meant and refrained from a frivolous answer. 'Not much to say really. I mean, at first it seemed a bit of a lark. There's something powerful about the Anti Aircraft guns. You feel in charge, sort of dominant. The Hun fighters come over and you see them in the searchlights and then you let them have it. They drone on and on and when you hit one there's the explosion and then the roar sound of it cascading down. Sometimes you see the parachutists. Sometimes not.

When you've got one everybody cheers and later you mark them up on your gun like scoring in a darts match.'

She nodded and touched his face with her free hand.

'I'm pretty good at it. Always had a good eye. The others seem to follow me as well which is why they promoted me I suppose. But then one morning when we'd had a really busy night I was lying in the billet, nobody around you see, and as usual I couldn't sleep, and I got to thinking. I thought I'm not just shooting down Jerry planes I'm shooting down Germans and those Germans are just like me except that they are Germans if you see what I mean.'

Doris thought of Vera and the parachutist. She decided not to mention it though she was sure his mother would have told him the story.

'I mean, young German boys, like I'm a young English boy who no more wanted to be a soldier than be a...ballet dancer or something. I mean I never ever got into a fight at school. I would back off. Not get involved. And here I am cheering like a looney when I kill someone. I had quite a problem with it, Doris, and there was no one I could talk to. They'd think I'd gone soft.'

She touched his cheek again, 'I expect a lot more of them were thinking just the same thing only they wouldn't mention it either,' she suggested.

'Do you think so?'

'Of course. It's only natural. But at the end of it all if we don't shoot them down they'd bomb our houses and people get killed; like some of those I deal with in my small way after the air raids.'

He shook her hand away, 'Doris I do know that. I'm not entirely stupid.'

She was taken aback and he continued, 'Sometimes I think you think I'm not very bright. Just because you got a scholarship and are learning to mix up medicines and things you think I'm not clever enough for you. But I'm not stupid. I was just lazy at school. Too interested in football and cricket.' He was shouting and she didn't know how to deal with him. Then he rolled back from her burying his face in the grass.

After what seemed an age he sat up and looked at her.

'Christ knows where all that came from,' he said, 'I'm sorry I didn't mean it. I....'

'Don't be,' she said, 'It's just me being clumsy but I really didn't know what you were going through. It's not the sort of thing we can say in letters is it? But I understand now and it's all right, isn't it?'

He grinned, 'Yes it is. I think I needed to shout at someone and you were the obvious one. Sorry.'

'You are OK though aren't you. In your head, I mean, about the guns and that?'

'Yes, of course I am. I had worked it all out but needed to say it.'

She looked at him carefully, ' I love you. I know I've never had another serious boy friend nor you a girlfriend but I know I love you and I know I shall never love anyone else.'

'And I love you that way, Doris Harper,' he said and they rolled together feeling their bodies against each other, excited by the fervour of their kisses. Her hands fondled him and his slid beneath her skirt. Then he was on top of her, smelling her hair and her body, wanting her desperately.

'Come here Whisky, come here,' a woman's voice rang out from the towpath.

'Whisky where are you.' Whisky was down the bank jumping around the young couple with great delight. 'Whisky. Good Heavens. Whisky come here, NOW'.

Whisky, somewhat reluctantly, obeyed the final command from a woman out of sight from Doris and Jimmy but she must have seen them earlier since they heard her mutter as she hurried down the path, 'This war has ruined the moral fibre of the country.'

By then both Doris and Jimmy were in fits of laughter. 'I told you once before we had to wait,' Jimmy said pulling her to her feet.

'I don't think I can for too much longer. You better hurry up and finish this war,' she said.

'Victory at all costs, Victory in spite of all terror, Victory however long and hard the road may be, without Victory there is no survival.' - Winston Churchill

Some people look like they are somebody what ever they are wearing, Doris thought, eyeing up the young woman who entered the shop. She was dressed in a long military style raincoat and a red beret; hair, that was almost black, was pulled back under the hat, her skin was smooth and olive and her mouth glistened with bright red lipstick.

'I wonder if you could be good enough to let me have these pills for my mother. Shes suffers from the most atrocious headaches and these are the only things that seem to help. I got her to sign this note to say that I am her daughter and I've got a chit from the doctor.'

Doris looked at the correspondence, she recognised the doctor's name as one who practised in Fonnereau Road and the fine headed personal paper told her that the mother lived at Playford. Bet it's one of those big old houses that stand back from the road, she thought.

'Yes, Miss umm, Mrs. Cameron, that will be fine. I won't keep you a moment.'

She disappeared out to the dispensary, where Mr. French was busy with the pestle and mortar, leaving Joyce to deal with any other customers.

'Guess what, got one of the Grimstone family in the shop. We are coming up in the world, Mr. French,' she confided in the owner.

'My Goodness, we'll be having King George himself in soon,' he chuckled, leaving his task and sorting the required tablets. After carefully labelling the bottle he handed it to Doris slipping his hand around her waist as he did so, 'Right off you go and hob-knob,' he said.

'Thanks awfully,' the young woman said and smiled, then hesitating, 'I say, I know this seems silly but I feel sure we have met somewhere recently.'

'We have met?' replied Doris, certain that their paths were unlikely to have crossed.

'I've got it. Landseer Road, last week. The air raid, you were one of the first aiders. You fixed up a mother and two little boys who had splinter wounds from the blast. I remember thinking how easy you were with them. I'm WVS. I was organising the homeless off to Holywells Rest Centre. I do a lot of work there.'

Doris looked hard at the customer. She wasn't sure that she remembered, so much had been going on. The noise of sirens, fire engines, bells, whistles, falling debris, everyone shouting meant that she had to block everything out and concentrate on the job in hand.

'It was a pretty nasty one, Landseer Road,' she said.

'They all are in a way. I'm Sylvia by the way, Sylvia Cameron,' then she laughed, 'Oh. You know that, it was on the note for mother's pills.'

'I'm Doris, Doris Harper,' Gosh, I'm sounding like one of them, she thought.

'Well if you're ever near Holywells Park call in at the Rest Centre. I'm usually there most days. 'Bye Doris, thanks.'

The shop had emptied. 'My you are coming up in the world' Joyce chirped.

'She was very nice though. You know something, this war is a bit of a leveller in some ways.'

'Oh. My, that's far too clever for me,' Joyce ran a duster over the glass counter.

It was one of those crisp, clear November days and Doris, having cycled half way up Bishops Hill, decided to enter the park and wheel her bike to the gates on Cliff Lane on her way to visit Vera. It was Wednesday, her half day, and she was going to make the best of it.

She was well wrapped up for the Winter, her hair pulled back into a wooden comb, a thick wool scarf, that she had fashioned from two very old jumpers, wound round her neck and under her old black coat she wore slacks. This was a new departure introduced to her, she was ashamed to admit, by her mother who wore them all the time nowadays. The magazines insisted that to be fashionable one had to be shabby and so she had sown bright coloured patches on her slacks which she thought were fun. Mr. French had made some remark which she translated as meaning he preferred looking at her legs but she made a joke of it.

Once inside the park she took a deep breath, smelling fern and bracken. The leaves had virtually all fallen leaving black stark tree trunks bordering the pathway. The lawns and grassy areas of the park had been allowed to grow for hay, which had been harvested in late summer. The perimeters were now carved into small allotments and she could hear the cut of spades and forks as one or two local men took advantage of the dry weather, tidying their plots in readiness for next year's planting.

The pathway began to slope towards the Cliff Lane Gate and Holywells Mansion loomed into view. She wondered whether Sylvia would be there and whether she should pluck up courage and call at the Rest Centre as invited. She admitted to herself that the thought of seeing Sylvia was one of the reasons she had decided to walk through the park. Why not she decided, in for a penny in for a pound.

She propped her bike on the sandbags piled around the building in the company of a dozen or so others and walked up the steps to the grand entrance. The front door was open and she went in, not exactly on tiptoes, but cautiously. Arriving in the hall the first thing that struck her was the noise; voices from all angles, young children shouting to each other, babies crying, echoing high heels, the squeak and grind of furniture being moved. Then there were the smells, strong flavoured cooking, drying clothes and disinfectant.

A woman in the green WVS uniform came from a room on the left of the hall, scurrying towards the end of the corridor.

'Excuse me, do you know if Sylvia Cameron is around.'

The woman turned, almost spinning on the recently mopped floor, 'Sylvia, yes I think she is out the back. Who shall I say?'

'Doris, Doris Harper,' she felt like some pathetic character in a Dickens novel.

Suddenly a door to the right opened and out popped Sylvia. Green uniform, hair pulled back in the latest style, lips bright red. She looked pleased.

'Doris, how good that you called on us. Have you time for the grand tour?'

Before the war Doris had once visited Helmingham Hall with a school party and Sylvia took on the mantle of the guide who had told them all the family secrets on that far off day. The difference being that what Sylvia showed Doris was how the mansion had been furnished with simple beds, occasional chairs and a whole range of different styled tables and cupboards. Comforting fires warmed the rooms and worn rugs attempted to give a feeling of homeliness. Bathrooms were clean and towels were piled high on well-scrubbed floors. Most of the women exchanged words with Sylvia and she with them. Doris noticed that in some rooms the WVS were sitting talking with the air raid victims, sometimes making notes, sometimes just nodding . In one of the larger rooms a group of old men, whose lodging house in Fore Street had apparently been badly damaged by incendiary bombs, were huddled over bowls of soup. In the kitchen a number of WVS women were busy preparing meals for later in the day, chatting and laughing with each other.

They came back into the hall again, 'There, so now you see what we do, or try to do,' Sylvia said.

'It's amazing,' Doris replied in a quiet voice, 'we all take our homes for granted don't we? It doesn't matter if they're mansions or cottages, they are our homes. I hadn't really thought about that before.'

'Nor me until I got into this, I can tell you. I'd always been a real selfish cow.'

Doris was a bit taken aback and then Sylvia said, 'Listen I could do with a breather and a fag as a matter of fact. Do you fancy a stroll?'

They went outside, Doris refused a cigarette as Sylvia lit up a Craven A. She even looks stylish when she smokes, Doris thought. She led the way across the terrace and into a small garden area, now prepared for vegetable cultivation, and passed what were once green houses. They emerged on the far side of the park and started to walk down a hill of stubble.

'So you work in the chemists, you are a member of The Mobile First Aiders, what else do I need to know about you? Do you have a boy friend?'

'Yes I do, Jimmy, he's a gunner in the Artillery, stationed at Folkestone. You know on the Anti Aircraft guns. But he thinks he will be posted soon.'

'Doesn't know where no doubt. They never do know where and then they spring it on you out of the blue, don't they? Was he at Dunkirk?'

'Yes, he says he was lucky. Got picked up quickly,' then Doris went quiet, ' but his sister's boyfriend wasn't so lucky.'

'I'm sorry. My husband... I'm married,' she stretched her left hand towards Doris,' 'He had a bit of a rough time. Got out in the end but had a rough time.'

They walked on in silence for a while, kicking at the remnants of hay.

'I think it affects them more than they want to say. Men are funny like that. Don't like to admit to being scared.'

'And maybe don't like telling us how awful it really is. War, I mean.'

'Jimmy was exhausted last time he was home and a bit disturbed in a way. He said it had suddenly occurred to him that he wasn't just shooting at enemy planes he was actually killing young German boys.'

'Then he seems a decent person, your Jimmy. Did you manage to talk to him about it?'

'Eventually I did and he seemed better. I think he just needed to say it to someone,' Doris suddenly went very red, ' Here, I don't know why I'm telling you all this, I mean I hardly know you and you being who you are and all that.'

'Sylvia, my name is Sylvia that's who I am. Sometimes it's good to confide in someone you don't know too well. I promise I don't blab.'

Don't blab, Doris thought, and smiled.

They got back to the Rest Centre, 'I'm really glad you called in to see us.' Sylvia said, 'I'll tell you what, I'll call in at your Chemist's and invite you over to my cottage sometime,' she noticed Doris looked a bit worried, 'It's nothing grand. 'Bye then Doris.'

Doris watched her disappear up the steps. I would never have spoken to her if it wasn't for this war, she thought.

'You're late, good job I waited to make the tea,' Vera greeted her.

'Sorry, got a bit delayed,' Doris didn't want to explain where she had been.

'I'm only teasing,' Vera laughed, 'Surely you know when I'm teasing by now.

'They took their tea into the front room, 'How's work?' she asked Vera.

'Do you know I really enjoy it now that I know what I'm doing and the others are a good laugh. I caused a bit of a rumpus the other night though. I refused to let this bloke into the Exchange as he wouldn't show me his pass. He only turned out to be the Regional Telephone Manager. How about you? Still learning things off that Mr. French?'

'Yeah. Don't know what good it will do me but I like learning things. Always have.'

I didn't realise 'til the other day that you got a scholarship at school, bet your mum and dad were pleased.'

Doris realised she didn't know whether they had been or not. She assumed they were but they'd never said, 'Mrs. French is none too good. I think he is very worried.'

'Poor man. We forget that in spite of a war going on people still get ill and some die. Though I'll tell you one thing, there won't be so many babies born if all our men eventually end up overseas.'

'Not all our men. Mr. Wright and his wardens and my dad and his Home Guard. They'll still be here.'

Vera laughed, 'I think Jack and me are a bit old for babies.'

For the second time that day Doris blushed, 'I didn't mean that.'

'I know you didn't, but you've got to laugh sometimes haven't you. If not we'd all go mad.'

'You sound just like Kitty .'

'Poor old Kitty. Jack doesn't approve of all her RAF types but she insists none of them are serious. He was having a real go at her the other night. Jerry was making a din over head and Kitty and I were in the dug-out with Jack doing his usual BBC War Correspondent bit then he paused and started on about her needing to settle down. Luckily there was a really big explosion and he dashed over to the porch.'

'Why doesn't he ever go down the shelter?' Doris asked.

'Search me, he's says he likes to see what's going on but I'm not so sure it's as simple as that...'

'He'll be pleased Jimmy's coming home again this week-end.'

'Yes, he will, silly old sod never says much but he's sort of proud of young Jimmy. I just wish he'd try to understand Kitty a bit better sometimes.'

Doris knew what Vera was thinking but said nothing.

'Right then, young lady, I better get back to the kitchen. Jack's on earlies tonight but he's pleased as punch it's lates tomorrow so he can listen to ITMA.'

' I don't know how they do it, every week like that,' Doris said, 'Joyce said Tommy Handley is a genius. I said he must be he even makes my dad laugh.'

'Doris!'

'I was only joking. ITMA does really make me laugh but my favourite is The Brains Trust. I'd love to meet that Professor Joad.'

Vera heaved herself out of the chair, ' See, I said you were a clever clogs.'

Doris thought Vera looked tired but then most people did.

Jimmy came home at the weekend and Doris knew that he was determined not to mope; he was keen to make her laugh, keen to let her know he was all right. She loved him for that but would choose her moment and make sure that he knew he could talk to her about anything that was worrying him.

She had to work on the Saturday and he went with his father to watch another Army team draw three all with another Navy team. He told her they stood together at the Alderman Road end and threw their hats in the air whenever the Army scored. He had given Jimmy an update on the recent increase in raids in and around Ipswich and confided in him his fear that with its docks and factories they might be singled out for a special attack. How Lord Haw Haw had said as much and some silly people believed him. Jack said that being a warden meant he was the 'eyes and ears' and he included scotching such talk as part of his responsibilities.

In the evening they went and joined the long queues to see *Gone with the Wind*. They stood in line holding hands and smiling at each other in eager anticipation of what the papers said was the best film ever. Usually when the lights went down for the main feature Jimmy would give Doris a squeeze and they would often miss quite a lot of the film, kissing and cuddling low into their seats. Doris noticed that with *Gone with the Wind* Jimmy's amorous attentions tailed off after about twenty minutes and he watched spell bound throughout. When they stood at the end for *God Save the King* they, and the rest of the audience, had tears streaming down their faces.

Once outside in the cold night they looked at each other.

'That was the best film I have ever seen,' Doris said. 'Didn't you think so, Jimmy?'

'Frankly I don't give a damn,' he said.

She dug him in the ribs, 'You always do that but it was lovely wasn't it?'

'Yeah, it was really good. I tell you something else, the siren went about half way through and no one moved, I even heard the rumble of bombing but I couldn't have left *The Odeon* for some old raid.'

'I heard the siren and looked at you but I didn't hear any bombing. Wasn't Clark Gable fantastic?'

He laughed again and hugged her close and they walked through the dark streets to French's where they had stored their bikes in the shed at the back. She took his hand and guided him, knowing the terrain, and then put her arms around him and snuggled her head under his chin. Jimmy smelt her hair and began kissing the top of her head, then her neck and mouth, 'God, I have missed you,' he said and she pulled back, tears streaming down her face, 'I love you so much,' she said.

The cold night and the need to concentrate in the blackout cooled their ardour as they cycled back to her house in Avondale Road.

'I told mother we would be late back since it was a very long film. She said she knew it was a long film.'

Doris unlocked the front door like a burglar and led him on tiptoes into the front room. She shut the door and started to unbutton his coat and he slowly unwound her scarf,

'This is very smart,' he whispered, ' it goes on for ever.'

Before long they were entwined on the sofa, eager for each other but aware that Mr. and Mrs. Harper were only a staircase away. After a while Jimmy got up and put the light on. Then he went to his coat pocket, 'I can't wait,' he said, 'Doris Harper will you marry me?'

She threw herself at him, 'Marry you, marry you. Yes, of course I'll marry you', she was yelling at him. Suddenly there was a loud banging from upstairs accompanied by a muffled voice, which seemed to be asking whether she was drunk. She put her finger to her mouth and then they both dissolved into laughter.

'Since you've said yes you had better have this,' Jimmy whispered and gave her a small diamond ring.

Doris slipped it on her finger and looked at it,' 'That's the most beautiful ring I have ever seen' she said.

'Well there's not much to spend your pay on down at Folkestone,' Jimmy joked as he always did when embarrassed, ' I still think we shouldn't plan on getting married until we've finished this war. I mean, you do agree don't you?'

'I don't know what I think anymore, I am just so happy being engaged to you,' she said. 'We've got all tomorrow to talk. Come and kiss me again.'

The noise from above subsided and Doris had no idea what time it was when she gently let him out of the front door.

On the Sunday Jimmy called at the Harper home at ten o'clock and apologised to her father for not talking to him before he proposed to Doris. Bert Harper even managed a smile saying the war was changing lots of traditions. He wished them well and said he only hoped they wouldn't have to start their married life in a country ruled by Germans.

Jack and Vera had been delighted when he broke the news to them over toast and honey – a fellow ARP warden kept bees – and Jimmy promised to bring Doris round to the house later in the morning.

In the afternoon, well wrapped against the cold, the newly engaged couple walked down the hill and through the park, pausing at the icy pond where he kissed her cold face.

'There is something I have to tell you,' he began, 'I wanted us to be engaged because I love you and want to marry you when all this is over but I'm soon to be posted. We were told last week to be ready. They didn't say where but the rumour is that it's Greece. Apparently the Greeks are putting up a great fight against the Italians but need some back-up,' he took a deep breath, 'there, I've told you, now.'

Doris didn't cry, she understood and had been anticipating that it wouldn't be long before he was posted to the front, 'Well it will be warmer than this,' she said, 'We will write all the time won't we? And I'll get Vera Lynn to sing something on *Sincerely Yours*.'

She went with him to the station that evening. Neither of them said very much. The platform was full of couples saying goodbye. They kissed for as long as they could and she watched him climb into the crowded carriage. She waved with the others as the train disappeared down the tunnel then touched the ring on her left hand.

IOWA

'The weather isn't always extreme here, it just seems like it.' -
anonymous.

'Tom, fetch that big old pickaxe from the barn could you. We're going to have to break the ice so the cattle can get a drink.'

Tom tugged at the hood of his thick jacket, bent his head into the wind and made his way to the comparative warmth of the main barn. The pick was hanging in its allotted place along the west wall with the rest of the hand tools.

He banged his gloved hands together. Not much more to do this morning, he thought, I've nearly finished giving the cattle their hay and I won't take long feeding the chickens. An hour outside in weather such as this and he was ready for his Thanksgiving meal.

He took the pick outside where his father was huddled by the water troughs, 'Stand back, Dad,' he shouted and swung the axe which bounced as it hit the ice.

'Some frost last night,' Karl grunted.

Tom swung again and this time there was some penetration. After a few more efforts he succeeded in cracking the ice and from then on in his task was easier.

'Build your muscles up for baseball', Karl laughed but, as always, he was impressed by his son's natural co-ordination.

The cows, as if sensing their water supply was now available, looked up from munching hay and moo'd.

'Someone appreciates you,' said Karl, 'come on, let's get inside and watch your mother flap over the meal.'

Lois was not one to flap but at Thanksgiving she did like to have everything just right and so the men knew it was best to treat her with care.

'What time are Ellen and Ben coming over, mother?' Tom asked.

'And Luke, don't forget Luke,' she said, ' about eleven o'clock but in this weather they could be a bit late.'

'Not for Thanksgiving, they won't.'

The men had removed their outside clothes and had their hands outstretched in front of the pot-belly stove. After a while Karl got out his pipe and stuffed tobacco from the pouch down into the bowl. He examined it carefully before striking a match and giving a few quick sucks on the stem. A thick blue-white puff of smoke curled upwards towards the wooden ceiling.

'Don't know why you don't take up the pipe, Tom,' he said, 'most satisfying feeling in the world if you ask me.'

'No thank you, Dad. I don't have the patience. In fact I don't even have the patience to smoke cigarettes. But think of the money I save.'

Lois turned round from preparing the green beans, 'Just leave the boy alone, Karl, two of you puffing at pipes in this kitchen and I wouldn't be able to breathe.'

Ben made good time with the rest of the Nelson family arriving just after eleven. Ellen left him looking after baby Luke and went to help her mother, quietly taking responsibility for the sweet corn and potatoes.

'How are things then, Ben?' Karl asked his son-in-law,' Thomas D. Murphy and Co. still treating you well?'

'Sure are, Mr. Nelson, I'm doing a spell in Accounts at present. I like working with figures, always have.'

His brother-in-law's manicured fingers fascinated Tom whose hands were already calloused and rough. He looked at Luke playing happily at his father's feet with a wooden horse on wheels; the baby's hands and feet were chubby and red.

Ellen looked round from the sink, 'Tom Nelson just what are you dreaming about? You have that glazed over look on your face I remember when we were kids. You're not mooning over some girl, are you?'

Tom blushed, 'Certainly not' he said and blushed again when everyone, except baby Luke, laughed.

'It's not Letha Linquist is it?' Ellen continued to tease her brother.

'I was not thinking about any girl I was just thinking...' instead of finishing the sentence he scooped Luke up into his arms, 'Now then Luke you're on my side aren't you' he said, extending his arms so that Luke was high in the air and gurgling. Ben looked concerned but said nothing.

By mid afternoon, having said grace, the Nelson family were seated around the sturdy wooden table in the warm kitchen watching Karl carve the turkey. Plates were soon piled high with the stuffed bird, mashed potatoes, sweet potatoes, green beans and sweet corn.

'This is as good a Thanksgiving meal as I can remember,' Karl announced, ' wonderful turkey Lois, and the vegetables all done to perfection.'

'It has to be the best ever,' Ellen added,' since now we have Luke to share it with us.'

They continued to enjoy the meal in silence. Tom wondered why Ellen had mentioned Letha Linquist. Probably the first name that came into her head, he thought. Strange things sisters, since he did wonder whether he would ever pluck up the courage to ask Letha for a date. She'd probably already got a steady, some college boy with smooth hands and manicured fingers. She wouldn't have time for a fresh off the farm boy like him.

The plates were cleared and stacked and then Lois produced the pumpkin pie.

'I married Lois for her pumpkin pie, you know Ben' Karl announced.

'And I can see why, Mr. Nelson.'

It was the turn of Lois to blush, 'Karl Nelson you do talk rubbish sometimes' she said.

1941

'Fry's cocoa – Rich in nerve food!' - Advertisement

1941 started in a blizzard and the cold weather continued for some months. Petrol rationing had already cut down the number of private cars on the roads and day after day of snow and ice reduced the numbers even further. Trolley-bus services became erratic and people slithered and slid to work on bicycle or trudged back and forth through the snow. The only good news was that the number of air raids declined; they were having bad weather on the continent of Europe as well.

Towards the end of January Mrs. French died of cancer and the shop was shut for the day of the funeral. Doris and Joyce joined the small band of mourners first at St. Augustine's Church and then at the cemetery. They shivered together, standing back from the few relatives, as the body was lowered into the ground and Mr. French walked forward murmuring his personal goodbye.

In the church Doris had closed her eyes and prayed for Mr. French, he was going to be so alone. She also prayed for Jimmy screwing her eyes tight trying to bring him close but it was Alan's face that came vividly to her as she knelt. He was looking right at her with his kind eyes, like he'd looked at her that day when she first went to Jimmy's to tea. She was sure he was trying to tell her not to worry and that everything would be all right.

It started to snow. Joyce took Doris by the arm and together they went over to Mr. French to say a few words. He wasn't wearing a hat, snowflakes glistened on his bald head before melting and running down his face. Instead of the usual twinkle his eyes were red rimmed. He reached out his hands to them.

'Thank you for coming, dear girls,' he said. They both muttered something inaudible then made their way towards the entrance of the cemetery where they had propped their bikes.

The quiet that snow brings gave a feeling of peace and Joyce and Doris walked in silence along an avenue of sprinkled yew. Small groups of people stooped to place fresh flowers on gravestones knowing they would not last long in the cold.

The girls reached their bikes and dusted the snow off the cold seats not relishing the ride home. Joyce looked up, 'Doris, the shop is closed so why don't we go somewhere posh, like Limmers, for tea. Cheer ourselves up?'

'That would be really nice, Joyce. Are you sure you really want to go to Limmers and not Lyons?'

'Of course I am. It's not often we look as smart as this. I mean, just for once you're not wearing that awful scarf.'

A few days later Sylvia invited Doris to the cottage for the evening. The skies had cleared and there was a full moon enabling her to find her way quite easily as she pedalled through the snow.

Sylvia prepared cocoa and they huddled around the fire making toast. Glen Miller crackled on the gramophone.

'You've got some really good records,' Doris said with a tinge of envy in her voice. 'My dad won't contemplate a gramophone. Says there's enough row from Jerry every night without having any more from us girls.'

'I suppose that's one advantage in being married. You can play what you like without being told it's a racket. Mind you, old stick-in-the-mud Francis is a classical man.'

'I don't know much about classical. Sometimes I hear a really nice piece on the wireless but then they don't say what it's called.'

'I know what you mean. We did it at school, of course, and I had piano lessons but was never much good. The more popular classics, as Francis would have it, are rather good but I get them all mixed up. Here, butter these bits and help yourself to some of Mrs. Moore's plum jam.'

'Have you heard from Francis, lately?' Doris spoke his name as though she knew him.

'The usual careful letter. He must be the only soldier whose letters are never censored. Says we are doing well, taking lots of Italian prisoners and it's hot and dusty. It isn't all awful, they still manage to have fun, good chaps in the mess, lots of stuff about this pal called Bruce and by the way, he misses me.'

Doris laughed, not quite sure whether Sylvia's dismissive descriptions of her relationship with Francis were part of her upbringing or whether they disguised seeds of doubt. In a way she was pleased that her letters from Jimmy, though heavily censored, were full of plans and hopes. He wrote to her all the time and she read them over and over again.

'I'll go and make some more cocoa, if you like. Have a browse through the records and pick some out, that'll be fun.' Sylvia rose easily from her chair, balancing her cup. She was wearing slacks and a cashmere jumper.

One day, Doris thought, Jimmy and I will have a cottage like this, big chunky, patterned chairs, fluffy rugs and an enormous fire. It will be a welcoming house, warm, friendly and cluttered.

A pile of records, some peeping out of their brown sleeves, spilled over the floor by the gramophone and she began to sift through the collection. She chose a Frank Sinatra singing with the Dorsey band, *This is a lovely way to spend an evening* with the B side *I didn't sleep a wink last night*, Glen Miller's *Moonlight Serenade* and then something by Debussy she couldn't pronounce. Doris had failed her matric because she was hopeless at languages.

Sylvia returned, handed her a steaming cup and glanced at the selection, 'You are an incurable romantic, Doris, even *L'apres midi d'un faune'* is sort of dreamy.'

'I picked that because the title sounded nice.'

'But you are a romantic, aren't you?'

'I think I'm just very lucky. I mean, Jimmy always says he never thought I'd go out with him but I'd wanted to for ages. When he did pluck up the courage to ask me it worked right away. I mean not just the love bit but the way we get on, we're real friends as well, Jimmy and me,' then she paused realising she was chattering on.

'I don't want you to think I'm just some soppy date, though.'

'I certainly don't think that but I do agree you are very lucky. Sometimes I'm not sure whether I.......... You see I've changed quite a bit since this war began, you know. I don't think you would have liked the old Sylvia, much.'

There were times when she surprised Doris. Sometimes the barriers between them almost came down, sometimes Sylvia said things that made Doris want to hug her and yet, other times, she realised they were worlds apart. She didn't tell anyone about her blossoming friendship with Sylvia, not even Jimmy; it was better being a secret.

'So is there really nothing about this Jimmy, this paragon, that concerns you?'

'No, not really,' Doris thought a bit, ' just sometimes he seems to worry that I'm cleverer than he is. You know I got a scholarship and he just did his apprenticeship but I can't see that it matters, can you?'

Sylvia stabbed a piece of bread with the toasting fork and nestled it in front of the flames, 'Not at all. So why does he worry?'

'Well, I told you that Mr. French teaches me a lot about making up all the medicines and that and he lends me books on pharmacy which I really ought to spend more time studying,' she looked at the fire not sure whether to continue, 'Look, I've never told anyone else this but he thinks if we win the war I should become a proper chemist. You know, like him. He says he could register that he is teaching me, like I'm an apprentice chemist, and then after a number of years I'd have to take exams. I don't know why but I'm not sure what Jimmy would think.'

'He'd be as pleased as Punch, I should think. Doris you should do it and don't worry we have to win this war. I mean I couldn't possibly survive under the rule of those ghastly Germans.'

Doris laughed 'Oh Sylvia, you are funny but you're quite right, as usual.'

'Right let's put Frank Sinatra on and you can dream romantic things and I can hope.'

They played more records, and watched the fire dwindle until, eventually, Doris said she had to go. Sylvia stood at the cottage door and watched her wobbling off down the driveway making tracks in the snow, scarf and hair flowing behind her like a circus clown on a unicycle. Doris is all right, she thought, I really like her and then, she bit her lip, and I wish I could love a man like she does.

The following afternoon Sylvia had agreed to attend a Civil Defence meeting with her mother. It was to be chaired by her father-in-law and later the Camerons were coming to Hall Farm for supper and bridge.

At one thirty on the dot the Morris Eight crunched up the drive and Elizabeth hooted her arrival. Sylvia, well wrapped up against the cold, emerged from the cottage and squeezed into the passenger seat, 'Hello mother, I won't ask where you got the petrol but it's better than cycling in this weather. It's what the girls call Brass Monkey weather.'

'Hello darling, what are you wittering on about? God, this drive is lethal, I'll get Old Moore to clear it next time he's up at the house.' With a crash of gears the motor car slithered forward until it reached the main road where limited traffic had at least compacted the snow.

'Were you on duty last night, you didn't come up to see us?'

'No, a friend came round. We made toast and played records, it was fun.'

'Old school chum?'

'No, just a friend.'

Elizabeth changed from first up to third, having negotiated the junction at Rushmere Road, 'Female, I hope!'

'Mother! Of course she was female. Her name is Doris.'

'Doris, Doris, Don't recall meeting anyone called Doris.'

Sylvia smiled to herself. I wonder what mother would make of Doris, she thought or indeed what Doris would make of mother. They reached the county hall and parked at an interesting angle at the back of the building.

Sylvia was relieved she was only present in a back-up role this time and that her mother would do most of the talking on behalf of the WVS. They made their way to the basement where a meagre fire had been lit. The shiny yellowish paint was flaking somewhat on walls recently decorated with new posters; the gruesome *Britain shall not burn* vying with *Grow your own food* and the more rousing *Let 'em all come* entreating all men between 41 and 45 to join the Home Guard.

Robert Cameron was already at the head of the table going through some papers with a senior policeman as representatives from the Fire Service, Home Guard, ARP and First Aid teams took their places alongside Army, Naval and RAF officers. Robert looked up, smiled at Elizabeth and Sylvia, then banged his gavel and the meeting commenced. He began by thanking those present for the amazing work that they were doing saying that everyone recognised that it was not easy maintaining support for their various organisations at a time when people were working long hours at their day time jobs. He said that although the bad weather, which stretched across Europe, had curtailed bombing somewhat we were not to be complacent since Jerry would strike again as sure as eggs were eggs. Some wag interjected that he didn't know what eggs were anymore which Sylvia thought was funny, Robert ignored the interruption and continued to stress the need for a high level of alertness. The Battle of Britain, he said, had certainly dented the Luftwaffe but their resources were enormous and an invasion remained on the cards. As before, Sylvia was impressed with his voice and ease of speaking but wondered whether he was possibly becoming seduced by power. She could understand why Francis was slightly in awe of his father, could see where he got his serious side from but, nonetheless, hoped he wouldn't grow to be too much like him.

The various representatives gave their reports and took questions, Robert ensuring that nobody over elaborated. Elizabeth responded by giving various statistics covering the number of volunteers now in the Service, call out figures, numbers of Rest Centres, vehicles, and details of victims accommodated. She could have been addressing the Womens Institute, Sylvia thought, but everyone nodded appreciating her thoroughness.

The meeting moved on to set out in detail various plans in case of an invasion. All private telephones were to be disconnected, private cars immobilised, named roads were to be kept clear, the Home Guard was to man the railway line from Tuddenham Road Bridge, the occupants of the Harwich naval base were to move to Ipswich on Eastern Counties buses, all petrol installations be set alight and, for reasons Sylvia couldn't fathom, all pigeons were to be killed by the police.

Robert wound up the meeting just before four o'clock saying that he was confident that Ipswich would be ready to repel Hitler. The sombre group ambled out and were pleasantly surprised to find that the sun was shining.

Sylvia went up to the main house to find that the Camerons had already arrived and were enjoying a glass of Chablis in the sitting room.

'Must have heard the bottle open, Sylvia,' Robert greeted her, 'I've still got one or two hidden in a dark corner of the house so I thought why not bring one along. The only decent thing to come out of France is a fine bottle of Chablis, don't you agree Edward?'

'What? Oh. Absolutely.'

'You were on good form this afternoon, father-in-law,' Sylvia said accepting the proffered glass, 'Quite Churchillian.'

'Oh, really? Thanks,' Robert Cameron never knows whether I'm teasing or serious, she thought, like father like son. Must be something to do with their Scottish ancestry.

'A meeting of so many different types needs a firm chairman,' Elizabeth chimed in, rescuing her life long friend from digging himself into a deep hole. She knew what her daughter could be like once she got going. Nonetheless Sylvia continued, this time more seriously,

'I'm not sure what *different types* means any more. The one thing I find this war is doing is making everyone stand together. Sort of a team thing and nothing to do with where you live or where you went to school. You've only got to be on duty at an air raid to feel that.'

The others nodded, aware that though they were at the heart of organising the various Civil Defence duties Sylvia was the only one getting her hands dirty. Once again it was Elizabeth who filled the pause,

'Sylvia is working all the hours God made. Sometimes she's quite exhausted, aren't you darling?'

' I'm young, as everyone keeps telling me, and in a twisted sort of way I enjoy it. I don't mean the awfulness of people being killed and injured or the sadness of the homeless but I've met some really nice people, made new friends, that sort of thing..'

'I'd be absolutely hopeless,' Valerie Cameron muttered and nobody disagreed.

'Well do sit down everybody,' Elizabeth said, 'supper won't be ready for a quarter of an hour and even then it's nothing special. Not like the old days. My, we had some suppers before the war. It'll never be like that again.'

Edward sunk heavily into an easy chair, 'The situation in Greece is looking interesting. They were saying on the wireless the other day that the Greeks are pushing Musso back into Albania. We're sending back-up and the Yanks are sending a load of planes that were destined for the RAF. Must think it's important.'

109

Robert carefully sipped his Chablis, 'Between ourselves, I think the feeling is that the Italians haven't really got the heart for this war and we have the where-with-all to push them out of the Med and North Africa.'

'Then the Germans would have to send in re-enforcements which would take the pressure of invading us, is that it?'

'Something like that. But although Churchill still persistently warns about invasion of our shores I still think, just a personal view mind you, that Hitler lost his chance last Summer.'

Oddly, Sylvia's first thoughts went to Jimmy, Doris had said he was in Greece, then, almost as an afterthought she wondered about Francis fighting the North African campaign.

They went into supper in sombre mood. Elizabeth had done something to a small portion of pork and the potatoes and greens had come to no harm in the frost. For sweet she had concocted a roly-poly using the famous plum jam.

'I heard from Francis, yesterday, as far as one can tell he is OK. Hotter than round here at least,' Sylvia ventured.

'We heard earlier in the week, as you know Sylvia,' Valerie said addressing the Grimstones. 'His letters are always so serious but he seems to have made some good chums. This chap Bruce seems a character, organising entertainment in the mess and such. I couldn't imagine Francis doing a turn but then I read on a bit and found out he helped behind the scenes.'

He didn't tell me any of that, Sylvia thought, I only get complaints about mosquitoes and sand flies.

After supper the four old friends set up the bridge table and went through the ritual of cutting for dealer. Sylvia said she would sit in the corner with a book since she had not lit a fire in the cottage and preferred to stay warm until it was time for bed.

'You know you can always sleep here. Your room hasn't changed even though you're married', Elizabeth made her usual offer and Sylvia, as always, declined. Instead she curled up by the fire and opened Scott Fitzgerald's *The Last Tycoon* and began to read. She was aware of calls of suits and no trumps, of the occasional *Well done partner* and more regularly Robert Cameron admonishing Valerie with *Surely you understood what I meant by that*. Whilst the book, lent to her by a school-teacher member of the WVS, was interesting it wasn't long before she dozed off. She dreamed that she was in a play with Francis and a chap called Bruce to whom she had given a face, a flabby, jowly face. She kept annoying Francis by forgetting her lines and then suddenly the stage was bombed. She woke up with a jolt.

Her book had fallen to the floor but the bridge players hadn't noticed.

*'At least 13 high explosive bombs were dropped in the dock
area during a raid on the night of 10thApril 1941.' - Ipswich
at War, A Military History.*

Vera was working the evening shift with Margaret, Eva and May. It
was ITMA night and they were not too busy so, as usual in the
exchange, they were working on their sewing. Vera was concentrating
on embroidering a cushion, something she regarded as a luxury in
view of the ever pressing need to make do and mend. Suddenly Eva
shouted from her post 'Yellow Warning'. Embroidery was abandoned
and they reached under their seats for tin hats. They'd long since
abandoned the gas masks.

'Red Warning'.

Vera jumped up and went to the lever that operated the siren and
pulled on it. Many more raids and I'll have muscles like a man, she
thought. The wail that would be heard all over Ipswich and beyond
shook the building. Margaret was passing the six key tickets down the
line and the four of them contacted, fire, police, ambulance, ARP,
Home Guard and WVS.

The switchboard began to light up and the women began talking as
instructed, in calm, clear voices, plugging in the callers, connecting up
the services.

'I take it we're not going to the basement?' Eva shouted to the other
three. They nodded their tin-hatted heads.

'Pay nineteens, lets see then George you win two, Fred you lose
three.'

'Good job they're only match-sticks, Jack.'

'Match-sticks they may be Fred Butcher but at the end of the game
match-sticks get converted into chocolate.'

'Christ, I was forgetting we were playing for high stakes.'

They were sitting in the ARP post in Cliff Lane having completed
their nightly patrols. The hut was built of brick but was draughty.
Sand bags were stacked against the outside walls where a green and

white sign indicated that this was a Civil Defence Warden's Post. Posters gave instructions about what to do in event of a gas attack and warned of the dangers of butterfly bombs; buckets and stirrup pumps stood ready by the entrance. Suddenly the telephone vibrated on the wall, Jack grabbed it, shouted a loud 'will do' then turned to the others, 'could be a big one. Waves of Dorniers and Heinkels coming this way.' George, who was already relaying the warning by telephone, had to shout to be heard above the whine of the siren.

Sylvia was woken by someone knocking on the front door of the cottage, accompanied by the now familiar sound of the siren. She pulled on her dressing gown and found her father, in full Home Guard Uniform, on the doorstep. 'Big raid, you're on standby aren't you. Step to it and I'll give you a lift. It's the docks again. We've been expecting it.' He sounded as though he was addressing his men.

Her uniform was at the ready and it took her no time at all to get dressed and tumble into the Riley. As Edward raced along the lane she gathered her thoughts whilst, at the same time, managing to apply a bit of lipstick.

Hanging on to her seat she watched searchlights sweep the skies, 'It'll be the docks,' Edward repeated in his military voice, 'I'll drop you at your post and then go on to HQ'.

As he spoke they heard the steady drone of German bombers interposed by the crackle of anti-aircraft fire. Then the eerie whistle of bombs falling towards their targets followed by loud explosions. The sky turned orange.

Doris never slept well at Heathfields and woke as soon as the siren sounded. She pulled on her uniform and dashed out into the yard where the converted van was already filling up with other members of the Mobile team.

Looking up she saw black silhouettes of enemy aircraft caught in the searchlights. Her thoughts immediately went to Jimmy. Then she shook herself and climbed into the van. Even inside the vehicle the noise was deafening. Fire engines with bells clanging raced past and before long they became part of a convoy of vans all painted in non-descriptive colours with neat white stencilling indicating their ownership. Someone in the front shouted that Jerry was attacking the docks and various factory sites around Ipswich. They were assigned to Fairfield Road where petrol installations had been blown up destroying a whole row of houses.

Jack assembled with his team in the dock area where they were told that already six H.E. bombs had fallen plus loads of incendiaries. The scene that greeted them was unlike anything they had witnessed so far. Several warehouses were on fire, bombs had opened up enormous craters in the ground, heavy steel structures were buckling under the intense heat, small boats were on fire in the docks. About a dozen private cars and a number of lorries were exploding and burning in what had been a garage. Jack identified Morris Eights, Hilmans and a couple of Austin Tens. All around firemen were un-reeling hoses, one group told him they had come from Woodbridge. The word had gone out to all surrounding towns and villages that Ipswich had been specifically targeted. Bloody Old Haw Haw was right after all, he thought.

His group was sent to take rapid action to extinguish incendiary bombs dropped on a group of wooden sheds just back from the major area of devastation. They set to work with their stirrup pumps.

'Round the back Fred, Jack, quick as you can.' As they moved Jack heard the familiar whistle of a H.E. followed by a thud. He threw himself on the ground. The bomb, they decided later, had been intended for more petrol storage units but had missed its target hitting a nearby warehouse causing timber and corrugated iron to fly in all directions. Police and fireman arrived from further down the road .

'Are you all right mate,' a special policeman said, looking down on Jack and Fred spread-eagled on the ground. They got gingerly to their feet, 'Fine thanks,' Jack puffed, 'We were just seeing to the....'

'Constable.' He was interrupted by a voice shouting from the smoke. ' There's a warden here in trouble.' He blew his whistle and sent a runner for First Aid.

'Let's see,' said Jack, pushing forward. Then he stopped suddenly. A warden, his blue tunic scorched by fire lay trapped under a section of corrugated iron that had cut into his arm and neck. He was bleeding badly.

Jack grabbed Fred by the arm, 'It's George. Jesus Christ Fred, it's George.'

'Where are you assembling the victims?' Sylvia asked the ARP Chief whose men were backing up the various fire services dowsing the Fairfield Road houses with water. He pointed to a hastily erected sign and shielding her eyes from the smoke she saw wardens leading people from the houses and away from immediate danger.

'Pam, Brenda, let's go, shall we,' she shouted. Their eyes smarted from smoke and grit, even from a distance the heat was intense. The situation, though on a larger scale than usual, was the familiar one. Dazed people clinging to one another in disbelief, mothers frantically searching for children, tiny mites crying for missing mothers. She and the others checked labels and gently led the bemused gathering away from the chaos in preparation for evacuating them to the nearest Rest Centre.

'Your mummy will be here soon, Emma,' she whispered, lifting the little girl into her arms, gazing at the sooty face streaked with tears.' 'We'll just take you to somewhere a bit safer and mummy will come and join us.' As always, she said a silent prayer that mummy would be all right.

Momentarily she thought of Francis. She wondered how different her war was from the one he was fighting in the desert.

Doris didn't see Sylvia at Fairfield Road. She spent most of her time treating people in the back of one of the mobile vans. She had never been squeamish and was able to distance herself from the awfulness of what she was seeing in order to help. That's how she had been trained.

Sometimes I can't believe it's me doing this, she thought, I seem to become a different person as soon as I put on the uniform. She even managed a smile remembering Jimmy once telling her he liked her in her white overall at work because she looked like a nurse. God, she hoped he was all right. The wireless kept saying how difficult it was for our troops now the Germans had arrived in Greece.

'This lady needs her leg cleaning up and bandaging. Just an abrasion, no burns.'

A male first aider led the woman in and Doris took over. ' Just sit down here and we'll have a look at it,' she said. The woman did as she was told. She was crying.

'I reckon it does hurt a bit but it will be better for a clean and a good bandage. What's you name?'

'Mrs. Tomlinson,' the woman sobbed, 'It's not the arm, miss, it's my old dad. He's been hit by shrapnel, they've taken him off but I think he's dead.'

'Anything under the counter?' – war time expression.

Later in the month, on a Saturday, Doris called on Vera. She hadn't heard from Jimmy for some time which was unusual and she was worried. She found Vera with Jack in the front room waiting for the next news bulletin.

'I've brought you a present, it's from a friend of mine,' she said handing Vera a jar of Mrs. Moore's plum jam.

'Thank you dear, that's lovely. Fancy your friend making jam.'

'Shsssh. The news,' announced Jack and the three of them craned forward.

'At 10. p.m. today the Greek Army surrendered to the Italians.....'

'Bloody Wops, they surrendered to bloody Wops.'

Vera glanced at Doris, 'We don't swear in this house,' she said.

'Enough to make a parson swear. And what about our Jimmy? Where is he in all this?'

'The Greek government is insisting that the Allies should not waste any more men and resources and is supporting the retreat of some 45,000 troops to the nearby island of Crete....'

'I hope he gets out all right,' muttered Doris.

Jack sat back and looked at her, 'He'll be all right,' he said, unconvincingly.

Vera pulled herself out of the chair, ' Let's go and put the kettle on, we've got a bit of milk and we can have some of that plum jam.'

Doris went with her into the kitchen.

'How is Jack, Mr. Wright I mean, after the other night?'

'He took it hard. Said it was like being back in the First War. Something about it not even being a battle ground. But, Jack being Jack went to work the next day and off to warden duties for his shift soon after.'

'I looked for him last night. I was up at Landseer Road.'

'No he was off last night. Stood in the garden during the raid after he'd shoved me down the dugout. Plane spotting from his silhouettes.'

'When did you last hear from Jimmy?' she asked.

Vera filled the kettle from the tap, rattling around, not looking at Doris, ' A week or two now but you heard last week didn't you?'

'The beginning of last week. He was going on about the Australians and New Zealanders. Really likes them he does.'

Vera turned round, hovering with the kettle, ' He'll be all right,' she said.

Doris, who now treated the kitchen like her own, started to cut the bread.' 'Got enough butter?' she asked.

Vera pushed the kitchen door shut, 'Now don't say anything, especially to him, but mysterious little gifts keep appearing in my kitchen in the mornings. This week it was butter, last week a bar of that plain chocolate. I think we have fairies at the bottom of the garden.'

'Doesn't he tell you where they come from?'

'It's not Jack. Jack never comes into the kitchen. It's Kitty but she's not saying anything either. She's got this new boyfriend, well man friend; he's quite a bit older than she is. She says he's a businessman. Black market business, more like. I know it's wrong and I'll have to say something to her but, to be honest, it's a Godsend what with all this extra rationing and that.'

On cue, Kitty came into the kitchen, she was wearing a dressing gown and her hair was pinned up, 'Doris I thought I heard you. You couldn't spare a minute could you I need someone to do the lines on my legs.'

'Lines on your legs whatever next, eh Doris? She only browns them with a bit of gravy powder to make up for having no stockings and someone has to put the seams down the back. Good job it's not going to rain, my girl.'

The three of them laughed, ' Make do and mend, mum, that's what it is. Come on Doris come up to my room before Dad cottons on and then I'll be for it.' Kitty was half way out of the door.

The first impression of Kitty's bedroom was that it was a heap of clothes with a bed buried beneath them. Closer examination detected make up, articles cut from magazines and a few booklets encouraging the nation to *make do and mend*. Kitty handed Doris an eyebrow pencil and lay down on the bed so that Doris could get to work on the backs of her browned legs. Doris thought the whole thing hilarious and couldn't stop laughing.

'For God's sake stop giggling, you've got to keep the line straight.'

Taking a deep breath Doris commenced her task but after the first leg was complete she viewed her work and giggled even more.

'I hope you're doing a good job,' Kitty remonstrated from the prone position.

'You won't be able to see if I am or not.'

'Oh Yes I can. I'll look in the mirror in a minute and check you out,' Kitty said, jumping up when Doris had completed her artwork. She threw some flowered material to the floor revealing a long mirror and craning her neck examined the bottom of her legs.

'Yeah. Not bad at all, Doris. I'll do the same for you one day.' She sat back on the bed and started to apply her make-up.

'So what's this Len like then?' Doris asked her.

Kitty pursed her lips, painted them a coral colour and grinned, 'Well he thinks he looks like Clark Gable but the only resemblance, as far as I can make out, is the moustache and that tickles when he kisses me.'

'And?'

'And I met him when I was out with my mates and some of those RAF types. It was at a private club in a big old house near Woodbridge. The boys seemed to know this Len quite well and I got talking to him. He said he could get me things if I knew how to keep my mouth shut. I said I did most of the time and gave him one of my looks and he laughed and said I was his sort of girl. From then on he's taken me to parties and other clubs and places. No expense spared, if you know what I mean.'

'What does he do then?'

'Do? Well he's a businessman. Quite a successful one I would say.'

'What does your dad think of him?'

'God, Doris all these questions. I don't know what dad thinks of him since I haven't introduced them. Originally I made him pick me up at the end of the road but just lately he drives up to the house and hoots the horn and I fly out of the door. Here, tell you what, let's have a bit of chocolate.' Kitty went to a small dressing table, pulled out a drawer, rummaged around and produced the first milk chocolate bar Doris had seen for some time. She broke a large piece off and handed it over, 'There we are, a present from Len.'

On Sunday morning Kitty came down to breakfast on time but looking awful.

'Think I had one or two too many last night,' she muttered.

'More than one or two by the noise you made. Whatever time did you get in? My one night off and I get woken up with you crashing and banging around,' Jack took a swig from his tea,' and another thing when are we going to meet this latest boyfriend of yours?'

'Soon I suppose but he's more of a man friend than boyfriend. He's about thirty I reckon.'

'So why is he not in the army then?'

'Got polio when he was young. Walks with a limp so he failed the medical.'

'Skiver is he?'

'You can't fake polio, dad.'

'What's he do then?'

'God! Everyone keeps asking me questions. I am over twenty-one. I can do what I want and go out with who I like without all these questions.'

'Not whilst you're under my roof you can't. He must do something fancy. I mean that motor car of his, Sunbeam Talbot isn't it, that doesn't come cheap and what about the petrol?'

'He's got businesses.'

Jack took another swig of his tea, 'Businesses,' he repeated looking at her over the rim of his cup. Vera came in carrying two plates of bacon and toast. Kitty looked up,

'Don't know if I can cope with all that,' she said.

'Bacon. Where the hell's all that bacon come from?' Jack couldn't believe his eyes,' why are we eating a months supply at one go. It's not Christmas is it?'

'Kitty's young man sent it to us as a present,' Vera said in her quietest voice.

Jack tipped back on his chair, 'Oh! Now I see it. You must think I'm stupid. This Len is in business, you say. Black Market business, that's what he's about. Well I am having none of it,' he was shouting, 'none of his bloody Black Market stuff whilst my mate George died last week trying to rescue bombed out people and your brother is out somewhere in Greece retreating under enemy fire.' In one movement Jack rocked his seat forward and sent the plate of bacon spinning across the table smashing into Kitty's cup of tea spilling the contents into her lap. She jumped up screaming and ran from the room. Jack looked at the scene for a moment, then he slowly stood up.

Vera heard the back door slam and buried her head in her hands. Oh Jimmy, she thought, how I miss your cheeky face.

IOWA

'Our liberties we prize and our rights we will maintain.' - Iowa State Motto

Iowa came out of a hard Winter to a Spring that warmed and softened the land. The farmers turned the grey soil into furrows of black earth and planted seed. Soon the hot, humid Summer ripened the corn and the fields swayed gold in the breeze. Iowa was a state of extremes as far as weather was concerned but the inhabitants of Red Oak were descendants of Swedish pioneers possessed of a calm temperament and a desire to work the land hard.

One Sunday after church in June 1941 the Nelsons had invited the Linquists over for a meal and having enjoyed chicken roast, mashed potatoes, green beans and some rather special pickled cucumber, they were sitting out on the veranda drinking coffee. Karl Nelson rocked back in his chair, 'I love this time of year, never fail to have a kind of eagerness to see the corn grow high and strong. Bit sentimental I know but that's how I feel. How about you Lester, do you feel that?'

'Sure I guess I feel kind of relieved that it's coming on OK but you and I are wise enough and old enough to know that in Iowa a sudden Summer storm can ruin everything. But you know what? I never stop thanking God that our forefathers came here and gave us the opportunity to farm this wonderful land.'

'Why Lester you're becoming quite the poet' his wife Patty chipped in.

'They're all poets when it comes to talking about their farms; now anyone for more coffee?' Lois said. She went round filling up their cups, a tall elegant woman, hair pulled off her face into a bun, 'And how's your Letha getting on at college?'

'She is just loving it. You know Letha, never happier than we she's a book in her hands.'

Lois sighed, 'I just wish Tom would be keener on studying. He's never happier than when he has a hammer in his hands.'

'Yeah, but he's a useful boy to have around, your Tom, isn't that right Karl?' Lester said. Whilst he was proud of his daughter he often looked at Tom and was saddened that they hadn't been able to have any more children and, as a farmer, he felt deprived of a natural heir to his land.

'Fix anything can Tom' Karl said, not wishing to get into the education argument.

'I gather there are disturbing things happenings in Europe,' Lester said, addressing his oldest friend,' they were talking about it in the hardware store today.'

'I don't pay that much attention, I'm afraid. There's enough to do here to worry me. If I do have a view it's that we would do best to stay neutral. Fair enough supplying old allies with arms, I guess, but stay out of any fighting this time, that's what I say. You've only got to go down to the cemetery to see the gravestones from the last war to know that I'm right.'

They were all quiet for a while, each dwelling on private thoughts, none wanting to voice them. Then they talked of local things, of repairs needed to the Mamrelund Lutheran church, of the new manager at The Montgomery State Bank and of the Nelson son-in-law's promotion up at Thomas D Murphy and Co.

Their talk was interrupted by the sound of a truck drawing up followed by the slamming of the door. A few seconds later Tom appeared framed in the doorway. His close cropped fair hair accentuated his fresh, round face. He smiled at the small gathering.

'Hi Mom, Dad. Good to see you Mr Linquist, Mrs Linquist.'

'Hi Tom.'

'Why don't you draw up a chair and join us?' Lester suggested. He liked Tom, and enjoyed talking to the boy.

'No thank you sir, things to do,' Tom replied and started to go back inside, then he turned,' and how is Letha doing at Lincoln?'

'She's doing just fine,' Patty leaned forward in her chair and looked around at the others, proud of her daughter. 'She'll be home at the weekend. Why don't you call over? I'm sure she'd be glad to see you?'

'Sure, Ma'am, I might just do that, if it's OK with you?'

Patty laughed, 'Of course it is, why else would I have said it and I'm sure it would be OK with Letha, too.'

'Right. Well, I'll say goodnight then and he scuttled away inside the house.

'This really is my favourite time of year,' Letha confided in Tom as they walked together through the woodland that backed onto the Linquists' holding, 'It can get so hot and humid in high Summer and folks get a bit jumpy in case there's a storm or something.'

'Well mostly they've put a lot a work into the corn and one of those giant storms can soon ruin everything.'

'You really are your father's son,' Letha teased, ' Fresh off the farm Tom Nelson, that's you.'

'Well I never was one for books, I'm afraid. Does that mean you think I'm dull?'

'Now Tom, I never said that. Besides I was only teasing. It's just that I can see you living and dying in Montgomery County whereas I want to see everything there is to see and know everything there is to know. Did that sound ungrateful? I didn't mean it to.'

Letha was a year older than Tom and whilst he knew her fairly well on account of the family friendship his own buddies tended to be from his own grade. That's the way it was. Besides, there was something about her manner that had always made him back away. In truth, he was a little in awe of Letha Linguist and it had taken quite a bit of courage for him to call on her. On the other hand, she seemed pleased to see him and had suggested the walk.

Tom was talking more freely now and went on, trying to justify his point, 'As I see it we're real lucky to have been born in Iowa. OK some times the weather can be a bit extreme and OK we're coming out of the Depression but so is the rest of America as far as I can make out. But, we have good homes, the people are neighbourly and help one another, I've got some great friends and we have this,' he swept his arms forward indicating the great expanse of undulating fields peppered with neat white farmsteads and steep roofed red barns. 'This takes some beating.'

'I do know that Tom and my folks would kill me if they heard of my lofty ambitions. You see I don't aim to stay around Iowa all my life but that's our secret, right?'

He was to share a secret, that's progress he thought and smiled, 'Our secret,' he repeated.

'I like it when you smile at me,' Letha said, slowing her walk and looking back at him with her blue-grey Scandanavian eyes.

Tom knew enough about girls to realise that she was teasing him, even flirting with him a little but he also calculated that with her looks she would have a lot of admirers.

'So Tom,' she continued, changing the subject, ' Don't you just love all this new music? We have wonderful dances at university you know with swing bands like Glen Miller and singers who sound just like Frank Sinatra.'

'Now he can sing, can't he. Though my dad says he'll never be as good as Bing.'

'All dads say that' she said and they looked at each other and laughed.

Tom still wasn't sure about her or indeed sure about himself but he took a deep breath and heard himself say,' Letha, you wouldn't like to come on a date with me when you're next home, I suppose. I mean it doesn't have to be anything serious, just a date.'

Letha stopped and fixed him with those eyes again, 'I was wondering when you'd ask me,' she said, it was her turn to smile, ' and I agree it doesn't have to be serious or anything; what with me being at university and having my secret plans to travel.'

'Of course,' he murmured. They had completed a circuit and were moving back into the wood by the stream.

'Tom, you can kiss me if you want' he heard her say.

IOWA

'All men shall be enabled to live in freedom from fear and want.' - The Atlantic Charter. '

The pioneers who built The Mamrelund Lutheran Church clearly expected all those who lived in and around Red Oak to attend on a regular basis. It was an impressive spacious, wooden building with a fine high ceiling. They would have been gratified to see that in 1941 a fair proportion of the local community still attended on a Sunday and, it being the month of August, were pleased that their predecessors had constructed such an airy building.

The congregation emerged from the service, paused for a word with Pastor Michael Winstrom, and then greeted one another as neighbours. The men shook hands then raised their hats to the women. It was nearing mid morning and the temperature was already in the eighties.

Tom Nelson stood behind his parents, fidgeting with the brim of his hat, whilst they engaged in conversation with Mr. and Mrs. Lindell who were visiting from nearby Stanton. He glanced around to see if Letha was home from college that weekend. He saw the Linquists in a group emerging from the church and then, as if she always had to surprise him, Letha appeared at his elbow.

'Morning Tom, sorry I couldn't make the other week. Something important came up at College and I had to re-arrange. You must think me awful?'

'I could never think you awful, Letha, and you know it.' Tom didn't blush anymore when he spoke to her.

'Well now, I am in this afternoon, why don't you drop by about four o'clock. It'll be cooler then.'

'I'll do that then,' he said, replacing his hat with some vigour. He looked at her and grinned. There was not a bead of perspiration on her lightly tanned face.

'I'll be waiting,' she turned and walked across to her parents nodding and smiling at various neighbours on her way.

At lunch he consumed double helpings of hog roast and a large portion of apple pie.

'My Tom, you've a good appetite today. Must have been something Pastor Michael said in his sermon.'

'More likely on account of my being up early hacking out some of that rogue corn. What are the other farmers saying about their harvests, Dad?'

Karl leaned back on his chair, 'Well, Tom, you know these farming folk as well as me by now. None of them are admitting they have a bumper harvest coming up but I think they're all pretty content with what they got. As long as we keep clear of tornadoes and such.'

'Talking of storms what was Sam Lindell saying to you about Europe and that terrible war they're having?' Lois asked.

'Nothing for you to worry about, Lois. Nothing to worry about.'

'Karl Nelson, I may be just a woman but I am not stupid. I hear talk of President Roosevelt signing........ What is it again?'

'The Atlantic Charter, mom, that's what they called it,' Tom chipped in.

'Atlantic Charter, you see even Tom hears things, and they say that the whole of the USA thought he was on a fishing trip. What do they make of that?'

'Sam was just saying what we all think. We in America should do all we can to help the British but our President is going about it the right way. Most folk I talk to think sending them planes and munitions and now even food is the most we should do. Now, Lois, are we going to get any coffee today?'

Karl got to his feet, stretched and strolled out onto the veranda. Tom followed him, 'Is that it then? What Mr. Lindell was saying. I mean I've heard President Roosevelt on the radio and he was talking about helping the British and...'

'My Tom, now you're getting political, I don't know what's got into everyone today. And I thought all you worried about was the harvest?'

'That's all I want to worry about, Dad,' Tom looked at his feet before lowering himself into one of the old wicker chairs; his father was already rocking backwards and forwards fiddling with his pipe.

'Listen son, if you really want to know what I think it is that our government is more worried about what the Japanese are up to than how to help out in Europe. So there's something else for you to think about when you're not fretting about the farm......or Letha Linquist.'

This time Tom knew he was blushing, ' Whatever has Letha Linquist got to do with it?' ' he said. Karl smiled and put a match to his pipe.

His mother appeared with the coffee, 'You could do far worse than Letha Linquist, if you want my opinion' she said.

Later in the day Tom declined his parents suggestion that he went with them to visit Ellen, Ben and baby Luke saying that he had one or two things to do. His mother gave his father a knowing look.

It took about half an hour to walk to the Linquists place and with the temperature remaining in the lower eighties Tom had changed out of his church going clothes. He strolled along by the vast fields of swaying corn and, not for the first time, thought about how much he loved the Iowan Summers just before harvest. He wanted to reach his arms up and take it all in. After about twenty minutes he went past the Swansons farm and down into the woods. He remembered the first time he had walked with Letha and how she had surprised him with a kiss. He smiled to himself thinking that since that time she had never stopped surprising him, exciting him and downright annoying him. One moment she made him feel he was the most important person in her world and the next that he meant nothing. Soon after that first kiss he took her to a movie and they hardly saw the film yet the following week-end she sat with her hands clasped on her lap looking and behaving like a prim Sunday School teacher. Once, when her parents were out, she guided his farmer's hands to her soft breasts yet later in the dusk of the orchard she pushed him away. Tom had put this erratic behaviour down to her being female but he couldn't figure why, having entreated him to meet her someplace, she would fail to turn up or why she teased him about her dates with college boys. Her defence was always the same. She had plans. Plans that would see her leave Red Oak, Montgomery County and even Iowa itself. Letha Linquist was not for settling down. Tom didn't think he was for settling down either. He simply wanted her to be his girl. He didn't want other girls so why did she want other guys but he knew she just liked to string him along and figured that he was not the only one subjected to this kind of treatment. Yet, there she was that very same morning, demure and respectable, a credit to her family, pristine and pure, coming out of church like butter wouldn't melt in her beautiful mouth.

As he emerged from the woods the Linquist farmstead came into view in the distance. He wondered whether she had told her folks that he would be calling. He need not have worried since, once again, she surprised him by appearing at the top of the slope. She had been waiting, she explained, in the shade of the orchard.

'You've changed,' she announced, looking him up and down, 'I think I prefer the farm boy Tom to the trussed up one at church. You look more of a man this way.'

'You've changed as well,' he said.

'I'm a woman, Tom, women are changeable,' she laughed. 'Come on, this way,' and she took his hand and let him through the rustling orchard and back to fields.

'Don't you just love it now,' he said, ' ten feet tall, miles and miles of shimmering corn, like some great golden sea.'

'My and you said you weren't a literary man.'

'And you want to leave all this?' Tom ignored her jibe.

'It doesn't mean I don't like it. It means....well, you just called it a golden sea. Have you ever seen a real sea?'

'No, the nearest I ever got to seeing one big expanse of water was Chicago and I've only been there once,' Tom admitted.

'Me, too. So can't you understand that I don't want just to look at the sea I want to travel on it to far off places.'

'You know me, Letha, fresh off the farm, as they say.'

She laughed, she had an open bell-ringing laugh, 'Come on then let's go and listen to the corn grow, as they say,' and she ran with him into the fields of ripe maize.

Holding hands they skipped and twirled down the avenues of high corn until they came to an area where the rogue weed had been hacked back making a small clearing. He took hold of her with strong hands and began to swing her round; faster and faster as if on a carousel. His head was spinning and the walls of corn blurred before his eyes until, dizzy and laughing, he fell with her to the ground. He felt her arms round his neck pulling him to her. A sudden breath of breeze caused the corn to sing out and he spiralled downwards. The sun filtered by stalks and husks created a dappled pattern on their bodies; the earth, soft and giving moulded a bed. He heard the words 'farm boy,' heard other cries that were not cries of pain as he felt her fingers dig into his back. And then all he felt was Letha.

Suddenly she pulled on her clothes and stood over him, 'Tom Nelson, you're my guy,' she said.

He looked back at her, confused, 'You mean you and me we are...?'

She laughed, 'Heavens no. It was just my way of saying thank you that's all. Tom, I'm sorry, but I have to go back. I really shouldn't have come at all but I did promise. The folks have people over for supper and I have to be there. I'll write and maybe we can go someplace again when I'm next home.' She bent down and kissed him lightly on the mouth, 'and for what it's worth I really did hear the corn grow.'

Propped up on one elbow he watched her disappear through a pathway of gold like Moses parting The Red Sea. The touch of his shirt on his raw back made him wince, he pulled on his muddy dungarees, stood up and rammed his hat back on his head. Was that the same girl I saw this morning smiling sweetly at all the neighbours after church, he wondered?

He trudged slowly back towards the woods in something of a dream.

'Come to spy on my harvest have you?' said a voice. He looked up and saw Lester Linquist, hands on hips, looking out over the fields.

'Certainly not, sir,' he said seriously before realising that the other man was laughing,' Just out for a bit of a stroll. Mom and Dad have gone to visit my sister Ellen. You know she has a baby now, I guess,' he was rambling.

'Sure, so how are things with you then, Tom?'

'Fine thank you Mr Linquist, had a bit of rogue corn but we have been up early, before it gets too hot, hacking it out and I think it's under control but apart from that it looks pretty good.'

'Letha's been home this week-end. You should have called round but you know Letha she always chasing after something so you might have missed her anyhow. I think she's gone out just now if not I would say come up to the house and say hello.'

'Oh! No thanks, sir, I have to get back and do a few jobs before the folks get home and besides you've probably got supper on the go.'

'No nothing special,' he said, 'See you around then Tom.'

'It's that man again.' - Radio programme starring Tommy Hanley

'Jack's been out in the garden all morning. Says it'll tone him up for the football this afternoon; it's one of those Army versus Navy matches. Not like the old days of Mick Burns and Jimmy McLuckie he says. Silly really, he thinks I know all about it but I've never been to a match in my life, I remember all their names though,' Vera paused, 'He's going with Syd Green from the ARP but between you and me he misses going with Jimmy. They would argue about the match for days.'

'Sunday mornings used to be football, football, football. It was so bad that I started going to church,' Kitty chipped in, then looking at Vera,' 'Come on Mum, take the weight of your feet and I'll make a cuppa. Even take one to Dad if he's still talking to me.'

'What ever have you done now, Kitty?' Doris asked. In spite of herself Doris enjoyed the little dramas at the Wrights; all she ever got at home was her mother boasting of her promotion in the world of the welders and her father still convinced we had to be ready for the invasion any minute. Alice, her sister, had made a wise move joining the Land Army up in Norfolk.

Kitty smiled at her, 'Nothing new Doris. We had a little tiff about Len, of course. He said when I went out with *that man* I looked like mutton dressed up as lamb. I told him I was twenty-one, made my own clothes and was not as stupid as he thought. I was just cheering myself up, that's all.'

'What did he say?'

'He put on a silly voice and said *It's being so cheerful that keeps you going.* You know like on ITMA. Then he reminded me that as an ARP he was still the *eyes and ears* of the neighbourhood, whatever that was supposed to mean.'

'So that wasn't so bad was it. He was sort of laughing at you. Now who's stolen the strainer?' Vera got up to supervise the tea making.

'I reckon it's that fairy you keep going on about,' Kitty laughed, 'The one that used to bring you little presents until Dad found out it was stuff I got from Len. Some fairy!'

'Would that be the same fairy that did my ironing the other night when I dozed off?'

Vera said, giving Kitty a hug as she triumphantly waved the strainer above her head.

Kitty looked at Doris and grinned. Jack appeared at the back door looking hot, sweaty and thirsty.

'You must smell the tea pot, Jack,' Vera said, ' Kitty's just brewed up.'

'We hadn't forgotten you Dad,' Kitty handed him a cup.

'*Don't forget the diver*,' Jack quipped..

' What has got into everyone today, you all trying to make up for me missing ITMA this week? Someone has to keep the telephones going.'

Kitty leaned on the sink and looked down at her high heels, 'Well you all might as well know I've some more good news for you. I've finished with Len. Apparently I wasn't his only girl friend so I told him what he could do with his high life. And guess what? I heard from some of the girls that he's been caught out. Someone gave the nod to the police about his shady little dealings. Serve him right I say.'

Jack sucked noisily on his pipe, '*Eyes and ears, a couple of beers, don't mind if I do, sir*' then he turned on his heels and went back to the garden.

The following Monday Vera was on day shift at an exchange near the centre of the town when Eva noticed a queue forming at Grimstones.

'Queue alert,' she shouted to the others, 'Grimstones. I'll plug into Tavern Street.'

Vera had been indoctrinated into the routine devised by Margaret for ensuring they did not miss out on any potential bargains. Any woman worth her salt would join a queue as soon as it formed never knowing what it was for but in the hope that there was something worthwhile at the other end. The lucky ones would emerge from the shop and someone would always make a call from the phone box. Margaret's system entailed plugging into the line of the nearest call box thereby obtaining speedy knowledge of the nature of the merchandise. If it interested the telephonists one of them would sacrifice their ten-minute break and join the queue.

'Material, material for dresses. A sudden supply arrived. Anyone interested?'

'I am,'

'And me.'

'OK Vera, I'll go for both of us,' Margaret, the ring-leader, announced.

The others nodded and she was off like a shot.

That evening, Kitty came home from fire watch and flopped into the old leather sofa in the front room. Vera brought her the inevitable cup of tea.

'My eyes are coming out of their sockets,' she said, 'how was your day, mum?'

'Oh. We're always busy but there were no emergencies so I suppose you could say it was OK. Had a letter from Jimmy. He's in Egypt. Got there by boat. Says he slept on a hammock because the boat was full of rats. Horrible isn't it? But he made it sound funny. You know Jimmy. Trouble is the letters all arrive out of order and miles out of date.'

'Yeah. Doris said she had five at once the other day but before that she hadn't heard for a fortnight. Still he's fine, mum, that's the main thing. Right, I'll go upstairs and change.'

Vera watched her go from the room and then tiptoed to the foot of the stairs and listened.

There was a scream and Kitty shouted from the top of the stairs, 'Mum that fairy has been again. I've got this lovely material.' She clattered down the stairs and hugged Vera, 'You are the best Mum in the world' she said.

Joyce was off sick. She'd had this awful cold for days and Doris told her that sneezing over customers was not the best advertisement for a chemist shop.

Mr. French had sold his bungalow and moved into the flat above the shop and though initially Doris had thought he would be spending more time at work, his attendance had become more erratic. She worried about him living up there alone, she wondered whether he ate proper meals and whether he kept the place clean. She had never been up to the flat and common sense told her she should keep her concerns at a distance. Nonetheless she did worry about him.

It had been a quiet morning and she had turned her attention to checking the stock, a task neglected by Mr. French of late. She began making a list of requirements, zinc oxide, zinc compound, emulsifying ointment, aromatic cardamom tincture. She looked in the records to check the quantities she should order and what the cost would be.

'Now then, what are you up to now?' She hadn't heard him come into the dispensary.

'Morning Mr. French, how are you today?' He had cut himself shaving and a small piece of cotton wool adhered to his chin to stem the bleeding.

'Not so bad for an old 'un.' He looked at the clock on the wall above the cabinets,' 'Gosh is it ten o'clock already. Joyce in the shop?'

'She's not come in. Remember she had that awful cold and I did say she shouldn't spread it around. So she's taken my advice for once.'

'Quite. So it's you and me to cure the ills of Ipswich, then? What are you up to here then, my dear.' He came and stood behind her as she perched on the stool over the books.

'The stocks are a bit low but to be honest I don't really know what sort of quantities to order. I was looking back to what we've done before.'

He leaned over placing his hands on her shoulders. She could smell his stale breath.

'What would I do without you Doris, ' he said. ' It's my fault I've been neglecting things a bit since....'

She turned abruptly so that his fingers left her shoulders and looked at him, 'Are you all right, Mr. French. I mean all right in your flat by yourself. I worry about you. I know it's nothing to do with me but you do have friends don't you?' She wasn't quite sure why the words tumbled out.

Now he was facing her. He placed his hands on her shoulders again, leaning towards her. 'Oh Doris you are a sweet girl. I didn't know you cared about me like that.'

She felt herself turn red, 'I didn't mean....'

'Naturally I am a bit lonely, after Mrs. French was taken from me. I have my records and my stamps. Friends from the stamp club invite me round sometimes.'

'Oh well, that's good then...'

'But I'm touched by your concern, Doris. I've grown very fond of you. And as I said I am a bit lonely. You could come round one evening, if you like, and I'll play you some of my favourites. I have quite a collection.' Before she knew it his grip tightened and he kissed her clumsily on the mouth.

Suddenly the door bell clanged. She almost fell off the stool, 'Shop,' she croaked, dashing out to tend to a list of supplies for an ARP warden.

'And that's all that happened really. It was all a bit silly. He didn't say or do anything else out of the ordinary all day and I didn't say anything. Joyce came back the next day and so every thing was back to normal.'

Doris was walking around the farm at Playford with Sylvia. The fields had been ploughed up and a watery sun caught the furrows causing the brown soil to shine blue and purple. Sylvia had found an extra pair of Wellingtons that just about fitted Doris and they both tied scarves around their heads. Doris continued, ' I don't know why I'm telling you all this.'

Sylvia didn't reply sensing Doris needed to elaborate.

'You see I really like Mr. French. He's been so good to me. Showing me things, giving me responsibility and as I've told you before he hinted that I could become a proper pharmacist after the war. Most of the time he is a really good boss. He is considerate and can be really funny but I think over the last two years or so he's been so busy nursing his poor wife that now she's gone he's lost his way a bit.'

'Poor old you. I can see the problem. I suppose men have always been like that in situations when girls can't really object. You know the old Lord of the Manor and servant girl thing. It's the same thing, isn't it? You obviously like your work, want to progress, even like this Mr. French in a boss sort of way but you shouldn't have to put up with this. No woman should.'

Doris took a deep breath and felt the misty air in her lungs. She heard a dog bark in the distance. 'Sorry, this is a lovely morning. I shouldn't bore you with all my problems.'

'That's what friends are for, aren't they?' Sylvia said.

'Yes they are and you've become a good friend to me, Sylvia. I can't imagine why. I mean we come from such different backgrounds.'

'I think the war is making a bit of nonsense of that sort of thing. For some people anyhow. Sometimes I wonder what Francis thinks. Does he see it very much as officers and other ranks or does the battle situation make him closer to all the men around him.'

'Jimmy certainly has respect for some of his officers. Sees them as being a bit different still though. He is quite rude about some of the others; in a funny sort of way, that is.'

'Yesss. Anyhow your Mr. French. I think with Joyce back he won't have many opportunities to get frisky again but I'm sure he'll repeat his invitation for you to visit the flat. So simply remind him you are engaged to Jimmy and intend to be totally true to him and you don't think Jimmy would like it if you went to any man's flat for an evening. That way he won't be made to feel too awful, but with luck, he'll get the message. If he tries anything again then you'll simply have to kick him in the balls.'

Doris burst into laughter. She couldn't believe what Sylvia had just said. Yet at the same time she had been given good advice. 'Thanks Sylvia' she said, 'thanks for being a good friend.'

They completed the circuit of fields around Hall Farm talking of other things. Of letters from North Africa, of clothes rationing, of J.B Priestley's *Postscripts*, and of Glen Miller's *Chattanooga Choo Choo* . Then Sylvia became a bit serious and confided her desire to give up her role at Grimstones in order to devote herself totally to Civil Defence.

Before they knew it they were back at the cottage where a woman in tweeds stood with a black Labrador. On seeing Sylvia the dog sprinted and she fondled it.

'Hello Lucky,' she laughed, 'had a good walk?' Then she realised that Doris and her mother had never met. ' Mother come and meet my friend Doris. She's one of those brave girls from the Mobile First Aid teams.'

Elizabeth advanced proffering a hand, 'How nice to meet you....Doris.'

Doris thought perhaps she should curtsey but took the hand instead, 'And you Mrs. Grimstone.'

'You girls do a wonderful job.'

'Well Sylvia's pretty impressive with her WVS too.' Doris replied.

'Are you an Ipswich family, Doris?' asked Elizabeth.

'Oh yes, born and bred. From the Rivers estate.'

'The Rivers Estate that's Nacton way isn't it? Now then Sylvia, I called to see what you are doing for lunch. Doris could join us if you like, we're only having scraps.'

'That's very kind of you but I have to be getting along,' Doris said, ' Nice to have met you. I'll see you soon Sylvia, and thanks again.'

'I'll pop in the shop and we'll fix something up, then. Bye.'

The two Grimstone women watched Doris weave her way down the lane,

'Nice girl, shame about the accent,' said Elizabeth.

'She's become a very good friend,' her daughter replied.

'Our enemies have performed a brilliant feat of deception, perfectly timed and executed with great skill.' President Roosevelt

December 7th 1941

'Vera, wake up Vera, I've just heard it on the late news.'

Vera sat up, rubbed her eyes, and stared at Jack who was sitting on the bed still dressed in his warden's uniform.

'Jack, what ever is the matter? It's not about Jimmy is it?'

'No, nothing like that. It's just been on the news. The Japs have attacked Pearl Harbour.'

She looked at him in disbelief. 'Jack every night someone is attacking someone, somewhere and you are waking me up to tell me that.'

'You don't understand. Pearl Harbour is a big American base. Freddy Grisewood said on the news that they have damaged hundreds of ships and aircraft and killed over two thousand Americans.'

'Good God.'

'So you see the Americans will have to be in the war properly now with us against the Japs, Germans and *Eyties*.'

Vera climbed slowly out of bed and fumbled for her dressing gown. 'I can't take it all in. Come on Jack let's go downstairs and have a cup of tea and you can tell me it all over again.'

In Iowa, the Nelson family had been to church and were driving home through a sprinkling of snow. They sat in the big kitchen where the pot-belly stove gave out a good heat. They tended to live in the kitchen, especially in the colder months; colourful rugs on wooden floors, chunky chairs and smell of cooking made the room cosy against the severity of Iowan Winters.

Ellen took hold of Luke's hand, 'Come on Luke, Grandma's got something to show us in the bedroom. She's been busy with her sewing machine again. Let's go and see what she's made.'

'Grandma,' said Luke and tottered towards the door, 'Grandma, cookie.'

Ellen laughed, 'No cookies yet,' she told him.

'He's coming on fine, that little fella of yours.' Karl was sitting with Ben.

He and Tom had changed out of their church going clothes on coming back from the service. Ben feeling uncomfortable, trussed up in his Sunday best, loosened his tie, 'So is Luke going to be a businessman or a farmer? he asked.

'Got good firm legs like a farmer but who knows what will have happened to the world by the time he's grown up,' Karl said speaking slowly.

Tom came in with a basket full of logs and stacked them beside the stove.

'The old hogs are snorting a bit out in the cold,' he said.

'So was I first thing this morning,' Karl said, laughing at his own joke. The boys joined in and Karl settled to light his first pipe of the day.

Tom went over to the radio in the corner of the room, 'I'll just tune in to see if they say anything about the weather,' he said.

'Aren't you just the worrier, Tom, we have survived harsher Winter's than this before, you know.'

'Just checking. No harm in that,' Tom shrugged and twiddled with the knobs.

Rock of Ages cleft to me crackled the radio and Tom twiddled some more.

We interrupt this programme to bring you some important National News . The three men craned forward in their seats. *The White House has announced that at 2.22 pm today the Japanese attacked The US Pacific Fleet's home base at Pearl Harbour. Reports say that over 300 Japanese aircraft were involved in this surprise attack and that US battleships, smaller ships and aircraft have been destroyed or damaged. Many service personnel are feared dead or injured. The Japanese also attacked bases in the Phillipines,*

Guam and Wake islands. President Roosevelt is meeting with his top war ministers and a statement is expected shortly.

It seemed an age before anyone spoke until eventually Karl took his pipe from his mouth and looked at the two boys who minutes before had been enjoying a joke in the warmth of his home. 'You know what this means, boys. The United States is now at war with Japan and by my reckoning we'll be at war with Germany as well in no time at all.'

Lois and Ellen with baby Luke in tow came back into the room. Ellen was holding up a tiny pair of dungarees.

'What's wrong, Karl. Something is wrong isn't it?'

'You better all sit down,' he said and explained in a slow, calm voice what they had all just heard.

Ellen burst into tears and went to her mother who cradled her like a baby. Luke confused by what was going on started to cry and put his small arms round his mother's legs.

'Does this mean that you and me will be drafted, Tom?' Ben blurted out and then added, 'All I ever wanted was a decent job, a wife and a family. I don't want to go and fight in some damn war.'

Karl re-lit his pipe, 'All along I've had no interest in whatever is going on in Europe but this if different. They have attacked The United States of America.'

'But it isn't fair,' Ellen sobbed, 'they can't take Luke's daddy away.'

'There being no further business I declare the meeting closed,' said Robert Cameron and the members of the Local Invasion Committee shuffled their papers, creaked back their chairs and rose from the table. The small annex at The Ipswich Institute Club was an ideal venue being in the centre of the town and close to the businesses where most of the committee members worked.

'What do you make of this dreadful business in America, Robert?' Stephen Bywater asked the chairman as he pulled on his heavy overcoat.

'I agree it is dreadful in terms of the sheer audacity and devastation of the attack. It's also amazing that the Japs seem to fear no one rather like Hitler thinks he can conquer the world. Together they conjure up a terrible threat to the world but any day now I can hear Churchill telling us that with America and Russia we, too, have a mighty powerful force.'

'True but the poor old Ruskies are being knocked right back to Moscow aren't they?'

'They were but the latest info suggests that the Panzers underestimated just how cold Mother Russia gets in the Winter and the weather had slowed them to a halt.'

'Napoleon all over again, eh?'

'Absolutely.'

'So now it really is a World War?'

'Quite, but for the first time for a long while I feel strangely optimistic.'

Bywater fumbled in his pocket, 'Cigarette?' Robert took one and waited for the lighter to be proffered. He inhaled and blew smoke towards the already stained ceiling, 'As we know the Yanks have been building tanks, ships, planes and just about everything else for months. A lot has come to us but now they'll be supplying manpower as well. I can see a whole new challenge for us in all this.'

'You mean the Yanks will come over here?'

'I think it's a strong possibility.'

The two men pulled up their collars, put on trilby hats and went out of the doors and into the cold rain.

'We'll meet again.' popular song

November 14th 1941 – Libya

Dear Sylvia,

The war here in the desert keeps seesawing between the Allies and the enemy but today spirits lifted since we are on the offensive again. General Auchinleck himself addressed the troops and the mood became buoyant.

It is cooler now, which helps, but the dust and flies still get everywhere.

At times the battle is fierce as the enemy under Rommel are a tough nut to crack but General Auchinleck seems convinced we will see them out of North Africa with this latest effort. I do hope so; I've had enough of sand.

However, it is not all awful as I have said before. In between offensives we manage to keep our spirits up. They are a grand bunch of chaps in the mess and we need their sort of camaraderie to lift us when things get really bloody.

You seem to be as active as ever with your WVS and the air raids do sound pretty frightful. It is difficult to imagine Ipswich being under fire as you describe it but logically I can understand why Jerry and his evil friends target places like our town.

Still, you seem to be keeping your pecker up, you always were a girl of spirit. I didn't quite understand what you meant about meeting different sorts of people though, on reflection, I realise that an awful lot of our friends (particularly the chaps) are now away on duty somewhere in the world.

I heard from mother the other day and she seems a bit confused with everything though she says father is in the thick of things with his Civil Defence duties. I read Bruce your passage about the meeting you attended when father was in the chair and we laughed at the Churchillian reference. Still it's good that everyone is doing his or her bit.

The longer we spend in this hell of a place the more difficult it is to remember the sort of life we used to lead but I have to believe that we will win through and then rebuild our country albeit, as you say, in a different way.

Your letters, dear Sylvia, are a wonderful tonic,
Love from
Francis

PS. By the way it's Captain Cameron now so I must be doing something right – or too many of my friends aren't around anymore.

My darling Doris,

I am writing from a place called Bardia which I don't think they will cross out since the way things are at present we will be somewhere else tomorrow and somewhere else again the day after.

They say this recent offensive is the Big One and the New Zealanders, to whom we are attached, have done ever so well to take this place back but we all know how strong the Africa Korps (I think that's how you spell it) can be. Still these Kiwis are a good lot – they call us Pommies like the Aussies do but it's better than me being called Swede as I have been on account of my coming from Suffolk.

When this is all over the last thing I will want to do is go to the seaside. I have seen enough sand to last a lifetime. It gets everywhere and so do the flies. You wouldn't believe them. They even drink the ink out of your fountain pen.

I don't remember telling you that I bought a leather photograph holder thing – there's a lot of leather out here. Anyhow, you look wonderful in it and I can look at you all the time. I even kiss you every night before I go to bed.

You seem busy in this awful blitz that you're having but you would be wouldn't you?

Sorry to hear about Mrs. French but it is good that Mr. French is teaching you so much. Sometimes I think you are so much cleverer than I am and you might find me a bit dull. I don't know what I'll do when all this is over – I don't fancy going back to the factory much. Don't tell Dad I said that.

It's really nice that you and Mum get on so well and even you and Kitty. She's always been a bit wild, Kitty not Mum, but she has a heart of gold as you have obviously found out. I think Dad knows that really but he would never let on.

I'm signing off now to get some shut-eye after I've kissed you goodnight.

143

I really love you Doris and can't wait to marry you,

All my love

Jimmy

XXXXXXXXX

PS. by the way it's Bombadier Wright now so watch out.

'You're more than the whole world to me.' – line from the song
'Sally' sang by Gracie Fields.

'What luxury! A whole one all to myself and it's not even Sunday.'
Sylvia sliced the top of her boiled egg, dipped in her spoon and
examined the result with relish.

'We only keep our allotted quota,' Edward mumbled, 'and you know
jolly well that you get your share from time to time.'

Sylvia laughed, 'I was only teasing, father,' she said popping an
unattractive piece of grey bread into her mouth.

Over the last few days Suffolk had experienced some of its worst
winter weather. It had snowed, thawed and then cold winds and frosts
had returned causing havoc for cyclists, trolley buses and the
occasional motor car. Walking was not much easier but somehow the
population had managed to get to work and to report for their various
Civil Defence duties in the evenings. Sylvia had been persuaded to
stay up at Hall Farm and though she enjoyed being pampered she was
anxious to return to her cottage. She also had some pressing WVS
administration to see to and had announced that she would not be
going into Grimstones that morning. This decision was met by a grunt
from her father.

'Seven o'clock news not too good,' he said, searching for some jam,
'that Rommel chap has pushed us right back to Benghazi. It's the
armoury you know, they're out gunning us.'

Not for the first time Sylvia's thoughts went to Doris and her
boyfriend Jimmy. He was a gunner, and if her father were right, would
be in the thick of it. Why, she wondered, isn't my first concern for
Francis? What is wrong with me?

Edward got up from the table, wiping his mouth on a serviette,
'Some of us have to go to work,' he announced glaring at Sylvia, 'I'll
be off then.' He kissed Elizabeth lightly on the cheek, then hesitated,
before bestowing the same dubious favour on his daughter.

'Oh dear! You've upset the boss this morning, skiving off work,'
Elizabeth said but she was smiling, 'come on let's take our tea into the
lounge and have a chat.'

Relaxed in one of the chunky chairs Sylvia looked around the room. She had always liked it, always felt safe there but nowadays she preferred the comparative frugality of her own cottage.

'Any more news from Francis?' Elizabeth began.

'I'm not sure how up to date you are, mummy. All his letters are very much the same and they on those little air mail things these days so there's not much room to say a lot. It's obviously very frustrating for them having done so well and now having the Afrika Korps push them right back. He doesn't say much about casualties but I gather there are quite a lot but he does say the army doctors and nurses are wonderful. Hasn't had much leave lately but when he does they seem to explore the old towns digging into the ancient culture. He enjoys all that sort of thing, probably end up being an Egyptologist or whatever they call them.'

'Well I'm glad he's all right. And you?'

'Me, I'm fine. At least I think I'm fine. Actually, mummy, there is something I need to talk to you about', she took a deep breath, 'it's about the job I have at Grimstones. You know the trainee buyer thing. Well, there's not a lot of sophisticated buying going on these days. Sometimes I feel I'm a bit in the way and other times a sort of a general dogs-body. I don't mind that. Don't mind what I do but when everyone else is working their socks off I feel I should be more useful, somehow.'

'Useful! My God Sylvia you do wonders with your WVS efforts.'

'Well that's just it, you see WVS has opened my eyes. There is so much more I could do. I mean if I could spend more time at all the centres making sure we really are doing our best for the growing number of homeless people then that would be far more worthwhile than checking the stock of black out material at Grimstones.'

Elizabeth took a long look at her daughter. She saw eagerness coupled with anxiety, determination and compassion. 'This war is changing you isn't it darling?'

'Perhaps I'm just growing up. But what do you think? It would help you and the committee if I were full time WVS wouldn't it?'

'What you mean is that we're out of touch, just a bunch of old fuddy-duddies who are doing our best. Strangely enough I wouldn't argue with that. Certainly your energy would be a Godsend but what's your father going to say?'

Sylvia put down her tea, it had gone cold, 'I thought perhaps you could talk to him. You know, from the committee point of view, heavy workload and all that. How I could be the answer if I were full-time.'

'My, you're right. You are growing up.' Elizabeth chuckled, 'Oh very well then I'll have a go but it won't be easy. He is keen on you becoming a cog in the Grimstones empire when all this is over.'

Sylvia got up and kissed her mother, 'Thank you mummy, I'm sure he'll listen to you.'

Vera sat on the trolley bus as it slushed through the melting snow along Clapgate Lane and wondered just what Jack was up to. She was under strict instructions to be at the main factory gates at twelve o'clock sharp. The female conductor punched out her ticket and complained about the weather.

Jack had been in a funny mood lately which she put down to him being worried about Jimmy. The news from North Africa hadn't been good and there had been no letters for a fortnight. She knew that Doris was worried too but Doris got in a stew if she hadn't heard anything for a week. Then there was the question of the Japs who were on the rampage in somewhere called the Far East. Jack had theories about their part in the war as well.

Now, quite out of the blue, he had checked that she was on evening shifts and told her to meet him at Andersons. He'd never done that before. Something was amiss.

She got off the trolley at the bottom of Bishop's Hill, told the conductress that she was sure the weather was improving, and set off along Fore Hamlet. She had put on her only pair of decent shoes and was upset that they were soon splattered with muck.

Turning the corner she noticed two or three cloth capped men puffing at cigarettes outside the main entrance. She spotted Jack in his foreman's overalls and waved. He looked up, didn't return her wave, but hurried towards her.

'Well done love,' he was speaking quietly, almost whispering.

'This is all a bit of a mystery, Jack. What are we doing, planning a robbery?'

'Something like that,' he said, still speaking in a funny voice, 'now pin this on. I fixed it with the gatekeepers. The head one is in my ARP group.'

He handed her a pass which she attached to the lapel of her coat. You wouldn't get in my telephone exchange as easy as this she thought, but didn't say anything. Instead she walked with Jack past the other men and through the gates.

She'd only been inside Andersons once before and that was long before the war. She was struck by the dirt and grime which was made worse by the grey slush. The windows were covered in soot, the paintwork peeling off the windows and the smoke belching from the chimneys made her cough. There were very few people about.

'This way,' he snapped, as if she knew exactly where they were going, 'step on it.'

He opened a door at the end of the main block and they went into an enormous area full of half made tractors.

'I thought you made military equipment?' she asked.

'That's in the main area. The country still needs tractors as well. An army marches on its stomach.'

Where does he get these sayings from she wondered, not for the first time?

Halfway along, on the left, they came to some double doors. Jack led her through and Vera stopped and gaped. The room was packed like a football ground. Just about everyone who worked at Andersons must be here, she thought, no wonder it was so quiet outside. She started to look around. The vast majority were women dressed in dungarees with their hair pulled up under scarves tied in turban fashion. She searched for Doris's mum or other women she might know who had become lathe operators and welders but they all looked the same.

Jack pushed through the crowd and she noticed that a stage had been erected at the front of the canteen. A band sat poised to play.

'If you'd told me we were going dancing I would have worn my best dress,' she whispered to Jack.

'Don't be stupid, woman,' he muttered, 'I got you in didn't I?'

Then the band started to play and everyone cheered. A slick looking man in a striped suit and bright blue tie walked onto the stage. Vera thought he looked like Len the Black Market racketeer but Kitty had said he was in prison.

'Good Morning Ladies and Gentlemen of Andersons,'
'Good Morning,' they all shouted back.
'I'm sure you don't want to hear a lot from me so without further
ado I will introduce the person you have all been waiting for. Ladies
and Gentlemen, our own Gracie Fields.'
The band struck up *Sally* and she walked on. Gracie Fields, in the
flesh, wearing a smart cornflower blue suit and shiny high heels. She
smiled that famous smile and began to sing. *Sally, Sally, pride of our
alley. You're more than the whole world to me.*

Doris came into the dispensary leaving Joyce to deal with a man
asking for cough sweets. Mr. French was gazing up at the rows of
brown and green bottles adjusting his glasses so he could distinguish
between them.
'One more prescription to make up, Doris, then we're up to date.
Been busy in the shop?'
He's full of himself today, she thought, ' Not too bad considering
half of Ipswich seem to be suffering from colds and coughs. It's this
awful weather I suppose.'
'Well you and I both know you don't get colds and coughs just
because it's damp but I suppose the resistance gets low and you
become susceptible.'
'Suppose so,' she muttered.
He selected the bottle he wanted and turned round, 'Heard from
that Jimmy of yours?'
Her face lit up. 'Yes, thank God, there was an airogram waiting when
I got home yesterday. He's fine. Been heavily engaged for days on end.
He can't say much, of course, but my father says we're on the retreat
and it all looks very bad. Mind you, everything looks bad to my
father.'
'Good news that's what we need, a bit of good news,' Mr. French
repeated turning his attentions to the chest of drawers where the
powders were stored. His eyesight was not good, even with the
stronger spectacles he wore these days.
'What are you looking for, Mr. French?'
'Zinc Oxide. Ah! There she is.'

He turned and beamed at her.

'I'm going to the pictures with Kitty after work. She'll be calling in the shop so I can tell her about my letter. You doing anything interesting, Mr. French?' In spite of the episode before Christmas she still worried about his lonely existence in the flat.

'No, not tonight. Quiet night tonight. Last night was very enjoyable though. Mrs. Fox came round and we listened to some Chopin.'

'Mrs. Fox?' she asked.

'Yes, you remember I told you my philately friends the Brownlows introduced me to their neighbour at Christmas. Mrs. Fox, charming lady, plays the piano beautifully. Well since we have this mutual interest I invited her round for the evening. What she doesn't know about Chopin isn't worth knowing.'

Doris was aware that her mouth opened and closed like a ventriloquist's dummy.

'Yes, charming woman, Mrs. Fox.'

He perched himself on one of the high stools and looked over Doris to the shop where he could see Joyce busy with a customer,

'Doris,' he began, 'look I'm really sorry about that incident. You know when I.....Well I shouldn't have done what I did and I'm sorry. You see I'm very fond of you and I promise it will never happen again.'

The shop bell clanged. 'Gosh! There's a whole mob of coughing customers out there. I'd better go and help Joyce,' she said and scurried out. When the shop cleared she felt that Joyce was looking at her.

'What are you smiling about?' Joyce said.

'Nothing. Well maybe it's just knowing Jimmy is safe,' she said but she was thinking about good old Mrs. Fox who loved Chopin.

She was still smiling when she met Kitty and they walked through town to The Odeon.

'What about Gracie Fields then?' Kitty gushed, ' Mum is driving me mad going about the house singing all those songs in a screechy voice. It's got so bad that I don't even care whose aspidistra is the biggest in the world.'

'Yea. My mum, too and she's no ear for music.'

'And dad he's just going about looking pleased with himself. Taken him out of his gloom, it has..'

'Well, it was a nice thing that he did. Smuggling her in to Andersons.'

'Silly old sod,' Kitty said.

'So who are we going to moon over tonight. Humphrey Bogart, isn't it?'

It was starting to snow and Doris pulled her scarf tighter around her neck.

1942

'It is very much more probable than not that at some point before the end of the war Hitler will see fit to order invasion.' The Regional Commissioner of Cambridge

Since her decision to quit Grimstones Sylvia had taken on more and more work for WVS and related Civil Defence duties. Elizabeth remained the titular head but it was Sylvia who supervised work at the twenty or so Rest Centres, thirty mobile units and more recently the establishment of the government sponsored British Restaurant. She'd taken Doris to the opening and they had sampled roast beef and cabbage followed by rice pudding for the reasonable sum of nine pence. As part of her increased responsibilities she found herself attending a meeting of the recently constituted Ipswich Invasion Committee. Inevitably this was chaired by her father in law, Robert Cameron.

Robert was explaining to attentive ears that though the enemy was fully engaged in Russia and North Africa the invasion of our shores remained a very real threat. Ipswich was what was known as a *nodal point* controlling all communications and movement of essentials over a wide area. Sylvia, as always, thought how much Robert enjoyed his war-time authority. *Secrecy is Power* was an expression that sprang to mind. She liked her father in law, even admired him, but the more she saw him in action in his various roles the more she understood certain aspects of her husband's personality.

'...Conditions which would be likely to prevail in the town in case of an invasion have been carefully examined from every angle,' he was sounding Churchillian again.

'Close co-operation between locally based army personnel and all aspects of Civil Defence is essential. Anti-tank ditches and roadblocks will be constructed within the next few weeks and....'

Sylvia's mind went back to the early days of the war and conversations with her mother when she had difficulty accepting what was prophesied. She didn't believe Britain would be invaded in 1939 and she didn't believe it now. She glanced at Elizabeth, sitting next to her, and wasn't sure whether she had dozed off.

Robert continued to talk of emergency water supplies, evacuating the majority of the population including those in hospital since all available beds would be needed for war casualties. He explained that the special police would visit all homes and explain procedures and then he asked for questions, gazing around the room as if daring someone to ask one. A few did and the meeting broke up in sombre mood.

Robert came over to Elizabeth and Sylvia looking pleased with himself.

'When are we going to hear some good news, Robert?' Elizabeth asked.

'Mother's right, the people around here, well, everywhere I suppose, are taking an awful pounding one way and another and all they hear is gloom and doom,' Sylvia added.

'We'll pull through,' he said,' bull dog spirit you know,' and turning briskly on his heels he walked across the floor to talk with the Chief of Police.

The bombing had been so frequent lately that the various units of the Civil Defence were existing on very little sleep. For two nights in succession Jack and Vera slept right through air raids only waking up when the all clear sounded. The night after Jack found himself on duty dealing with a particularly unpleasant bombing on Foxhall Road. The pattern was the usual one; chandelier flares lighting up the sky followed by a rain of incendiaries and later heavy explosives. Jack and fellow wardens helped the medics pull out five people from three bombed houses. One elderly man was killed. During the operation Jack noticed a young WVS woman leading a group to take charge of those made homeless. Her accent identified her as being upper class but he couldn't help being impressed with the way she helped the victims. Somehow she was able to be both strong and caring and the stunned group responded to her. He told Vera about her at teatime the next day but she had other things on her mind.. A member of the special police had called about half an hour ago with some instructions for all Ipswich householders.

'He said not to panic but the Invasion Committee, or some such group, were convinced we would still be invaded at some time and we had to be aware that we would be given three weeks notice at the most to get out. He didn't say where we would go, mind you, just we would have to get out. He knew you were a warden and that I was a telephonist and said we would probably get advance warning.'

'Piffle,' Jack replied with his mouth full of bread and jam, ' Hitler has far too much on his plate with Russia and North Africa.'

'He's got more on his plate than you judging by the way you're attacking your tea,' Kitty came into the kitchen.

'That's enough of your jokes, thank you very much.'

'George, he's the sailor I met from HMS Bunting, he said that there's something funny going on. They keep being put on special alert and such.'

'Doesn't this George know that Careless Talk Costs lives?' Jack grumbled.

'No but everyone is a bit nervous Jack. At the exchange the other day the boss told us Ipswich was a *Nodal Point* and we telephonists would have an even more important role in handling emergency communications.'

'Well then your boss is as bad as her sailor mentioning Nodal Points.'

'What exactly is a *Nodal Point* then Jack?'

Jack grabbed the last piece of bread and jam. 'Search me,' he said, ' so what else did you learn at your gossip centre today?'

Vera stood up and cut two more slices of bread, 'The girls are very upset about delivery boys.'

'Yea, how about that, no more delivery boys. I remember when Jimmy was a delivery boy for Fowlers and Alan for Chaplin the butchers......poor old sod.'

Jack was about to remonstrate with his daughter about her language but thought better of it, instead he changed the subject. 'It's like I'm always saying all they do is hit the working man, I mean take this latest budget.'

'The girls at Pipers were moaning about cigarettes going up again, I can tell you. I bet that wasn't too popular at your place either, dad?'

Jack, as if in protest, started to fill his pipe, 'They had other things on their minds, poor devils, a whole lot of their boys are reported missing after the fall of Singapore. The Suffolks and The Norfolks are out there, of course, a lot of them either dead or in Jap Prisoner of War camps. Can't think which is worse.' He got up from the table and went into the garden and lit his pipe. After a while Vera joined him. Kitty watched through the kitchen window as her mother placed both her hands on his shoulders. Neither of them appeared to say anything but they stood together for some time before coming back in.

'Here I've made some fresh tea,' Kitty said, 'and I've had an idea. Why don't we all go the pictures tomorrow it's that new film with Noel Coward, *In which we serve*? You'd like that dad.'

'The desert was an infinite sandy rubbish-tip.' Penelope Lively
– Moon Tiger

Sylvia examined the rabbit, picked up her sharpest knife and commenced to cut it into joints. Apart from lessons at school she had learned her cooking from Mrs. Moore during the holidays. She was prepared to experiment and so, having invited Doris over for a Sunday meal, she decided to try jugged rabbit. The sleeves of her beige blouse were rolled up and she wore sensible brown slacks and a striped apron.

She had to admit that Old Moore had done a good job skinning the rabbit having assured her that it was possible to carry out this operation in one go, *head and all!* Sylvia had chosen not to watch him perform this skilled task but had gratefully accepted the result which was about to be fried in a pan on her tiny cooker.

She was looking forward to seeing Doris again. In her head she had listed a number of things that she wanted to chat about but experience had taught her that their conversations would take a whole variety of turns.

The other evening she had re-read her collection of letters from Francis trying to imagine just what his life was like. He was not one to discuss emotions and so she set about analysing the factual side of his neatly penned correspondence. The conclusion she came to was that his war was nothing like a war in Europe, where armies secured towns and villages and advanced down roads. It was more like the battles of former times, the sort she had studied at school, where armies lined up against each other and fought for territorial gain on some vast wasteland. The desert, according to Francis, was a great expanse of nothing; a dirty, dusty nothing splattered with burnt and bombed out vehicles.

Engineers would go ahead to identify the mines. Then soldiers would advance in tanks, armoured vehicles and on foot supported by ground artillery and aircraft. Obviously tactics were important but it seemed to Sylvia that the side who had the most effective equipment would win. She wondered whether the letters that Doris received from her boyfriend would confirm this. But from what Doris had told her the letters she received were more cheery and optimistic than those from Francis. They were certainly more romantic.

She sliced the carrots and onions and dropped them into the pan.

Quite naturally most of the letters were written either when things on the battlefront were quiet or when he had a few days leave. Presumably the Generals considered that their officers had to have a break from time to time and Francis would leave the battle and return to base at somewhere more civilised like Cairo or Alex. There, for officers at least, life was totally different. There seemed to be a cocooned world to which they retreated before returning to the awfulness. A world of cafes, restaurants, polo, dancing and exploration. Frances had reported trips to the Pyramids, to ancient tombs, to the Valley of the Kings. He had even waxed poetic about the Nile at night and of a different desert, a desert sculptured by the wind into soft and undulating shapes. She thought of the whole scene as rather like a microcosm of what she had learned about the First World War when thousands of soldiers were dying in France but in England the subject was seldom discussed.

Sylvia transferred the rabbit and vegetables to a stew pot and added water and some cheap red wine scrounged from her father and then she placed the lid on the pot and put it in the oven. According to the pencilled instructions given to her by Mrs. Moore this would take two hours.

She wiped her hands on her apron, poured herself a glass of water and perched on a wooden chair. Who does he go on these trips with? Presumably other officers who are on leave at the same time, like this Bruce, or maybe one of the nurses? He is always full of praise for the nurses. Curiously she didn't feel any pangs of jealousy. It was almost as if she wanted him to relax, shed the tension when away from the Front. After all she was building a new life for herself. A war time life as opposed to a married life. Francis had become a chum she cared about, an old friend, a pen pal. They had had so little married time together and just when she thought she might be getting close to this most private of men he had been whisked away again and she was back to square one. She realised that in re-reading his letters the other night she had been searching for some clue as to how he really felt about her and that she had found nothing.

She shrugged and rose from her chair, put her hand to her hair, which was trussed up in a comb, and checked that she had the necessary ingredients for the sauce. She thought her jugged rabbit was a good choice on such a blustery late Spring Sunday. The tinned peaches and carnation milk were less exciting.

Just before mid-day Sylvia looked out of the window and laughed. Doris appeared down the track pedalling furiously against the wind, a large black beret rammed on her head and the scarf flapping about her. She skidded to a halt outside the door, stood her bicycle against the shed, noticed Sylvia, and grinned.

'Gosh what a wind!' she said when the door was opened.

'It's about time we had some decent weather,' Sylvia added, ushering her friend into the sitting room.

'Something smells good.' Doris had taken off her wet clothes and was standing in front of the mirror prodding at her tangled red hair. She felt at home in Sylvia's cottage.

'You've had your haircut. It looks nice,' Sylvia said.

'Kitty trimmed it the other night. I think it's better shorter.'

They sat down opposite each other in front of the fire. 'I know it's May but the weather has been so awful so I've treated us to some warmth. And the smell you noticed was rabbit. I'm attempting to cook jugged rabbit. An old recipe of Mrs. Moore's, but it was jugged hare then.'

'She should go on the wireless. She'd be better than that Mabel Constantinople or whatever her name is.'

'Constanduros,' they were both laughing, ' but you knew that Doris Harper, you were just having me on. So, what have you to report?'

Doris stretched and then relaxed into the armchair,' Now let me see, where shall I begin. I know, I'll update you on Mr. French. You remember I told you he had a fancy woman, Mrs. Fox who plays the piano, well the other day a big van drew up outside the shop and these two men came in. It was Joyce who served them but actually they didn't want anything except to know where the entrance was to the upstairs flat. She went and got Mr. French and he came out grinning like a Cheshire Cat. *It'll be the piano* he said and then went outside with the men. Joyce was in hysterics, *A piano for Mrs Fox so she can serenade him* she said and we both went into fits of laughter. Lucky no one came in the shop. Well, they spent virtually the whole afternoon getting this piano up the outside stairs to the flat. Tied it up with rope and eased it up with blankets. Mr. French was a very funny colour when he eventually came back into the shop demanding tea for the three.'

'Doris you are priceless.' Sylvia wiped her eyes with a handkerchief, then she paused, 'Is he all right with you now?'

'Right as rain. I think he has been lonely for a long time what with Mrs. French having that long illness. That's all it was. He was lonely. Mrs. Fox has filled a gap in his life, someone with similar interests. That's nice, isn't it?'

Sylvia didn't say anything for a while then she got up and went to the window. She started to speak with her back to Doris, 'I've been reading my letters from Francis,' she said, 'trying to understand what he's going through out there. What does your Jimmy say? Does he explain it so it makes sense?'

Doris thought for a while, 'Not a lot about the war I'm afraid. They're not allowed to are they? But as far as I can make out it's all backwards and forwards on miles of sandy nothing; weeks on what they call The Front where all the action is and then a few days back in the main towns. They play football and have a few drinks and, no doubt, some of them go out with women. I know Jimmy wouldn't do that. But I agree with you it is so hard to make out just what it's really like.'

Sylvia continued to speak looking out of the window as if Doris wasn't there, 'Sometimes I think I should never have married him. I was in too much of a hurry.'

'That's the war speaking. I'm sure you don't....'

'Don't get me wrong. I was sure I loved him. Sure he was right for me but I didn't really give the poor chap a chance.' She turned round and there were tears running down her face. 'Sorry, not much of a host, am I?'

Doris stood up and Sylvia came towards her, 'Don't ever tell anyone I said that will you?'

'Of course not,' Doris said, 'of course not but everyone's a bit down at the moment, aren't they. People who come in the shop, the First Aiders, my Dad, but there again he's always down. We're all tired out; working all day and most nights, no good news on the wireless, more and more rationing. See I'm beginning to sound like my Dad?'

Sylvia wiped her eyes and smiled, ' Thanks you're right. We could do with some good news to cheer us all up. Come on let's go and look at that rabbit.'

They sat in the kitchen licking their lips. 'That was really good. How annoying you being able to cook as well.'

'As well as what?'

'As well as....well, you were talking about letters earlier and I was thinking about how both our men must have changed like we have changed. . You see two of Jimmy's best mates have been killed and that has made him think in quite a different way about the Germans. Then in other ways he hasn't changed. I told him about you and I told him about how, in spite of our backgrounds, we had become really good friends.'

'And?'

'Oh. He went on about who did I think I was getting in with posh people.'

'Well I am posh, aren't I? But there's not much I can do about it. I shall always be posh but my head isn't buried in the sand anymore,' she paused and laughed aloud, 'Oh that's a terrible way to put it but you know what I mean, don't you?'

'Absolutely. Oh gosh, listen to me! Absolutely that's what posh people say isn't it?'

This time they both laughed until Sylvia stood up and announced that for sweet she could only produce tinned peaches and pretend cream. Doris said she liked tinned peaches.

Later they took their tea back into the sitting room and Sylvia put on some records. Doris requested Chopin and to her surprise she really liked the intricate piano pieces. She closed her eyes and let the music float all around her.

Vera fed the wet washing into the mangle whilst Kitty cranked the handle wringing out the surplus water. Then, they roughly folded the clothes and sheets and placed them in a wicker basket.

'Come on let's put this lot on the line, there's a good old drying wind out today.'

They came back into the kitchen and plumped down onto the only two chairs.

'Where's dad?'

'He heard there's some slack going at Snows coal yard so he's taken the barrow down to stock up for next winter. We're right out and he says he's allowed three loads. Waste of time if you ask me but it makes him think he's doing his bit.'

'He's been a bit down lately hasn't he?'

'Everyone's been a bit down lately. We could do with some good news.'

'Talking of news it's nearly twelve, we'd better put the wireless on, he's sure to want a full report.'

They scurried into the front room and switched on to the Home Service just in time for the pips.

'Here is the twelve o'clock news and this is Bruce Belfrage reading it. The RAF has carried out a successful bombing raid on Cologne destroying at least two hundred factories. A thousand planes took part on what was the biggest raid ever on Germany's industrial areas. In the desert the German panzer division have launched their long expected offensive. There are no further reports as yet. The Russian army is staving of German attempts to advance and are stubbornly defending an area around Kharkov. Japan is said to be shocked by US bombing raids on Tokyo.....

'I hope Jimmy is all right.'

'What's that about Jimmy?' They hadn't heard Jack come in. He's face was red and his hands covered in coal dust.

'Take your shoes off Jack, I polished that lino this morning.'

'Don't fuss woman. Now what's all this about Jimmy?'

'Nothing except that there's another big battle somewhere or other out there.'

'Somewhere or other. What sort of information is that? I can see I shall have to listen to the next bulletin myself and then I might get to know what's really going on. Women!' He took off his shoes and padded off into the kitchen. They heard him turn on the tap and wash his hands.

After a while Kitty stood up, 'I'll go and make it. What do you want, Bovril or tea?'

'Ask your dad. He can choose.'

Later the three of them sat down together and Vera attempted again to relay the details of the news. This time Jack listened and nodded and then told them he'd been involved in two minor incidents the previous night but nothing to worry about. All the wardens seemed weary, he said, maybe this news about bombing the Germans would cheer people up a bit.

'I was thinking Jack, those people in Cologne that we bombed, they're probably just ordinary folk like us.'

'Nonsense woman, they're Germans aren't they?' Jack stuck his hands in his pockets searching for his tobacco.

IOWA

'To work – to work. It is such an infinite delight to know we still have the best things to do.' Katherine Mansfield.

The work ethic of the American Midwest dates back to the first settlers. The pioneers had no choice but to take care of everything themselves and basic practical skills were passed down from generation to generation. Tom, with his preference for working on the land to academic studies, was in many ways a typical descendent and he defended his love of things mechanical to this inherited need for self-sufficiency.

One Saturday in the spring of 1942 his father found him in the large barn next to the corn crib covered in grease leaning over the open hood of the Cherokee truck.

'Just what are you up to now?' Karl asked.

'I think the big end has gone.'

'She was making a funny old noise last time I used her,' Karl admitted.

Tom gave a wrench and then turned to his father, his face smudged with oil, 'I've drained the oil and removed the sump so we'll know soon enough.'

'Well supper's in about fifteen minutes and by my reckoning you're gonna need five of those to clean up.' Both of them knew it was a sin to be late for a meal in the Nelson household.

'What's Mom cooking. Something special?'

'You could call it special since I fished it myself only yesterday. You remember the bull-head I caught, big brute he was but he'll taste good when your Mom has finished with him.'

'Right I'd best be getting finished. I've got the replacement so it won't be too difficult if I'm right about the big end.'

Karl walked out of the barn into the Spring evening and lit his pipe. He looked out over his rolling fields and rejoiced in the calmer, warmer weather and in the prospect of sowing another crop. His hogs were doing well, the beef cattle had survived the winter and even the prairie hens seemed to be chuckling again. Normally this would be enough for Karl, normally life in and around Red Oak represented his world and all he wanted from it but this war was changing all that.

164

Why even Lois had joined with some women from the church in sorting out bundles of clothes and blankets to send to England. Boys were enlisting, women going to work in the factories; some crazy folk even rumoured that the Japanese were about to invade the west coast of the United States. Karl thought it was hard enough being a farmer let alone having to worry about all these other things.

The ugly old bull-head made an excellent meal with green beans and peas and the apple pies that followed put him in better humour. Tom reported that he had fixed the truck and Lois confirmed that Ellen, Ben and, of course, Luke would be coming over after church the next day.

After the meal Karl went outside for another pipe and was surprised that Tom followed him.

'Can I talk to you, Dad?' he said.

'I don't think that's ever been a problem, has it son?'

Tom looked at his hands, 'No, of course not but this is important. You see I have made a decision. I was talking to Randal Bergson and some of the others after soft-ball and we got round to discussing enlisting.'

Karl looked up sharply, taking the pipe from his mouth.

'You see, Dad, if I enlisted then I could choose what sort of training I wanted. What I want to do in this war whereas, if I wait for the draft then there would be no choice. Randal has been to see the army people and it makes sense.'

'What do mean it makes sense?'

'Well you see, I could enlist to become an aircraft fitter or mechanic or something technical and they would train me over about six months and then assign me to a Squadron. That's what Randal is doing. I could learn things that might be useful to us here on the farm when the war ends.'

Karl sucked his pipe. It had gone out. ' I didn't know we had plans to fly aeroplanes off the farm?' he said.

'Of course not but I would improve my knowledge of engineering in general and in the future we're bound to use far more complicated machinery on the farm.'

'You've thought this all out haven't you Tom.'

Tom dug his hands into the pockets of his dungarees, 'Yes. I guess I have.'

Karl didn't say anything for a while and then he sighed, 'I hate this damn war. Just when we were starting to get things going again this war has to come along and put us right back where we started. But, I guess there is something in what you say. Far better to have a say in what you're letting yourself in for than leaving it to the army.' Karl was not a tactile man but, standing out in the dusk on this cool Spring evening, he put his arm around his son's shoulders, ' Don't think I'm not proud of you, Tom, because I am. I know it's right that you should go and fight for your country but we're gonna miss you around the place, your mom and me.'

'Thanks and I'm gonna miss you and this place. Hell Dad, all I ever wanted was to leave school and work on the farm. I've never wanted to go anywhere but it seems I don't really have any choice.'

Karl sighed again, 'Right, now for the difficult part. Let's go and explain all this to your mom.'

The biggest British harvest in living memory.' - NFU spokesman

'I cannot believe you didn't respond to my two hearts second bid, Valerie.'

'Which one was that?'

'The one where I opened one heart and then repeated my hearts. Our opponents had passed and you said nothing even though it transpired you had eight points and a singleton.'

'You know I can never remember my hands once I've played them, Robert.'

'But they'd both passed, surely that told you something?'

The Grimstones and the Camerons steadfastly kept their fortnightly bridge going in spite of what Hitler was throwing at them and at times became more concerned about the game than they did about the war. They were sitting in the front reception room in the Cameron's Park Road house; the late afternoon sun was shafting through the high windows at the end of what had been a particularly warm early summer's day.

'All the analysis in the world won't change the result, Robert, I make the final score 1200 to us, agreed?'

Robert pored over his score sheet. 'Agreed,' he sighed.

'They say we're having a wonderful harvest.' Edward was keen to change the subject.

'Yes indeed, nice to get some good news in the middle of all the gloom.'

Valerie got up from the table and suggested they sat on more comfortable chairs in the lounge then announced she would go and fetch the sherry. Valerie liked a drop of sherry even though it was the cooking variety.

Once settled Elizabeth took up the topic, 'And in spite of the do-gooders protesting I think the youngsters are enjoying helping get the harvest in,' she said.

'I agree, Elizabeth, I mean surely we only got rid of delivery boys so they could help on the farms and factories where we are so desperately short of labour.'

'I agree,' said Valerie, returning with four Sherries on a silver tray, 'Much as I miss my deliveries I think the youngsters are better off helping on the farms.'

Robert sipped his sherry thinking how much he would have preferred a whisky and soda. 'Of course the current dilemma is that on the one hand the farmers are doing a magnificent job utilising every inch of space for production and on the other a number are being told to give up some of their acreage for the expansion of the air fields.'

'So what's that all about then?' Edward leaned forward.

'Mainly it's about the Americans,' Robert explained, 'they are quietly moving in around here in considerable numbers and by this time next year they'll be everywhere. And the reason is that they will be flying their enormous bombers on raids over Germany. Big bombers need two thousand yards of concrete runways not grassy slopes like we have at present.'

'I've seen their massive lorries trundling along the Woodbridge Road,' chipped in Valerie, and then looking around the others with wide eyes, ' and they were being driven by black Americans.'

'It's the black Americans who are helping our chaps build the new runways.' Robert sat back folding his hands over his waistcoat.

'They won't all be black will they, these Americans that you say will be coming over in numbers, Robert?'

'No Valerie, of course not, the air crew are all white.'

''Cause a few problems, an influx of young Americans. Ipswich is full of unattached girls and a few attached ones who haven't seen husbands and boyfriends for a while.'

Elizabeth wasn't one to mince words.

Valerie thought this new turn in the conversation warranted a refill of sherry and hastened from the room. When she returned the men were discussing cricket so she turned to Elizabeth, 'Robert says Sylvia is everywhere and anywhere these days, taking on loads of responsibility.'

Elizabeth laughed, 'She was never short on enthusiasm but at times I wonder what direction she is moving in. All this work with the less fortunate is giving her strange ideas. She's mixing with all sorts. There's a girl called Doris who seems to have come on the scene. Wouldn't be surprised if she's a socialist.'

It was such a pleasant evening that after her meal Doris had gone into the garden, and sat on a chair in front of the shelter feeling the last of the day's sun on her face. More freckles she thought but who cares. She hadn't heard from Jimmy for a while but neither had Jack and Vera and from what she heard on the news there were high hopes that this Monty might perform miracles in stemming Rommel's advance at somewhere called El Alamein. It was two weeks now and whilst he never moaned, she sensed that Jimmy was weary of the ups and downs of desert warfare. When she wrote to him she tried to cheer him with stories about Mr. French and Mrs. Fox, or Joyce's latest attempts in finding the man of her dreams. She constantly worried how much the experiences in the desert had changed him. He had been such an optimist, so refreshingly innocent and although the war must certainly have hardened him she prayed that deep down he hadn't lost his gentleness.

She knew that she had changed. She knew that the work she did with the mobile first aid team had made her realise how quickly life could be taken away, how easily injury could ruin someone's future.

She fished for a comb in her handbag and pulled her hair back from her face. Her sister had been home at the weekend and she always had her hair back. They'd talked a lot about the land army, tales of other girls, of an airman based up in Norfolk that Alice had taken a fancy to and of their parents. Doris had explained how she worried about her father's depressed state and how, particularly since her mother had entered so enthusiastically into work, they seemed to have little in common any more. Alice had shrugged and said it was the war. It was easy for her she was going back to Norfolk; Doris had to stay at home.

She stood up and stretched up to the sun. I shouldn't go on so, she thought, considering everything I have a good life, good friends and out there somewhere a man who really loves me. Still looking upwards she whispered, 'Please keep him safe.'

A few days later Doris was serving a customer with a bottle of camomile lotion when a small, neat woman came into the shop. She had a face that reminded Doris of a cat, a Lewis Carol, smiley cat.

'Is Mr. French about?' the cat woman purred.

'He's out the back in the dispensary. Perhaps I can help?' Doris thought I can do virtually anything he can do, anyway.

'No it's personal, dear. Could you tell him it's Mrs. Fox.'

Doris was aware that her mouth was open for some time before she replied, 'Right, Mrs. Fox. I'll tell him.' She hastened from the shop and down the single stair at the same time as Joyce was coming up, 'Mrs. Fox' she mimed but Joyce just said, 'What?'

'Mrs. Fox to see you, Mr. French,' Doris announced.

For a moment he coloured up, then taking a handkerchief from the pocket under his white coat he wiped his brow, 'Thank you Doris, thank you,' he said and bustled up into the shop. She heard his excited voice but couldn't distinguish the words and by that time a couple of tall black American servicemen had appeared in front of Joyce with a list of requirements. Joyce came out to the back of the shop.

'Look out there, Doris. They're American. Black as the ace of spades they are. But they're ever so polite and their uniforms have been tailored in heaven.'

'Never mind them did you see Mrs. Fox?'

'And their voices are all slow and drawly.'

'Mrs. Fox,' hissed Doris, 'Mr. French is talking to Mrs. Fox.'

'He's always talking about her. Aren't you interested in my Americans. I've never seen such black faces. In a way they're fascinating.'

'Not about her, to her. The smart little woman with Mr. French is Mrs. Fox.'

'Where?' Joyce almost screamed, ' Mrs. Fox in person and two black Americans. I don't think I can cope with much more. Here this is what they want,' and thrusting a list into Doris' hand she tripped back to the shop.

Later when Joyce had left and Doris was completing the drugs' list she said, as casually as she could, that she thought Mrs. Fox seemed a very pleasant lady.

170

'One in a million,' beamed Mr. French, ' and such a pianist. Did you notice her fingers? She has such expressive fingers.'

'No I'm afraid I didn't,' Doris replied, 'Mr. French, I hope you don't think I'm nosy but is there a Mr. Fox.'

Mr. French looked shocked, 'Surely you don't think.....Oh dear no. Poor man was killed in the blackout early on in the war. Cycled into the back of a coal cart going at speed down Constitution Hill. Tragic. Tragic.'

IOWA

'Fun is a good thing but only when it spoils nothing better' –
George Sanayana.

The Montgomery State Fair was the high spot in the County's year
and the organisers saw no point in making any changes because their
country was now at war. On the contrary, they argued, the job of the
Mid-West was to provide food for the nation, which now included
feeding an army, and thus it was even more important to demonstrate
their pride in this role.

So it was that when Tom and his friend Randal arrived at Des
Moines, ferris wheels still spun, carousels waltzed, banners looped
from trees and the Stars and Stripes proliferated. Once inside the
people of this small part of Iowa showed off their livestock hoping for
winners' ribbons. They displayed all forms of produce from pumpkins
to pies; cheered on the children at their races; applauded the
demonstrations of old crafts and skills; enjoyed the bands whether
Sousa or modern swing and toured the art and craft stands seeking
bargains.

Tom and Randal were in uniform, both on a three-day furlough, and
since it was hot and humid their jackets were slung over their
shoulders. They headed for the large tent with the sign '4H'
emblazoned in large letters over the entrance.

'Remember when we were in 4H?' Tom asked his friend.

'They were good days. None of the animals I nurtured ever won
anything though.'

'Me neither, but boy we worked hard on them. Hey, look at this little
fella over here.'

They stopped by a pen where a young boy, no more than twelve, was
busy grooming a good looking cow, 'You gonna win a ribbon?' Tom
shouted to the boy.

'I sure hope so.'

'The only ribbons we're gonna win now are the ones we'll stitch on
our uniforms.'

Tom shrugged, 'I don't know about that, Randal. So how's it going
with you? We've hardly had a chance to swap stories.'

'I didn't enjoy the basic training too much. The drill sergeant kept picking on me since I was a country boy and I didn't have the sense to keep my cool.'

'First thing my dad said to me before I went was to not let them rile you. So I just took it on the chin and they picked on some poor Jewish guy from Chicago.'

'But now it's fine. I'm a qualified technician on B42 Liberators. Get my sergeant's stripes soon and then off to somewhere called Camp Kilmer in New Jersey? After that they won't say. Could be Iceland or England or anywhere the B42s end up, I guess. How about you, what stage are you at now?'

They sauntered slowly down the aisle looking at the youngsters putting in the final work on their entries. Tom thought it didn't seem that long ago they he was one of them and now here he was in the army and going to war.

'Me? Well I've started my technical training but I'm on fighters, B47 Thunderbolts. Really sleek machines they are. Like you, I guess, I'm enjoying the engineering stuff but I've a long while to go before I get my stripes. The other guys are OK, in the main, but I'm still not used to sleeping in close quarters with so many men. You know we're country people. We're used to space.'

'Sure. All that snoring and smelly feet stuff takes some getting used to.'

They were both laughing when they came out into the air again.

'I suppose we should look on it as a sort of adventure. You know we'll be going on one of those big boats zig-zagging across the ocean to avoid the U-boats and ending up, God knows where.'

Tom grinned, 'And I still haven't even seen the ocean,' he said.

Randal was determined to be philosophical, 'At least we don't have steady girls to fret over. Who knows we might even find some friendly natives.'

Karl and Lois had travelled with Ellen, Ben and Luke who was tugging at his father's hand wanting to go where the noise was. The noise in question was a threshing machine demonstration which certainly brought back memories for Karl but in which Ben had no particular interest. However, devoted father that he was, he yielded to the pressure from the three year old and made his way over to the ring.

'He's a real daddy's boy, that one,' Lois observed. Ellen didn't reply.

'Are you all right Ellen?'

'Sure, I just can't imagine life without Ben and poor little Luke will be distraught.'

'Ben hasn't received his draft yet has he?'

'No, but it's any day now I guess. I mean my Ben a soldier, it's a joke, he's even kind to spiders.'

As always the farming folk from all over the county had turned out for this middle Saturday of the Fair but this year the crowds were sprinkled with a number of young men proudly strutting in their new uniforms. Lois had already noticed the familiar poster of a soldier grasping the Stars and Stripes. The caption read *To have and to hold, War Bonds* and a long line had formed outside the tent where some lesser-known movie star was promoting sales. When Luke had become bored with the machinery Lois, who was feeling the heat, suggested that it was time to drink some lemonade, sit in the shade and listen to the brass band.

'What time do they judge the cakes and pies today?' Karl asked her.

'Oh. Not until this afternoon,' she replied but she knew only too well that the judging started at three o'clock.

Lois was used to the heat and humidity, she had lived in Iowa all her life, but these days she preferred to seek the shade. The cloudless skies and almost white sun could make her feel quite giddy even though she wore a wide brimmed straw hat. She was relieved to plop down into the canvas chair and noticed that even Luke was content, sipping his lemonade, kicking his chubby legs in time with the music. She knew Ellen was heartbroken by the outbreak of war, wanting nothing more than a good husband, a family and a modest house in or around Red Oak. It wasn't much to ask but this war was about to take her husband away and she was dreading the day. Already boys were being killed and injured in the Pacific. It didn't bear thinking about. She wiped her brow with a handkerchief, sipped her lemonade and closed her eyes.

Karl excused himself and went over to the stock area where he met one or two farmer friends including Lester Linquist.

'Hi Lester, it's a hot one all right?'

'Sure is. You not showing any animals this year, Karl?'

174

'No, not this time. As you know we had quite a tough time during the winter, relieved to get them through it in one piece let alone go for any prizes. You the same I guess?'

'Sure. Still the harvest has come good. We had all the wild weather in the winter this time, probably get a tornado next year.'

'Don't go being such a Jonah. I'm going to be short handed, what with Tom away and no surplus labour around. Can't contemplate things like tornadoes.'

It was true he was gong to miss Tom in more ways than he could imagine. The boy worked hard and long on the farm and although Lois gave him unstinting support he couldn't expect her to do much more than deal with the vegetables, chickens and what he called the house farming. The talk was of younger women taking the place of their men folk in the factories and on the farms but there was no sign of this as yet in Montgomery.

'So he's doing OK, your Tom?'

'He's fine. Learning a lot about engineering too, so that might all come in handy one day but I told him I didn't plan buying an aeroplane. He's here somewhere with young Randal Bergson. Randal's in uniform too.'

'Letha's come home this weekend, says she wouldn't miss the State Fair for anything. Funny girl that daughter of mine, has some notion about moving away from these parts one day but then hankers after days like this. She's with this Dexter she seems to be fond of. He's about to graduate in medicine and then he'll be off as well I gather. Says he's going to enlist in the navy. They need doctors out there. Wherever there is.'

'Where's he from, this Dexter fella?'

'Not from round here. Detroit, that's where, Detroit. Not too many fields in Detroit. Still, Patty seems impressed, fussing all over him she is like he's a permanent fixture but I'm not so sure,' he paused and fanned his face with his hand. 'I had hopes, silly really, that maybe Letha and your Tom would get together one day but she's so full of ambition I can't see her settling too easily.'

Karl chewed his pipe, it wasn't alight but he enjoyed the taste, 'Funny old world Lester, on the one hand we have Tom not wanting to stray away from the farm and this war about to send him to the end of the earth whereas Letha will probably end up spending the war helping out around here someplace.'

'Hi Tom. My, don't you look smart. Hi Randal.' Letha appeared on the arm of a tall dark haired young man who neither Tom nor Randal recognised. They had drifted over to the pig roast and had their mouths full of pork and crackling when Letha spotted them.

'Dexter I'd like you to meet one of my best friends from way back, Tom Nelson.'

Tom attempted to wipe his lunch from his mouth with the paper napkin and was aware that it was a greasy hand that reached out to greet the newcomer.

'Pleased to meet you,' he managed trying to swallow a large piece of pork at the same time.

'Pleased to meet you, too,' Dexter replied.

'Oh. And this other smart young soldier is Randal Bergson, another old college friend,' Letha remembered her manners, 'Dexter is about to graduate as a doctor and then he's going to join the Navy, aren't you Dexter?'

'That's the plan, I guess.'

Tom noticed that she was clinging onto Dexter's arm in a manner that suggested some permanent attachment.

'I've only been enlisted for a while. I'm learning to be an aircraft technician, working on fighters. Randal here is on bombers.' Tom felt the need to clarify things.

'Well good luck guys, let's hope we clear this thing up in a hurry.'

'Sure,' they both said together. Dexter already sounded like an officer.

'It's just not fair,' Letha interjected, 'I was the one who wanted to travel now you are all off somewhere exciting and I get left behind.'

'The somewhere exciting is called war, Letha,' Dexter admonished and Tom had to stop himself from being impressed.

'Maybe we'll catch up later,' Letha said, feeling she was being whisked away towards the main arena.

'She is quite something that Letha,' said Randal, ' and she looks at you in a funny way, Tom. Are you sure...'

'Don't talk rubbish, Randal,' Tom interjected.

'Well I'd say Doctor Dexter, US Navy, was looking a bit jealous,' Randal teased.

'Come on, let's search out my folks. I haven't seen them all day.' Tom pushed his friend in the back.

The sun got lower in the sky and the temperature cooled somewhat. Dusk took over from sunshine, twinkling lights lit up the trees and tents and the soft sound of dance music hung in the balmy evening. The two boys made their way to the small fairground and tried their hands, unsuccessfully, at rifle shooting. 'Good job we're not going to be on the front line,' Randal laughed.

'Hi boys. Have you had a good day?'

It was Letha again but this time she had a girl friend in tow, 'Dexter had to go back to university to get ready for the graduation but I came across Jeanne, you remember Jeanne don't you?'

Jeanne was short and jolly and freckled. The two boys nodded.

'Come on then Tom, take me on the ferris wheel,' Letha was grabbing his hand.

The wheel took them slowly way above the fair and although it was dusk they could see the lights of Des Moines to the east and to the west just about make out the vast rolling fields and the occasional lights of Iowan farmsteads. She took his hand, 'I know what you're thinking,' she said, 'Dexter is a nice boy, he's been good for me at Nebraska but I've told him, like I told you once, I'm not ready for settling down. I guess in some ways this awful war has proved me right for once.'

Tom laughed, 'Maybe.'

'Oh Tom, it's so lovely up here. Away from everything, floating like birds, free from all life's worries.'

He squeezed her hand, he couldn't be concerned about the Dexters of this world, 'So what ever are your worries, Letha?'

'Oh. I don't know. Just worries but up here with you they all drift away.'

'Well my only worry is this old war which none of us planned for.'

She was looking down and didn't seem to hear him, then she turned, 'You will always be special to me, Tom Nelson,' she said.

Randal seemed to find Jeanne good fun and so the four of them toured the various stalls, trying their hand once again at shooting, pitching quoits and seeking to make their fortunes in the Penny

Arcade. Later they made their way to the area set aside for dancing and armed with cokes found themselves a table not too close to the band. The organisers hadn't managed to entice Glen Miller to play for them but the local band were doing a good job. Letha tried, with moderate success, to teach Tom to jitterbug and later they held each other close when the band swung to *Moonlight Serenade* and *I'll be seeing you*. Letha mouthed the words in his ear and for a while he didn't want it all to end. But end it did and Tom had to admit to having a slight transport problem since he and Randal had come in the truck but Randal persuaded Jeanne to sit with him in the back. Tom promised to drive slowly. He wasn't in a hurry anyway.

Tom, who never touched alcohol, was as good as his word and enjoyed toying with the wheel, Letha's head on his shoulder, her hand resting on his thigh.

'I shouldn't say this but I'm glad your friend Dexter had to go back to University.'

'Me too. It's like I told you earlier Tom he's just a good friend. He's a bit serious for me if you want the truth.'

'Your mom thinks your practically engaged from what I hear,' Tom told her.

'That's just mom being ambitious. You just have to believe me Tom, it's you that's special,' she paused, 'and me that's awkward.'

They travelled in silence for some time and just when he thought she was sleeping she kissed him gently on the cheek. Eventually they pulled into Fountain Square and Tom stepped out to see how the passengers had fared.

'Battered, bruised and still alive, buddy,' Randal laughed and struck out his hand to Tom, 'I'll let you know where I end up, Tom,' he said and they briefly hugged.

'Why look at you two,' laughed Jeanne grabbing Randal by the arm and marching him off.

Tom drove Letha back towards the Linquist farm and she made him stop along the lane before the house came into view. They kissed tenderly before she broke from him. 'Will you be home for Thanksgiving, Tom?'

'I doubt it,' he said, 'probably be Christmas before I'm back again.'

'She undid the door and swung it open, 'I'll think of a special present for you then,' she laughed, jumping nimbly off the board.

He watched her go down the lane to her home. She didn't turn round, just waved and was gone.

'This is not the end. It is not even the beginning of the end. But it is, perhaps, the end of the beginning.' Winston Churchill

'Monty has broken through. They're in full retreat. Did you hear that.' Jack was shouting from his front room ringside seat by the radio. Vera and Kitty came scurrying from the kitchen.

'We've taken nine thousand prisoners, destroyed three hundred tanks. Well done Jimmy, lad.' Jack jumped out of his chair grabbed Vera and waltzed her round the room.

Vera was laughing and wheezing at the same time, 'Stop it you daft old devil,' and she broke away, 'I do hope he's all right. Jimmy I mean.'

'He'll be fine. He's on the winning side.'

'What's that noise?' Kitty had her hand to her ear.

The three of them hurried out into the garden. They looked across at neighbours' gardens which stretched as far as the eye could see; people had gathered outside, standing on their shelters calling to one another and all of them listening to the peal of bells. The church bells all around Ipswich were ringing again.

'I'd promised Doris I would meet her for a drink later in The Catchpole,' Kitty said, 'by the looks of things we won't be the only people there.'

'We'll join you won't we Vera? It's a long time since we had something to celebrate.'

Jack put on his best suit and tie, Vera her utility blue floral dress and Kitty a new regulation short skirt. They wanted to look their best. They walked down Cliff Lane to the pub where numerous bicycles leaned against the red brick walls. It was a clear night and Jack was pleased he was not on call.

Inside the air was heavy with smoke and the level of laughter provided a barometer to the belief that, at last, things were starting to go the way of the Allies. People weren't stupid; they had heard Churchill on the wireless joyous in a victory but warning it was by no means the end. But, instead of the talk being of possible invasion by Hitler there was a feeling of hope that maybe, just maybe, the tide was beginning to turn.

Sam Evans was playing with a new energy responding to a request for *They'll always be an England.* Jack found a table by the darts board (nobody wanted to play darts tonight someone told him) and then went to the bar. He couldn't resist talking to his cronies on the way; Vera could hear him crowing about El Alamein then adding that he was now convinced the Ruskies were getting the upper hand at Stalingrad. Eventually he arrived back at the table with a shandy for Vera and a port and lemon for Kitty.

He raised his glass, 'We're on our way,' he announced.

'All we need now is a letter from Jimmy telling us that he is OK,' Vera said quietly.

Kitty patted her mother's hand, 'He'll be fine, mum, I just know he will.'

'Yes, of course he will. Talking of Jimmy where's that girl of his?'

Kitty peered through the crowded bar, 'I can't see her but I can see a couple of interesting men,' she announced.

'Not again Kitty. Who is it this time, Noel Coward and John Mills?' Jack laughed at his own joke.

'Not interesting like that. Interesting in a, let me think, curious way. Look over in the far corner. See? Two black Americans, sitting on their own. I don't think I've seen a black person close before.'

'What do you mean Darky Bailey from Derwent Road, she was blackish.'

'Nonsense,' said Vera, 'Darky Bailey was, well coffee coloured,' she raised herself from her seat, 'No those are really black. What are they doing here Jack?'

'Building aerodromes for the American airmen, putting in new runways. That's what I've been told. Soon they'll be all over the place with their bloody great bombers. About time too, if you ask me.'

'Careless talk, Jack' Vera added.

'No one can hear. They're all making too much noise.'

'Loads of Americans, well that will liven things up. Come on let's have another drink.' Kitty was beaming.

As she got up they saw Doris's red head bobbing towards them. She had a friend in tow. A tall dark girl with striking eyes and bright red lips.

'Sorry we're late. Had to go to a meeting at HQ and I bumped into Sylvia and persuaded her to come. Sylvia meet, Kitty and Mr. and Mrs. Wright, my sort of in-laws.'

Jack got up and stretched out his hand, ' Charmed I'm sure,' he said.

Vera smiled,' Any friend of Doris is a friend of ours, dear. What will you have to drink? Kitty is just about to get them in.'

'Oh a shandy would be fine, thanks', Sylvia was already organising a couple of chairs for Doris and herself.

'Live around here do you dear?' Vera asked.

'Playford, actually.'

'Oh! You're the.....'

'Posh friend. That's me.' Sylvia finished the sentence and Vera went into fits of laughter.

'You're all right you are. Here have a cigarette.'

Jack had been sitting back studying Sylvia making Doris feel a bit uneasy. Suddenly his face lit up, 'I've got it. It's been worrying me since you came in young lady. Foxhall Road the other night. Nasty old incident. You were there. Helping with the homeless. Remember Vera, I told you all about this young lady.'

'Yes I was there,' Sylvia said quietly, ' Pretty horrible situation wasn't it but the rescue people did a wonderful job getting those people out before the place collapsed. They might have lost their homes but their lives were saved.'

Jack smiled to himself, ' Well I never,' he said.

Kitty arrived back with the drinks which she put on the table and then excusing herself weaved her way to where the Americans were sitting. She refused their offer of a seat but stood talking to them for sometime.

The pianist struck up *White Cliffs of Dover*, Vera linked arms with Doris and Sylvia and they joined in the singing. Kitty came back but Doris thought she would leave it to another occasion before quizzing her about the Americans. They had more drinks and sang more songs and left the pub, slightly tipsy, but the happiest they had been for some time.

'It's been a pleasure meeting you,' Jack told Sylvia, ' especially on such an occasion', and then he added, sounding more Churchillian than Robert Cameron, ' At last Good is beginning to overcome Evil.'

'I'm dreaming of a white Christmas.' - *Irving Berlin*

Doris put on a brave face during the Christmas period of 1942. She hadn't heard from Jimmy for some time. She told herself that this was because he was heavily engaged in chasing Rommel as they kept saying on the wireless. Doris had worried before and then been rewarded by a whole heap of mail that had been held up somewhere along the line. The problem was it was Christmas and how could she enjoy it not knowing where he was and whether he was all right.

The news from North Africa, as recorded in newspapers and on the radio, was good. The Germans were in full retreat. The Allies had Rommel on the run. This was the sort of Christmas present the British people wanted even if the traditional fare was in short supply. Chickens seemed to spend their lives exclusively laying eggs these days; carrots replaced spices in the Christmas pudding and children's stockings no longer had oranges and nuts stuffed in the toe. None the less the effort was made. Families got together, determined to enjoy themselves and across the country stood to the National Anthem at the end of the King's broadcast.

Doris was pleased to see Alice and to learn more of her boyfriend who had apparently returned to Grimsby for three days seasonal leave. She smiled when shown the photograph of a young corporal looking like so many more with his short back and sides and fresh face. Her mother had done her best with the limitations of rationing and her favourite Aunt and Uncle came for Boxing Day tea. Her father was quiet and spent a lot of time in his chair listening to the radio with a silly paper hat perched on his head. Even Alice's land army stories failed to make him smile. He seemed to have retreated into some private world of his own.

Two days after her brave effort at enjoying the festivities Doris was rewarded. Her face visibly relaxed as the letter dropped through the letterbox.

December 15th 1942

North Africa

Darling Doris,
  I can't really tell you exactly where I am since the officers would only cross it out when they went through the letter. I think it's awful they have to do this and I wonder who goes through their letters. (They'll probably cross that bit out too!).
  Anyhow, here I am safe. We're chasing Jerry right out of North Africa now and after all this time every one is feeling excited. It hasn't all been one way; of course, we've lost a few. One of my best mates was badly injured by a mine and our football team goalie was killed in action, poor devil. We've also taken hundreds of prisoners and no one quite knows what to do with them. They look a raggle-taggle bunch – difficult to imagine them as the cream of Rommel's army.
  I really hope you get this by Christmas. I know what an old worrier you are but you just have to believe me when I say I will get through all this and come home to you and a better world. I've bought everyone little presents and though it's pointless sending them I shall pretend to give them out on Christmas Day. They're only silly things but one day the trinkets I've got for you will go on our mantlepiece and you and I will never be apart again.
  I can't believe old French having a girlfriend. There's life in the old devil yet, eh?
  How is Joyce these days? You haven't mentioned her recently. Give her my best.
  Have there been any more big raids on Ipswich? You must be just as careful as me, you know.
  I've written to mum and dad and the last letter they sent me was a tonic. Mum is very funny in her letters and seems to be enjoying her telephonist job. Dad seems almost used to the idea by now.
  I know war-time Suffolk is different from the Suffolk I knew but I still think of our walks at Flatford and down at Nacton shores, of the heath lands and the fields at harvest time. You think of such things when all you see is mucky

desert. Not much chance of a white Christmas out here I can tell you but we'll
have a special meal and sing some carols.

  Happy Christmas then my darling Doris.

I love you more than ever,

Jimmy

1943

'Wartime is socialism with its difficulties left out'. - A.J.P. Taylor

'So he's alive and well and not only that has bought you a Christmas present. That's more than Francis has me.'
Sylvia and Doris were sitting on a pillbox in Holywells Park.
'You've heard from Francis. Oh. That's great. Now we can both relax. I don't suppose he said where he is?'
Sylvia inhaled her cigarette, 'No. He wouldn't flaunt the rules, not Francis. He seemed pleased about the way things were going though. Said they'd have a better Christmas this year. Hoped I would too. Assumed I'd see his family as well as my own. Sent them his seasonal greetings. Was amazed that I'd been in a pub with you but said he supposed that's what happened in war time Britain.' She gave a dismissive laugh and inhaled again.
Doris, who had declined a cigarette nibbled at an annoying nail and looked out over the park where as a young girl she had raced down the grassy slopes and fed the ducks. Hay would be harvested from those same slopes in early summer and even now men were busy hoeing on the allotments that had sprung up on the flatter areas. She had no idea where the ducks had gone.
'He's going to find his Britain has changed quite a bit when this war is over. The working class, as he calls anyone who isn't privately educated, will want a bigger stake in society. Something they'll certainly deserve after all they're putting up with.'
'Everyone is putting up with it in a way.' Doris was thoughtful.
'You mean rationing has brought us all to the same level. Yes, you're right, of course, in a way it has. It may be pretty severe but it's the same for my mother and your mother except that my mother doesn't get her hands dirty.'
'She does an awful lot with the WVS Sylvia, I'm always reading things about her in the *Star*.'
'Yes but she's still aloof from what is actually happening. I don't mean to criticise her. I think the world of her, admire her even but, you know how this war has made me aware of so much, well it hasn't affected her that way at all..'

'We're younger, Sylvia, it's easier for us.' As the words came out Doris wondered whether Jimmy was changing. She sensed that for him it had to be officers and men, two distinct classes. That was the way of things out in the desert.

'You should be a diplomat, Doris Harper,' Sylvia was laughing, swinging her legs.

'And you should be a politician, Sylvia Cameron.'

'Now there's an idea,' Sylvia looked full of mischief. 'I've been reading this report by Lord Beveridge on Social Security.'

'You've lost me again.'

'You must have read about it in the papers. Someone called Lord Beveridge has written a report suggesting that the government should provide free health, education and even pensions. All sorts of benefits for people funded out of taxes and such.'

'And pigs might fly,' concluded Doris.

It had become a regular habit for Doris to visit her *mother in law to be* during her Wednesday half days. On this particular day she found Vera waiting at the front gate grinning like the proverbial Cheshire Cat.

'Got something to show you,' she said, pulling open the gate and hurrying around the side entrance and into the back garden.

'Down here, come on,' she was tugging at Doris's hand, ' what do you think?'

'My goodness, just look at them.'

At the bottom of the Wrights' garden a little wooden hut had appeared surrounded by a lot of wire. Three plump chickens were picking at scraps on the ground oblivious to the excitement they had caused.

'Got three eggs this morning. Lovely warm eggs for our breakfast. Beats those old white ones we used to get from Fowlers.'

'How many are you allowed?'

' You mean how many chickens? One per person per household. So that's three, of course, and there they are. Mary, Millie and Mandy.'

'Don't kid me you can tell the difference.'

'Jack can. Let me see now, Mary has the jaggered crop, Millie beady little eyes and Mary has lighter feathers; no that's not it Mary's the one with the beady eyes, Millie has the funny crop. Oh I don't know you'll have to ask Jack he's practically on first name terms with them.'

'When did they arrive?'

'At the weekend. Jack spent most of his spare time fixing the nesting hut and the run. As I said we've had to give up getting eggs from the shop but who cares.'

'Well I think it's all very exciting.' As Doris returned to the house with Vera she thought of Sylvia trying to explain how the war hadn't changed her mother. No doubt they had chickens up at Hall Farm and no doubt it was Old Moore who looked after them.

That night Kitty was on fire watch again at Pipers but Jack was off duty. At about ten o'clock the siren went and he hustled Vera into the shelter clutching her knitting. As always he stood sentry at the entrance where he reported that the sky had suddenly turned bright orange. Jerry was dropping flares over the docks. Jack explained that this was so they could take photos and know what to go for when they next targeted the area. 'Hope they didn't frighten my chickens,' he said.

Later in the week Doris was training up at Headquarters. The now familiar wail of the siren interrupted proceedings followed by the jangle of telephones. She rammed on her tin hat and ran to the mobile vans which were fully equipped for air raid incidents. Instructions were yelled at the driver and they were off into the black night.

From the beginning everything seemed more chaotic than usual. Searchlights weaved intricate patterns, ack acks rattled and scarred the sky. The grating sound of Focke Wulfs roared over head; someone said they counted six in all. Other aircraft, at the time unidentified, were caught in the glare. Louder guns pounded and juddered. The first aiders transport shook at a loud explosion not far away. They were to learn later that a large bomb had dropped in the Felixstowe Road area, jumped over the trees in Holywells park and landed in a row of houses near the docks. One of the Focke Wulfs diving to attack the gasometer was put off balance by the explosion and crashed into the river.

The unit arrived at a scene of complete devastation; houses reduced to rubble, firemen hosing, specialist rescue people moving into the debris searching for signs of life. Flames licked the air, black smoke choked both rescuers and victims alike, roofs, walls, timbers tumbled into the mess. The noise seemed more deafening than ever before, everyone seemed to be shouting out orders, wardens' whistles cut through the belching blackness, police cars, ambulances, fire-engines rang out in their determination to get to the heart of the trouble. And in a rare lull Doris heard the crying of children and the screaming of mothers.

A sooty faced warden instructed them where to set up and they prepared to receive those with minor injuries. The ambulance crews would ferry those with serious wounds to hospitals, the WVS would seek out and comfort the displaced and shocked.

Doris never knew why she strayed from the van. Why she walked, as if in a trance, towards those working at the centre of the awful destruction. A cacophony of sounds from hell echoed all around her. Her hands and faced were blackened within seconds. The heat was intense yet she shivered with cold. She was sweating profusely but still she slowly walked forward. Nobody took any notice of her. They were far too busy.

Some men were shouting that they had seen an arm stretching out of a heap of charred rubble and hastened to the scene. She saw them gently tug at the limb. It came easily to them. Just an arm. It wasn't attached to anything.

Still she shuffled on.

'Oh. My God!'

'What is it Pete?'

'Fetch a blanket, quickly.'

'Don't look miss. Don't look' someone was shouting at her.

She looked.

A torso with most of its head blown off lay in front of her. The face had virtually disappeared.

She felt the vomit reach up from the pit of her stomach. She retched and then everything was spinning.

'Miss. Are you all right. Charlie, come over here quickly.'

She kept seeing Jimmy's body with half a face. He was trying to grin. Trying to make her laugh. She screamed. Nobody heard.

She woke up wet with sweat. There was water on a table next to her bed and she gulped at it. She fell back onto the pillows and fell asleep. This time there were no faces.

Later she was aware of a shaft of sunlight. She blinked, pushed back a strand of thick hair from her face. She was in a strange bed, it smelt clean, and it smelt safe. The room was unfamiliar. It wasn't a hospital. It didn't look like a hospital. But then she didn't think she was wounded. The walls were crooked, the ceiling beamed, books tumbled on a bookshelf, a school photograph dangled precariously above an orange and yellow vase, a jug of water, a tumbler and a bowl perched on a bedside table..

What had happened? She screwed up her face and then the awfulness came back. It had been a raid. A God awful raid. For some absurd reason Jimmy seemed to be involved. Then she remembered the torso. Her stomach turned and just in time she remembered the enamel bowl. She turned her head towards it and was sick.

'My. What a way to wake up.' It was Sylvia. Why, of course, this must be the cottage.

Doris coughed and wiped her mouth on the back of her hand, 'Sorry. What am I doing here? How long have I been here? What's been happening?'

Sylvia handed her a towel and sat on the end of the bed. 'One thing at a time, please. Basically you passed out during an incident near the docks. Though what you were doing in that particular area seems a mystery. We were set up close to your unit and I suddenly realised it was you causing all the fuss. Your people treated you the best they could. Doctor McPherson was on duty and gave them some pills for you and you seemed to go into a sleep. As soon as the worst was over I brought you back to the cottage, cleaned you up a bit and here you are.'

Doris squeezed her friend's hand, 'Thanks. Thanks so much. What an idiot. I don't faint. It isn't something I do.'

'Some of the things we see when we're on duty would make the toughest Sergeant Major faint. That's how Doctor Mac put it, anyway. There's nothing to be ashamed of. It'll be my turn one day no doubt.'

Doris relaxed for a while and then sat up in bed with a start, 'Who knows where I am? What about my mother? Mr French?'

'Relax I called in on Mr. French this morning. He said you have to take a few days off. He's a real sweetie. Well at arms length anyhow.'

'And my mum. I know she's a bit odd but she will worry. I mean how long have I been here for heaven's sake?'

'Woah back! It's about four in the afternoon. You have been here one night and nearly a whole day. I think the pills made you sleep. And would you believe my mother went round in the Riley and told your mother all about it. She said you have a very sensible mother who lives in quite a pleasant little road with one or two nice trees.'

'Oh. My God.'

'My advice is to say put. Take the pills for another twenty-four hours and get some rest. Doctor Mac says you'll remain in shock for a day or so and then, depending on what sort of person you are, you'll work out how to come to terms with what happened.'

Doris nodded. 'Thanks and thank the doctor for the knock out pills, if you see him. I'll be all right.'

Doris stayed another night and after nibbling some toast for breakfast, dressed in the clothes Mrs. Grimstone had retrieved from her mother, went outside and took a deep breath of cold air. Sylvia had gone off early promising to get back as soon as she could in the afternoon. She told Doris to help herself to anything she wanted, adding there wasn't much that would do her any harm. Doris didn't feel much like eating.

It was a crisp, frosty morning and she decided to go for a walk along the field leading away from the house. As she walked she breathed deeply and, in spite of the cold, began to feel an inner warmth return to her body. She pulled back her hair and felt the welcome bite of a new day on her face. Although she occasionally attended Alan Road Methodist Church she didn't consider herself a religious person but on this particular morning she looked to the sky wanting to believe that there was a God.

As she walked she had a discussion with herself. She had to stop worrying so much about Jimmy. What was it he always said? He was a survivor and she had to believe him. Instead she began to think about how it would be after the war. Although only one victory, El Alamein had been Jimmy's victory and she believed that at last the allies were starting to win the war. She would talk again to Mr. French about qualifying as a pharmacist, Jimmy would finish his apprenticeship or maybe he would have other plans by then and most important of all they would get married. Doris slung her scarf around her neck and began to stride out briskly.

She walked further than she had intended and it was mid morning before she arrived back at the cottage where she indulged herself by having a bath and washing her hair. Sitting in the little bath she thought that she could get used to this. Perhaps she was meant to be a lady of leisure after all. Something else to explain to Jimmy!

Sylvia came home looking tired and Doris said a bowl of soup would be fine after which she really should return home. Apparently there was some meeting that Sylvia and her mother had to attend in town and so, in spite of protests, it was decided that they would drop Doris off on their way

Elizabeth enquired after her health in a way that appeared to show genuine concern.

She drove slowly, clutching the wheel rather tightly and leaning forward to peer through the windscreen. She didn't seem to care too much what gear she was in.

However, she did manage to stop the Riley outside the right house. Doris noticed one or two curtains move nearby.

Sylvia told her to take care and promised to be in touch shortly and Elizabeth surprised her by sticking her head out of the window and saying in a loud voice,

'Now don't take on everyone's troubles Doris. You're doing more than your bit to win this blasted war as it is.' Then, with an awful crashing of gears, she drove off.

IOWA AND BEYOND

'America is not training three million troops to play tiddly winks with Germany'.
Henry Hopkin – Adviser to the President.

Technical Sergeant Tom Nelson ticked the final items on his list, stuffed the requisite number of socks into his kit bag then he sat on the edge of his bed and looked around the room. He wanted to remember it all, the quilted bed cover, the solid chest of drawers, the framed picture of the High School Baseball team, the old wardrobe that tilted precariously on the sloping floor, the Indian rug, the smell of seasoned wood and a small photograph of him with Letha at the State Fair. He pondered on whether to take the picture with him but decided against.

Letha had continued to behave in her unpredictable way right up until last night when she had promised to come round to his house but failed to turn up. Letha who had thrilled him with her presence both physically and as someone to banter with; Letha whose mother had said was seriously dating a medical student at University but who still told Tom she needed to see him; Letha who on hearing that he would be going abroad was both proud of him and jealous of his unexpected opportunity to travel. Letha who, like many Americans, had no idea what war was about.

Tom looked at his watch. Still an hour to go before he left for the Depot and the long trip spanning America and eventually across the sea to a new world. The sea? What would it be like? What would a voyage on a troop ship be like?

When he first enlisted in September 42 and went to the basic training camp his father had told him to take whatever they threw at him unflinchingly, not to answer back, not to try to be clever. He had taken this advice and the Drill Sergeant soon realised that this particular country boy was not going to rise to the bait. Further more Tom, being fit and well co-ordinated, had no problems with the marching, rifle drill and endurance training. He hadn't enjoyed these first few weeks in uniform but had coped. But then came the technical training. Six months intensive work learning everything there was to know about fighters in general and B47 Thunderbolts in particular.

He had loved every minute of it and, having passed out as a Technical Sergeant, couldn't wait to put his new found knowledge into practice. He was now a member of 356 Squadron, Fighter command and was impatient to get to England even though he had no idea what England was like. Today he would be leaving Red Oak and travelling to Camp Kilmer, New Jersey, the first stage in his journey. The second stage, six weeks at sea, was another experience awaiting the boy who had never seen the ocean.

Tom ran his fingers through his hair and stood up. The May sunshine was filtering through the window casting symmetrical patterns on the floor and he decided to pay a final visit to the farm. He needed to say his goodbyes to the land he loved to work with. Coming downstairs he muttered something to his mother and went outside. There was no wind and it was warm. He wondered about the weather in England. In every movie he had ever seen about the place it was foggy. He walked through the yard and out onto the fields and took in the view. Miles and miles of cultivated land sloping off here and there into wooded areas, the occasional white farm buildings with their high roofs, grain stores and silos but mainly he saw this vast expanse of land.

He walked away from the farm and down into the nearest field and, once out of view of the house, stretched himself face downwards onto the soft soil. It moulded easily to his body and he spread his arms and legs to their limits. He smelt the rich earth and prayed that it would all be here, just the same, when he returned.

He wasn't sure how long he lay there. He knew he said a silent prayer for his Mom and Dad, for Ellen and young Luke whom he had visited the day before. He prayed for Ben, the unlikely soldier, now drafted and on his way to the war in the Pacific. Then he slowly got to his feet, shook himself down and decided he was ready to go. Ready to find out just what this next part of his life was all about.

Karl and Lois Nelson drove their son in comparative silence to the depot. They had said all there was to be said the evening before. They joined other similar groups on the platform and greeted acquaintances politely, wishing their sons well. After what seemed a very long time the big train shunted around the bend and drew to a halt. Tom hugged his Mom and Dad and promised to write as soon as he was able. He hoisted up his kit bag and prepared to climb up the iron steps to the nearest train door.

'Tom, wait, wait!'

He looked round and saw Letha scampering along the platform arms outstretched. She threw herself at him and kissed him not caring who saw her.

'You're going to see the world before me, Farm Boy,' she whispered, ' look after yourself and write to me. You'll always be my guy'. Tom looked at her and grinned then turned and mounted the train with other young men travelling to the unknown.

The young boy from Iowa who had never seen the sea found himself on one of the luxury liners of the pre war age, *The Queen Mary*. When writing home later Tom didn't mention the word *luxury* however. The famous liner accommodated ten times more troops than it had passengers; they were cramped into every available space, fed on awful English food and sea sick for most of the six weeks it took to cross the Atlantic. As if the motion of the boat and the rise and fall of the sea were not enough they were told that provided the *Queen* zig-zagged she would avoid the attempts by the German U-boats to sink her.

In his first letter home he was at pains to point out that he didn't actually arrive in England, more like Scotland, where the liner could easily berth. He wasn't sure whether his parents knew the difference between England and Scotland but it seemed to be important. The thousands of green faced young Americans were billeted in nissen huts before being allocated camps in various strategic parts of The United Kingdom. Tom found himself on a crowded train moving south east until, eventually, arriving at somewhere called Ipswich. He was then transported to USAAF Wattisham which was a maintenance depot. This he found disappointing since he was itching for action, keen to be allocated a fighter squadron, keen to feel he was doing his bit, putting his training into practice.

The months he spent at Wattisham were, as it turned out, useful in so far as he worked on both fighters and bombers; he also enjoyed the company of young men, who like him, were happiest covered in oil delving into the intricacies of aircraft engines. When not on duty the majority of his new buddies went into Ipswich and relieved their boredom and homesickness by drinking too much until herded up by the military police at eleven o'clock and driven back in liberty trucks. Tom had never been a drinker and decided he wasn't about to start just because he was holed up in some foreign country. He'd been allotted a bicycle and so took to cycling around the villages exploring the countryside. It didn't take him long to realise that the people were having a hard time. The place was in its way still beautiful, a sort of miniature Iowa, but the pill boxes, road blocks, lack of signs, shelters, intensive farming and gardening and the drab appearance of the people confirmed that the war was treating them badly. The booklet he had been issued was right when it said *The British do look a bit down on their luck but try to make the best of it. Just because we crossed the ocean we're not war heroes. There are housewives in aprons and youngsters in knee pants who have witnessed more high explosives than many soldiers saw in the last war.*

Tom's time at Wattisham enabled him to adjust, to select other young men with whom he had things in common and whilst the camp did its best to provide things American he decided he would try to use his limited free time finding out more about Britain and the British.

'Don't show off or brag or bluster.' - extract from 'A short guide to Great Britain' issued to American service personnel.

They had arrived as if pulled from a magician's top hat. One minute nobody had even considered their existence and the next minute they were everywhere. They lolled around the pubs trying not to complain about the warm beer; they slouched in Lloyd Loom chairs in the tea rooms sipping what they expected was going to be coffee; they greeted everyone they met as if they were on intimate terms; they were polite to the extreme, seemed to love the banter with youngsters, made instant advances to every girl they met and aggravated a fair number of local males.

For Joyce they could do no wrong. They came into French's regularly and made her feel like a film star. More and more she encouraged Doris to spend time in the dispensary and leave the shop to her.

'I'm taking Mrs. Fox up to London on Saturday to a Myra Hess lunch time concert', Mr. French informed Doris as she huddled over her pipette screwing up her eyes to read the levels. Mr. French, as always, was encouraging her in her quest to extend her pharmaceutical knowledge and she was enjoying every minute of it.

'She always sounds like a German to me. Myra Hess, I mean, not Mrs. Fox, 'she said.

Mr. French ignored the attempt at wit and continued, 'Of course she isn't German. She plays almost every day in the National Gallery. It's empty since they've taken the pictures away and so makes an excellent venue. Very fine acoustics.'

'Will she play Chopin, this Myra Hess?'

'We very much hope so. And then in the early evening Mrs Fox and I are going to The Albert Hall to a full orchestral concert.'

Doris looked up at the contented face of her employer and smiled. Catching her look Mr. French blushed and then busied himself reaching for a bottle of *Minodex* from a nearby shelf.

'I told you that I had made you official now, didn't I?' he said, glancing over his shoulder.

'What does that mean exactly, Mr. French?'

'It means that The Institute have agreed that over the next three years I have to make you acquainted with all there is to know about pharmacy and you have to study the books I shall lend you. Then you take an exam to qualify as a fully- fledged chemist. How about that?'

'It sounds wonderful to me, Mr. French. You are sure, aren't you? You are sure that I'm worth it. I mean, I really will try not to let you down.'

Doris knew that prior to the arrival of Mrs. Fox, Mr. French would have placed an arm around her, now he simply turned and smiled, ' I have great faith in you, Doris, and besides that I enjoy teaching you what little I know. I find it very gratifying.'

So, she thought, that's it then. Mr. French wants me to qualify and The Institute have agreed. She couldn't wait to tell Sylvia. As for Jimmy, she just wished he were nearer so she could explain what this meant to her, wished his silly face would appear, pressed against the window.

Instead it was Kitty's face that appeared as Joyce ushered her into the back room. 'Visitor,' she announced and then returned to the shop where yet another beautifully uniformed American airman needed her full attention.

'Sorry to butt in Mr. French but I only have a few minutes lunch break and I have to tell Doris she's invited out on Friday night.'

Doris looked up, ' Kitty, how are you? Now, could you start again? Who has invited me where?'

'Well the United States Airforce has invited you to their base at Debach.'

'What just me? What do they want a lesson in first aid?'

Kitty laughed, 'Not quite and I wasn't totally truthful either. They are laying on buses to take girls to a dance and the factory is doing its bit to welcome our allies. So I thought you and Joyce might like to come with me. It'll do you good to have night out. What do you think?'

'Oh. I don't know Kitty. What about Jimmy? He wouldn't like me dancing with Americans. I mean I wouldn't like him dancing with Egyptians or whoever, would I?'

'Don't be daft. You can't get up to much harm dancing. And Joyce, she'll just love it. It will be worth coming simply to see her enjoy herself.'

Mr. French had been listening to the conversation with mild amusement, 'Go on Doris, you deserve a bit of fun. Too much work and not enough play makes Doris a dull something or other.'

'Oh. All right. Just this once but I'm not going to drink too much or do anything silly.'

'Right I'll call for you at seven on Friday.'

On her way home Doris tried to convince herself that she had made the right decision. She had sorted herself out since the incident at the docks but they were right, she did deserve a night out and besides it was only fair to Kitty and to Joyce that she went along. Jimmy would understand. No he wouldn't, Jimmy would be jealous! She would be jealous if she knew he had gone to a nurses' dance. Perhaps he did. He deserved some fun, too, after all that terrible fighting she kept hearing about on the wireless.

Pushing her bike up the hill she nearly became entangled with a couple of men ahead of her. *Watch where you're going miss* was the only rebuke and she apologised.

If I'm being very honest with myself I am just a little intrigued to see what they're like, she admitted.

Doris and Kitty arrived at The Old Cattle Market bus depot at seven thirty amidst a frenzy of excited girls clambering for seats on the ten buses rented by the American base. After some difficulty they located a lip-sticked and well-powdered Joyce and linking arms they made for one of the vehicles that made up the end of the convoy.

On board they found a three-seater near the back and watched as more and more look-a-like females filled vacant places. One or two, spotting Kitty, shouted out a greeting. Doris looked around and thought that they had all made quite an effort and she hoped, though had her doubts, that the Yanks would appreciate how difficult it was for a girl to look good in wartime Britain. Whilst she possessed some dark pink lipstick she knew that some of the girls would have resorted to beetroot juice and eye brows would have been pencilled in with the same eye liner used to put seams on their legs.

200

Eventually the girls settled into their seats, lit up cigarettes and the bus jostled along behind the queue of similar vehicles wending their way out of town.

'I've no idea what this is going to be like,' Kitty confided.

'I don't think anyone has,' Doris agreed.

'It'll be like one of those Hollywood Parties,' Joyce re-assured them.

The bus was a cauldron of excitement and the noise level increased by the minute. Experiences with Yanks were discussed in detail, one girl started to hand around American cigarettes called *Lucky Strikes*, and another suggested they should chew gum. The latest Utility style clothing was mentioned with someone saying that at least raising the hem line was a good thing – Yanks liked a bit of leg, she added to laughter from some of the louder passengers. Looking around Doris realised that ninety per cent of the noise came from about ten per cent of those on board. The majority of the girls were talking quietly, even nervously, to those close to them. She was uncomfortable with those her mother would have termed *common* but quickly dismissed such thoughts as being snobbish. At the same time she couldn't imagine Sylvia being on such a bus.

They shuddered to a halt forming a queue at the entrance to the USAAF Debach. When they reached the gate the driver was waved down and questioned by two of the biggest men Doris had ever seen. Looking out of the window she felt a pang of nerves noticing that these white helmeted military policemen carried both guns and enormous batons. Joyce nudged her, 'I'm glad they're on our side,' she giggled.

The convoy of buses was directed down avenues of neat, recently painted buildings. Jeeps and trucks of various sizes were parked outside. Groups of stylishly dressed servicemen waved, shouting inaudible greetings. Most of the doors to the great hangars were closed but every now and then there was a glimpse inside where men were working on the giant bombers.

Eventually they stopped outside a smaller hangar and stepped into a new world. Doris felt like an evacuee and thought she should have a label on her dress stating her name and address. They filed past a number of airmen who welcomed them to the base in what, she at first thought, was an over polite manner. Later she realised she had a lot to learn about Americans.

En masse they stepped into Aladdin's Cave. Through the dimmed lighting she was aware that a large group of Americans had abandoned their previous pose of lolling around the bar and were moving easily towards the influx of girls. The Stars and Stripes hung from the high ceilings as did large models of aeroplanes, the walls were full of posters proclaiming the value of Coca Cola, Nestles chocolate and Camel cigarettes as well as those urging the need to *Fight for Freedom*. From the far end of the hangar saxophones swung with the latest Glen Miller tune and accents, previously only heard on film, hung in the air like smoke from the *Lucky Strike* cigarettes. Tables and chairs had been arranged around the sides of the hangar and Doris felt Kitty grab her by the elbow and propel her towards the nearest vacant seats.

No sooner had they sat down than three airmen appeared. 'Hi, I'm Tony, can I get you ladies something to drink,' one of them chirped.

'What do you suggest then Tony?' Kitty was never shy when drinks were being offered.

'Anything you like, ma'am, A cocktail, a beer, a coke?'

'A cocktail sounds interesting. You can choose,' Kitty was already enjoying herself.

'Right that will be three Mint Juleps,' and before Doris could suggest a more conventional alternative Tony went to the bar and the other two Americans dragged up chairs and joined them.

'I'm Dick from Denver, Colorado and this is Oakey, well he's from Oklahoma, naturally,' announced the dark haired one with the turned up nose. Oakey just looked at them and smiled. He has nice eyes, she thought.

'Well I'm Joyce from Ipswich and this is Doris from Ipswich and then there's Kitty from Ipswich. Ipswich, Suffolk that is.'

As always Joyce had broken the ice.

A singer was now fronting the band crooning *You'll Never Know*. Dick from Denver smiled at Joyce, 'Would you care to dance, Joyce from Ipswich, Suffolk?' Joyce, looking like she'd landed in heaven, tried not to leap to her feet and allowed herself to be escorted to the dance floor.

Doris looked up at Oakey; he's just a boy a long way from home she thought.

'How long have you been over here, Oakey?' she asked. He looked down at his hands and then back at her,

'Just a month. I haven't seen much of England yet. We've been kind of busy since we arrived. I'm part of the crew for one of the B42's but I have some time off soon so I will have a look around then, I guess.'

Doris noticed that Kitty was leaning back on her seat chatting away to another airman on the next table. She thought for a while, 'I suppose what they have done here is make a little America so you don't feel home sick' she ventured.

He laughed, 'Yes, I guess you could say that but it doesn't stop you being home sick. Before this I hadn't travelled very far in the USA let alone Europe. So when I do get off base it's gonna be real interesting.'

'It's such a pity you couldn't have seen England before the war. Everything and everyone are a bit sad these days but it wasn't always like that.' In spite of herself Doris was beginning to enjoy talking with this young boy from Oklahoma He wasn't so different from her Jimmy but on thinking that she felt a stab of guilt.

'Here we are folks.' Tony arrived with the drinks.

'They look really pretty,' Kitty remarked sipping at her Mint Julep,' 'mmm I think I'm going to like cocktails.'

'And so do you look real pretty. Can you jitterbug?'

'No but I'd love to learn,' Kitty was on her feet ready for her first lesson.

Oakey sipped his beer, 'I'm afraid I haven't got the hang of jitterbugging yet,' he admitted to Doris, 'but perhaps we could have the next slow one.'

'That would be nice,' Doris said, ' Oakey, you have noticed that I am engaged haven't you. He's fighting in the North African Campaign at the moment. I wouldn't want you to get the wrong idea.'

'To be truthful I hadn't noticed, but I kinda worked out that someone as nice as you would have a boyfriend. What's his name?'

'Jimmy.' She even felt guilty saying it.

'Then would Jimmy mind if I just borrowed you for the next dance, do you think?'

'As long as you bring me back in one piece' she said.

Oakey was taller than she had thought and held her tight, but not too tight, as they swayed together to *Moonlight Serenade*. They didn't talk but neither of them were in a hurry to leave the floor and so continued as the sad saxophones sang out *I'll never smile again*. Doris moved a little nearer to him and his face nuzzled her hair. It had been a long time since she had felt a boy close to her.

They talked and danced throughout the evening and she allowed herself one more delicious Mint Julep. She told him that she would understand if he wanted to dance with some of the other girls but he said he was having a good time. They watched with appreciation at Kitty's improving jitterbug technique and although Joyce never quite mastered the new art she was obviously having the time of her life. Doris thought that Yanks were going to be better for the local girls than any tonic that she could make up in the chemists.

She felt relaxed talking with Oakey and when the lights came up after the last waltz she stood looking at him for a while. 'Thanks for giving me such a good time,' she said and kissed him lightly on the cheek.

'Maybe we'll meet again,' he said in his quiet drawl.

Doris smiled and then walked slowly away looking for her two friends. She couldn't help grinning when she saw them both locked in passionate embraces. She walked to the bus and sat for a while by herself whilst other girls, babbling excitedly, clambered aboard. It was nice, she thought, but I won't come again.

Kitty came into the kitchen the next morning looking distinctly out of sorts. She muttered 'Good morning.'

'Had a good time then?' Vera enquired gently.

'It was wonderful, mother. I drank cocktails, learned to jitterbug and Tony is going to get me some nylons.'

Jack scraped at his pipe. 'I wish you wouldn't do that when we're having breakfast' Vera scolded. Jack made no reply but stuck the pipe back in his pocket.

'What about Joyce.......and Doris, did they learn to jitterbug?'

Kitty frowned at her mother, 'Joyce did and stop worrying about Doris, Mum, she was as good as gold.'

'Hope so with her fiancee fighting his way up Italy.' Jack stood up and looked out of the window at his vegetables.

'The Yanks are doing their bit too, Dad. This one I was dancing with he....'

Jack leant further towards the window studying his beetroot, 'They were a bit late on parade,' he muttered.

Kitty ignored the comment and spread some margarine thinly on her toast. She turned to her mother, 'They were very polite, treated us like real ladies, they did. And they were so generous...'

Jack swivelled round and faced them, 'Generous. They can afford to be generous can't they? I mean here we are living on the bare minimum, even the youngsters sweets are rationed, no one allowed to drive for pleasure as they put it and what are these Yanks doing? Handing out candy to the kids, all manner of goodies to the girls and racing around in those Jeep things on the wrong side of the road. Load of show offs if you ask me.'

He sat down with a thump and slapped open the *Evening Star*. Vera got up and started to clear the table. Nobody spoke for quite a while and then Jack took out his pipe and began to fill it with tobacco from his worn pouch, 'Syd's boy was killed last week,' he said quietly.' Two more sons of blokes on my line are reported missing and you go around having a good time with RAF types, Black Market crooks and now Yanks.'

Kitty stood up, 'I used to go around, as you put it, with a boy called Alan. Remember him, Dad?' and she walked from the room. They heard her go up the stairs. Jack lit his pipe and went out of the back door into the garden and started to count his carrots.

205

IOWA

'Our common tongue is a priceless inheritance.' - Winston Churchill.

War or no war the people of Red Oak continued to go into town on a Saturday night, to shop, sit around Fountain Square, gossip and watch the children play on the grass. The only army present were the Salvation Army whose band, depleted somewhat by the absence of young men, played steadfastly on Northside.

Karl, after wandering along the sidewalk chatting to a few farming friends, deposited himself on a seat in the shade and waited for Lois. Eventually he spied her coming out of The Ideal Pharmacy clutching two bags. She tried to wave with some difficulty, crossed the road and plumped down beside him.

'I'm getting old. A little bit of shopping and I'm ready to sit down,' she laughed.

'It is Saturday and you haven't exactly been slacking during the week.' Karl poured some lemonade. This war will put years on both of us by the time it's over, he thought. He was already missing Tom's contribution on the farm and in spite of what the Government said there wasn't much sign of young female labour. *Rosie the Riveter* appeared on posters everywhere but she and all the other Rosies obviously worked in the factories.

Lois put a hand on his, 'Just what are you fretting about now, sitting there all quiet like?'

'Usual thing, the farm, the crops, the animals, how I'm going cope without having Tom around.'

'Strange you should say that, as I was coming across the square it struck me, yet again, that there were no young men about. It made me shudder, Karl.'

Karl poked his tobacco down into the bowl of his pipe, 'I suppose we should be grateful that as far as Tom is concerned he's working on the aircraft and not flying in them. That way he's a reasonable chance of survival.'

'Pray to God you're right.' Lois sipped her drink, ' His last letter was a bit of a tonic in a way. He seems happier now he's gone to a fighter station. Seemed to enjoy the parade or whatever it was when they finally took the place over.'

'Hand Over Parade that's what he called it. Said the bands played and they all marched past the top brass and local dignitaries before there was a ceremonious taking down of one flag and raising another. The Brits had been there and now our boys have taken it over. Where was it again? Martlesham Heath, that's it, Martlesham Heath.'

'What are you two gossiping about?' As always on a Saturday their oldest friends the Linquists ambled over for chat.

'Hi Lester, Hi Patty, here we've saved your seats.'

'So how are you doing?' Lester began as always, ' Any more news from Sergeant Tom?'

'Surprise, surprise we were just saying he's moved to a new camp and seems really excited that he is now part of a team working on his beloved Thunderbolts. Seems to be what he's been waiting for. Apparently they escort the big bombers on the raids over Germany,' he sighed, ' I find it all so difficult to imagine.'

'I'm glad you said that,' Lois chipped in, ' I can't seem to visualise England at all. Tom tries to describe it in his letters but always ends up saying that the English folk are having a really tough time but he doesn't really tell us what the country looks like. Anyhow Patty, I'm sure glad we sent those blankets and bundles from the church.'

Patty, who had seemed quieter than usual, added, ' Sure, You know what, I was in Des Moines last week and saw these posters suggesting that we could all be bombed here in the USA, just like in England. But there's something more important I have to tell you.'

'Those posters are just trying to make sure that our boys know what they are going to fight for. Trying to scare them into enlisting, that's all. Sorry Patty what were you saying?' Karl realised he had butted in. Patty had tears in her eyes.

'It's Letha. She's got herself a deferment from University and has enlisted as a WAAC' she blurted in out in one breath.

'She's done what?' Lois was shocked.

'She says it's her duty and that at Nebraska they were encouraging girls to defer. Says not to worry she'll only be required to do administrative duties. She has no idea what war is about. Not that I know much but that daughter of ours knows even less.'

Lester took up the story, trying to sound calm, 'You know what I think? I think it's the lure of travel. She's dropped these hints from time to time about wanting to see the world. The odd little comment. Thought we didn't notice but we did.'

'I blame this Dexter. As soon as he qualified what did he do? He enlisted in the Navy. Some sort of romantic notion if you ask me. But there's no talking her out of it. It's her patriotic duty she says.'

'In a way you should be proud of her,' Karl said, sucking his now empty pipe, ' like we are of Tom. Miss him like mad but still proud of him.'

'Well, we are, of course. Letha has always made us proud of her.' Lester paused and looked around the square,' You know something? I always kindled a sort of hope that your Tom and our Letha might get together but then she met this Dexter guy and I guess that was it.'

'The Yanks are coming...so beware.' - line from song *'Over There.'*

'Of course you'll come. It's only a drinks thing. Probably be all over in an hour.'

Sylvia and Doris were in Limmers having tea.

Smart Ipswich ladies, who had frequented Limmers for years, leant back in their blue cane chairs craning their necks to look at the American clientele the restaurant now attracted. For their part the Americans slouched in the chairs like plasticine models. Obviously their parents had never rapped their knuckles for failing to sit up straight at the meal table. Early experience had taught them to order tea since the coffee tasted nothing like the beverage of the same name served back home. For that matter neither did the tea but they were prepared to accept that tea was a British habit and one that they should try to cultivate.

'It'll just be like coming here for tea but with alcohol instead.' Sylvia was persistent.

Doris hadn't confided in Sylvia about her trip to Debach and now, confronted with this latest request, decided that it was best to keep that experience to herself. She dribbled milk into the cups and poured the tea, 'But I won't know anyone. I'm not very good with people I don't know. Especially, you know, people who speak properly and all that.'

'Rubbish. Any way you're invited to socialise with the Yanks, I mean the American officers, not the Ipswich upper crust and I've a sneaking feeling they'll certainly want to chat to you.'

Doris was finding this difficult, ' And that's another thing, what about Jimmy? I am engaged you know.' She couldn't help thinking of Oakey and how nice he had been and of the guilt she had felt later.

'And I'm a married woman who's been instructed by my father-in-law that I jolly well have to socialise with them, like it or not. All part of his campaign for harmony with our US allies.'

Doris was certain the woman on the next table with the green pillbox hat had transferred her eves dropping from the pair of well-groomed Americans to this more interesting dilemma.

'And another thing. I haven't anything suitable to wear.'

'Good girl that means you'll come then.' The lady with the pillbox leant over the glass-topped table and whispered to her friend.

It was a warm evening for a change and Doris walked from the Bus Depot up towards the park trying to memorise the directions to the Sylvan House. She was wearing a new utility style mustard coloured dress and had decided to let her hair hang lose over her shoulders. Sylvia, who was about her size, had lent her some fancy shoes which not only looked good but also were comfortable and, joy of joys, Kitty had given her a pair of nylons.

Doris found the house easily and walked up the steps to the impressive entrance. The front door was open. She heard the hubbub of voices and stepping in was aware that everyone seemed to have their backs to her. Coffee coloured smooth uniformed backs, dark brown gabardine backs, posh frock backs.

'Sherry madam?' said a girl dressed as a waitress.

'Thank you,' she said taking a deep breath. She couldn't see Sylvia anywhere and so taking care with her sherry she wormed her way into a reception room off the hall.

'You look as lost as I am.' He had a soft drawl.

'Oh. Sorry, did I really. I've only just arrived and was looking for Sylvia. You know Sylvia Cameron,' she blurted looking up at a tanned face.

' I'm Sam Rogers. Lieutenant Sam Rogers,' he pronounced it *Lootenant*

'Doris,' she said, 'Doris Harper.'

'So where are you from Captain?' Sylvia asked automatically, whilst craning her neck to see if Doris had arrived.

'A little place called Sausalito, California but you wouldn't have heard of it.'

'How do you know that?' she asked, feeling he was putting her down.

His eyes lit up, 'You have heard of it? You have heard of Sausalito?'

'Well no, I haven't actually, but you had no right to assume that I hadn't.'

Chuck Taylor looked bemused, he found American women difficult to understand at times but these British ones were even more perverse.

210

'Point taken Mrs. Cameron,' he said, 'but you would love it. Or you would have loved it before they started building the liberty ships. Now it's one big marine works.'

What a smoothie, she thought, and then out of the corner of her eye spotted Doris by the door, 'Will you excuse me Captain, I have to look after a guest who has just arrived. Perhaps you could tell me more about your Saulsal... whatever, later.'

'Wonderful news about the Italian surrender, colonel.'

'Sure is but the Germans are piling in to put up a stiff resistance down at the toe.'

Robert was enjoying his conversation with this surprisingly articulate and informed American. 'Things look more promising though. We have been in retreat everywhere for far too long.'

'Too right. You know something the longer we are here in England and the more we are finding out about the blitz. We begin to wonder how much more the British people can put up with.'

'As much as it takes, colonel, as much as it takes.'

'There you are darling. You couldn't pop into the kitchen could you? Valerie is in a bit of a flap,' Elizabeth resplendent in turquoise confronted her daughter.

'What! I was just off to greet Doris but yes, OK, I'll trot along in a minute.'

Sylvia slid past her mother and found her friend surrounded by the overseas guests.

And this was the girl who had worried about socialising?

'Doris, sorry I did spot you but then mother intervened. Some panic with the catering.'

' I'm fine thanks, these chaps are looking after me very well.'

'Doris has been telling us all about the work you all do during the raids. Seems you've seen more of the war than all of us put together. On top of that you stage a welcome like this for us. I call that very...British,' Sam butted in.

Sylvia decided she liked him better than that arrogant Captain she had met earlier.

'More sherry, madam?'

'Here we are boys, this is what the British drink, sherry, loads of sherry.'

Sylvia looked closely at her friend and realised that some of the new found confidence was coming from the Dry Fly bottle, 'Back in a minute,' she announced and scuttled off to find mother-in-law.

'Oh Sylvia dear, thank goodness you've come. You see there seem to be far more Americans than anticipated. Robert's invitation was a shade too open, I'm afraid. I'm so worried there won't be enough nibbles to go round.'

The large solid table in the middle of the kitchen was laden with sausage rolls, cheese straws and all manner of tiny sandwiches. Four young girls, who she recognised as borrowed from Grimstones, stood nervously in their white aprons and black skirts.

'The Americans know there's a war on, if not they wouldn't be here and as long as there's plenty of liquor, as they call it, they'll be happy enough. I suggest the girls take a plate each and mingle. If they receive any adverse comments they should smile sweetly and remind them we're on rations over here.'

'Thank you dear, I'm sure you're right. Have you got that girls? Then off you go.'

The girls stepped timidly forward, nudging each other and giggling before picking up the plates and making their way to the reception rooms.

Sylvia, feeling the need for air, opened the back door and went into the garden. She remembered how beautiful it had been before the war. The brick walls covered in honeysuckle, ivy, climbing roses and clematis; the lawn lightly cut sloping upwards from a small terrace where Valerie always had pots full of seasonal blooms. An ancient apple tree jutting from the west wall and the borders resplendent with herbaceous perennials. Now it was all dug up, of course, a sheltered and successful vegetable patch spread around the gnarled apple tree whose branches had yielded well this year. It was still warm and she lit a cigarette.

'You escaping the party already?'

Damn, it was that cocky Captain. 'Just having a break and remembering how this garden used to be before the war,' she said.

'Tell me about it?'

And so she did and he listened. Then he asked where she lived and about her garden and soon, to her surprise, she found herself talking of Francis and of their hasty marriage and their little cottage, of their plans for something grander when all this was over. But then she told him that she wasn't sure whether she thought such things were important any more.

'Just to have him back would do,' he said.

Sylvia looked at him closely. She saw cropped hair, deep brown eyes and lips that were a shade too full. She saw a kinder man than the one she had encountered inside, 'Can I say something that may sound a trifle rude?'

'Well I don't think you're the sort who holds back.' He was smiling.

'I found you a bit annoying in there but out here you're much better.'

'Perhaps we better stay out here then. The fact is I'm not too good at the small talk thing. I didn't mean to be patronising in there it just came out all wrong. Can't we be friends?'

Sylvia looked again into his eyes and extended her hand, 'Friends,' she said, ' and talking of friends I really should be getting back inside to my friends, my other friends that is, they'll be wondering where I've been.'

'I don't usually drink much and certainly not sherry,' Doris was explaining to Sam who had insisted that she needed a gin and tonic to wash down the potted meat sandwich.

'What do you normally drink, Doris. If I took you to a pub what would you order?'

'Oh a shandy. That's not very alcoholic you see.'

'Do you have ice in that?'

'We don't have ice in anything.' Memories of the dance came into her head, 'You have ice in everything don't you. Your Mint Juleps have loads of ice in them.'

Sam burst into laughter, ' There's a lot more to you than meets the eye, Doris. I think you're wonderful. I might just take you to a pub and buy you a Mint Julep.'

Doris laughed with him placing a hand on his arm to steady herself.

'Some one is having a good time. Now Doris let me introduce you to Audrey, one of my dearest friends.' Sylvia appeared at her elbow with a tall blonde.

Doris looked up and smiled. She thought Audrey looked fun.

'Hello, I've heard all about you as well. You're in the WVS aren't you?' She felt she was speaking clearly, if a bit loudly.

'That's right and you're a First Aider.'

Sam was moving from one foot to another looking uncomfortable.

'Oh. Where are my manners,' said Doris, 'This is Sam, Lootenant Sam.'

'Lootenant Sam', mimed Sylvia. Sam looked confused and then shook hands with the two girls. Doris excused herself clutching her handbag. She was impressed to find that the Camerons had a downstairs toilet and after washing her hands she splashed cold water onto her face and examined herself in the mirror. Doris you are a little tipsy, she decided, so you'd better stop now before you do something really stupid. Then she applied some fresh lipstick, giggled, and returned to the party.

'Ladies and Gentleman, your attention for just a moment please,' Robert's voice rang out and after a few coughs the general conversation ceased. Robert continued, ' I just wanted to take this opportunity to officially welcome our friends from USAAF Martlesham Heath. We know that soon after moving in they and their men became engaged in some particularly dangerous missions and that as the months roll on they will continue to risk all to help rid the world of the Nazi scourge. We ask that you be patient with us Ipswich people as we get used to your ways and you ours but I am convinced your presence will help us believe in the sort of future we all crave for. Good Luck to all of you.'

Everybody clapped and Sylvia whispered to Doris that Robert liked to sound like Winston Churchill. Then the Colonel clapped his hands together. He was a big man.

'Robert, Valerie, Ladies and Gentlemen. On behalf of the officers of 356 Fighter Group may I thank you all for this wonderful gesture. Naturally I cannot give anything away since I have read your posters about Careless Words etc. but I can assure you that USAAF Martlesham Heath will be at the forefront of inflicting telling damage on the enemy. Our men, like yours all over the world, are under great pressure and when off duty or on furlough will no doubt seek to enjoy themselves as young men do but we have impressed upon them that they are visitors to your country and must respect that. God Bless you all.'

There was more applause and the Colonel shook hands with Robert and Valerie and made his way from the room. This seemed to be the signal for the party to break up and Sam turned to Doris and asked how she intended getting home. She muttered something which he didn't understand and then offered her a lift in his jeep. To her surprise she agreed.

Sylvia sought out Chuck Taylor, what a ridiculous name she thought, and they shook hands politely.

'Thank you ....Sylvia it has been good meeting you,' he said and left with a group of fellow officers.

Sam assured Doris that he hadn't had much to drink and knew he had to drive on the left-hand side of the road. She wondered who had travelled in the jeep with him to the party but he must have bribed whoever it was since she was the only passenger. He drove carefully through the blackout and, as directed by her, up the hill towards her home.

The breeze took her hair and she loved the sensation. She knew she had had far too much to drink but she was sensible enough to work out that she didn't want the jeep drawing up anywhere near her house so she directed Sam to the Levington Road crossing. It was a reasonably clear night and there was no sign of any activity from our boys or Jerry.

She could just about make out his face.

'Thank you Sam. You've been very kind. I'm not usually like this. As I said I don't drink this much as a rule..' She had hardly completed the sentence when his arms went around her and they were kissing. She didn't feel he had taken advantage of her it was simply that he took her by surprise and then she surprised herself by kissing him back. He was whispering to her but she couldn't hear, then his hands began to wander somewhat freely over her dress. She pulled away.

'Sam, I'm sorry. I don't know what came over me. We shouldn't be doing this. We really shouldn't.'

'I think you're lovely,' he murmured, his arms went around her again; firmer and more insistent this time. She managed to push him away.

He looked up, seemingly unabashed, 'Sorry was I going too fast. Here I have an idea why don't I buy you that shandy some time next week. How can I get in contact with you?'

'No Sam, you don't understand. I have a fiancée, he's fighting in Egypt and I don't cheat on him. It's not fair. It was just so lovely to have someone kiss me again and you are very nice to kiss.' She was aware that she was babbling as she climbed out of the jeep. 'Goodbye Sam. Look after yourself.'

As she walked down between the trees towards Avondale Road it started to rain.

Two nights later Doris was on duty when a major incident was reported at Kesgrave. Jerry had dropped three bombs, firemen and wardens were already working in the smouldering remains of what had once been a home. They were directed to what remained of an Anderson shelter and immediately started to help with the wounded. The shelter had received a direct hit killing a woman and her two children and badly injuring her husband. The house next door had also been damaged and Doris treated its occupants for minor injuries.

She returned home at three in the morning, collapsed onto her bed and sobbed uncontrollably.

She was working in her little garden, tidying up the leeks, when he arrived. There was a scrunch of wheels on the drive, the slamming of a door and there he was.

'Mrs. Cameron, how nice to see you.'

She ran her dirty fingers through her hair and stared at him. Then she grinned.

' How ever did you find me?'

'Simple, you told me your cottage was in the grounds of Hall Farm, Playford, where your parents lived, and so I looked you up on the map and here I am.'

Did she really give him her address? She couldn't remember or didn't want to admit it to herself. It was two weeks ago and a lot had happened. There had been a couple of big incidents and she had been busy at the centres sorting out the homeless. The welcome party seemed a long time ago. Sylvia propped her hoe against the cottage wall and wiped her grubby hands on her slacks. She was wearing wellies and must have looked a sight.

'As you can see you have caught me completely by surprise. Would you like a cup of tea?'

'That sounds so English. Yes please, I'd love a cup of tea.'

Sylvia grabbed a couple of care worn deck chairs from behind the shed, 'Let's have it out here. It's such a lovely day.'

Seeing she was struggling he took the chairs from her, 'I'll manage these while you put the tea on. I think that's the correct expression,' he said.

Sylvia scurried off into the cottage, filled the kettle and then went up the stairs two at a time to the bathroom. She quickly washed off the grime, checked her hair and applied a smidgen of lipstick. What was he doing here? Is this what Americans do? Drop in unannounced on people they hardly know.

When she returned to the garden he was sitting back in one of the deck chairs looking completely at home. The second chair was positioned close to the first with a small piece of grass between them where she placed the tray. 'I hope it's strong enough for you. The tea I mean not the chair.' She sat down noting a small rip in the canvas.

He offered her a cigarette and tapped it out of the packet like she had seen Americans do in films. For some reason this small action underlined the differences between them. Two countries speaking the same language divided by an ocean as someone had said.' 'So what have you been up to, Chuck?' She had not used his name in that way before.

'We've been pretty busy escorting the bombers on runs over Germany. This is the first time I've been off base since we met at the party.'

Very impressive but I haven't exactly been idling my time away she thought but decided not to say anything.

'I don't remember asking what it was that you do exactly. In your airforce I mean?'

'I fly,' he said, 'I fly B47 Thunderbolts. They're fighters, you've probably seen them roaring about overhead.'

For some reason she went cold. She hadn't imagined him as a pilot. Not that she thought of him much at all of course. Then she recalled their talk in the garden and how she found him easy to be with, how she probably told him far too much about herself. Then, ignoring her internal voice, she found herself telling him again. Telling him about Francis who she assumed had now left Sicily. Telling him how she understood that he couldn't write when in the middle of battle. Suddenly she had to know whether he was married. Was there a Mrs. Chuck Taylor? Were there children back in California? He told her he was married, to Helen, there were no children. They had tried but no luck. These things couldn't be planned. Quickly Sylvia changed the subject to where he lived. He was impressed she knew about the Golden Gate Bridge. He explained how this opened up the whole of Marin County including Sausalito, he reminded her that was where he lived. She didn't need reminding she had looked it up in her atlas.

So she gave him a tour of her small garden and since he wanted to use the bathroom as he called it (she couldn't imagine he wanted a bath) she showed him the downstairs rooms of her cottage. He said it was just what he imagined an English home would be like. Just like on the movies.

Then he announced he had to get back to base. 'I've had a really good time,' he said, 'I can't tell you how wonderful it is to get away from it all and talk of other things. Thank you Sylvia,' he held out a hand and she shook it politely.

'Drop in any time,' she heard herself say.

'I might just do that,' he said and she watched as he climbed easily into the jeep, spun the wheel and disappeared down the drive.

'Oakey was asking about you,' Kitty dug into her handbag and produced a packet of *Lucky Strike*. Would you like one?'

'Oh, go on just one,' Doris wasn't a great smoker but, there again, until the night of the party she didn't think she was a great drinker.

Kitty screwed up her face in concentration and tapped the end of the packet. About six cigarettes fell onto the ground. Both girls giggled helplessly.

'Less of that noise, I'm trying to work in here,' Mr. French's voice came from the dispensary.

'Miserable old sod,' whispered Kitty, 'it's your lunch hour.'

'He's only trying to be funny,' Doris assured her. She knew Mr. French liked to eaves'drop. He said he was going to write a book about Joyce and her one day.

'I hope you reminded this Oakey that I am engaged. After all you are virtually my sister-in-law.'

'Of course I have. But Doris, these Yanks are a breath of fresh air I can tell you and so generous. Fags, nylons, candy (that's sweets and things) and they love a bit of fun. They're only boys away from home and I take it as my duty to give them a bit of comfort and understanding. I mean, in spite of what my dad says, they are on our side. It's not as though I'm going out with Germans.'

Kitty was a tonic, no wonder the Yanks loved her. She wasn't stupid either. Played the field a bit, didn't get hooked on one particular chap.

'You know you never told me much about that posh party you went to, the one with the Yank officers. I got you the nylons, remember?'

'Oh it was OK, lovely house and lots of snobby people plus some Yanks. Nothing like the dances you go to.'

'Well we don't fit in with officers do we? So are you coming out tonight with Joyce and me to meet some of our Yank friends. Just a drink, that's all.'

'Thanks but no. I've really been busy lately. Quite a lot of raids and some first aid training. I'll take it easy for a while. I'm fine on my own really I am.'

Kitty stubbed out her cigarette, 'OK, I'll tell you what. You and me will go to the pictures again soon. Just the two of us.'

'Thanks Kitty. That would be great.'

Chuck was as good as his word. From time to time, usually when she was least expecting it, he would drop in at the cottage and because of this Sylvia spent more of her free time there. She worked hard on the garden and even tried her hand at decorating the kitchen.

Sometimes he would call when she was out working at the Rest Centres or involved in the latest drive for aluminium utensils and there would be a brief scribbled note awaiting her return. He had terrible handwriting. On such occasions she would shrug her shoulders and pretend it didn't matter but deep down she felt a pang of disappointment. She wasn't completely in charge of her emotions but convinced herself that she had nothing to be ashamed of. It was an innocent war time friendship.

He didn't talk much of his flying but she found herself worrying when she hadn't seen or heard from him for a while. She noticed the bombers and escorts go out early morning and watched for their return later in the day. She didn't count them in and out but wondered whether he was amongst them. What really worried her was that she didn't have the same fears for Francis but then, she tried to convince herself, that was because he was so far away. His letters came in fits and starts as ever. They were always brief and to the point and, for obvious reasons, contained little of the war itself. They were peppered with vague accounts of lighter moments with his friend Bruce and others. She had no way of knowing whether any of the 'others' were female. That was it really. Francis never wrote of feelings only facts. Inevitably he concluded by telling her not to worry but she did. She worried about Francis himself.

'It's so difficult to get to grips with the class system over here,' Chuck announced one day, 'it's something we don't have in the States.' They were sitting in the cottage sipping American beer for which Sylvia had developed a taste.

'Well that's because of our history, feudal times and all that. You don't have enough history for a class system to have developed. But it's changing over here. This war is changing it.'

'You really think so?' Sometimes he seemed to be spoiling for an argument.

'Yes, particularly among my generation. I mean take Doris, one of my best friends and she's from a humble background. She's bright and intelligent and we have loads in common.'

'So what does your mother think of Doris?'

'My mother! She hardly knows her. You're not suggesting my mother is a snob I hope?' but she was thinking of Elizabeth's comment when she first met Doris – *Nice girl, pity about the accent* .

He was laughing, 'Now don't go getting all prickly on me. I was simply suggesting your mother is from a generation who believe that the class system is the backbone of England.'

'Well at least you're admitting that my age group want to challenge that.'

'Of course,' He was still smiling.

'Anyhow you Americans have double standards as well, you know. Coming over here criticising our so called class system when you segregate your blacks from the whites.'

'That's different. It's better for both if we do that.'

'Nonsense. They're fighting for America aren't they? Taking the same risks. Wearing the same uniform.'

'They do different sort of jobs.' He knew that sounded lame.

'Exactly. How many black pilots are there?'

Chuck gazed out of the window and then took a packed of *Camel* from his top pocket, 'Cigarette?'

'Thanks.' She took the cigarette and waited for him to light it. He leaned over and she felt the touch of his hand. Stupid girl, she thought, you've been watching too many films.

He looked at her again, 'You're right, of course, I gave you the official answer but the truth is that you make me feel ashamed. Fighting alongside the black guys must change our attitudes. Like your class thing I hope that side of our country changes for the better when this war is over.'

They were quiet for a while and then she went to her record collection, 'Enough politics for one day, I think. Let's have some music. Tommy Dorsey all right?'

He stayed for about another hour and they talked of other things; of Hemingway and Orwell, of Noel Coward's new film, of Suffolk before the war. Finally he stood up and took both her hands, 'Still friends then?' he asked.

Sylvia smiled making no attempt to remove her hands, 'Of course. That's one of the things I like about you. We can talk seriously, even disagree, but you listen and try to understand where I'm coming from.'

She leaned forward and kissed him gently on the cheek, 'Come and see me soon,' she said.

'They're going to have their own club in Carr Street.'

'What do you mean club?'

It was Sunday and Kitty was updating Doris on Anglo-American relations over a cup of tea and a *Lucky Strike*. Vera had gone into the garden to dig up some vegetables. Doris, whose father was on duty and mother working overtime, had been invited to lunch. She had brought a cauliflower and some cheese.

'A club with their sort of things in. Coke and hot dogs and strong coffee. Set up by the Red Cross and run by some American Woman but they want English girls to help. Half a mind to volunteer. Beats Pipers any day. Mind you Brad says he'll still go the pubs.'

'Who's Brad? Is he the latest?'

'No just one of the many. He's a bit too fond of the whisky to be serious.'

'Judging by the stories people tell us in the shop some of them do sound a bit wild. Crashing their jeeps, falling off their bikes. Joyce says it's because all roads in the USA are straight so they're not used to going round corners. I said it's because they're not used to our whisky. I told her I wasn't born yesterday.'

'When were you born, dear? I ought to know when your birthday is?' Vera came in through the back door with a basket of potatoes and leeks. 'The leeks looked the best in the end. Now when did you say and I'll write it down.'

'October, October the tenth. So how are you, Mrs Wright?'

'Not too bad considering. Been busy at work but at least I was on the day shift.'

'And Mr Wright?'

'Same for him really, not too many visits from Jerry. Until last night that is, now he's gone off in a right old rage.'

Kitty was giggling and insisted in telling the story. Some incendiary bombs had missed their target and landed on the allotments in Holywells park setting fire to one or two sheds and causing havoc. Syd Green had been round that morning and reported that a whole load of kids had been sent by their parents to help themselves to the disturbed vegetables. Said they were anyones. On cue, Jack's head and shoulders went past the kitchen window. When he came in Doris didn't think he looked particularly grumpy.

'Well?' Vera demanded, 'rescued the veg, have you?'

'Sort of. It's not that bad really. But Syd was right, when we got there a handful of youngsters were helping themselves but they scampered off when they saw us coming. Apart from one lad, he couldn't have been more than six and was clinging to some of my best beetroot. I got him by the collar and asked him what he was up to. *My mum said it was all right,* he whimpered. *Well I say it isn't. What's your name son?* He looked at me with great big eyes and he said, *Tommy Handley.* I was laughing so much I had to let him go. *Tommy Handley* indeed.'

Vera wiped her eyes, 'You're a hard man Jack Wright. If that Hitler could see you in action he'd call off the war tomorrow.' They all laughed together. Doris wished her parents could laugh like that. Jack went to the sink and washed his hands, drying them on a tea towel. Vera looked at the girls and shrugged.

After lunch they sat back and Jack updated them on the war. He was enthusiastic about the RAF raids on Germany's industrial cities even admitting that the Yanks were doing their bit. He felt it was wonderful that the Ruskies were fighting so hard in Stalingrad and he was excited about our progress in Italy. Doris said that Jimmy had now left

223

Sicily, she had heard from him on Friday. She didn't tell them that she cried herself to sleep.

'Even your Yanks are getting into it a bit now. Pity they didn't join in a bit earlier.' Jack got in a dig at Kitty. She ignored him and attempting to change the subject turned to Doris.

'You still haven't said much about this posh party you went to?'

'It was nothing. I only went to please my friend Sylvia.'

'Is that the Sylvia we met in the pub once?' Vera liked to keep up to date.

'That's the one, she's what Kitty calls my swanky friend. She's married to an officer.'

Jack scratched his chin, 'You want to keep away from that lot. Stick to your own kind, I say. Always been like that around here and always will be.'

'I seem to remember you took quite a shine to her in the *Catchpole* that night,' Vera reminded him.

'That's nothing to do with it,' Jack grumbled.

'She's a very good friend. She says all this class nonsense will disappear after the war.' 'Doris felt her face go red.

'Bosses and workers don't mix. Officers and men don't mix. Jimmy would see it that way as well. He's seen it in the factory when one or the other steps over the line. Seeing it in the army as well, I reckon. The classes just don't mix.'

Doris stood up and started to clear away the dishes. Kitty joined her and whispered that she was sorry she ever mentioned the subject. Doris shrugged and clattered the plates in the sink. Jack lit up his pipe and went into the garden.

When the washing up was finished Doris announced that she ought to go and Vera put her arms around her and gave a squeeze without saying anything. Doris knew she had upset them.

She walked home with all sorts of thoughts swirling around in her head. She seemed to mess everything up these days. She was aware that the siren went and seconds later heard the guns from the docks and then a great ball of fire emerged from the clouds spiralling downwards. She crouched down by the nearest fence and heard a frightening crash. Lumps of shrapnel, like red hot metal hailstones, pinged on the road. It was a miracle that she wasn't hit.

'Got any gum chum?' – everyone under twelve.

The Christmas of 1943 was very much the same as those of 41 and 42 except that this times the Yanks were here.

Walking up the Buttermarket in mid December Doris was aware of the sparsely decorated shop windows; she knew stockings would be filled with home-made presents, chickens would only be eaten by those willing to trade on the black market, ancient family decorations would loop across ceilings, carollers would be urged not to ring hand bells and churches would black out stain-glass windows. She also knew that across Suffolk, as in the rest of the country, people would make the best of it; they would play silly games, laugh with Tommy Handley and Arthur Askey on the wireless, sing along with Vera Lynn and cry a little for loved ones across the war torn world.

She hadn't seen Sylvia for a week or two. Both of them busy with Civil Defence activities, with work, with families. It was, therefore, with a spring in her step that she entered Limmers for afternoon tea.

Sylvia was already there, seated in one of the tired looking Lloyd Loom chairs, elbows resting on the glass topped table, a cigarette dangling in her hand. The usual Ipswich ladies, blissfully unaware that the war had changed anything, sipped their drinks and exchanged gossip; the now familiar Americans slouched in their cane seats as if lolling on some Californian beach and the waitresses contrived to ignore everybody.

'You look like something out of a film,' Doris greeted her friend.

'As long as I'm not Mrs. Miniver.' Sylvia pushed back a chair.

'So how have you been?'

'Fine....I think.'

'You only think. This is not Sylvia the decision-maker talking,' Doris teased.

'Sorry I'm fine. Absolutely fine.'

'I had a letter yesterday. Jimmy's somewhere in Italy and seems in fine spirits. He's been so much better since they invaded Sicily. Says when we have a family he's never going to build sand castles for our kids. Fancy him thinking about our having kids?'

225

Sylvia stubbed out her cigarette, 'You're a lucky girl, Doris. I'm really looking forward to meeting this Jimmy, even if he will think I'm swanky.'

'You know you're not you're just a bit.....'

'Posh,' they both laughed at the shared joke.

'Right now, I've ordered tea so let's get down to business. The Yanks at Martlesham want to throw a huge Christmas party for the kids of Ipswich. You know the kids who have had a bad time, those who have lost their homes, and in some cases lost parents and there's some whose families just can't afford a Christmas at all. Chuck has officially asked me, on behalf of their committee, to produce a list of youngsters. He says they will arrange the liberty trucks to pick them up, they'll provide loads of food and entertainment. Chuck wants this to be the best day they've had for a long, long time.'

'Hold on, hold on. This all sounds wonderful but am I allowed one question. Who is this person with the funny name?' Doris seized her moment to interrupt the enthusing Sylvia.

'Chuck? I suppose it is rather a silly name, isn't it. I hadn't really thought about it. Well, anyway, the Yank with the silly name is one of the officers I met at the party and when he found out my role with the Civil Defence he decided I was the person to liaise with.'

'To liaise with?'

'He's on the liaison committee. He was the one I told you I wasn't sure about, remember? Well he is a bit better than I first thought and he is very keen on this Christmas party idea.'

A tall waitress bent over them and sniffed, 'Tea for two,' she announced.

'Thanks. Thanks very much,' Sylvia said and smiled at her. There was no response.

'I'll pour, so you can tell me more,' Doris said.

Sylvia took out her silver cigarette case and offered her friend a cigarette. They lit up. Doris watched the smoke drift upwards towards the yellow ceiling.

'Well you've got the gist of it I think. I'm busy consulting with the Rest centres and putting together this list and we'll take it from there. There is one thing however, although Chuck is adamant that the Yanks will do everything he does feel we need one or two British women to act a chaperones for the kids. You know some of them might be a bit frightened by it all and need someone not in uniform. I wondered whether you might like to help. I've asked Audrey and a couple of other WVS girls but then I thought about your sister-in-law as you call her?'

'Kitty. Oh yes. I'm sure Kitty will come anywhere there are Yanks,' and then feeling a bit guilty, she added, 'and she's got a heart of gold so she'd be ideal for the children. Obviously I'll be there. I want to see this Chuck.'

Sylvia laughed, 'Now stop it. I told you this is business.'

As they rose to leave Doris turned to Sylvia, 'I am sorry, what with all this flurry of excitement I forgot to ask if you had heard from Francis?'

Sylvia smiled, 'Yes I did get a letter. A few days ago. He's all right....as much as one can tell.'

Tom sat on the end of his bed re-reading a letter from his mother. Most of the guys were either working or had gone to investigate the recently opened Red X club so for once things were a bit quiet.

His mother insisted that although Ben and himself would be in their thoughts during the Christmas period she was determined to provide the usual spread for the remaining members of the Nelson family. Ellen and young Luke, who was now apparently running around talking to anyone who would listen, were coming for the Christmas Day meal. His mom and dad would, of course, be going to the carol service on Christmas Eve and he would be in their prayers. She had seen Betty Linquist recently and learned that Letha would be coming home for the holiday though it was likely that she would be posted overseas soon after. More and more young girls in the US were enlisting and the Linquists were getting used to the idea of Letha being in WAAC uniform. Tom smiled to himself thinking that Letha would look pretty good in any uniform. He flipped the page and sighed, wishing he could be with them all. The second page of the letter was virtually a string of questions since Lois seemed determined to build an accurate picture of this foreign place where her son was now living. He had tried to describe England to her but it seemed she still couldn't quite fathom it out. She went on to say she was pleased to hear he was getting out a bit more and finished by sending love from all the family, promising to say a special prayer for him at Christmas. Tom folded the letter and put it in his top pocket. His mom would be pleased to know that he was about to help entertain a load of local kids at a special party.

Two hundred youngsters, wrapped up against the cold, labelled by name and centre, holding onto one another with gloved hands let out one enormous cheer as the liberty trucks trundled into The Old Cattle Market. Held back by Sylvia and her helpers they jumped up and down in eager anticipation and as the US drivers climbed down from the cabs and came over quite a number shouted out *Got any gum chum?* Sylvia was pleased to see the Yanks laughed and shouted back that they had gum and lots of other goodies if the kids could now climb aboard in some sort of orderly fashion. As they said this they looked hopefully towards the English women who rather like a band of nannies walked purposely forward with their selected groups in tow. Eventually children and grown up escorts were all accounted for and the trucks ambled forward in convoy.

Doris suggested to her group that they should sing carols and before long the streets of Ipswich and lanes of Martlesham echoed to *Away in a manger*. One small girl confided that she wasn't quite sure what a manger was and Doris did her best to explain.

At last they arrived at USAAF Martlesham Heath where the convoy stopped outside a large hangar. The children were herded out and directed to the entrance door. Once inside, they stood open mouthed and silent and then unleashed a collective scream.

The whole hangar was decorated outrageously in all manner of trimmings and fairy lights; a giant Christmas tree (Sylvia later found out it had been cut down illegally) stood guard over a line of B47s which were almost as fascinating to the children as the glitter. Large tables were set up with a party hat and a tumbler containing coloured straws in front of each chair. Jugs of lemonade stood like sentries along the middle of the tables, tubes of tomato sauce and mustard abounded and army issue cutlery suggested something more substantial might appear any minute.

The children were shepherded to their seats and with a flourish US serviceman wearing white aprons appeared carrying plates full of what they called hot dogs.

Then the Americans instructed the youngsters in the art of squeezing the sauces onto what turned out to be sausages in the rolls. Soon the youngsters were laughing at each others faces smeared red and yellow like so many clowns.

'I hope there's some left for us,' Kitty nudged Doris, ' not that I want to deprive the kids of course.'

'They're good with them aren't they, the Yanks I mean, they're good with the kids. They don't seem to mind making fools of themselves?' Doris was intrigued.

The servicemen wiped faces with napkins, cleared away the remains of the hot dogs and led the cheering when iced buns, doughnuts and great dollops of ice cream were served.

Doris looked around and continued to be impressed. The Yanks seemed to be enjoying the occasion as much as the youngsters. Maybe, she thought, they are making up for missing Christmas at home. Maybe it was helping them deal with their own homesickness. Later she was able to chat to one or two of them and the ease with which they talked made her think of Oakey over at Debach and she hoped he was OK. The noise was deafening but it was a happy noise. She glanced about and saw Sylvia deep in conversation with a tall officer with closely cropped hair. That must be Chuck, she thought, craning her head to get a better view.

Although Sylvia's team expressed the desire to help with the fun the Americans politely told them that they were only present in case of emergency and to chaperone the children at the end of the party. Kitty, like the others, stood at the back watching the proceedings in awe. After a while she nudged Doris, 'He looks an interesting young airman, that one over in the corner, the blonde haired sergeant.' She was having trouble not pointing.

After making a few incorrect guesses Doris spotted a healthy looking individual who did indeed have fair hair and as far as she could make out blue eyes. He was laughing with two little boys who were unceremoniously demanding more ice cream.

'Not your type. He looks too normal,' she said but Kitty was having none of it.

'He's got wonderful cornflower blue eyes,' she announced.
'Don't be ridiculous, how can you see from here.'
'Because I've got pretty good eyes myself.'

'That was a simply marvellous spread, Chuck,' Sylvia enthused.
He was laughing, 'They seemed to enjoy it didn't they?'
'And so did your airmen. It was so lovely to see the rapport between them and the children.'
'Something to do with being away from home at Christmas, I guess.'
'Do you feel that?'
'A little, if I'm honest.'
'Thanks. Chuck, I want you always to be honest with me.'
He looked at her but said nothing.
A small band seemed to materialise on a raised platform. The one who appeared to be the leader went to the microphone, 'Right kids now it's your turn,' he announced. 'We're going to play and you're going to sing. Is that OK?'
A few small voices shouted *Yes*
'I said is that a deal,' he cupped his hand to his ear and they all shouted out a much louder *Yes*
The band started with some well known carols which the youngsters aided by the airmen joined in with increasing enthusiasm. Then the band leader said he would teach them some new songs and before long they were shouting out the words of *Don't fence me in* and *Chattanooga Choo Choo*. Kitty noticed that some of the Yanks, including the one with the eyes, were hoisting the youngsters onto their shoulders and dancing them around.
It was then suggested that the children might like to entertain the Americans and after a slow start one little boy mounted the platform and having had the microphone adjusted gave a hearty rendition of *Run Rabbit Run*. Others took to the stage and, with much encouragement from the audience, sang other war time favourites. The high spot being an impromptu piece by a little girl of no more than six who looked as though butter wouldn't melt in her mouth. She sang a version of *My Bonnie lies over the ocean*.

My Bonny is stationed at Bawdsey
It's just as hush hush as can be
So nobody knows he's at Bawdsey
Except all his relations and me.
The gun he is guarding at Bawdsey
Stretches seventy feet in the air
And although you don't say that you've seen it
You bloody well know that it's there.

'So much for your careless talk,' Chuck whispered to Sylvia.

After more singing a magician appeared in a wonderful sparkling costume and performed a series of amazing tricks.

The kids were then all given a bag of candies to take home and, with the Americans looking as sad as the youngsters, were told the trucks would be arriving shortly. Sylvia asked Chuck if she might say a few words and somewhat nervously bent into the microphone.

'We cannot leave without saying one enormous thank you on behalf of the children to you the officers and men of USAAF Martlesham Heath. You have given them a Christmas they will never forget,' she paused and looked around and then added, ' and one I shan't forget either. Happy Christmas to you all.'

There followed an enormous cheer and Kitty whispered to Doris, 'She's all right, your posh friend.' Doris turned to reply but Kitty wasn't there. She was making straight for the blonde sergeant in the far corner of the hangar.

The kids were escorted to toilets, herded into groups and checked onto the trucks.

On the way back to Ipswich they didn't sing, some munched on their candy, some saved it for later and quite a number nodded off, exhausted by all the fun.

Doris and Kitty were in charge of groups going to Holywells and met up after delivering their precious truckloads back to the centre. They walked up Cliff Lane hill together.

'They've had a great time, bless them,' Kitty said.

'Yes, I've got to hand it to those Yanks they really piled it on for them, didn't they?'

Kitty nodded, 'Yeah. They're OK you know. Different from us but OK.' Then she added,

'Especially the one with the cornflower blue eyes. I'm going out for a cycle ride with him on the Sunday after Christmas.'

Sylvia felt strangely elated when she arrived home from the children's Christmas party. The kids had had such a wonderful time. She knew that now, they had to face the reality of being homeless, desperately poor and lonely. She convinced herself that she would work even harder tracing relatives and friends who might take them in, badgering authorities for every possible kind of assistance and generally giving more of her time to whoever needed it.

The cottage was cold but Old Moore had recently left a pile of twigs and some logs since there was so little coal available. Once again she felt a pang at being privileged. She set about lighting a fire which soon crackled giving warmth to the room. Then she went to the kitchen and began to organise cheese on toast. The mixed emotions of the day had left her hungry.

Feeling better once she had eaten Sylvia decided on the luxury of a hot bath and even pampered herself with just the smallest amount of bath salts. She undressed, pinned back her hair and, with a sigh, felt the warm soapy water soothe her body. Random thoughts flitted around in her head. The *Beverage Report* was receiving more and more publicity; she was certain that it represented the way ahead. She had talked to Doris about it but Doris wasn't really interested in politics. Politics? Yes, she Sylvia was interested in politics. When the war was over she would do something positive in a political sense. The Labour Party was being talked about as the reforming party; the party that would do something about the less fortunate members of society; make their lives more tolerable. My God she thought, sponging herself with warm bubbles, mother would have a heart attack and father would disown me if I joined the Labour Party. And Francis? Well, not voting Conservative would surely be grounds for divorce! She would talk to Chuck about it. He enjoyed a good discussion. He would try to understand but also he would argue the opposite viewpoint if he thought it was valid. That was one of the things she liked about him. One of the things.....

She wasn't sure how long she stayed in the bath; she may even have dozed off but then she heard a noise, a knocking noise. Oh My God it's the door, she realised sliding out of the bath and quickly towelling herself down. At the same time she shouted out, though unsure that she would be heard, 'I'm coming mother.'

She wrapped her white towelling bath robe around herself and opened the front door,

'Sorry mother I was in the.......Chuck!'

He stood grinning, collar turned up against the cold. 'I've brought your Christmas present,' he said.

'What! My present! But I haven't got you anything. I didn't think....'

'Look I don't wish to appear impolite but are you going to invite me in, it's freezing out here?' He was still grinning.

'Oh yes, sorry, of course.' 'Sylvia led him into the lounge. 'Oh. The fire is going out. I've been in the bath for simply ages I think.' She went to the log basket.

He was taking off his hat and coat and tossing them over the sofa, 'I'll do it,' he said, 'you could put some music on and then I might give you that present.'

Sylvia caught a glimpse of herself in the mirror; she had forgotten she was only wearing a bathrobe, 'Oh my God. Just look at me. Straight out of the bath, I must look an absolute sight. Hang on, I'll go and get some clothes on.'

'Don't,' he said coming towards her, ' you look wonderful.'

'I've put on *White Christmas* is that all right?' she muttered.

'Perfect, will you dance with me,' he said and putting his arms around her they moved gently to the music. She put her face close to his and he kissed her softly on the cheek. Soon he was kissing her mouth and neck and she knew she wanted this more than any thing. 'Is this my present?' she whispered.

'No, this is both our presents,' he said.

His hands were caressing her body and before long the robe slipped to the floor. Later, she couldn't remember exactly how it happened but magically they were both naked, making love in a way she had never ever imagined possible. The fire flickered, dancing patterns on their bodies and she was vaguely aware that *Bing Crosby* had stopped singing. She seemed to have disappeared into some special place where she had no idea what she was saying or doing except that it was wonderful.

Eventually they fell apart but it seemed that he couldn't stop kissing her. After a while she took his hand and they stood up. Without saying a word she switched off the gramophone, placed a guard in front of the fire and then led him to the bedroom.   In the middle of the night she opened her eyes and found him awake. They kissed some more and then he whispered, 'I haven't given you your present.'

'Oh I think you have,' she said reaching for his face, ' but I'm feeling greedy.'

Specks of light permeated minor blemishes in the blackout and she was aware that he was getting out of bed. 'I have to go Sylvia. Duty calls even at Christmas time.'

He went from the bedroom and returned partially clothed. He handed her a badly wrapped package and sat on the edge of the bed. She dragged herself up, smiling at him, and pulled at the paper. 'Oh lovely,' she said, ' we were talking about Evelyn Waugh the other day.' She leaned over and kissed him for a long time then she looked at him. 'I want you to know that what happened last night is not something I do, you know. Not before I was married and certainly not since. Chuck I think I really am in love with you.'

He kissed her again, running his hands tenderly across her body, ' And I am afraid that I am very much in love with you, too, ' he whispered, ' and I have no idea what to do about it.'

'Let's worry about that later. I don't want anything to spoil what has happened between us.' Then Sylvia frowned at him, 'I know you have to go.'

She slid out of bed, slipped on her gown and went with him to the lounge where he finished putting on his uniform. They kissed again and she clung to him.

'When will I see you?' she asked.

'As soon as I possibly can. I am on duty over Christmas, but then you will have family things, I guess, so I will call here just as soon as I can after.'

She took him to the door and they hugged, 'I love you Sylvia,' he repeated and she let him out into the cold. It was five thirty in the morning.

Sylvia went back to bed and surprised herself by falling into a deep sleep. When she eventually woke it was nine o'clock. After the initial shock she remembered it was Sunday and so she need not hurry. She washed and dressed in a dream, thinking but not thinking about what had happened. She opened up the windows and went into the kitchen and made toast and tea, then she sat back and leafed through *Put out More Flags* by *Evelyn Waugh*. Looking out of the window she noticed that it was a clear day. A clear still day that was suddenly disturbed by the roar of two USAAF fighters. Oh no. Surely he's not up there already, she thought and then told herself she was being irrational, but she knew from now on there would be problems being rational. Every fighter that crossed the sky would be Chuck, every mission to Germany would be accompanied by him and every day he failed to make contact he would have been shot down. She had done this to herself and she was going to suffer for it.

She tidied up a bit around the cottage in a haphazard fashion and then nearly jumped through the roof when there was another tapping on the door. This time it was her mother.

'You look bright and perky this morning, darling. Must have been a good party.'

'It was wonderful.'

'Well done you, then. So you got all the little horrors there and back OK? Didn't lose any?' Elizabeth chuckled.

'They were lovely, mummy, they had such a good time. It was the best thing that had happened to them for so long. I know it was a bit like a fairy tale and there are now so many practical things we have to do for them but a least they had a few hours of magic.'

'My how poetic you are becoming. Must be all this stuff you read,' Elizabeth had picked up the book and was examining the cover.

Sylvia laughed, deciding not to explain. 'Would you like a coffee, mummy, I'm just about to make one?'

' No thanks, tea for me, Earl Grey. I am still English you know. Not like you turning into an American.'

'What does that mean?'

Elizabeth looked at her daughter carefully, 'The children's party, of course. You're so full of it.'

'I've always liked coffee,' Sylvia announced disappearing into the kitchen. Elizabeth followed.

'And how's that husband of yours? Valerie said they had a letter this week but Francis didn't say where he was exactly.'

'Well he can't can he? Last I heard he was half way up Italy and making good progress. Can't wait to get to Rome, apparently. So all appears well as far as one can ever tell.'

This time Elizabeth bridled, 'What do you mean by that?'

'He never really tells me how he is. Doris was saying that her Jimmy, just occasionally, tells her how he is feeling, how he is coping or struggling to cope. Francis never lets on that sort of thing.'

'I should think not, indeed. Francis is an officer and this Jimmy is...well he's not an officer is he? It's all to do with breeding. You know, public school, family regiment, proper background. This country is great because we understand that some are meant to lead and some are meant to follow and everyone accepts that. Makes Britain what it is, for heaven's sake. Sometimes, Sylvia, I wonder about the sort of people you mix with in this war. I mean Doris seems a nice enough girl but I can't help but think it's people like her who are filling your head with all sorts of notions.'

Sylvia opened her mouth to reply but no words came out. Sometimes it is better to say nothing, she thought. Stiff upper lip and all that.

'I don't know what you think is funny,' Elizabeth detected a smile.

'Oh nothing important mummy. Here we are one Earl Grey and one English coffee. Let's go back into the lounge.'

No sooner had they sat down when the cottage walls shuddered as more Thunderbolts flew low overhead.

'Bloody Americans. Your father says they do that to show off,' Elizabeth said, sipping her tea.

1944

*'Unbelievable things are happening in some of our villages' –
Ipswich Probation Officer.*

He parked the jeep at the top of the lane and they meandered down
towards the river.

There was a bite in the air but no real breeze and they breathed in
deeply, feeling free and at peace with each other. Sylvia held his hand
and guided him down a familiar pathway which, eventually, broke
through the trees by the shore. Stopping for a while they took in the
swaying reeds, the gently rippling water and the fine sweep of soft
mud, its subtle colours glinting in the fading sun.

'We won't get muddy if we stick to the grass verge. That way we
might get round to that church you can see in the distance. I really
want to show it to you, the site dates back to six hundred and
something when it was a monastery'.

'Maybe that's why it's so peaceful and quiet here,' he said, 'tell me
there isn't such a thing as war.'

Sylvia reached up, put her arms around his neck and kissed him, 'I
wish I could,' she murmured.

Suddenly a black labrador came scampering towards them carrying a
stick in its mouth and wagging its tail. Skidding to a halt it began to
shake its wet coat. Sylvia backed behind Chuck laughing, 'Don't you
dare take that stick and throw it unless you want an extra companion
for the afternoon.'

'What a spoilsport you are. Come on boy. Just the once,' He threw
the stick out over the purple mud into the river. The dog scampered
off returning in record time, muddy and wet, dropping the stick at his
feet.

'What did I tell you?'

'Its OK, look here come the owners.' A couple had appeared in front
of them having reached the shore from another direction.

'Sorry, we couldn't resist playing with your dog.'

'Don't belong to us. Think he's from the cottage back there,' the
man said. The woman managed to smile whilst looking intently at the
American officer and then back to Sylvia.

Seeing there was no more fun to be had the dog ran away from the
shore towards the fields.

'Shall we have a rest. It's not that cold,' Chuck indicated a fallen tree trunk. Sylvia snuggled up to him.

'I can't seem to leave you alone. Chuck, what on earth are we going to do?'

'The simple answer is I don't know. The situation is both wonderful and hopeless.'

'You mean because we're both married to people who are a long way away?'

'In a way. I get letters from Helen and I feel as guilty as hell. She's done nothing wrong and neither has Francis. Don't you feel awful sometimes?'

'Of course I do but somehow it's different. I've tried to tell myself that it was pre war Sylvia who married Francis and wartime Sylvia who has fallen in love for the first time. God knows what post war Sylvia will turn out like.'

'She'll turn out just fine.'

'But it isn't like that for you Chuck is it? Be honest.'

'No because before I met you I was certain that Helen and I were fine for each other. And now this experience, the way we are together, is showing me something so different.' He took out his cigarettes and offered one to Sylvia whom, to his surprise, declined. He lit up, inhaled deeply, and looked out at the river.

'Do you want to finish it?' She asked.

He looked at her and inhaled again slowly blowing smoke into the crisp air, 'Life is so precious at the moment. Every day I fly out with the bombers, everyday a lot of my buddies don't come back and everyday I thank God I am still alive to come and see you. I'm certain I'm in love with you but in a world where future is so fragile we have no future.'

She was quiet for a long time, 'Thank you for being honest,' she said. 'Come on let's see if we can get to the church. If the sun fades we'll walk back to the jeep by road.'

They stood up and continued along the verge, the sun was lower in the sky and it was getting colder.

'Tell me what's new. Your man Eisenhower is now Supreme Commander so you must know more than me when the second front is coming?'

He laughed, 'I know no more than you do on that one. It can't be long though. There is so much movement on the roads, troops everywhere. England is turning into one big military training ground. It can't be long.'

'And you'll be involved?'

'Everyone in uniform will be involved. Say, what brought this serious conversation on?'

She shrugged, 'I thought we should change the subject, that's all.'

Chuck stopped and took her in his arms.

They drove back to the cottage in comparative silence. He parked the jeep, came inside and they took off their heavy coats. Sylvia took both his hands and looked at him for a long time before leading him to the bedroom.

Afterwards she made coffee.

'Can I be practical?' he said, 'I think it might be best if I cycled over in future. The jeep looks pretty obvious.'

She took his hand and looked at his strong, young, American face. 'Yes, of course. My mother is sure to ask questions sooner or later.'

'What will you say?'

'I've really no idea. I'll think of something, don't worry,' another pause, 'when do you think I will I see you again?'

'Nowadays we tend to fly out most mornings escorting the bombers over occupied Europe and Germany itself; those who get back return early in the afternoons. I'll come over when I can but some days it won't be possible. Some days I just won't be much company.'

Sylvia kissed him gently on the cheek, ' Come whenever you can and if all you want is to sit and be quiet just tell me. I'll understand.'

Later, when he had gone Sylvia tried to work out what was happening to her, what she was letting herself in for, what this man was doing to her? Her experience with men was comparatively limited. An all girls boarding school had been an unhealthy way to grow up; she had left at eighteen almost totally inexperienced as far as boys were concerned. This was followed by a number of dalliances with equally inexperienced former public school boys who told her she was pretty whilst struggling to undo her bra. There had been a boy called Gregory who she quite liked since at least he would talk to her like a human being but he ended up falling for Fiona Buttersmith. Her mother talked to her about finding a suitable husband, settling down, having a family, being part of the county set which all seemed so appealing. When she met Francis he seemed to fit the criteria. He was good looking, privately educated, from a good family, a trifle serious but, in some ways, she even liked this side of him. She decided he could provide what she wanted. Poor Francis didn't really have a chance.

The war, she knew, had changed her. The horror of airs raids, the despair of the victims, the bravery of those around her. She found there were other sorts of men, men who treated her as an equal, men who discussed problems with her, men who laughed with her. There were women too, women, like Doris, who became real friends. Background no longer mattered. She was meeting genuine people. Her mother may have categorised them as common but, through the awfulness of war, Sylvia had become somebody different. Certainly somebody different from the girl who had married Francis Cameron.

Struggling to come to terms with this the last thing she was looking for was a new man in her life. She smiled, thinking of her first encounter with Chuck Taylor. At first she had found him arrogant and, at times, she still bridled at some of the things he said or apparently believed in. The colour issue, for example, was a subject he continually glossed over, telling her, in a patronising way, that you had to live in America to understand what it was all about. Colour seemed to be the only subject that he wouldn't discuss openly with her. That apart they both enjoyed the cut and thrust of an argument.. They discussed everything from books to music to politics and they talked of their feelings in a way she had never been able to with Francis.

She knew the situation was hopeless, she even knew she was brewing up a whole load of trouble for herself since people were bound to talk. She knew she might embarrass her parents and her friends but she also knew that she loved him in a way she had never thought possible. With her lack of experience of men in general she couldn't believe he loved her the same way. She was totally absorbed by him but understood that he faced death every day and so had other things on his mind.

Air raids became less frequent and although Sylvia spent a lot of time ensuring that all possible was being done to assist the hundreds of homeless she also devoted time on various collections for the war effort. The latest was an ambitious campaign to collect thousands of books firstly to send to the forces overseas and secondly to be ground down as pulp. This involved house to house visits, since it would have been hypocritical to send a written note of their intentions; there was also the tremendous problem of storage and distribution. Thus, whilst still working many hours, she was able to organise her schedule arriving back at the cottage in the afternoon, heart thumping, stomach churning in the hope that he might cycle up the drive.

Sometimes he would arrive cheerful with the news of a successful mission, other times he would be low and say little of the day's activities, on occasions he would be completely shattered and fall asleep in a comfortable arm chair. Some days he would not arrive at all and she would look to the sky and pray.

'I think I deserve a drink after all that exercise,' Kitty was puffing as she stacked her bike against the wall in the yard at the back of The Crown.

'OK you win but don't you just love days like this. Makes you feel kinda healthy just being outside. Tom was thinking of Red Oak winters but had the sense not to start any boasting about how wonderful they were. He had read the guide on what and what not to say to the English.

They went inside the old coaching inn where a log fire was burning. Tom was immediately fascinated by the Grandmother clock under which a rusting metal sign announcing that coaches arrived daily. He also noticed that there were quite a number of American servicemen lolling around and quite a number of girls from Framlingham and neighbouring villages keeping them company.

'Have you got used to our warm beer yet, Tom?' Kitty asked him.

'No I'm afraid I haven't. I don't drink alcohol as it happens.'

'You don't drink alc....' What have I let myself in for here, Kitty wondered, hoping Tom was not one of those mid west religious freaks she had heard about.

'I'm happy to buy you whatever you want. My problem is your pubs don't sell coke so I have to drink this funny sort of soda you call lemonade.'

'Don't you have lemonade where you come from, Tom?'

'Sure but it's what my mom makes and it tastes wonderful. It's not a soda if you understand what I mean.'

He really is a strange one Kitty thought and asked for a shandy. She liked a drink and wasn't going to give up the demon alcohol for some cowboy. In fact she was surprised she only ordered a shandy. Having a few drinks bought for her was one of the few genuine treats left to a war time factory girl.

They took their drinks to the quietest corner of the busy inn. He grinned at her. He had an uncomplicated face.

He looks all right, she thought, but I doubt if he's much fun. Since he hadn't offered she fished in her bag for her cigarettes, 'I suppose you don't smoke either?' she joked.

'As a matter of fact I don't,' he was laughing, 'I guess you are finding me a pretty dull sort of guy?'

'Not dull but certainly different. You're the first yank I've come across who isn't set on ruining himself on wine, women and song.'

'It's only the wine I don't do,' he said, 'though come to think of it my singing isn't that special.'

At least he's got a sense of humour she thought.

He was looking around at the wooden panelling and beamed ceiling, the thick oak doors and the pictures of hunting scenes hanging crooked on the walls.

'How old is this place?' he asked.

She had no idea, never having been remotely interested in history. At school all she had wanted to do was leave and earn some money.

'I don't really know. Tudor I should think, the old flagstones on the floor look really old, don't they?' She was guessing, trying to sound knowledgeable, 'We'll ask before we go, someone might have a book or something.'

'Sorry I must sound very American. But I decided since I am here in England I ought to find out something about its history. Don't worry I wasn't the studious type at school. Disappointed my mom but dad understood that all I wanted was to help out on the farm.'

She breathed a sigh of relief that he wasn't a University Professor, 'You wait until you see the castle then. Now that is very old.'

'Sounds great. As I said I must sound pretty dull to you. Bit of a, what did you call me earlier?'

'A Stick in the Mud. So come on Sergeant Stick in the Mud tell me something about this place in the middle of nowhere that you come from.'

He smiled again, 'I'll try but the book says us Americans must not brag or bluster saying everything we have is bigger and better. The truth is, from what little I've seen of Suffolk and hearing you explain how it was before the war, it is like a tiny version of Montgomery. The nearest town to where we farm is called Red Oak. It's in the county of Montgomery, which is in the state of Iowa.'

'Hey, this is like a geography lesson. I have a feeling it could go on for a while so why don't you get me another shandy, teacher.'

She watched him walk slowly and deliberately to the bar, one or two other yanks said something to him, others gave her the once over whilst he was ordering. She ignored them, which she knew was not like her at all.

He returned, sat easily in his chair and continued. He told her that the main difference between Red Oak and this part of England was the population. Hardly anyone seemed to live in Montgomery County except a few farmers. He explained that he was descended from Swedish pioneers as were the vast majority of the inhabitants of the area; in other parts of Iowa the people were descended from Norwegians, Czechs, Poles, Danes as well as those who had moved west from the Eastern Seaboard of the USA. They grew corn but mainly what we would call maize as opposed to wheat and barley; they reared cattle for dairy and for beef and hogs. Tom seemed particularly fond of the hogs. Winters were cold, summers hot and humid and every now and then great winds swept across the land flattening the crops. His family had struggled during the Depression but, until the war hit them, were starting to prosper again. Hard work seemed all-important and this seemed to be linked to some deep love of the land.

To Kitty's amazement the stream of facts he set before her didn't bore her. Maybe it was his slow voice that she found attractive, maybe it was his pride in where he came from and what he did, maybe it was the look in his eyes when he talked of home. She leaned forward and held his hand. She hadn't touched her drink nor lit another cigarette.

Tom looked up and grinned, 'Sorry I do go on a bit sometimes,' he said.

'No it's interesting. You see we English girls think America is all like it is on the pictures. All Hollywood, California, New York, Chicago. All big towns, hustle, bustle and glamour. Either that or you're all cowboys. Not too many farmers.'

At the far end of the room a group of girls and their American companions burst into riotous laughter but either Tom didn't hear them or thought them unimportant. He asked her about her family and her life and they sat holding hands and swapping stories until the landlord called time. The other occupants staggered off into the town and Tom got slowly to his feet.

'I don't have a whole lot of time I'm afraid but I would sure love to see this castle.'

They left their bikes at the back of the inn and walked up the gentle hill past the little theatre and the Georgian Conservative club whose pastel colours were flaking through lack of attention. Many of the small shops were shuttered up. She pointed out St.Michaels church on their left but insisted that they didn't have time to look in. When they came to the grassy area in front of yet another pub he understood why. There in the distance, sharply defined against the crisp blue sky stood Framilingham castle.

'Oh. My! I have never seen anything like that. That is really something, Kitty.' He grasped her hand and almost ran to the entrance. In these days of frugality she was pleased he was able to obtain a small guidebook and he thumbed its pages enthusiastically reading aloud to her, greedy for knowledge of the 12th century fortress with it's 13 towers.

After about an hour Kitty felt she had learned more local history in the company of this American than she had in her previous twenty-four years. For a boy who said he wasn't keen on studying his enthusiasm was overwhelming.

Finally, crossing the drawbridge he stuffed the little book into his tunic saying he couldn't wait to write home. She made him take a short detour down the sloping pathway in order to look across the meadow to the college and then, taking his hand, they scrambled back over the little bridge and up the hill.

'I have had my best day since I've been in England. Thank you Kitty. I know all this history is old hat to you but to me it has been fascinating. Sorry if I may have been a bit of a bore.'

She squeezed his hand, looked up and kissed him gently on the mouth, 'Am I going to get the chance to be bored again, then?'

'You bet. The sooner the better,' he said.

'...and then I took him to the castle. Well, it was like I'd given him a Christmas present. He was so interested. Said it was the best day he'd had since he'd been in England.'

'You never learn, my girl, do you? Never learn. These Yanks are just a bunch of smooth talking womanisers. I mean it's only human nature when you think about it. Thousands of young, lonely blokes with too much money, many of whom have wives and girlfriends, back home. So what do they want? I'll tell you what they want. They want booze and girls. And what do we have in England? Thousands of young, lonely girls, blokes away at war, and what do they want? They want a good time. The sooner the Second Front comes the better. For everyone's sake if you ask me'

'That's the longest speech I've heard you make since our wedding,' Vera tried to lighten the conversation sensing yet another row.

'All very well for you to laugh. I'm just trying to point something out to Miss Yanky Bait here.'

'Why do you always have to spoil things for me?' Kitty was red in the face and shouting, 'You think you have all the answers but sometimes you know nothing. It so happens that Tom does not drink, he does not smoke and I'm the first English girl he's even been out with.'

'That's what he tells you.'

Kitty burst into tears and roared out of the room. Jack went to the fireplace, fiddled with his pipe and spat into the remnants of a fire.

'You handled that well,' Vera muttered and started to clear away the plates.

A severe bout of influenza was rife in the country and Suffolk did not escape. This resulted in staffing shortages everywhere and Vera was asked to put in more hours including relieving at the small exchange at Rushmere.

The local subscribers not knowing that their usual operator had the flu came through with the usual bewildering requests.

'Put me through to the doctors, there's a dear.'

'Can I have Mrs. Parsons up at the rectory?'

Even when she explained her situation they didn't always understand but by the end of the week she was starting to know the regulars and their requests and was beginning to enjoy herself. It certainly wasn't as busy as the central Ipswich exchange and she had time to do a bit of embroidery in between calls.

She also had time to think a bit. Something of a luxury for Vera but since everywhere she turned she encountered problems she came to the conclusion that you could spend too much time pondering.

The war had been going on now for over four years. Like everyone else she was prepared to scrimp and scrape but she was a woman, not a rich woman, but she still had a pride in her home. It hurt her that it was beginning to look so sad. The carpets and rugs were worn and there was no money for new ones, material for curtains was just not available in the shops, there were burn marks on the lino and the bath and toilet had stains that would never come out. They had very little coal and had to rely on sticks that Jack gathered from the woods and some logs that he scrounged off a neighbour. The only thing that looked new about their house was the green plaque on the gate, which announced to the world that an air raid warden lived at number twenty four.

'Hello Gladys, Get me Sally Whitehouse will you, it's a bit urgent.'

Vera explained that Gladys had the flu and that she would need a number. Eventually the caller was satisfied.

Then there was Jack. Good old honest Jack who still couldn't get used to his wife working. He still had no idea how to deal with Kitty even though he knew she was a good girl at heart. He couldn't abide her *live for today* attitude. Poor old Jack who she knew deep down hated the idea of this war. His obsession with the progress of the various campaigns, his encyclopaedic knowledge of combat aircraft was somehow linked to experiences during the First World War that she would never be part of. In Footmans the other day he wouldn't go in the lift and she realised, for the first time, that this was linked to his determination not to go into the dug outs which, in turn, harped back to something more sinister in that war to end all wars. She knew he worried about Jimmy. He poured over the letters from his son as if searching for some hidden clue about how the boy was really coping.

'Gladys, Hilda here, get me the bank could you?'

Kitty had been on fire watch and by the time she arrived home her father had gone out to an Air Warden training exercise at the Drill Hall. She went round the back of the house and let herself into the kitchen. She was surprised to see that the dirty dishes had not been washed. Her mother was in the front room sitting in the worn leather sofa, head in hands, sobbing quietly.

Kitty went to her, 'Mum, whatever's the matter. Not Jimmy is it?'

'No, no, thank God. Just me feeling sorry for myself. I didn't hear you come in.'

Kitty sat down and cradled her mother's head to her, 'It's me who should say sorry. I shouldn't keep arguing with Dad like I do.'

'It's not that. It's lots of things. All got on top of me.'

'I know I've played around a bit, tried to have a good time in spite of the war and that but it's just my way of coping. Honest mum, I haven't been a bad girl or anything. Haven't been sleeping with any of them.'

Vera looked up red-eyed, 'I know that love.'

'Yes, but dad doesn't does he?'

'I have no idea what he thinks most of the time.'

'The thing is mum this one, this yank called Tom, well, I think I really like him. You know really like him.'

Vera got out a handkerchief and blew her nose, 'Then why don't you invite him round?'

'In time, maybe, in time. Now just you sit there and I'll make us a cuppa then you can tell me what else has brought all this on.'

Vera turned on the radio. The news was ending confirming the allies had just inflicted the heaviest bombing raids to date on Berlin.

Kitty came back with the tea. 'What about Jimmy? Do you think he's a lot like Dad?'

Vera sipped her tea carefully, 'Like father like son. What brings this on?'

'It's something Doris said the other day. She keeps trying to explain to Jimmy in letters what it means to her to become a proper chemist but he doesn't seem to get too excited about it. You know the idea of her working after they are married, possibly earning more than him.'

'Now that is a new one,' something else for me to worry about Vera thought, 'I see what you mean though. Your father still doesn't really like me working even though it's the law now. Still thinks he should provide but is happy enough to pool the money and then dish back to me what he thinks I need for housekeeping,' she paused. 'Doesn't realise I keep a little bit back that he knows nothing about now.'

Kitty laughed and Vera managed a wry smile,' Well done mum, that's more like it.' She gave her mother a hug.

'Seriously though,' Vera continued, 'Jimmy is the son of a very working class type of father. My parents both died when I was fairly young as you know but they weren't strictly what Jack would call working class. Even left me a little bit of money that helped us buy this house. Don't ever mention that to your father will you? It's this silly pride thing. Jack does think he should be the provider. A woman's place is still in the home. The classes shouldn't mix but know their place. A lot of that will have rubbed off on Jimmy. He wouldn't understand how things have changed during the war here at home whilst he's been fighting in other parts of the world, would he?'

'No I suppose not. It's all going to be a bit interesting after the war when they all come back isn't it?'

Vera smiled again, 'Whatever else you are, Kitty, you are a tonic. Thanks for getting me out of my gloom. The important thing is that for the first time people really believe we are going over to Europe to finish off that Hitler and that has to be good news.' She thought a bit, 'When I next write to Jimmy I'll touch on the Doris thing, just a hint like. He'd be a very silly boy if he ever let her slip through his fingers. He'd have to go a long way to find another Doris, I can tell you.'

'Against infection and the hand of war.' – Shakespeare · *Richard II*

Doris was standing at the top of the grass slope in front of the mansion in Holywells park. The pill boxes had gone, the shelter had gone, the allotments had gone; everywhere was green, there were no signs of grass being grown for hay. Children were playing happily with bat and ball and kites were cutting into the blue sky, mothers pushed prams along the paths chatting cheerfully.

She looked down towards the pond and saw the back of a soldier. He was feeding the ducks in an easy, almost lazy way. She recognised his movements immediately.

'Jimmy,' she cried out, 'Jimmy it's me. I'm coming,' and she ran towards him laughing.

She reached him in seconds and he turned towards her. She knew it was him but this Jimmy had no face. It had been blown off leaving a mass of blood and bone.

She screamed out his name, 'Jimmy, Jimmy, Jimmy.'

'Jimmy, Jimmy,'

'What ever is the matter girl. You'll wake the whole road.'

She was in bed. She was sweating heavily yet shuddering with cold.

'Mother. I've had this terrible dream. You see...'

Her mother leaned forward and touched her forehead, 'You've got the flu my girl. That's what you've got. There's a lot of it about. Lots away at the factory. I'm having to get people to work extra hours. Here I'll get you some water. That's what you need lots of water. Not much else will do any good, they say.'

Doris pulled herself up. She was still shaking. It had all been so real.

She heard her mother coming up the stairs and into her room. She grabbed the water and greedily gulped it down. Then without realising it she slipped down between the bed clothes and fell asleep.

When she woke up her night dress was sticking to her body. Someone had pulled away the blackout curtains and daylight was creeping into the room. She found she didn't want the light in her eyes and her head was splitting in two. A jug of water and a glass had been left by the bed. Her mother had scribbled a note.

Your dad and I have gone to work. Stay in bed and drink lots of water. I will get a message to Mr. French, love mother.

Doris had no wish to do otherwise. During the day she dozed off quite a bit but couldn't stop shivering and her headache would not go away.

Her mother informed her that the influenza epidemic was said to last about a week if one was young and strong. Her father popped his head gingerly around the door when he came home from work and seemed to delight in telling her how many people had already died from it.

Over the next few days Doris experienced variations of the nightmare. On one occasion Jimmy was sitting in front of her on a bus; on another he was looking in French's shop window trying to press his faceless face against it. Every time she woke up screaming which gave way to sobbing and shaking.

But she was healthy and the fever subsided. By the end of the week she was eating bread and soup and beginning to feel better. On the Friday she got out of bed when her parents had gone to work and went down the stairs with wobbly legs. She made herself some tea without milk or sugar, sat in the lounge and wrote to Jimmy. She told him she had been off work with flu but nothing about the dreams. In his last letter he had included a sentence or two about his hopes for when the war ended. He had hinted that he might not want to go back to the factory but she wasn't to worry because whatever he did he would always provide for her. She realised that, like his father, he thought a wife's place should be at home but she also knew that she would not give up the opportunity presented to her to become a qualified pharmacist. She wished he were with her so that they could discuss things properly. It was useless to try to talk of such things in a letter. Especially when he was enduring the continued horrors of war as the 8th Army progressed doggedly up Italy. He needed letters of love and understanding, nothing more.

After work, before her parents arrived back home, Joyce called to see how she was feeling. She made Doris laugh with stories about regular customers as well as updating her on the Mr. French and Mrs. Fox romance of the century, as she had named it. Then, suddenly, Joyce, for once, looked a little embarrassed, 'I think I've got a steady,' she announced.

'Oh Joyce that's great news. Who is he? Do I know him?'

'You may have seen him. He comes in to the shop from time to time. I realise now it was to see me, after the first time that is. He drives one of those great big lorries between the bases delivering bombs and things. He...'

'He's a yank then, an American?'

'Oh. Yes, his name is Leroy.'

'Leroy'

'Yes and he's black. The black ones do all the driving you know.'

In spite of herself Doris was lost for words.

Joyce bubbled on, 'He's so polite and so kind and he has a lovely face. In America it's awful how they treat the blacks. They're not allowed to talk to white girls so he just loves talking to me. If I didn't have other ideas he'd talk all night. All evening I mean, of course. He has that slow voice the ones from the South have.'

'Is he treated all right here. There are some terrible stories.'

'Well he says he's used to having to go to separate places from the whites back home so for him it's no problem but he did say the military police are very quick to attack the blacks if there's any sign of trouble.'

'I'll have to get back to work as soon as possible Joyce, I'm missing out on every thing,' Doris said.

The sound of a key being turned in the front door brought an end to their gossiping. Joyce, sensibly, had no wish to share her news with Mrs. Harper who bustled in greeting Doris with, 'Oh. So you're up. Hello Joyce, finish early today did you?'

'Mr. French let me off so I could come and see how Doris was, Mrs. Harper.'

'All right for some. Wouldn't do at Andersons, I can tell you. Still good of you to come.'

'Thanks. Well Doris I'd better be going then. Hope to see you on Monday.'

'Thanks for coming Joyce and for your special news.'

'Don't fence me in.' - popular song

My dearest Doris,

As I write we feel we are making real progress at last in Italy and although I cannot give you details they are saying we have one more major obstacle and then it's Rome. Hope they don't censor all that since I want you to know roughly where I am and you will realise I am OK.

We keep hearing of all the activity in Britain and all the lads are excited and already talking of what they will do after the war.

The more I think about it the most important thing is to marry you, darling Doris, and then we can live happily ever after as they say in the books. The other thing is I don't think I want to go back to Andersons and working in a factory all my life. I know my dad has but that doesn't mean I have to does it? My big mate here Dick, his father has a garage business in Bury St. Edmunds and he keeps on about me joining up with him. His dad hasn't been too well and will probably want to move over and let Dick take over. Dick says a lot more people will have cars after the war and the business is a gold mine. I think I might like that – the garage work I mean not the gold mine. I'd like to be outside more and I like meeting people. Also I am mechanical so I could soon qualify to do engines I'm sure. You wouldn't mind living in Bury would you? As long as we're together we'd be fine, you and me.

I love all your news and gossipy things about Mr. French and Joyce and now Kitty, you say, has a yank. Well, as long as you don't find one that's great. Ipswich must seem very strange with all the yanks and the poles and the others you describe.

I'm glad the bombing has calmed down a bit because I worry about you like you worry about me.

Must get some shuteye now,
All my love as ever,
Jimmy

'I don't think he reads my letters properly. He just doesn't seem to understand what I have been saying about my job here.'

Joyce thought for a while, 'It's probably very difficult for him Doris. You see the England he left isn't the England we have now is it?'

'I know that but I get so frustrated. Instead of feeling excited having read his letter I feel really depressed.'

Mr. French came into the dispensary catching the back end of a conversation as usual but wanting to add his opinion, 'Does that to you, influenza, makes you very low for a few days, even weeks. So try not to worry Doris. Have you done that prescription for Mrs. Greenway?'

'No not yet. I've been up and down like a yoyo helping out in the shop. It's been really busy.'

'It's the flu. Good for business influenza. Mrs. Greenway will be back about eleven so chop, chop.' He bustled out into the back yard before Doris had a chance to answer.

Joyce put her fingers to her mouth, 'Don't say it,' she advised, then, changing the subject, 'Leroy says there was an awful fight in town last night. Black and Whites again until the Snowdrops arrived at eleven and went in with their truncheons. One of his buddies was knocked out. It's so unfair.'

'Was Leroy all right?'

'Oh. He wasn't there. He stays out of trouble, my Leroy. Taking me to the pictures tonight, *Meet me in St. Louis.*'

'You really like him, don't you?'

'Yeah. I've never met such a kind person.'

'What do your parents think of him?'

'I'm still plucking up courage to tell them.'

'Joyce, for goodness sake, you have to tell them if you think it's serious.'

The shop bell rang and Joyce went to serve an elderly couple. The man was coughing. Mr. French came in from the yard, 'Nasty cough that old chap's got. The flu, you know, nasty thing this influenza.'

He stood at the opening between shop and dispensary, his arms folded. Doris finished the linctus for Mrs. Greenway, completed the label and stuck it on the bottle. Mr. French coughed, not an influenza cough more like a, I've got something to say, cough,

'I wish to talk to you both,' he announced. 'The fact is Mrs Fox has done me the honour of agreeing to be my wife. It'll be a small-do, just a few friends, including you two of course.'

There was a silence broken eventually by Joyce, 'Mr. French that is wonderful news.'

'Yes it is. Congratulations Mr. French.'

'And Joyce,' he added, 'Please invite your boyfriend to the wedding and the little reception in the Picture House Tea Room. Leroy you said his name was didn't you? Add a bit of colour to the proceedings having an American serviceman present.'

'Good job I picked a coloured American then,' Joyce laughed,' 'and thank you Mr. French. It's a very kind gesture to invite Leroy.'

After work Doris went to meet Sylvia in a more cheerful frame of mind than her gloom of the morning. Her initial reaction to Mr. French's announcement had been that it was a bit soon after his wife's death but then she thought Good Luck to them, they're not young and there's a war on. He'd been a different man since he'd met Mrs. Fox, hadn't tried to touch her up once!

Doris hoped things would turn out all right for Joyce. She was such a decent girl and deserved to be happy. Like most Ipswich people she had no problems with the black Americans who were said to be far more courteous than their white counter parts. She found it difficult to accept the American insistence on segregation when they were all fighting the same war.

Then there was Jimmy's letter. Clearly he was not happy with the idea of her pursuing her own career after they were married. She longed for him to be back so she could look in his eyes and explain. She was certain she could make him understand.

Determined to find out if she were over reacting she spoke to Sylvia who, as anticipated, agreed with her. She added that convincing Jimmy of her intentions was nothing compared with the anticipated effect on Francis and his family when she announced she had joined the Labour Party. Somehow, Doris sensed that Sylvia found it difficult to talk of Francis when her head and heart it seemed, were so full of Chuck. She didn't judge her friend since she knew what Sylvia felt about the American officer was genuine. As for Chuck, who knew that every time he climbed into his Thunderbolt his chances of survival were at best fifty percent, how could you blame him for wanting someone as lovely as Sylvia waiting to comfort him. It was wartime and they both knew the score.

As usual Sylvia left Doris with another dilemma. Sensing she needed cheering up she urged her to come with her to the base on Saturday to a party in the Officers Quarters. Nothing big or serious, just a little band, a bit of dancing, a couple of drinks, it would do her good, cheer her up.

The next day at the shop Mr. French posed yet more problems. He asked Doris to speak with him privately and then explained that he and Foxy, apparently his pet name for his intended, had been doing some thinking. After the war they intended to travel the country, and even Europe, in search of good music and as such he would not spend so much time at the shop. Assuming Doris qualified, Foxy thought it might be an idea if Mr. French made her the manager and employed another young assistant in the shop. Then, smiling as if it were all settled, he went on to explain that in time he would be moving to Mrs. Fox's house which would free up the flat above the shop. They, Mrs Fox and himself that was, thought that when she and Jimmy got married it might provide their first home. It could be made part of her remuneration, so to speak.

Doris stopped him in his tracks, 'Hold on Mr. French I am having difficulty taking all this in. You're giving me an awful lot to think about and I can't even talk to Jimmy. It's not the sort of thing I can say in a letter,' she paused and sat down heavily on a high stool. ' It's not that I'm not grateful, in fact it seems to be exactly what I've always wanted it's just....'

'My dear girl. I'm not asking for any decisions. Foxy is so good with ideas you see. Leaves me standing. All we are doing is telling you how we are thinking. No decisions until we've won the war. And that's still sometime off I fear.'

Later, Doris cycled home her head in a whirl. There was no doubt about one thing, however. Foxy was going to be quite an influence on poor old Mr. French. Still, the ideas they had suggested were very appealing. The problem was the old one, Jimmy's apparent conviction that she would end up a carbon copy of his mother and whilst Doris was extremely fond of Vera there was no way she was going to have that. What the hell, she would tell Sylvia that she would go to the party. She was fed up with being Agony Aunt to Joyce, Kitty and Sylvia. Fed up too with agonising over her own future. She deserved a bit of fun.

The grandly named Officers Club was no more than one of the larger nissen huts. Through the dim light Doris could make out crew photographs on the walls and wondered how many of the smiling young faces were still alive. Simple wooden furniture was scattered in random fashion about the room and, in an attempt to cheer the place up, blue and white gingham tablecloths were spread over the tables. At one end a bar was dispensing drinks as if it were celebrating the end of prohibition and at the other a five piece band were making a spirited effort at playing *I'll be seeing you*. American officers poured themselves over chairs in their usual casual manner, smoking and chatting with girls in short dresses showing off recently acquired nylon stockings. Already Doris was having grave misgivings.

Chuck spotted them almost as soon as they entered and came over giving Sylvia a polite kiss on the cheek and smiling at Doris, ' Good to see you again Doris,' he said as if he had known her all his life, ' hope you're feeling better.'

'Yes thanks, much better but Sylvia insisted I needed a night out.'

'In a smoky atmosphere,' added Sylvia, ' very good after a bout of flu.'

They sat at a table as far away from the band as possible and Chuck asked what they would drink. Doris was careful to say she would just have an American beer which she gathered from Joyce was quite different from the English equivalent. Sylvia had a gin and tonic.

When Chuck returned Sylvia put her hand on his, 'How has it been. I haven't seen you for days so obviously you are pretty busy.'

He looked tired, 'Yeah, you could say that. All I can tell you is we are what they call softening the enemy up. Targeting their airfields and depots as opposed to the cities. It's all part of you know what.'

They sipped their drinks and although both Chuck and Sylvia could not have been nicer to her Doris was beginning to feel like a gooseberry.

'Hey! I thought it was you,' a vaguely familiar voice sounded in Doris'ear. She looked round.

'Lootenant Sam.' She couldn't resist the attempt at mimicry.

'We met at that party in the smart house in town. God knows how long ago now,' he explained to the others, 'So how are you doing, Doris?'

'I'm impressed that you remember my name,' she said.

'You remembered mine. Say, may I join you, Chuck?'

'Sure. Good idea. We were about to dance weren't we Sylvia?'

'If you say so.'

One of the saxophonists had turned vocalist and was attempting a solo version of *Into each life some rain must fall.*

'Please notice Sam, I am sober and have no intentions of making a fool of myself tonight. Sylvia felt I needed cheering up a bit and dragged me here.'

'Hope she didn't harm that wonderful red hair,' he drawled.

She took a sip of her beer, it was fizzy and quite refreshing; she looked at him over the top of the glass. She had been right about one thing, he was good looking in an American sort of way. How did he keep that tan during the English winter or was his skin always that almond colour?

'Have you seen lots of action, as they say?'

'Yeah, a fair bit. A lot more to come, I guess but I'd rather not talk about that tonight OK?'

'Sorry, I was just...'

'...being very polite and very English and I thank you. Now why don't we dance?'

He held her firmly but politely and for a moment she thought of the young airman from Oakland she had met when the yanks had first come over. She hoped he was OK. Above all she hoped he was alive. They swayed to the music, she enjoyed the feel of him and surprisingly the smell of him. American men, she had learned, used cologne, a habit regarded as sissy amongst the British who scrubbed themselves with *Lifebouy.* The band finished and they clapped politely making no attempt to return to their table. *Moonlight Serenade* was now a standard and they danced to the lilting Glen Miller sound plus two other classics made famous by the great orchestra. Sam didn't talk much and she allowed her head to rest upon his chest feeling surprisingly at ease.

Later they returned to the table but Chuck and Sylvia had gone to the bar and were talking to another couple.

'Would you like another drink?' he said.

'Not really but you have one.'

'No I'm fine.' He looked weary but sounded calmer than she remembered. She had no idea what these American flyers were going

259

through only what she had learned from Sylvia that they had lost a lot of men on daytime missions over Europe.

'I know nothing about you Sam. Can I ask you silly things like where are you from in America?'

He smiled at her, looking relaxed, 'Me I'm from a little town called Hingham which is near Boston, Mass.'

'What's the Mass?'

For the first time he laughed, ' Massachusetts. We always do that. Put the town in front of the State.' She remembered Joyce joking she was from Ipswich, Suffolk.

Sam continued, 'It's a typical New England small town. We call the whole area New England because that's where the Pilgrim Fathers first landed. Lots of the places have English names. There's even an Ipswich. I've never been there but I know there is one.'

'Gosh. An Ipwich, Mass,' she said and they both laughed.

'I studied law and was about to start to practice in Boston when all this started. I'd always wanted to fly and decided I would take the opportunity of the war to learn. No idea what I was letting myself in for at the time.'

'Do you have a...?'

'Nobody serious. But I know you do. You made that pretty clear last time we met.'

She thought she was blushing but the lights was so dim even he wouldn't see, ' Listen Sam it's not that I don't find you attractive. I mean I...'

'Tell you what let's dance again. We're better at that.'

This time she danced really close to him, putting her arms around his neck and her face against his. The war had marked this young boy from Boston, Mass and she wanted to soothe the invisible wounds.

From time to time during the evening they bumped into Sylvia and Chuck, both of whom had had quite a bit to drink. The party broke up at about midnight and Sylvia came over to speak to Doris when she noticed Sam wasn't about.

'Are you in a fearful hurry to leave?' she whispered, 'only I was wondering, you know, could you give us an hour or so?'

'What! God, I don't know.' Sam was coming back, ' One o'clock then. Are you OK to drive Sylvia?'

'Absolutely. I won't touch another drop and I'll see you back here in one hour. You're a sport Doris.'

'What was all that about?' Sam asked.

'Looks like you and I are going to stay here and drink coffee for an hour,' she laughed.

'I do have a better idea.'

'How did I know you were going to say that.'

'Listen I know the rules. Your rules I mean but I do have my own room and I do have coffee.'

Here I go again, Doris thought, but she was enjoying him so much more this time.

Back in his small billet he made her a very strong coffee which she sipped sitting on the side of his bed. She looked around for tell tale photos but saw only ones that were obviously family. He pointed out his parents and his kid sister, as he called her. Then he took her coffee from her and they kissed.

She didn't remember how they eventually got into the bed, or who removed whose clothes but the presence of a man around her, a cologne smelling man with olive skin, was wonderful. For a moment it seemed the most natural thing in the world that they should make love but when he forgot the rules, as he called them, somehow she resisted.

'I mustn't Sam. It's not that I don't want you. I do. But you see I'm still a virgin and..'

He raised himself on one elbow and looked at her for a long time then he kissed her gently, 'OK Cinderella. I guess it's time to go any how.'

They dressed in silence and he escorted her towards the parking area, 'Listen this sounds very corny, Doris, but could I take you to a movie or something next week?'

To her surprise she said yes.

'Into each life some rain must fall.' – song recorded by Ella Fitzgerald and the Ink Spots

Doris had been in a state of total confusion since Saturday. Her nerves were jangling, she was off her food, she both hated Jimmy and loved him to bits and she both longed to see Sam again and wished she had never been so stupid as to agree to the date.

But she had agreed which is why she found herself standing outside *The Cricketers* on the following Wednesday evening nervously looking at the clock. The least he could do was to be on time she muttered to herself. What if someone sees me meet him? What if Joyce and Leroy are in the pictures? What if Jimmy's father is returning from Air Warden duty?

As she stood waiting, the liberty trucks from the bases came in to town disgorging more and more uniformed Americans to fill the pubs or meet their girls. She felt cheap. He was fifteen minutes late. He had decided not to come. He was doing the decent thing. She couldn't make out whether she was relieved or disappointed.

Half an hour. How long should she wait?

Then she heard the honk of a jeep as it drew up a few yards down the road. Her heart missed a beat. He had come. She knew then that she really did want to see him.

But it wasn't Sam that was walking towards her it was Chuck. There had been some mix up. Sylvia was the only person who knew about her date. She must have told Chuck.

He walked up to her and placed his hands on her shoulders.

'Doris I have bad news, I'm afraid. Sam didn't come back today.'

Doris went home. Both her parents were out. She undressed, laid down on her bed and sobbed herself to sleep. She must have slept for about ten hours when her mother woke her. Thankfully there had been no re-occurrence of the nightmares.

'Don't count your chickens before they're hatched.' - proverb.

'Come in Millie, off you go. Let's see what you've got.'

Doris walked up the garden path.

'The Ruskies are doing well, captured the whole of the Crimea they have and at last we've got a breakthrough in Monte Cassino. Reckon Jimmy might be there by now. What's more it won't be long before we're back over in Europe in force. Oh. Good girl Millie, two lovely ones.'

'Just who are you talking to?'

Jack looked round, his face red from either bending down or embarrassment.

'The girls like to be updated. I usually tell them what's going on. Helps to relax them then we get a whole lot of eggs. How are you then? Got over it have you?'

It was her turn to turn red, 'Got over what?'

Jack looked a bit startled at her reaction, 'The flu, of course, last I heard you had the flu.'

'Oh yes. I'm over that, thanks. It's the war I'm not over. I really hate this bloody war.'

'I hate all wars. This one, the last one and probably the one before as well if I could remember what it was.'

'But you're so interested in what's going on. I mean even talking to the chickens.'

Jack stood up straight and grinned, He didn't do that much these days, 'They're the only ones who'll listen to me. Mary, Millie and Mandy have turned out to be the best friends I've got. I seem to upset Kitty most of the time, even the old woman's fed up with me and now Jimmy writes to say he doesn't think he'll go back to the factory when all this is over. Is that what he tells you by the way?'

Doris looked at the ground. A worm wriggled on the soft earth, 'Let's just get him home in one piece first.'

'You're right I suppose. Vera's popped up to Fowlers for what groceries she can scrounge from her few remaining coupons. She won't be long.' He took out his pipe and fiddled with it, ' Met Kitty's yank yet, have you?'

'Just the once. She brought him into the shop. He seems a very nice bloke don't you think?'

263

'How should I know?' he muttered, then he looked at her carefully, 'You still look a bit peeky girl. Come on let's go up and sort the kettle out. She'll be back soon. Sure you feel all right?'

'I'm fine. It's just that life seems really depressing all of a sudden.'

Then, to her surprise, he put his arm around her shoulders and gave a squeeze, 'Not like you to be down, girl. You're the one who keeps everyone's spirits up.'

IOWA

'Is this Heaven? No it's Iowa.' - dialogue from the film Field
of Dreams

Karl stood at the kitchen door, a mug of coffee in his hand, looking
out at the rolling prairie. He loved the late spring as much as any time
of year. Blossoms were fluttering to the ground in the apple orchard at
the side of the barns and to the south every thing was green as the
new shoots were flourishing as far as the eye could see. Over the next
few months he would watch them turn to gold and grow ten feet tall.
He would pray that the winds stayed kind and that he wasn't troubled
by rogue corn.

In the barns his recently acquired help Sarah was tending to the
latest batch of calves.

Lois came and stood behind him; she was holding a letter. 'More
news from Tom,' she said, eager to share the contents with her
husband, 'I think he's met a girl. Well, I know he's met a girl what I
mean is I think he really likes her. I mean an English girl Karl.'

Karl turned round and smiled at his wife, 'Easy now Lois, he's not
actually said he's going to marry this English girl, has he?'

'Kitty, she is called Kitty. Nice enough name I guess. They've been
going out on bicycle rides and she's been showing him the countryside
around the base. He's fascinated by the history of everything. Talks
about this old castle they went to.'

'It doesn't sound as if she's actually leading him astray, Lois. Can't
get up to much harm on bikes in the sort of climate he's been
describing in his letters.'

'Ah he says it's getting warmer. Not all the time but in the main.'

'Stop fretting woman. Next time he writes it will be some other girl.
He's at an age, you know. What does he say about the war?'

'Well, as usual he can't say much except that his fighters are real
busy. Going out with the bombers as far as Berlin itself. He says a lot
of his buddies don't make it back. How does he live with that, Karl?'

Karl took the final swig from his mug, 'Good coffee,' he said.

Lois turned the page, ' Oh and he also says that England is full of
servicemen from all over. Something big is going to happen soon, he

thinks. Sends his love to Ellen and Luke, wants to know how Ben is doing and that's just about it.'

Karl sighs, 'When he first volunteered to be a mechanic I wasn't too sure but now I'm just mighty glad he did since at least he's in a relatively safe place. If there is such a thing in wartime.'

'Safer than poor old Ben, the reluctant soldier.'

'We have to look New Guinea up in our atlas Lois. I get kinda confused by where everywhere is in the Pacific. But I'm no longer sure about Ben except that he misses his wife and not seeing Luke growing up which I know must be really sad for him. What I mean is he's just been promoted to Sergeant and this is the boy who didn't want to go to war. Could be the making of him.'

Lois went back to the table where she was about to peel some potatoes, 'Typical man sort of thing to say that is. Could be the making of him, indeed.'

Karl shrugged, put down his coffee and ambled out towards the barns.

Later, when they had finished their meal and Sarah had gone to her room, Karl sank into his chair and lit a pipe and Lois fetched her quilting. They always enjoyed half an hour or so of quiet in an evening before Karl would switch on the radio to catch up on the war news and maybe listen to a little music. On this particular evening this ritual was disturbed by the sound of a truck crunching on the drive. It was unusual for anyone to visit unannounced this late and Karl went to the window and peered out.

'Why it's Lester. What do you think he wants at this hour?'

'You won't know unless you let him in.'

Lester came in muttering a greeting. The usually tall, tanned man stooped slightly, the colour seemed to have drained from his face.

It's Letha,' he said, ' her troop ship was torpedoed just off somewhere called Biak island, near the Philippines. There were no survivors. I thought I best come and tell you. Had to tell someone.'

Lois dropped her quilt and went to him, 'Oh. My God Lester, this is awful news. Where's Patty? Is she not with you?'

He sat down heavily, ' The pastor's with her and a couple of near neighbours. She wanted me to come and tell you personally. You're our oldest friends and we wouldn't want you to hear from anyone else and...'

'Here Lois, fetch Lester some coffee. It's still hot in the pot.'

Lois went to the range. She had difficulty in pouring her hands were shaking so much. Lester just sat and stared ahead. He'd given them the news and that was that. There was nothing to add.

'Would you like me to go and be with Patty tonight, Lester?'

'No thanks. She's got plenty of folks around. Perhaps tomorrow. Yes, tomorrow, that would be kind,' he paused,' It just won't sink in. I mean it's not like she had a motor car accident in town or something. It's all those miles away and we'll never see her again. She was so pleased to be going but she'd no idea what she was going to. It was just an adventure to Letha. The adventure she'd always wanted......'

'She was a wonderful girl, a wonderful daughter...'

'Our only child. Patty couldn't have any more, as you know. What on earth are we going to do, Karl? What are we going to live for?' Tears trickled down his fine features and he hastily searched his pockets for a handkerchief.

'We'll do all we can. We'll help you both through this just like you would us if any thing happened to Tom.'

'Tom, I had hopes for Letha and Tom, you know. Wouldn't that have been something? But she met this doctor fella and when he went off to war she seemed determined to do her bit, too. Not that I'm blaming him or anything. It's just if it had been her and Tom maybe things might have turned out different.'

Lois took his coffee from him, it had gone cold and he'd only sipped at it. He stood up, 'I'd best be getting back to Patty but she wanted me to tell you.'

'I'll be over first thing tomorrow. God bless you both,' Lois said, kissing him on the cheek.

Karl put an arm around his friend's shoulder, 'I'll be here for you, Lester and we'll both be praying for you and Patty.'

Tom read the letter again and again. He was used to death. Used to air-crew buddies not returning. Used to news of pals from other bases being killed or injured in air raids. But Letha? Letha had so much life in her she was virtually indestructible. And what was she doing in the Pacific anyway? Why the hell had she volunteered? He knew, of course, she had this ridiculous thing about getting away from Iowa and seeing something of the world. She had reminded him at the depot that day when she rushed up to say goodbye. She'd never written. Letha wasn't the sort who wrote letters so he had never written to her. Maybe he should have. Maybe it would have been a decent thing to have done. To have kept in touch. But in spite of the fact that he had been more intimate with her than any other girl she made no claims. She wasn't his girl. She belonged to a much bigger world and now she was dead. The beautiful, intelligent, intriguing Letha Linquist was dead. He stuffed the letter in his pocket, walked out of the hut, mounted his bike and cycled the few miles to Waldringfield.

Once by the river he left his bicycle at the back of *The Maybush* and went down to the muddy shore. There was no one around. The pub hadn't opened and most people were at work. He wasn't sure how long he walked kicking at the pebbles and weed beneath his feet but he went past the few loosely secured dinghies climbing over the wet ropes and on towards a copse across the mud flats. It was surprisingly warm and the copse reminded him of home and of times in the orchard with Letha. There were tears in his eyes but he did not cry. He'd lost too many friends to cry but he would always know that she was special.

That evening Tom met up with Kitty as arranged and they went to see a movie, it was a thriller called *Double Indemnity* but he didn't remember anything about it. He simply sat in the fourth row holding her hand. Thankfully, she was totally absorbed in the film, craning forward in her seat in concentration. Afterwards, after gushing about the performance of Fred McMurray, she sensed something was wrong.

'Have I done anything to upset you Tom?' she said quietly.

'I'm sorry. No, of course you haven't. It's me, had some really bad news today, that's all.'

She stopped, and made him sit next to her on the wall of a bombed out house, she took hold of both his hands, 'Tell me about it Tom. Sometimes it helps to talk to someone.'

So he did, he tried to explain the extraordinary person that Letha was. She was so different from him in hopes and aspirations. Her parents and his parents were the best of friends, maybe they thought he and Letha would get together but it would never have worked out. He even told Kitty how unpredictable she was but that somehow he always forgave her. He explained that she went to college when he decided to work with his father on the farm. She was too bright, too beautiful and far too good for him.

Kitty turned his face towards her and kissed him gently, 'Nobody could be too good for you, Tom Nelson,' she said and he kissed her back. 'Maybe it would help if I told you more about how I was before I met you?'

He nodded, not quite sure what to expect. So she told him about Alan. How Alan had been such a decent human being. How he was totally against war, thought there should be better ways of settling the differences, probably scared out of his wits by the idea of fighting. But how he was a gentle and kind boy whom she took for granted and led a merry dance at times. And then how he was killed so early on in the war. She explained to Tom that she made up her mind there and then that she was not going to get close to anyone until the war was over. She was simply going to have a good time. And in some ways she had until recently when she realised that having a good time didn't mean quite what it said.

'I met you, you see, and I think I fell in love.'

They clung to each other for a long time perched on the wrecked wall of a bombed out house in Grove Lane.

'The eyes of the world are upon you.' – General Eisenhower

'Stop fussing woman, he's only a Yankee sergeant not General Eisenhower.'

'He's Kitty's boyfriend and he's a visitor to our house, that's what he is.'

'Well I'm going to talk to the chickens. There's a lot going on at the moment.' Jack shuffled out of the back door his newspaper tucked under his arm.

'Those chickens know more about the war than I do,' Vera muttered smoothing out the table cloth then stepping back to check that her efforts looked all right. Jam, egg and potted meat sandwiches, neatly cut and nicely arranged, some cheese, bread and a few sticks of celery from the allotment. The chickens had come in handy again since she had been able to make a jam sponge of which she was particularly proud. As a final English offering she had saved up some tinned peaches and made a trifle.

She went into the hall and looked at herself in the mirror, patting her hair into place; those grey hairs were never there before the war, she thought. She applied a little lipstick, straightened her dress around her hips and went to the back door.

'Jack, it's half past four,' she shouted, 'that gives you half an hour to spruce yourself up. Can't have this boy writing home to his parents saying we're a load of scruffs.'

After a while he ambled down the path, pipe clamped firmly in his mouth.

'Just look at your hands and nails,' she grumbled, 'filthy habit, smoking that old pipe.'

'I also work in a factory,' he muttered, going past her into the kitchen where he picked up the kettle full of hot water and stomped up stairs. Vera listened and after a few minutes smiled, hearing the noise of scrubbing coming from the bathroom.

After spending what had seemed like hours getting ready Kitty had cycled off to meet Tom. She'd made it clear to him that he shouldn't

270

bring any presents and he had understood. He'd read the bit in his little book about the English being a poor but proud nation.

At five o'clock there was a knock on the front door. Vera hurried to open it and saw her daughter hanging on the arm of a tall, blond, healthy looking young man. He had honest blue eyes.

'You must be Tom,' she said extending her hand.

He shook it firmly, 'Nice to meet you ma'am,' he said, ' and you, too, sir.' Unbeknown to Vera, Jack had crept up behind her. Kitty smiled to herself, she'd seldom seen her father look so smart; clean shirt, regimental tie, hair smarmed down with some sort of grease.

'Make yourself at home Tom,' Vera said, ' here, take off your jacket. It's really a warm day for a change.'

Jack fingered his tie, 'We don't stand on ceremony here,' he explained.

Vera decided they should eat right away and Tom tried to sound enthusiastic about what were called potted meat sandwiches; he was more comfortable with the egg and later the jam.

'Good eggs, Mrs. Wright,' he commented.

'That's because we have our own hens,' Jack announced.

'Really, I'd like to see them some time.'

'Dad would love to show you Mary, Millie and Mandy. They're the only women in his life who ever listen to him.'

'Do you have chickens at home, son?'

'Sure do, and cows and hogs.' Kitty felt Tom relax, he was never happier than when he talked of home and the farm.

Vera poured the tea, 'You do like tea, I hope Tom?'

'I'm getting to,' he laughed.

'So tell us more about where you live? Kitty has showed me where it is on her old atlas but I'm really none the wiser.'

Kitty sat back and watched him, seeing his eyes shine as he described the wheat lands of America. The hot humid summers that ripened the miles and miles of corn; the small copses and orchards that nestled near the tributaries of the Mississippi; the simple white farmsteads with their steep red roofs. He explained that the climate was extreme, the winters could be bitter, the winds could wreck the sturdiest of crops.

271

'We live close to the land,' he paused and looked at his captive audience, 'Sorry, Kitty will tell you I'm not really a talkative guy but when someone asks me about home well I....'

'Don't apologise son, it's interesting. You see it would be easy for us to think you all come from big cities and industrial places without realising that a lot of you boys are from the countryside. Now mother, how about cutting Tom some cake?'

Kitty was surprisingly quiet, content for her parents to get to know him. Vera found this both interesting and worrying. He was polite enough to let them know how much he was getting to like Suffolk, how the history intrigued him, how Kitty had told him what it had been like before the war. He went on to say that his ancestors were Swedish and that, in fact, just about everyone who lived in and around Red Oak had descended from Swedish pioneers. He told them, with a smile, that in many households they still said grace in Swedish before their meals.

'Heavens, we didn't say grace before tea,' Vera blurted out.

Kitty went into a fit of giggles, 'Dad should have said it in Swedish,' she laughed.

'What are you going on about now?' Jack muttered, ' Come on Vera give Tom a dollop of your trifle.'

After the meal Jack announced that he was going to show Tom his garden and his chickens leaving the women to clear away and wash up.

As soon as they were out of earshot Kitty whispered to her mother, 'Well, what do you think of him?'

' Me? I think he seems a very polite, nice type of boy who obviously comes from a decent family, even if they do live in the middle of nowhere. As for you, it's very plain to see what you think of him.'

The first thing Tom did when he walked down the garden was to stoop and pick up a handful of soil rubbing it gently before letting it fall through his fingers and back onto the ground.

'Feels good, the soil, bit clayish, maybe?'

'Used to break it up with compost but we have to put it all in bins now for pigswill'.

They discussed the vegetables, Jack telling him about his allotment in the park, and then finally came to the hens. Tom reached into the run and expertly picked one up,' Fine birds, sir' he said.

Jack turned and looked at this young man from across the world, 'So when's it all going to happen then?'

'You mean the invasion. I'm only a technical sergeant, nobody consults me but our boys have been really busy softening up the enemy as they call it. And I don't have to tell you about all the troop movement on the roads. So it's any day now I'd say.'

'It's what we've all been praying for,' Jack said quietly and then with a grin he added, 'in English that is, not Swedish.'

This is the ten o'clock news on Tuesday June 6ᵗʰ and this is Frank Phillips reading it. Under the command of General Eisenhower allied naval forces, supported by strong air forces, began landing allied armies this morning on the northern coast of France.

'Knew it was coming, of course, factory been building pontoon bridges, tank landing equipment and all manner of invasion stuff for months now. Most of it transported out over the last couple of weeks. Never seen troop movements like the ones on the roads recently. Yanks have been increasing the bombing according to what I heard at a recent Liaison Meeting.' Robert had decided to tidy up some of his Defence Committee papers before going to work and had come into the kitchen for the news.

Valerie preferred it when he was at work, he didn't mean it, but he disturbed her routine. 'That's very good news, isn't it. Perhaps we can finish off these Germans and end this silly war once and for all.'

'Still a lot to do, it's by no means over yet. This war is being fought all over the world.'

'I know that. We haven't heard from Francis for some time, have we? I mean he should be in Rome by now according to last night's news.'

Robert sucked the pencil he was holding in his hand, 'Has Sylvia heard recently?'

'Sylvia? Haven't seen her for ages. Bit elusive these days.'

Elizabeth bustled into the cottage. Sylvia, crouched over the radio, turned and put a finger to her mouth, 'Wonderful news,' she mouthed.

US 8th Army airforce bombers and fighters are raiding continuously, Liberators, Mustangs, Thunderbolts and Lightnings from east coast bases in constant action.....................

'Your friend from Martlesham will be there,' Elizabeth said, looking carefully at her daughter.

'Who?'

'Your Martlesham Captain.'

'Oh. You mean Chuck from the Liaison Committee, yes he'll be one of them, I should think.'

Elizabeth thought her daughter looked tense, 'It's so good it's all happening at last though.'

'Yes, it is. This war has gone on far too long.'

'And it's changed us all.'

'Most of us, certainly me. And the whole country will need to change once it's over.'

'Well, I don't know about that. Now then, heard from that husband of your?'

'Francis. No I haven't and it's over two weeks now. Monte Casino and then nothing. Still, no news is good news, they say.'

.....four thousand ships and at least 11,000 aircraft are involved in what is becoming the largest invasion in history.....

'Did you hear that? Eleven thousand aircraft', Jack relayed the news to Vera.

' By the amount of noise most of them seem to have flown over here,' she replied. 'Your Tom will be busy what with all the fighters going over there,' Jack shouted to Kitty who had just come home from Fire Fighting duty. She had Doris with her.

'Yeah, I doubt whether I shall be seeing much of him over the next few weeks. He says he'll contact me as soon as he can. You wouldn't mind if he cycled over here on the off chance would you?'

'Course not,' said Jack. Vera looked at Doris and raised an eyebrow.

'We haven't heard from Jimmy this week, have you love?'

'Last letter I got he seemed sort of relieved. I think the Monte Cassino thing was pretty awful and once they'd won there and the yanks (sorry Kitty the Americans) had won at somewhere called Anzio then they all felt things were on the up. He finished his letter by saying *Rome next stop*.'

'Wonderful to have so much good news all at once, I'm going to tell the girls,' Jack grinned and went off into the garden.

'Tom seems to have made a hit?' Doris said to Kitty who had walked into the kitchen and put the kettle on.

'I think it's because he knows a bit about chickens,' she said.

'And a bit about people, he's no mug that young man of yours,' Vera added.

'I have called this meeting to discuss the new German weapon the V-I rocket or Doodlebug as the RAF have named it.

Just when we are heady with success following the invasion of France the enemy have retaliated by launching over a thousand of these pilotless aircraft carrying about a ton of high explosive each and they say they have plans for even more frightening weapons. The V.I's are being launched from the coastal areas of France and we can hope that as the allies advance the lauching sites will be wiped out on the ground. In the meantime our gunners are shooting them down as they would any other enemy aircraft but many are getting through. In the main they are aimed at London where already there have been many deaths and many made homeless. An evacuation programme is being mounted I am told.

Doodlebugs are programmed to stall when they run out of petrol and explode on impact. Therefore, to some extent as long as you can hear the engine then you are safe. At night they emit an orange flame and when this goes out one should take cover.

As far as we, in Suffolk, are concerned then all areas of the Civil Defence should be on the alert to ensure that people take to the shelters when such indications occur. Fire watchers at our factories and other places of work should be particularly vigilant.

Whilst it is likely that most of these cowardly weapons will be targeted on London I need not remind you that we are a strategic area.

Once again I ask for your co-operation but at least this time, it is against a back drop of the success of our troops in Europe supported by our Navy and Airforce in what we all pray is the final thrust of this war.

Any questions?'

Robert looked around the room. There were no questions. As always, Sylvia was impressed. He's going to miss all this power when the war is eventually over, she thought. He'll probably stand for parliament. Then she smiled to herself thinking, not for the first time, that her father in law wouldn't be too pleased to learn that she had joined The Labour Party.

The meeting broke up into small groups and Robert came over to where she was standing with Elizabeth,

'Heard anything from Francis?' he asked.

'All quiet on that front, I'm afraid,' she said.

' We shall hear something soon, I'm sure. You're keeping occupied I gather.'

She said nothing, unsure whether there was some hidden message she was meant to interpret.

Elizabeth broke off from her conversation with the representative of the Education Committee concerning school shelters, 'Well done Robert. Beastly things these buzz bombs. How's Valerie?'

'Very well thank you Elizabeth, we must fix a date before long,' then, spotting someone he wished to talk to, he was gone.

Elizabeth dropped Sylvia off at the cottage declining the offer of a cup of tea since she had things to do up at the house before Edward came home. Sylvia was relieved hoping, as always, that Chuck would call.

Since the invasion his visits had, naturally, been spasmodic. Invariably he arrived on his bike looking exhausted; sometimes she would coax him to sleep, other times he wanted to talk, often they would go to bed in order to be close and share the pain.

He was being asked to fly more and more hours and many of his friends were being shot down but underneath the stress of it all there was a sense that, at last, they were winning. She didn't ask anything of him, deep down she knew that she provided comfort to this man and that she shared everything with him. She also knew that she Sylvia Cameron, an intelligent, sensible, practical woman had a hopeless need to be with him.

She hadn't been back from the meeting long when she heard a vehicle draw up on the gravel. She almost the dropped a saucepan in the kitchen in her haste to get to the front door. She released the catch and pulled it open. And there he was, looking pale and thin, leaning heavily on a stick.

'Francis!' she mouthed.

They both stood, looking at each other for what seemed ages. The silence was broken by the RAF driver, 'Shall I bring the luggage into the cottage for you, ma'am?'

'Of course, oh thank you, yes. Just dump it down in the hall would you, I'll deal with it later.'

There was no embrace, no kiss, no hug. Francis simply smiled at her, 'Hello Sylvia', he said and limped into the lounge where he slumped into one of the comfortable chairs. 'That's better,' he said.

Her head was whirling. Why did she not know he was coming? Why had nobody told her? Obviously his parents didn't know since she had only seen Robert that morning. What if Chuck suddenly turned up? Chuck! Oh. My God, Chuck.! Tea, she thought, when in doubt the English make tea.

'Have you time for a cup of tea, corporal?' she asked the driver.

'No thank you ma'am. Better if I got going.'

'Thank you Corporal,' the unfamiliar voice from the lounge interjected.

'Sir.'

'Right then Francis, tea first then you can update me. Are you OK there?'

'Perhaps you could just move the pouffe across then I can rest the gammy leg on it.'

He sounded the same, if a little tired. Still had that somewhat superior way of telling her what to do.

Whilst she busied with the tea she took a few deep breaths and began to think more clearly. She would get a message to Chuck. He hadn't called for a week and she was praying he was all right but she knew if anything happened one of his buddies would let her know. They knew the score.

'Tea. Good old English tea,' she announced, sitting herself down opposite Francis on the other chair, 'So tell me how you arrived here without so much as a post card?'

He didn't laugh just looked at her as if he was wondering who she was. Then, after sipping his tea he said, ' I was in a military hospital just outside Rome. They'd treated the wound the best they could but said I had to rest it for a while, then to do exercises whilst gradually using it again. They wrote it all down for me.' He fumbled in the tunic of his battle dress and produced a scruffy piece of paper which he handed to her. 'Then, quite out of the blue, one of the medic wallers told me that a transporter had landed on the strip bringing in some more casualties after which it was due to return to base in England. Would I like a lift?'

'Just like that?'

'Absolutely. They said there was nothing they could do for the leg that couldn't be done over here and that they would make an appointment for me in London to get it checked out in a few weeks time. So I jumped at it. The plane landed at Coltishall in Norfolk, would you believe, and they organised the transport here.'

He reeled off the information like he was reporting to his CO. She thought he looked more than tired. Almost vacant. In some other world. Understandable, of course, he must feel both exhausted and strange. It had all happened so quickly.

'So how did you get wounded, Francis?'

He looked up at her, eyes bloodshot, 'I'll talk more in the morning. Feel pretty tired. The leg's giving me a bit of gyp. Could you be a pal and fetch my pills. They are in my haversack then, if you don't mind, I'll go to bed,' he seemed to be working something out, ' spare bed I think. The leg is very tender.'

'Of course. I'll get the pills and then go and make the bed up. Anything else you need?'

'No thanks. Sorry to be such a pest.'

'Don't be ridiculous. I'm sorry to be in such a dither. It's the shock of you being here,' she turned back to face him. 'Do your parents know you're home?'

'No. Nobody. Only you. Don't tell them tonight. Plenty of time in the morning.'

'I've hardly seen him. Poor boy has been working round the clock what with supporting the invasion and trying to knock out the doodle bug sites his Thunderbolts have been in the air non stop. Is there any wonder they lose so many? They're all buggered. Sorry, I don't swear any more, do I?'

Kitty was having tea with Doris in Lyons. Since D Day England was suddenly full of girls pining for boyfriends who were too busy to even think about them.

'Funny how it's all swung about isn't it. Jimmy's now in Rome, of course, with all those Latin lovers pouring all over him and enjoying every minute of it I reckon.'

Kitty giggled, 'I don't think Jimmy would know what to do with a Latin lover.'

'Don't you be so sure,' Doris laughed and then went a little quiet thinking that most people thought her a demure little Suffolk girl and yet she had been with Sam the night before he died.

'Here, you all right? Look as though you've seen a ghost.'

'Sorry, no I'm fine. Do you want a piece of this rock bun? I don't think I can eat any more.'

'Thanks, don't mind if I do.'

'Kitty, I want to ask you a favour. Or, to be honest, my friend Sylvia wants to ask you a favour. I told her I was meeting you and she'll be popping in any minute.'

Kitty tried to swallow her rock bun but it got stuck in her throat and she washed in down with a swig of tea, 'I wish you wouldn't fill me with intrigue when I'm trying to eat my bun,' she managed.

'It's just a letter she wants delivering to an officer at the base. I've told her all about you and Tom and she wondered whether he could act as a sort of messenger. Only it's very secret. She needs someone she can trust.'

'Go on then. Tell me what it's all about?'

'I can't. You know I can't but she's been a very good friend to me and I'd like to help.'

'OK. I understand. Well, I think I understand. There is a war on. I'm sure Tom will do it and he certainly wouldn't gossip. Not his style at all. Only problem is I don't know when I'm going to see him.'

Sylvia had heard him moving around in the spare bed and later crying out but he must have got some rest since he was in a deep sleep when she tip toed in with a cup of tea at eight the following morning.

Over a late breakfast of scrambled egg and toast he managed to explain that he was injured just east of Monte Cassino.

'We were in this armed vehicle on a pretty ropy bit of road when we. I encountered enemy fire.' It seemed he could only explain things if he spoke in an official army manner,' 'The driver took a direct hit, I bought it in my left leg and the vehicle toppled over. I was thrown into the scrub. Then, there was more machine gun fire and the whole thing went up in flames.'

He pushed his breakfast to one side.

'Sorry I shouldn't have asked you so soon. I.....Well, I suppose in a way you were lucky. To be thrown free, I mean....'

He started to shout, 'Bloody lucky, yes I was bloody lucky. But not Bruce. Not Bruce. He was trapped under the armed car. Burned alive, poor sod. Bruce, burned alive.' Francis, his injury momentarily forgotten, struggled to get up but fell back into his seat, tears streaming down his face.

'Oh. My God. I'm sorry. I didn't....I mean he was your pal wasn't he? The one you went around with?'

'Something like that,' he said and fell silent.

She got up and went to him, placing her hands on his shoulders. He didn't shake her off but he didn't seem to welcome her either.

'Try and eat your breakfast,' she said, 'later we'll work out what we're going to do. Telling your parents you're home, I mean.'

'Thank you,' he said, playing with his plate.

Robert and Valerie came over as soon as Sylvia got word to them. Robert treating his son like a hero and Valerie fussing like an old hen. Sylvia provided tea and tried to stay out of the way but Robert came and found her in the kitchen and gave her instructions on how to look after him to ensure recovery was as speedy as possible. Valerie said she would come over to be with him if and when Sylvia had work to go to. They seemed to be taking over but she sensed that all Francis wanted was to be left alone to come to terms with what had happened, to try to find some peace. She thought that she could provide that need for him. She owed him that, at least.

Making up her mind about her priorities didn't stop her thinking constantly of Chuck. She hoped the note had reached him; she didn't want him to think that she was shunting him off because her husband had turned up on the doorstep. She never stopped thinking about him, pining for him even, and knew that Francis or not, she had to see him as soon as they were able to meet.

A few days after her note was despatched she received a message back suggesting a brief rendezvous late one Wednesday afternoon in the small parking area at the back of the Martlesham Red Lion. It all seemed rather sordid but she knew she had to go. Francis had been going through his books and even showing her photographs of his sorties with Bruce to explore the archaeological wonders of Egypt. At one stage he said, 'I would have liked you to have met him. You would have loved him Sylvia,' adding in a hurried voice, 'he was such a grand chap.' When she announced she had to pop out he seemed quite content to continue to browse.

The pub had closed and when she arrived there was just the solitary jeep parked in the shade of an oak tree. A few bicycles were stacked against an old brick wall but there was no sign that anyone else was about. She leaned her bike against the oak and the door of the jeep opened.

He looked tired, but then everyone looked tired these days, and before he could say anything she collapsed in his arms.

Eventually she looked at his concerned face, 'Everything is so absolutely hopeless and all I know is that I love you so terribly,' she said.

'I knew Francis was home before the note came,' he was smoothing her hair, ' I came around to see you and just as I approached the drive some old guy waved me down and shouted into the window, 'The captain's home. Wounded he is and not to be disturbed.'

Sylvia managed a smile, 'That would be Old Moore, protecting the master. Very feudal and rather sweet.'

'So tell me about it. How is he? Is the wound bad?'

'There are several wounds. Physical and mental. The physical ones will heal quickly,' she said and then began pouring out a torrent of words, making sense and not making sense, an incoherent mixture of fact and fears.

'You always hurt the one you love.' – song recorded by *The Mills Brothers*

Old Doctor Pearce, now in his seventies, dressed the wounds on Francis' leg and declared that he was making good progress. He was now able to walk quite easily with the aid of a stick and the pain had receded.

The early Summer months were warm and generally pleasant enough for him to go for walks around Rushmere and Playford or to sit in a deck chair by the cottage where he would read or study his photographs. Sometimes, when Sylvia returned from some job or other he would shuffle them away under his chair, but occasionally he'd select one or two and show them to her. He would explain how they had gone to the purple hills of Mokattam one night or why they were standing at the foot of the Great Pyramid surrounded by donkeys and camels.

When she was not involved in work she would go with him to Christchurch Park and sit listening to the band of the Home Guard; often the music would cause him to doze but even then he would jerk and twitch in his sleep.

If his parents or sister visited he would put on a veneer of the old Francis but as soon as they had gone would sink back exhausted by the effort. He didn't pretend with her which in some ways was a compliment since she had become much more of a friend than a wife. She was happy with this, judging that what he needed most at the time was a friend.

The leg was an accepted unspoken excuse by both of them that he should continue to sleep in the spare bed and whilst, from time to time, she would spontaneously kiss him on the cheek whilst he rested, there was little physical contact between them.

Over the few weeks of his convalescence she made no attempt to contact Chuck nor he her but she shuddered whenever an American plane passed overhead, prayed for his safety and longed for his arms about her.

A month went by and then Francis received a letter from the army instructing him to report to an Army doctor at Guys for an assessment of his progress from which would follow recommendations as to his future service. He told her he would, most probably, be offered a desk job. On hearing the news his parents announced that they intended to hold a family dinner party on the Saturday before. Both Francis and Sylvia dreaded the prospect but felt it was their duty to accept.

There were seven for dinner at Sylvan House, both sets of parents, Sylvia and Francis and his sister Victoria whose husband Mike was a naval commander currently engaged just off the coast of France.

Sylvia wasn't sure where her in-laws had managed to get such a liberal portion of beef from but the vegetables were home-grown and the apple charlotte that followed was delicious. Francis was holding his own asking Vicky for the latest news on her husband; Robert was pontificating about when he expected the allies to enter Paris though his efforts to draw Francis in on this conversation failed to elicit any response. Valerie had been with the Rotary Club and wives to a review at The Hippodrome which she said was very funny and cheered them all up. Then they all had stories to tell of the doodlebugs that passed over the town and in particular the one that came down at Woolverstone.

'They're causing havoc in London,' Sylvia ventured, ' thousands homeless, poor things.'

'Cowardly devils,' muttered Edward, 'more claret anyone?'

'So what with having your husband home I don't suppose you've been anywhere exciting, if you know see what I mean?' Robert suddenly said to Sylvia.

'I don't think I ever go anywhere too exciting,' she ventured, 'though I did manage to get to the Public Hall to hear Lord Beveridge. That was a few days before Francis got back, of course.'

'A lot of socialist waffle, this Welfare State stuff, if you ask me. How do they think they are going to pay for it all? That's what I'd like to know.'

'Lord Beveridge is a Liberal, I think, and he got a standing ovation at the end. The place was packed.'

'All this free health and free schooling. I was brought up to believe that a man had to provide these things for his family. His responsibility not the Government's.'

'Not everyone can afford to do that and certainly after the war poverty is not going to disappear overnight. Anyhow, it's this government, the Coalition Government, that is welcoming the proposals and promising a National Health Service, a new education system and a substantial house building programme. It's not simply a socialist ideal.'

Everyone else had stopped talking intrigued, in their various ways, with the passion of Sylvia's argument and her courage or foolhardiness at taking on Robert. It was her mother who intervened.

'Wasn't there something I learned at school about not discussing politics or religion at dinner,' she said.

'Sorry,' muttered Sylvia.

'So Francis, what are your plans now that the leg is healing, so to speak?' Elizabeth enquired, changing the subject.

He was staring across the table and out of the window, 'I just saw a couple of grey squirrels jumping along the branches. Remember Sylvia, a long time ago, we saw some in the park?'

She patted his hand, 'Yes I do remember. What a long time ago.'

The next day she went with him to the station. He was in full uniform and carried a haversack with his overnight clothes saying that since the appointment was early it was best if he stayed at his club in Pall Mall. He seemed chirpy but she knew he was putting it on for her sake. As the train was coming in he put the bag down and hugged her, 'Thanks for being so good to me and trying to understand,' he said.

'You'll be fine,' she muttered, ' see you on Wednesday with a full bill of health.'

He looked at her and smiled then climbed into the carriage pulling on the leather strap and shutting the window. The female guard waved her flag and blew the whistle with gusto and the train disappeared down the tunnel.

She didn't hear the car. She was busy in the kitchen washing the bed linen.

'Can we come in?' they said, filing past her into the room, 'It's best if you sit down.'

Sylvia did what she was told, 'What is this all about?' she said.

There were four of them, a driver who stood by the door, two officers and for some ridiculous reason an army padre.

'We have some bad news,' one of the officers said,' there's no simple way of telling you I'm afraid. Your husband, Captain Francis Cameron, was found dead in his club this morning. It would appear that he had shot himself in the head.'

She didn't exactly faint but everything swam around her. Then, for a moment, she thought she was going to vomit. The driver appeared before her with a tumbler of water; the officers' distorted faces looked grotesquely into hers, like crazy mirrors at a fair ground.

She screamed out, ' No, no, no.' and then 'the poor, stupid boy. He knew I understood. He knew I would have helped him.'

Nobody said anything. Nobody came near her. They were trained in this sort of thing. After some time one of them said, 'He wrote you a letter,' and handed her a sealed envelope, 'There is another letter, to his parents. We have to go there next and tell them. Will they be in do you think?'

'I've no idea. His mother will I expect,' then she added, 'but don't tell her without Robert being there. You could contact him at the factory, at Andersons, he's the managing director.'

'One further thing Mrs Cameron, and I know this is terrible for you, we will need to see the contents of your letter. Evidence if you see what I mean. If it is suicide we need evidence.'

She looked at the letter and then at him in disbelief.

' The padre will stay with you. We'll come back when we have seen the Captain's parents'.

'No,' she shouted, 'I don't want any padre. You all go. Go. Get out of my house.'

The padre spoke for the first time, 'That's fine. I will go then but you shouldn't be alone. Is there anyone near?'

She looked at him. He was trying to help, 'My mother. She's at the big house up the main drive. She'll come.'

'Right then, that's what we'll do.'

They filed out closing the door quietly. Tears streamed down her face and she slowly opened the letter.

My Dear Sylvia,

Please forgive me for doing this. I know that it will cause you much distress but I have gone over and over things these last few weeks and concluded that this is the best way out for all of us.

Since I have been back you have been a brick. You have not pried or bombarded me with questions; you have befriended me in a way that we never knew in our earlier time together.

However, I realise now that I should never have married you. Never have married anyone, of course. Knowing now what sort of man I am I would have loved to have simply been your friend.

You understand what I am saying, of course, you have realised over the last weeks that I am not a man who can love women, even you, the best of all women. It was Bruce who turned out to be the person I could love. Maybe if he had not been killed it would have been possible to work something out. He and I talked of living together after the war in somewhere more tolerant than England. You may have even forgiven me. But he didn't live, he died and there is no way out but for me to die too. I will write another letter to my parents but would implore you to destroy this once you have read it and never divulge to them the contents..

I know that if could I have loved any woman it would have been you Sylvia but you must now go forward and find someone who is right for you in the fulfilled life you deserve.

Good bye

Francis

Tears fell onto the letter as she muttered again and again, 'You silly boy, why didn't you let me help you.'

She read it again and again and then, fearing the Army would return, went into the kitchen fumbled for her cigarette lighter and set fire to the letter letting the smouldering fragments fall into the sink. She turned on the tap and tried to wash them away but some pieces simply would not go, remaining black and shrivelled and stubborn.

'What does farewell mean, if not death?' – *Honore de Balzac*

Sylvia had to do something so she went to work. She went to Holywells and talked with the current temporary residents; she heard about how they had lost homes, loved ones, everything they owned whilst their husbands were fighting in places with strange names, Caen, Marseilles, Burma. She scribbled in her notebook, promised to look into things, to locate relatives, to find accommodation. Then she went back to the office telling herself that it was time she stopped feeling so angry inside.

She made a few telephone calls, drafted a couple of letters and started to read a report from the chairman of the Education Committee. There was a knock on the door. Shouting 'Come in' she looked up from her reading.

'I only just heard,' he said, shutting the door behind him and pulling up a chair on the opposite side of the desk, 'Sylvia I'm so very sorry.'

'How did you hear?'

'These things get around.'

'Yes I suppose they do. Even in wartime,' she ran her fingers through her hair. It was hanging loose, not held back in a comb as usual when she worked. She had, at least, applied a modicum of make-up.

'Do you want to tell me about it? I mean what drove the poor man to do it? It wasn't because of us was it? You didn't tell him about us?'

She sighed, 'No, Chuck, you needn't worry I didn't tell him about us. I don't think he knew. He hadn't talked to many people since he came back. Only family.'

Chuck seemed relieved, 'You were obviously very worried about him when we last met at Martlesham. You opened up about all sorts of theories as to his depression but I never thought it would come to this.'

'Me neither. That's the trouble, I keep thinking that I should have got him to talk more about the things going on in his head. I keep thinking I failed him. Not only as a wife but as a friend.'

Chuck started to fumble for his cigarettes but changed his mind, 'What are you going to do?'

'Do you mean what are we going to do?'

'Maybe. I don't know. I have to be so careful. I mean, because of what has happened, if the Colonel got to know about us I could be in trouble. He's very determined that his officers should present a good image to the community and to the men, of course. That's why we have the liaison committee.'

She looked at him unable to respond. He licked his lips and then continued, 'Then there's Helen. I mean if there was a scandal and she found out ....'

Sylvia shouted at him, 'Chuck, for God's sakes stop it. You didn't seem to worry about your precious Helen before or about the Colonel for that matter. What are you trying to say? That it's over. OK so it's over. I'm in no fit state to be much of a companion at the moment anyway.'

He stood up and started to move around to her side of the desk. Calmly she told him to sit down.

'I'm sorry. As you can imagine I'm not thinking rationally these days.' She took a deep breath,' 'You are right of course Chuck, you have to walk out of here and forget me. You have to concentrate on doing your job and keeping alive. Then when this evil war is over you have to go back to your wife. Just think of me sometimes when something happens to jog a memory, you know, a song, an expression, a face in a crowd. You see, I loved you with everything I'd got. I really did.'

'But I feel the same way.'

'No Chuck, it's not your fault, but you didn't love me enough.'

'I did, Sylvia, I....'

'Please, no discussion. Just stand up, smile at me, and walk out of the door.'

He sat for ages before getting up then in his soft, slow voice said, 'I love you Sylvia.'

She heard the door close behind him and burst into tears, 'Not enough you bastard,' she shouted,' not enough.'

A few days later Sylvia elected to take the trolley bus from the Playford Road terminal rather than cycle into town. It was a pleasant late Summer day and she decided to wear her grey slacks with a crisp white blouse; her hair was pulled back and held in place with a tortoiseshell comb and she applied a little bit more make-up than usual. She didn't want Robert Cameron to see the tired rings under her eyes.

A cheerful conductress swung on the pole as the trolley shuddered to a halt and Sylvia climbed on board deciding to travel upstairs. The lack of money available made the old buses look grubby and worn which Sylvia thought was sad; they were an important part of Ipswich. A bell signalled that they were on their way swinging round towards the town in a tight circle.

Over the last few days Sylvia had struggled to come to terms with the loss of the two most important men in her life. She was continually nagged by the feeling that she should have tried to talk more to Francis since, in a strange way, she felt she had become his friend rather than his wife over that last desperate period of his life. That was how it should have always been. She had been wrong to push him into a marriage he had no heart for. Of one thing she was certain however, the contents of the letter would never be divulged to anyone.

The trolley pulled up at the top of Woodbridge Road near the Ambulance centre where Doris did her training; a squad of women in overalls were hosing down the vehicles. At one time Sylvia had considered sharing the whole story with Doris who, like the good friend she had become, had called at the cottage when she heard the news. On reflection, she was not prepared to betray the trust that Francis had shown in her to anyone. She owed him that.

Chuck, his resistance lowered by countless dangerous sorties over Europe with more and more of his friends being killed everyday, couldn't face the possibility of a scandal. His colonel, it would seem, turned a blind eye to the dalliances of his officers unless something out of the ordinary caused embarrassment. Chuck just hadn't anything left in him to deal with that possibility and the chance of his wife finding out.   Sylvia knew that she had acted emotionally but she had given him the choice and he had elected to walk out of the door and out of her life.

Ideas were forming in her head about her immediate future as she walked slowly up the hill to the Cameron residence.

He was sitting behind a large mahogany desk in an impressive, ornate chair. Papers were stacked neatly in leather tooled trays and a

matching fountain pen and pencil were positioned in parallel before his clasped hands. She felt that she was back at school
waiting to be admonished by the head teacher but that, in her case, it would have been a woman and not Robert Cameron.

He didn't get up, nor smile but gestured her to sit opposite him in a much lowlier position. His face displayed little emotion.

'How are you?'

'Still trying to come to terms with it all but I think I feel a bit better in myself. And you and mother-in-law?'

'Valerie's in a bad way. Finds it difficult to believe, always knew he might be killed in some campaign or other but never this.' He unclasped his hands,' I haven't discussed this with her, of course, but I'm not stupid Sylvia, I know why he did it and I shall never forgive you for the way you behaved. Naturally Francis was a gentleman until the end.'

She looked at him not understanding exactly what he meant. He fixed her with his steel blue eyes and continued, 'You see Sylvia, you and I do not have to pretend that it was the scars of war that caused him to take his awful decision. We know differently. We know that he came home, a wounded war hero, having campaigned right through the desert and up into Italy. And what did he find? He found his wife in the middle of some wild, reckless affair with an American officer. A married American officer, to boot.'

'Did he say that in his letter to you?' She was struggling to remain calm. She wasn't quite sure what she had expected when she had been summoned to Sylvan House but she hadn't reckoned on this instant assault.

'Not in so many words but as I said earlier Francis was brought up to be a gentleman.'

'I see. Well, it won't surprise you, I'm sure, to hear that I don't agree. However, I don't think any purpose will be served by our discussing it. Francis certainly wouldn't have wanted that.'

Robert leaned over the desk, fingers steepled, apparently not having heard what she said, 'And talking of letters. Why, if you had nothing to hide, did you destroy your letter? A letter that the investigating officers told me they needed as part of their enquiries. In view of the fact that...'

'I destroyed his letter because he asked me to. I carried out his wishes, as a properly brought up young lady should.'

'There's no need to be facetious.'

'I shall be whatever I chose.'

'What if the law instructs you to divulge the contents?'

'I shall refuse.'

He stood up, red in the face, his small neatly cut moustache quivering, 'Your affair with that American, whom you even had the cheek to see when Francis was at home convalescing, is what caused his death, young woman. Deny that if you dare.'

'Have you been spying on me?'

'Don't prevaricate. Answer my question.'

She managed to stay calm. He appeared to be suspended in mid air, knuckles white on the desk. Sylvia took a deep breath, 'I'm surprised you even ask since you seem to have made up your mind even though Francis did not mention my affair, as you call it, in his letter to you nor indeed in his letter to me.' She paused and he lowered himself back into his chair. She looked at him carefully,' To be perfectly honest with you I can't believe this conversation is taking place. I came here to sympathise with you and Mrs. Cameron, to share our grief as a family and I am amazed that you are talking to me like this at a time like this. I am your daughter in law not one of your minions.' She was close to tears but the anger inside her made her determined not to let him see this.

'Don't try to be clever with me. You sound more like one of your lefty political friends every minute.'

Sylvia stood up and walked to the window. She looked out at the garden, the garden where she had first talked with Chuck. My God so much had happened since then. Robert didn't move. He remained in his chair drumming his finger tips on the leather topped desk. She took a deep breath, turned and faced him, 'Ah. So that's it isn't it? You don't know what you feel worse about do you? Your daughter in law joining the Labour Party or your son's terrible death. Well Robert Cameron, I will tell you this for the last time, I am grieving over Francis' death far more than you could ever imagine and it will be with me for the rest of my life. I may not have behaved properly in the eyes of the world but I know for certain that you are wrong about the reason for him taking his life.' She looked at him again very carefully and continued, 'I'm leaving now. I doubt whether we will be seeing each other again.' Then she turned and walked slowly from the room closing the door gently behind her.

The main gates to Christchurch park are situated about a hundred yards down the road from Sylvan House. Without really thinking about where she was going Sylvia walked through them and sat on a wooden bench under one of the huge oaks. She looked through the branches to sky and smiled and then she buried her head in her hands and sobbed uncontrollably.

The few people walked by ignored her. She was just another victim of the war, another poor girl whose boyfriend or husband had been killed.

'I've emptied all the drawers and packed things the best I could. You did say you could put them in my old room and most of the furniture is yours anyway and...'

'Don't fuss. I'll take care of it,' Elizabeth looked around, ' All this is so terribly sad. Oh and don't forget it's not your old room it's simply your room.'

'Thank you but you do understand that I can't live in this cottage a moment longer. It can no longer be my home. I would like you to find some really deserving homeless family to come here, at least until after the war. Out of all this we could at least make someone really happy.'

' I knew you'd say something like that.'

'I've spent the last few years finding the homeless homes so this is the least we can do. Now I'm going to have to do the same in London plus dealing with the evacuees, of course.'

'It's a bit of a coincidence really the Doodlebug evacuees being sent to East Anglia. At least you'll be able to tell them what it's like out here.'

Sylvia went to the bookshelf and selected a few books, 'Hemingway, Steinbeck, bloody Americans,' she said.

'You are going to be all right, aren't you darling?'

'Yes, I'll be so busy I'm bound to be all right. Doris says once I've settled she'll come up for a week-end and check me over.'

'That's good of her.'

Sylvia picked up a book from the pile on the table and idly flipped through the pages, she gazed at the title *Put out more flags by Evelyn Waugh*. 'Mother, there is something I want to say. You and daddy probably think I have behaved very badly but you see the truth is the worst thing I did was to talk poor Francis into marrying me in the first place. We weren't the first to have rushed into a wartime wedding I know but probably the last thing he needed was to be saddled with a wife. In spite of that you have to know that he did not take his life because of my relationship with Chuck.'

Elizabeth came over and took hold of her daughter's shoulders, 'You think I don't know all that,' she said and then she looked out of the window for a second before continuing, 'I had a theory once that most people meet someone in their lives who is special. Sometimes it works out, often it doesn't. In wartime the chances of happy endings are pretty slim.'

Sylvia hugged her mother, 'Thanks for trying to understand, mummy.'

Elizabeth smiled.

'What about daddy, do you think he understands?'

'Of course not, he's a man.'

'The sense of space and sky – ample room to walk, think and dream.' – Susan Alan Toth.

'I always said it would be August and I was right. Paris liberated, now that is wonderful news. Not that the French deserve it, of course.'

'He's talking to those chickens again,' Kitty and Tom were walking up the path, hand in hand.

'Nothing wrong with that,' Tom said, 'I do it all the time back home.' He looked across at the other gardens; rows and rows of same size plots, all with shelters humped somewhere near to same size houses, all full to the brim with vegetables. In Iowa he would have been looking at miles and miles of corn, here it seemed it was simply miles and miles of gardens.

Jack heard them coming and turned round, 'It's good news for a change. Just heard it all on the wireless before I came out here. Paris liberated, Allies landed in Marseilles, then your lot moving in on Manila. Good news all round.'

'Do you think Jimmy's in Marseilles then Dad?'

'That would be my guess.' He turned to Tom, 'I wasn't sure where Manila was so I looked it up on Kitty's old atlas and I can understand now why it's so important.'

'That's where Ben will be,' Tom said, talking to himself.

'Ben is Tom's brother in law,' Kitty explained.

'The reluctant soldier, that was Ben. Never wanted to go to war. Didn't really believe in it. Wanted to stay at home with Ellen, that's my sister, and their little boy Luke. Poor old Ben, never wanted to go.'

Kitty suddenly turned on her heels and went quickly back towards the house.

'Have I said something wrong, do you think sir?'

Jack stroked his chin, ' Kitty had a boyfriend, right at the beginning of the war, he didn't want to go either only he was killed at Dunkirk.'

'Oh. My God, of course. She told me, Alan wasn't it?'

'Yes, Alan. He was as bit like you in some ways.'

Jack and Kitty had set up chairs on the small concrete area in between the kitchen and the shelter. He puffed at his pipe and she bent to pick up one of his shirts from the basket full of mending. It was a warm evening and, for once, reasonably quiet. Somewhere up the road a baby was crying, muffled radios were playing and a couple of cats were squabbling but there were no sounds of war.

'Where've they gone?'

'Just for a walk. It's a nice evening. Sometimes he seems a bit hemmed in.'

'Used to a lot more space than there is round here.'

Vera licked the end of a piece of cotton before squinting to thread it through the needle, 'How's Kitty going to react to all that space then?'

'What do you mean, woman?'

'I mean if she marries him.'

'Marries him, who says she's going to marry him?'

'I'd bet a week's wages on it. You're not blind are you, Jack Wright. She's never been like this over a boy.'

'We were talking about Alan today,' Jack sucked but the pipe was not alight.

'If you listen to Tom it really is the middle of nowhere, that place where he lives. Do you think she'd be all right? She couldn't come running home to mum from the middle of nowhere could she?'

'He reminds me of Alan sometimes. Except he's an American, of course.'

Vera put down the shirt and picked up one of Kitty's blouses, then she searched in a small tin box for a suitable button, 'You do realise that if she does marry him and goes to live in, where is it, Red Oak Iowa, that we'll probably never see her again.'

'Neither of them has mentioned marriage as far as I know,' he said.

Lois sat on the old rocking chair in the porch listening to the evening sounds of the farm. She had made her famous chowder, chopping and dicing onions, celery, potatoes; mixing them in flour and water and adding corn, bay leaves, salt, pepper and ham. There was enough for Karl and her for supper as well as for Ellen and Luke on Sunday. She reached into the pocket of her apron and pulled out the latest letter from Tom enclosing the photograph of Kitty. Lois looked again at the girl smiling at her. She could have been Swedish with her blond hair and blue eyes; not the skin though, not the tanned skin, this girl was pale and a bit on the thin side.

Tom seemed very serious about this Kitty from England but what did he know about girls. As far as Lois knew he'd only ever been out with poor Letha and even that wasn't serious. Yet, reading between the lines, this one was really special. And even if she was as perfect as he said how was she ever going to settle in remote, slow moving Montgomery County? A girl from a busy town with all sorts of things going on. She wondered what her parents thought. Tom said they had been very kind to him, welcoming him into their home; they were hard working people with very little money but that, he said, was typical of so many English folk in their war battered country. He hadn't said he wanted to marry her as such but he was obviously brooding on it. Why couldn't he simply come home after the war and find himself a nice local girl. A girl who understood what it was like living in Iowa.

She heard the truck draw up on the drive. Karl had been down to the copse at the far end of the farm. It was no use talking to him though. When she'd shown him the photograph all he said was 'Looks a pretty girl.'

Lois stuffed the letter back in her apron. She would write a careful letter back; she would tell him to think carefully about what he would be letting this English girl in for if he really was contemplating asking her to marry him.

With Mr. French on his honeymoon in Oxford, in common with most shops hit by staff and stock shortages, the chemists now closed for an hour at lunch time. Kitty had missed out on her usual canteen lunch at Pipers and arranged to meet Doris in Christchurch Park. They sat on a seat near the mansion nibbling at marmite sandwiches provided by Doris.

'So, tell me about the wedding then?'

'Oh. It was sweet. They are really suited you know though Joyce and I are convinced that Foxy, as he calls her, will be the boss.'

'I don't know who's the boss with Tom and me. Sorry, go on.'

'They got married in the Registry Office, just a few friends and relatives. Oh. He also invited Leroy, that's Joyce's boyfriend so that was nice.

They took over the restaurant at The Ritz for the reception and Mr. French made a funny speech and we all had the usual tea with a special wedding cake. One of his friends took some photographs and, would you believe it, as he was taking them someone shouted *Look out!* and one of those horrible doodlebugs came over. The bloke taking the photo said *Never mind the doodlebug, just smile.*'

'I hate those doodlebugs. The noise they make gives me the creeps. They don't seem to have landed around here though, do they?'

Doris took a bite of her sandwich, ' No they're nearly all aimed at London. It's been terrible there. We've been doing some extra training up at the depot but apart from one crashing harmlessly by mistake and a lot of false alarms there hasn't been too much for us First Aiders to do. Not like the old days, thank God.'

'You know I've got to quite like marmite. Don't suppose they have that in Red Oak. Sorry I keep going off the point. Tell me more about the wedding.'

Doris laughed, there was something infectious about Kitty, 'The marriage of Foxy and Frenchy as Joyce calls it. It was a happy day and that's what mattered. One more funny thing though, you know that they are both musical and that Foxy is a piano teacher?'

Kitty nodded.

'Well, Mrs French as she is now, she was talking about her music and asked Leroy if he was musical. He said he played a bit and she, thinking he meant classical, pointed to the piano in the corner of the restaurant and asked him to play something. At first he went all shy, he's ever so nice this Leroy, then we all urged him on and he played the most wonderful jazz and swing music I've ever heard. Joyce was so proud of him.'

'That's nice. Really nice.'

By now most of the park benches were occupied with people like themselves, enjoying sandwiches in the sun, listening to the birds, feeling the benefit of space.

Doris turned to Kitty, 'So how are things with Tom?'

Kitty looked at her hands, 'I've never felt like this before, Doris. It's serious. I want to marry him and I don't care if I end up living in the middle of nowhere, as Mum keeps calling it. I just want to be with him.'

'Have you talked about getting married then, with Tom I mean?'

'Not in so many words. I think he's worried about taking me away from my family and from a life I understand. I think he feels that would be asking too much of me but I want to tell him I'll be fine. Of course I'd miss everyone, of course there would be times when I'd be homesick, but I'd live on the bloody north pole with him, Doris.'

'Stille Nacht.' – Christmas carol.

In the months leading up to Christmas 1944 the Allies made good progress in Europe liberating Brussels early in September. Later in that month the skies over Ipswich were thick with gliders and Jack and Vera were amongst others who watched spellbound. Sadly the assault on Arnhem was a failure and thousands were killed. In general, however, the wireless reported good news all round with the enemy on the run throughout Europe. Only in December was any real resistance reported when the Germans staged a last ditch effort in the Ardennes.

At home there were signs that the war was drawing to a close as the Home Guard was disbanded and the black out partially lifted. Christmas, however, was little different from other war years with rationing and shortages limiting the seasonal spread.

As always, Jack and Vera made the best of it and the fact that lamb and not chicken was served on Christmas day was more due to Jack's request than any shortage in that direction. They decorated the house liberally with old trimmings, home made paper chains and streamers and after enjoying their family meal listened to a more optimistic speech from the King. There were four of them standing for the National Anthem, paper hats in their hands; Doris had promised to call round later.

'His stutter is getting worse, you know,' Vera said as they sat down.

'Has your King always had a stammer or is it the war that's brought it on?' Tom enquired.

'Always been there but, like Vera says, it's got worse. He's been a good King though during this war, and so has she, if you know what I mean. Stayed in London throughout they have. Right, are we going to try some of these sweets you've brought from the base then, Tom?'

'Just a selection of candies. See which ones you like.'

Kitty opened the box and they gazed in wonder at the selection, 'Me first,' she said picking out a marshmallow.

'You did the kids proud again, this year, I heard,' said Vera popping a chocolate cream into her mouth.

'Sure. It's such fun though. The noise they made would have drowned a Flying Fortress.'

Kitty took hold of his hand, 'Doesn't seem a whole year since we first met, does it?'

'So what made you pick me out from all of those other handsome guys?'

'Because you were the biggest kid of the lot,' she laughed.

Jack who had been quiet for a while started to fill up four glasses with some port that he had stored in the cupboard under the stairs. Although Tom declined, asking for water, he joined the family in a toast proposed by Jack. 'To Jimmy. Where ever you are. Happy Christmas son.'

'To Jimmy.'

'Happy Christmas everyone.' They all looked up then hastily gulped their port.

Doris had let herself in and come through into the back room, 'Sorry, have I interrupted something. You all look as though you've seen a ghost.'

'No, no dear. Come in. Did you have a nice lunch?'

'Yes very nice thanks. Not too jolly but very nice all the same.'

Doris was given a drink, a hat and the choice of the remaining candies, as Tom insisted in calling them. They asked him about how Christmas would be celebrated in Iowa and he explained that it would certainly be a white one, bitterly cold probably, that they would all go to church and then come back for a similar traditional meal. Jack switched on the wireless and they listened for a while to Vera Lynn's Christmas show though Jack was really looking forward to ITMA. After a while Vera started to clear the plates and Doris and Kitty got up to help her.

When they were in the kitchen Doris turned to Vera, 'I don't supposed you've heard anything?' she said.

'From Jimmy? No I'm afraid not but we've been through times like this before when we haven't heard for a time and then a whole load of letters come at once, haven't we?'

Doris picked up a tea towel, ' But it's Christmas. You'd think we would hear something at Christmas.'

'It happened once before at Christmas,' Kitty reminded them, 'He'll be all right. He's Jimmy, he'll always come up smiling.'

Doris had tears in her eyes, 'I keep telling myself that and yet I feel so worried. Sorry, I shouldn't be such a baby, especially at Christmas.

Just look at me crying my eyes out wearing this silly hat. He'd laugh at that wouldn't he?'

They started on the chores, Vera washed, Doris wiped and Kitty stacked the things away.

'I keep thinking about something you said the other day Kitty. Do you remember you said you could live on the North Pole as long as you were with Tom and I'd been moaning on about Jimmy wanting to work in Bury St. Edmunds.'

Vera stopped suddenly, 'Did you really mean that Kitty? About living on the North Pole.'

Doris realised that in blurting out her feelings she had said something wrong. She looked at Kitty trying to say she was sorry. Kitty blinked and then replied, 'Oh. They were just words. I was trying to make a point. I couldn't really live on the North Pole. Too bloody cold and those polar bears can be a bit nasty they say.'

Nothing more was said on the subject.

In the evening Tom was introduced to the Wright's traditional Christmas game of playing pontoon for matches. He couldn't stop laughing at them solemnly placing their bets, arguing over who said what and then accusing one another of cheating.

'What's so funny, Tom?' Kitty asked him.

'They're only matches,' he said.

'Question of pride, son,' Jack told him,' question of pride.'

Kitty left with Tom at ten o'clock accompanying him to the bus depot where he would catch the last Liberty truck back to base. It wasn't too cold and they walked slowly, their arms around each other. There were very few people about. When they came to the top of Bishops Hill he guided her towards the indent by the park gates and slid his arms around her waist. She waited for him to kiss her but he didn't; instead he spoke to her in his soft, slow voice, 'Kitty, this may not be the right place but I just have to know. Will you marry me?'

She threw her arms around his neck and hugged him but before she could reply he said, ' I know I am asking an awful lot of you. I know you have little idea of what living in Iowa is about. I know that the idea of leaving your folks and all this must be an awful thing to do but you see, I love you, and I have to ask. If the answer is 'No' then I'll understand but....'

'Don't be so ridiculous. The answer is Yes.Yes, Yes, Yes.'

'You're sure?'

'Aren't you listening. Tom, I've thought about all the things you said and I know that at times I will miss them terribly but I'll have you and maybe in time we'll have children of our own and Iowa sounds a wonderful place to bring up a family.'

He picked her up and swung her round in the air. Then they kissed for a long time.

'There's just one thing,' Kitty was out of breath.' 'We can't say anything until we know about Jimmy. I'm sure he'll be all right but the way Doris was today shook me up a bit and I wouldn't want to give Mum and Dad anything else to worry about just now.'

'I understand. Of course I understand but you won't change your mind will you?'

'Never,' she said.

When Tom got back to base he dumped his presents on his bunk and went outside needing some time on his own. It had turned colder but the cold never worried him. He recalled breaking the ice in the drinking troughs so that the cattle could get a drink in the sub zero Iowan winters. He wondered how they were all spending Christmas, without him, without Ben but with little Luke running wild with excitement. He missed them all. It was time to go home and when he did there would be two of them. Tom prayed that he had done the right thing in persuading this Suffolk girl to come with him leaving her family behind. He knew his folks would do their best to help her settle to the slow pace of life in Montgomery County. But he also knew it would be up to him to take special care of her and to understand that there would be times when she would yearn for the clang of the Ipswich trolleys, the smoke from the engineering works, the small fields of Suffolk and the people who spoke her language.

Vera lay awake trying to wrestle with the fact that she could lose both her children.

Doris had only let slip what she had known for some time that Kitty and Tom were in love. She knew he was a decent enough young man and, in spite of all the obvious pitfalls, they would get married and live in America.

Kitty was resilient, she was perky, quick tempered too, but she soon got over it. But America was such a long way away and she knew deep down when they married and left England she would never see her daughter again.

And Jimmy, the cheeky son who bounced back like a ball whenever things didn't work out. He was no world-beater and the girl he wanted to marry was brainier than him by a mile but they'd work it out when he got back. If he got back. It seemed impossible to think that he wouldn't but this war had taken so many young boys, so many cheeky Jimmys had been killed.

My God, she thought, I could be spending the rest of my life with just Jack for company. She looked across at him. On the table next to the bed were his torch, his tin hat and his pipe. He was snoring loudly.

Doris got into bed feeling weary. She'd tried to keep up a cheerful face for Vera's sake but failed. She let Kitty down by blurting out things about her and Tom. She'd done it again. Got it all wrong.

The Christmas meal had been wonderful. Turkey and all the trimmings. Crackers and silly hats, and church bells ringing everywhere. Suddenly the church bells became deafening and she clutched at her ears. Jimmy wearing a bright blue shiny cardboard hat turned to her. His face had gone. Blown off. Just blood and shattered bones.

'Jimmy.' she screamed, 'Jimmy, Jimmy, Jimmy.'

1945

'I'll be seeing you in all the old familiar places.' - *popular song.*

Vera couldn't open it until Jack came home. She was on the afternoon shift and went to the exchange in something of a daze.

Later they sat together in silence, neither knowing what to say to the other. Eventually he spoke, his voice hoarse, 'It only says missing. Not missing presumed dead. That has to give us some hope.'

She had tried so hard not to cry but her voice was spoken through tears, 'Is that right? Is that what they say if there's no hope – missing presumed dead?'

'Yes that's what they say,' then trying to sound optimistic, ' believe me Vera it'll be an absolute shambles over there. War isn't all orderly and neat and tidy like, it comes over on the wireless. It's a mess. People do go missing in battles, they may get a bit woozy from the effects of an explosion and before they know where they are all their mates have moved on. They end up behind enemy lines and have to hide. Get captured. There are loads of reasons why Jimmy is missing but he is not presumed dead.'

'Yes. I do see that,' she kept turning the letter over in her hands, 'we have to tell Doris. Can you explain all that to her. Like you just said. I think that might help.'

Doris tried to be brave. Jack did what Vera asked and more besides. He told her that Ipswich Town Football Club were being reformed and that the Cobbold family had come to their rescue financially. They'd be back in the Third Division South. Jimmy would not want to miss that, he said. Doris had smiled and touched his hand.

A few days later Tom found Jack at his allotment in Holywells Park forking over the hard ground, there was a great deal of banter with the other allotment holders. It seemed to Tom that a lot of British humour consisted of being unkind to people you liked.. Perhaps the mid west Americans were too polite. He'd have to talk to Kitty about it but then he doubted whether she would ever stop her teasing and he wouldn't want her to either. Jack explained his plans for his small plot to Tom whom he treated as an expert on such things and was pleased to get a nod of agreement.

'I gather there's no news of Jimmy?'

'No news is good news.'

'I sure hope so. It's a worrying time though. Difficult to deal with,' Tom sounded thoughtful. He was witnessing what he had heard about before he came over to England. He thought the word was stoicism but he wasn't good with words. The three women in Jimmy's life, his mother, sister and girlfriend were individually worried sick but tried to convince one another that it would all turn out OK. Jack was behaving in the same way.

Jack leaned on his hoe and looked at Tom, ' Now then Tom,' he began.' 'There's something I have to say to you. You may be surprised to learn that I am not as stupid as Vera thinks. I realise that you want to marry my daughter and I know that she will be fine living in where ever it is that you live. She's full of spirit that one, as I know to my cost over the years. At times she can be down right contrary but her heart is in the right place. Of course, we're all worried about Jimmy but, that aside, you have to marry the girl.'

Tom looked at this man long and hard, 'Thank you sir,' he said, ' I appreciate that. I will marry your daughter and I will look after her but we've talked and we have to wait a while for Jimmy before we say anything. We've agreed that, Kitty and me.'

Jack extended his grubby hand.

Over the next two months they all tried to carry on as if nothing was wrong. Each putting on a brave face in public but going through private agonies. Sylvia had been in touch with Doris suggesting a get together in London and Doris decided it might take her mind off things if she spent the weekend with her friend. The friend whom Jimmy had referred to in his letters as 'swanky.'

It was a long time since she had travelled on the trains and clambering up the step nearly tripped over her small suitcase. A sailor, who was sitting near the door, helped her in and then closing the door pulled the window shut with the leather strap. There were four other occupants in the compartment all of whom were in uniform. She thanked the sailor and sat in the far corner burying herself immediately in a newspaper. She had no wish to talk with anyone.

The train pulled out on time and she looked over the top of the *Herald* and felt how shabby it all was. The whole compartment looked in need of a good scrub, including the water colour prints of East Anglian towns framed in smoke stained glass. She fantasised that if she bounced up and down on the seat a cloud of dust would puff up and she would rise like a genie in a pantomime.

The two sailors, airman and nurse struck up conversation with one another checking on where they had served and where they were now stationed. Occasionally she felt one of them gaze in her direction but she concentrated on the paper; they must have thought her a slow reader.

Eventually the train arrived at Liverpool Street, the same sailor waited to see if she alighted with more elegance than when she arrived and she smiled and thanked him.

Like the train, the station itself was awash with uniforms. She wondered why they were all there. Why weren't they in Europe finishing off the war? Or looking for Jimmy? She remonstrated with herself for such a stupid thought and made her way to where Sylvia had told her she could get a taxi. *It will cost a bit more but it's worth it in the end* she had said. Searching for the scrap of paper in her handbag she thrust the address in front of the driver who grinned and said he would get her there in no time.

Sylvia was sharing a flat in South Kensington with three other girls, all working in their various and different war time jobs. It was a small flat in a terrace of similar residences and Sylvia herself came to the door almost as soon as the doorbell rang.

Doris climbed the steps. They looked at each other for a few seconds then spontaneously threw open their arms and hugged.

'Come in. Come in, the others are all out so we can have a cup of tea in the lounge and you can tell me all the news.'

The lounge was small but comfortable, magazines, books and newspapers were scattered all over the place, as well as a couple of discarded cups and a half used packed of Craven A. Sylvia picked this up and offered Doris a cigarette then excused herself to make the tea. Doris thought that her friend looked a bit pale but that was London for you; other than that she gave the appearance of having regained some of her former sparkle.

Over tea they swapped stories and news. Sylvia was working hard with evacuating mothers and children away from the capital to East Anglia and other safer areas. It was a massive exercise. Over a million evacuees were being moved out as a result of what had been a dreadful assault by the doodlebugs and now V2 rockets. Sylvia said nearly three thousand people had been killed and eight thousand injured. The allies were winning the war but the Germans last act was of cowardly proportions. The bulk of the exercise had been completed and as we got closer to winning the war then the rocket sites were being destroyed and the scale of the attacks was lessening.

'But that's enough facts and figures from me sounding more like a politician every day. How about you? Where is that Jimmy of yours these days?'

'I wish I knew. He's missing. I mean he's officially missing. We've had one of those awful brown war office letters. It's three months now and no word.'

'Oh. You poor girl. Why didn't you write and tell me?'

'You've got enough to do. Enough to worry about. And you've had your share of the tragedies in this bloody war. We're coping. I'm coping. Supporting each other. Not giving up hope until we hear for certain. But Sylvia, I don't want to be moping all weekend, it's so good to see you. I want to see London with you.'

That evening they went into the West End which was thronging with armed forces from just about every country involved in the war, Canadians, Americans, South Africans, Australians, New Zealanders, Poles, Czechs. Sylvia enjoyed herself identifying them by their uniforms. They lost count of how many times they were propositioned for dinner or dancing or just a drink but on each occasion they grinned and politely declined.

They walked through Piccadilly where a crowd was sitting beneath the hoarded-up Eros, on to Leicester Square and into Soho where Sylvia guided Doris into a small restaurant in Greek Street. The food was good and sensibly priced and the clientele reasonably well behaved. They talked of happier times and of the real hope that the war was, at last, drawing to a close. Sylvia had, apparently, found time to link up with the local Labour party and was brimming with news of what the next government, a socialist government of course, was going to do. Later the conversation lulled and Sylvia looked across at Doris,

'Tell me what you feel inside. About Jimmy I mean.'

'Inside, what do you mean?'

'I mean have you had a jolt, or a sudden feeling that you've been punched in the stomach when you least expect it?'

'Obviously when I first found out he was officially missing.'

'No, since then. A sudden feeling of dread.'

'No, not really. You see I can't believe he's dead. I know that's unrealistic but I can't.'

'Then he isn't. He's alive somewhere. I am convinced that you know, one knows, if someone close has died. Doris, he has to be alive.'

Over the course of the weekend Sylvia gave Doris the tourists guide to wartime London. They went down the Mall to the palace, to the Houses of Parliament where Sylvia said she would one day be an MP, to Westminster Abbey and bomb damaged St.Pauls. They went to a concert at the Albert Hall and dined at a small restaurant in Kensington near to where Sylvia lived. Doris slept in a made up bed in the lounge, briefly met Sylvia's flat mates who never seemed to sit still for a minute and then, exhausted, Sylvia piled her into a taxi and back to Liverpool Street.

On the train, which was not so crowded, she thought of what Sylvia had said and returned to Suffolk with hope.

'There ain't no cure for love.' - Leonard Cohen

'What you want is Meggazones, good for all sorts of things these Meggazones, coughs, catarrh, bad throats. Look it says so on the label.'

The elderly woman shuffled out of the shop clutching her cure. Joyce turned to Doris, 'They should give me an award, those people who produce Meggazones. I recommend to everyone for just about everything.'

'I don't think there is much cure for what I've got,' Doris replied. She had perked up a bit after seeing Sylvia but two more weeks had passed and still there was no news.

'Remember what your friend said,' Joyce told her turning to serve another customer with a cough.

Doris went into the dispensary where Mr. French was half balanced on a stool weighing what looked like calcium on the delicate scales. He rocked back nearly falling off his perch.

'We're busy this morning,' he said.

'Everyone seems to be coughing,' she picked up a prescription and read it, 'there we are, more cough medicine required.'

He looked at her over his glasses, 'Now we're back Foxy is keen that we should put some of our plans into action,' he told her.

'Good.'

'I mean plans about this flat and making you our manager and all that. You know, like I mentioned some time ago. I know this might not be a very good time for you to.......'

Doris swivelled round, flushed, 'No. It's not a very good time, Mr. French. The last time I wrote to Jimmy I was arguing about staying here when he wanted to live in Bury St. Edmunds. Now all that seems trivial. I don't care about anything except getting him back.'

'Yes. Well I did tell Foxy maybe we should wait a bit.'

Doris fetched the small stepladder and clattered it in to position before climbing up to reach a bottle of linctus from the top shelf.

Joyce burst into the dispensary, 'Doris you're wanted in the shop.'

'For God's sake Joyce can't you see I'm busy.'

'Well this customer specifically asked for you.'

'Too bad. You deal with it.'

'Sorry Doris but you do have to come.'

Mr. French raised an eyebrow and followed the two girls into the shop keen to see what the fuss was about.

'There's nobody here,' Doris announced glaring at her friend, ' I'm in no mood for jokes, Joyce, you should know that.'

Joyce pointed to the window, ' Out there,' she said.

Doris looked, seeing nothing at first. Then she noticed a face, a face of a soldier, a face pressed against the window. It was intact and it was grinning. It wasn't a dream, it wasn't a nightmare. It was him.

'Jimmy,' she yelled at the top of her voice and ran out of the shop.

He was standing on the pavement still grinning. She threw her arms around him, 'Where the hell have you been?' she shouted.

'It's a long story,' he said, ' but I'm here now and it's all right.'

May 8th 1945

'Land of Hope and Glory.' – *Edward Elgar*

'I don't know where Sheila got this muslin from but it's the very devil to stitch.'

Vera was crouched over her sewing machine on the kitchen table surrounded by all manner of fabrics scrounged from friends at work and helpful neighbours.

'It was good of her to let you have it', Kitty remarked, trying to make some sense of the wedding dress pattern that one of the girls at Pipers had lent her, 'Oh Mum it's going to be a lovely dress.'

'Don't count your chickens, as your father would say.' She cranked the handle of the old *Singer* as Kitty fed in the muslin. 'Got everything organised have you?'

'I think so. They were very nice at Alan Road, we met the circuit minister who's going to marry us and he said we only got fitted in because Jimmy and I used to go to the youth club. Tom wouldn't have been happy with a Registry Office. He said his parents would never forgive him if he didn't get married in church and Methodist is close to Lutheran which is where they go apparently.'

'That was really nice of his parents to write to Jack and me. Lovely letter it was. Thanked us for welcoming Tom into our home and now the family. Promised me they would look after you and help you settle in' Vera stopped sewing and looked at her daughter there were tears in her eyes,' Kitty, you will be all right, won't you?'

Kitty stood up and hugged her, 'I'll be fine. Tom will take care of that. I'll miss you though Mum, miss you terribly. You're the best Mum in the world, you are.'

Jack walked into the kitchen and found both his wife and daughter crying.

'We have won the war haven't we?' he muttered going out of the back door, ' and don't forget we're all due at the street party outside *The Catchpole* at three.'

They looked at each other and laughed,' He'll miss you too in his way, funny old bugger,' Vera said.

Kitty wiped her eyes, 'I know. But listen mum, Tom says in a few years time they'll be loads more aeroplanes flying ordinary people all over the place. One day, he says, you and Dad will be able to come and visit us.'

'Don't be ridiculous, your Dad in an aeroplane? He won't even get in the lift at *Footmans.'*

The noise outside *The Margaret Catchpole* was deafening. Tressle tables had been erected, white paper sheets acted as table cloths and every child from the district was seated in front of an enormous spread. All manner of Christmas decorations and trimmings had been strung up and the union jack fluttered from every window of the pub. Sam Evans the butcher was doing his best on the piano but could hardly be heard above the joyful noise of happy children. Church bells were ringing all over Ipswich, their muffled tones a cheerful change from the drone of doodlebugs and enemy aircraft.

The pub was open all day and a miscellany of men stood at the back of the celebrations gripping their pints and puffing at cigarettes. The women, resplendent in their best floral dresses, busied themselves making sure that the children had the best party of their young lives.

'This is a bit like the parties we held at the base for the kids at Christmas like the one where I first met Kitty,' Tom was chatting to Jimmy.

'Poor little sods. I bet they enjoyed that.' Jimmy found he could talk easily to his prospective brother in law. He'd always had a bit of a love-hate relationship with his sister but was glad she had met a good bloke in the end.

'You did well to get a slot at the Methodist Church. We've been making enquiries and just about every church in Suffolk is booked for weddings for the next six months. Doris and I decided we'd wait a while. Let all the excitement die down a bit.'

'Something to do with Kitty being in the youth club, apparently.' Tom told him.

314

Jimmy smiled to himself. Alan Road Methodist Church Youth Club had a lot to answer for. That was where he met Doris; where he first plucked up the courage to ask her to the pictures. All that seemed a century ago. He looked across at the party.

Doris and Kitty were dishing out ice cream to the little ones in high chairs behind the main tables, laughing together as more of this special treat went on faces than in mouths. When they had finished they came over to where Jack and Vera had joined the two boys.

'I just have to pinch myself that it's all over at last,' Doris said.

'In Europe it is. Just hope we mop up the Japs pretty soon,' Tom reminded them.

'It won't be long, son. I heard a special bulletin on the wireless,' Jack re-assured him in his knowledgeable way.

For some reason Doris glanced over towards the road, 'Oh My God. Look who's come to the party,' then she started to wave frantically, 'Sylvia, Sylvia, over here.'

'I thought this is where you'd be.' Sylvia looked more relaxed than Doris could remember, 'I'm here for a while herding the evacuees back to where they belong,' she explained. Doris introduced her friend to Jimmy. Sylvia fixed him with a smile, 'I'm the swanky one,' she said.

'All I know is that you're the one who gave her hope and you were right weren't you? I can never thank you enough, it must have been terrible for Doris not knowing and all that.'

'And not much fun for you either so I gather but it's really good to meet you at last, Jimmy.'

'And you, Sylvia, you don't seem too swanky.'

'It's Mrs. Cameron isn't it?' A young woman with a little girl pulling at her arm appeared in front of them, 'Remember me? I'm Mrs. Wilson and this is Thelma. You helped us so much when we were bombed right at the beginning of things. You took time with us, listened to us and now it's all turned out OK. I'm still with the distant cousins you found but been promised one of those pre-fabs up near Sidegate Lane. What's more my old man is on his way home; should be here next week. Sorry to interrupt but seeing you there I just wanted to tell you that you were the one who pulled us up when we were down. We'll never forget that.'

Sylvia didn't know what to say so she bent her knees and looked at the little girl, 'So Thelma, going to school now are you?'

The little girl grinned, 'I'm in Mrs. Green's class. She's ever so nice,' then she looked up and saw Tom in his uniform, 'Got any gum chum?' she shouted and then burst into laughter.

Sam Evans was now attracting more attention playing a number of war time hits. Soon everyone was singing and when he paused and triumphantly went into the opening bars of *Land of Hope and Glory* their voices must have been heard all over Ipswich. At the end everyone clapped themselves and the pianist decided it was time for a dance, 'Everybody Conga,' he shouted hitting the keys in a way that would have made Mrs. Fox cringe.

'Come on then,' Kitty shouted, grabbing hands with Doris and Sylvia, 'let's show them how to do it,' and they soon had a whole string of revellers snaking behind them. Round the trestle tables, down to the gates of Holywells Park where they swivelled and danced back towards the pub. '*Everybody Conga, Everybody Conga.*'

Jack turned to Vera, 'Look at those three girls leading the way,' he said, 'they're the real heroes of this war.'

'You mean heroines,' Vera replied.

'No I don't. I mean heroes. It's all the same these days.'

She linked her arm in his.' 'You're a funny old thing, Jack Wright,' she said.